BREAKING
NEWS OF TOMORROW

IGOR CHIRASHNYA

Publishing Services provided by Paper Raven Books LLC

Printed in the United States of America

First Printing, 2023

Paperback ISBN: 979-8-9879821-1-2
Hardback ISBN: 979-8-9879821-0-5
Ebook ISBN: 979-8-9879821-2-9

PRAISE FOR *BREAKING NEWS OF TOMORROW*

"Igor Chirashnya's debut novel, Breaking News of Tomorrow, is a well-crafted work of suspense, compelling characters, and moral decisions as one man carries the weight of the future. It's a must-read for readers of all kinds!"

—Steven Pressfield, Bestselling Author of *The War of Art* and *Gates of Fire*

"A smartly plotted thriller of seeing and betting on the future."

—BookLife Reviews

"As a debut novel, this is one of the best thrillers I have ever had the pleasure of reading, and it will keep you on your toes all the way through."

—Anne-Marie Reynolds for Readers' Favorite

"A brilliant novel. Keeps you on the edge of your seat."

—Trudi LoPreto for Readers' Favorite

"Breaking News of Tomorrow is a brilliant, fast-paced, political thriller novel that will take its readers on a wild and shocking journey from start to finish."

 —Aimee Ann for Red-Headed Book Lover

"Breaking News of Tomorrow was an exciting read that was truly unforgettable...I highly recommend reading this story if you're looking for something new, exciting, and captivating - it'll definitely surprise you."

 —Robin Ginther-Venneri for Robin's Review

"Igor gives the reader a thrill right from the start... Breaking News of Tomorrow is an interesting read with fascinating characters that come to life...Excitement galore."

 —Claudia Trindade for Reedsy Discovery

"A smart and exciting political thriller."

 —Alma Boucher for Readers' Favorite

"A spectacular introduction to the world of science fiction. Chirashnya is an author to watch out for in the future."

 —Essien Asian for Readers' Favorite

"An engrossing plot...kept me on edge. Chirashnya effortlessly switches between the scenes...giving the storyline a beautiful flow as the plot unfolds."

 —Keith Mbuya for Readers' Favorite

*In loving memory of my father.
He would not be able to read this book, but he would
be the proudest man on Earth to see it published.*

PART 1
GOOD SAMARITAN

CHAPTER 1

As Mike was about to hit the "Send" button, he had an unpleasant sense of growing uneasiness, despite all the reasons to feel the opposite. He couldn't explain a sudden and disobliging tremble inside his chest, manifesting itself with rapidly intensifying and loud heartbeats he never experienced before. The previously almost unnoticeable modest wall clock abruptly announced its presence with a thunderous ticking, as if purposely synchronizing itself with Mike's pulse, which resonated simultaneously in his ears and in both temples. Mike involuntary put a palm on his left side, trying to pacify the alarming clenching of his heart, and took a few deep breaths, sitting motionless until his anxiety finally faded away.

He decided to read the email one last time and found it a bit too bold. He erased most of the text and spent the next ten minutes composing the message over and over again. He was still unhappy with it, as with each rewriting attempt his main points were interchangeably either too blunt or too dire. He glanced at the wall clock: six p.m. He'd been running late. With a deep sigh, he crossed out two strong adjectives from the last sentence and pressed the button. He'd finally made it.

It was quite a challenging task to finalize the proposal and make it look presentable. He knew he shaped some forecast numbers a bit more favorably to convince the board that Solutry Corporation had only one plausible direction in which to move forward, and that was to switch to his new software or face a slow but inevitable death. Unfortunately, all the damn board cared about was the next quarter's profit. It would take a lot of convincing for them to agree on changing direction. Mike hoped that the numbers and the prospects in his presentation could win Houston's approval this time. He closed his laptop, stuffed it into his backpack, and finally left the office.

The evening smelled very fresh. An early rain swept away all the dust and smog, and the air was uncharacteristically clear and crisp. Typically, downtown stank with heavy layer upon layer of city vapors, which created a cacophony of smells from smog and stiff airwaves coming from different corners and alleys. Today was an unusual day, with cloudless skies that miraculously cleared after the rain, like somebody took a heavenly broom and swept away all the clouds and, with them, all foul odors of the city, leaving the purest of the air for people to enjoy as long as it lasted.

Mike tried to shake off a thought about the next day's possible battle with Solutry management prior to the board meeting as he stepped outside, hardly trying to convince himself that these were the worries of tomorrow. Today was the time to celebrate. Today was the day he would propose to Jenn.

Jenn, or Zhenya, as she was named at her birth, was the opposite of what you would expect from a Russian beauty: she never let her looks define and dominate her. That was her uncanny quality; she knew she was beautiful, yet this was secondary. She carried herself in a way that men weren't afraid to talk to her, and she engaged in conversation as a friend or a sister and without any hint of sexuality or flirtation.

Jenn's parents emigrated when she was nine years old, and despite her perfect, accent-free Russian, she felt much more American than Russian. Lacking any money and working at low-paying jobs, all her parents could afford to rent was a small one-bedroom apartment in a southern neighborhood, one of the most disadvantaged areas of the city. The warmth of her parents and her family's strong connection to their cultural roots kept her from following the bad influence of the majority of her school-mates. She was the only one in her class to get a college degree and, declining several promising high-salary job proposals, joined a nonprofit organization working with troubled kids. Despite a very modest income, she'd found her life's calling.

Mike and Jenn were a bit of an odd couple; she was a beautiful five-ten, outgoing, and charming woman who quickly and naturally joined any social gathering, while Mike, looking unremarkable and taciturn, made great effort and worked hard to not be perceived as such. Small talk was a natural thing for Jenn. She could engage in conversation in the most flawless manner. For Mike, it was always an internal struggle. But with years of training, he became quite successful at hiding it. People could understand why Mike was in love with Jenn, but they were often puzzled by what she found in him.

But most people missed the real reason behind Mike and Jenn's union. With constant self-doubt, despite his intelligence,

Mike needed Jenn's belief in him and her support; on his side, he gave her a feeling of being herself, and he genuinely accepted her as a person and not just as a beautiful woman, a feeling she'd never had with any other man. And, as she often told her friends, he made her laugh, with his sharp sense of humor and hilarious remarks that touched her own perspective with sniper's precision.

Mike parked in front of Perfecto, an upscale Italian restaurant near downtown, trying very hard to justify its name and one Michelin Star. He patted a small box in his right pocket and climbed the stairs, sensing that today would mark the start of a completely different life. He had chosen this place for its sparse and deep niches, and it was the best location for the occasion, despite its prohibitive cost. You didn't want to look stingy in such moments. He was surprised that Jenn was already waiting for him inside, browsing the menu when Mike entered.

"Hi, Mike." Jenn smiled and gave him a quick kiss on the cheek. "There are so many things I want to try here! Let's share, if you don't mind."

Jenn always took charge of choosing the food for both of them, and their typical dining experience involved ordering different dishes she wanted to try and sharing. Mike didn't care. For him, food was rather a binary decision: either a juicy hamburger and fries, or whatever else. Perfecto didn't offer hamburgers, and in any case, hamburgers did not fit the occasion, so anything Jenn had chosen would serve him well.

"Do you know how much they charge for just breathing their air?" asked Jenn when they were finally seated.

"That's OK," Mike said, his face turning red and big drops of sweat emerging on his forehead. He wiped them away with his sleeve and, catching a surprising look of Jenn, took a napkin. "Lis-s-s-ten, kh-kh, Jenn," he stammered, then cleared his throat, tried to pour himself water from a bottle, spilling some on the table, and began to wipe it off with a napkin, which he still held in his hand. Jenn continued to look at him in astonishment, as his strange behavior was rather unusual. "Kh-kh, I am not sure how this should be done. Will you marry me?" If anything, Mike wasn't a romantic person.

"Just like that, plain and without a ring?"

"Oh, sorry—here it is." He searched for the ring in the wrong pocket, making the situation even more awkward.

"Mike, I love you a lot, and I will marry you! But what story will we tell our future kids about such a dull proposal? Where is a helicopter, where is the music, where are the flowers, and where is kneeling for me? What will I tell them? You forgot the ring and proposed over dinner with hamburgers?" Jenn laughed.

"It's Perfecto, the most luxurious place in town. They don't serve hamburgers!"

"Well, I will spice it up for the dramatization of the moment." And with that, Jenn hugged and kissed her anti-romantic fiancé.

IT WAS ALMOST midnight, and Jenn was quietly sleeping on Mike's shoulder. Mike was still wildly restless; events of the day continued to play in his mind, fiddling with his consciousness. Afraid to wake Jenn up, Mike eased out of the bed, put on shorts and a shirt, and went to the kitchen.

It's March 31, thought Mike, realizing that April 1 was just about to hit the calendar. Every year, he brought a new prank to the office, and eventually, it had become a tradition. This time, however, April Fool's was the last thing on his mind, thanks to all his preparation for new software development and the proposal to Jenn. He typed a few typical April Fool's keywords into the search prompt. Skimming through the results, his glance stopped on an entry that piqued his curiosity.

"Breaking News of Tomorrow" was flashing with big and ugly red letters on the screen. It looked like a six-year-old's experiment with size and color and immediately grabbed Mike's attention. He visualized how he could play this idea in the office, and although the look of the opened page left no doubt about the author's infantile design skills, Mike could not resist reading the content.

However, after he read the first few news items, he lost any possible respect for the page creator, the initially intriguing promise falling flat. The reported news was boring and lacked any sense of humor or originality. *What a waste of such a brilliant idea*, he thought, yet he continued to scroll through the rest of the page in hope that the real reason for this site was concealed at the bottom. His eyes came upon on the last item, mentioning a neighborhood and an apartment complex with the same name as his own.

HOMICIDE IN WEST PARK

A man and woman, husband and wife, were shot and killed late afternoon on April 2 in the West Park neighborhood in the Evergreen apartment complex. The shooting was reported at about one p.m., according to the police. The victims were inside their second-floor apartment when they were fatally shot. Their names were not immediately released, pending formal identification and notification of their next of kin by the County Medical Examiner—Coroner's Office. Police have not released any suspect information or a potential motive behind the shooting.

Geotagging, assumed Mike. Couldn't be a coincidence, as it was apparent to him that the author used his IP address to insert his location name for authenticity. Some fleeting thought kept Mike from closing the page, but he could not identify what, exactly, felt misplaced. Clearly, whatever point the website author wanted to make was lost, and what initially seemed like a good idea was poorly executed. Disappointed, Mike opened a new tab in the browser and looked for other pranks, until he finally had chosen one and decided it was time to go to sleep.

ALREADY TWO DAYS engaged and feeling like a new man of a different status, a status confirming his worthiness in his own eyes, Mike was in a great mood as he drove home from the office, and he almost ran into a completely unexpected police barrier on his street.

"Sorry, sir, this street is closed for traffic." A noticeably tired policeman tried to guide everybody to a detour.

"I live over there, the sixth house on the right. Can I park in my garage?" Mike knew it wouldn't convince the officer.

"Sorry, sir, no exceptions."

"What happened?" asked Mike, not expecting a reply.

"Homicide, sir."

"Homicide, here?" This was truly a crime-free neighborhood, where running a four-way stop sign was the most severe violation. "What happened?"

"Sir, you're blocking traffic, please move on." The police officer impatiently waved for him to continue and went on to direct other passersby.

Mike parked his car on an adjacent street and was startled by Sam and John, who appeared out of nowhere in front of him as if they were ambushing him for precisely this moment. John and Sam were a lovely couple in their mid-sixties, comfortably retired, who spent most of their waking moments on their porch, feeding on every hint of something worth mentioning at least once to anyone in the area. Usually, Mike tried to avoid them, as he despised their gossiping, but now, his curiosity prevailed over his opinion about his neighbors. He walked toward his house quietly, trying to decipher relevant facts from Sam's and John's uninterrupted torrent of information.

"Can you believe it, Mike, somebody killed Martinez and his wife! You know the Martinezes, right? They are from 2F. Somebody shot them both to death! You know, here, right under our noses!" Sam chattered nonstop and with such enthusiasm, as if describing not a murder but a visiting rock star.

"I was the one who called the police!" added John, ignoring Sam's angry look for his interruption.

"You called the police because I told you to!" Sam was unable to hold his annoyance at John. "I ran outside to see what happened and told you to call the police! If it weren't for me, the police wouldn't have even thought to come! Who can call them in the middle of the day in such a quiet neighborhood: everybody's at work!" He turned to Mike again.

"I am sure that because of us, the police will be able to catch the killer in no time!" John added with visible pride.

Mike was struck with a strange sense of déjà vu. A man and his wife, homicide… He felt that he already somehow knew every detail. And then it occurred to him: this was the story he had read a couple of nights ago on that poorly designed webpage he'd stumbled across. A strange, uneasy feeling started to crawl inside his stomach, a feeling that he couldn't yet attribute to anything.

Sam and John continued filling Mike in with every possible detail until, much to Mike's relief, the police allowed him to go into his building.

Mike walked up the stairs to the second-floor apartment he and Jenn shared in an unnoticeable gray corner unit of the Evergreen apartment complex, with faded wall colors long overdue to be refreshed. Their apartment was as dull as the building itself and consisted of a living room, a tiny bedroom, and an uncharacteristically large kitchen.

"Do you know what happened?" Jenn greeted Mike with a kiss, pulling her earbuds off.

"No way, dear, you missed all this commotion!" Mike exclaimed, surprised by how Jenn could remain so oblivious to what was looking like a battle zone outside.

A single glance at the dining table in the kitchen confirmed his suspicion. The table was littered with dozens of glossy bridal magazines, made to test the nerve of the newly minted groom-to-be. Stopping himself from inquiring why a $10 magazine, let alone a dozen of them, was better than a free internet search,

Mike kissed Jenn, mentally subtracting these costs from their already modest budget.

Jenn had stayed home to work on a presentation for new funding initiatives, but by the looks of it, she'd spent most of her time reading these bridal magazines, which she'd methodically bookmarked, judging by the Post-it notes sticking out of different pages. They had not yet set the date or venue or discussed any details, but Jenn said that merely fantasizing about the wedding yesterday made her day brighter and demanded that she take today off to continue dwelling on this subject. The first few days after a proposal were the sweetest, as the planning at this stage belonged more to a fantasyland than to the harsh reality of actual logistics, expenses, and arguments. She had been so engaged in her research, looking at different ideas and listening to her music, that she'd written off all the commotion outside as a noisy background.

"Since noon, there've been dozens of police cars on the street. Is there an accident?" she asked.

"Worse, a murder, a terrible one." Mike told Jenn everything he'd heard on his way from where he'd parked the car. "You know, the rumors spread fast when John and Sam are around. Those guys have too much time on their hands, but I guess they will be useful to the detectives now. They live for this."

Dinner was a Central Asian dish resembling pilaf. Well, that's how it was defined in the recipe book. Mike's one-word description of Jenn's cooking was "unpredictability." Jenn loved to experiment with the food, and she called herself a world-class assembler. Every dish she made was completely different each time. You wouldn't be surprised if today it were pho, tomorrow a poke, then Russian pelmeni, or something Indian or Mexican,

Italian or fusion. There was only one rule in her kitchen—she should not spend more than twenty minutes preparing the dish, excluding the time of actual cooking. And so her dinner planning was quite hectic—a little before dinnertime, she would search online for a quick recipe based on non-spoiled ingredients she found in a fridge or kitchen cabinets. Often, the recipe called for some additional ingredients, but such nuances never stopped Jenn from improvising, for who could say that fresh lamb with a bit of fat on it couldn't be replaced with a lean chicken breast?

"You know, Jenn," said Mike, forking unidentified pieces onto his plate and shoveling them into the mouth. "There's something strange about this murder. It's freaking me out."

"Of course, it's terrible! Poor family! I cannot even imagine it! So shocking!"

"Well, not that. I mean, of course, it's terrible and all, don't get me wrong, but something else bothers me. Errhh, it's like I knew about it all along. Like, errhh...I read about the victims and their murder a couple of days ago."

Jenn gave him a strange look. "You couldn't have read about the victims and their murder a couple of days ago—it happened just a few hours ago. Maybe you read something about some other murder."

"No, every detail of this case, including the name of our neighborhood and our apartment complex, is exactly as it was described." And with that, Mike told Jenn he hadn't been able to fall asleep from his excitement on the day of their engagement and had silently gone to the kitchen and opened his computer, and then he'd stumbled upon this archaically designed page that portended tomorrow's news.

"My first thought was that predicting tomorrow's news is a great idea for an office prank. But now, after the precisely described murder really happened in our complex, I think this is something else."

"What can it be?" asked Jenn, totally confused.

"I now think that the murderer wanted to announce his plans for some sick reason. Look at the details—the place, the time, the family all match the real story. It couldn't be a coincidence. Let me show you." Mike turned on his laptop and launched the browser.

"Why would he do it?" asked Jenn, waiting for Mike to fetch the page. Her tone showed little signs of buying into his story. "Wouldn't a killer want to avoid being caught?"

"I think he would, but… Here it is!" Mike found a link in his browser history and hit the "Enter" button.

"Breaking News of Tomorrow" was flashing with the same big ugly red letters, except the page was empty of any content but a single line under the title, typed in all-capital green letters, almost as big as the title: "NEXT UPDATE—APRIL 3, 12:01 A.M."

MIKE WAS ALMOST finished with his work emails when he looked at his antique wall clock, which loudly announced midnight. Some vague feeling of curiosity pulled him back to his browser. He hit the "Refresh" button, and for a second, the screen went blank. Then the same ugly red flashing letters appeared, followed by new articles, loading one after another.

"Jenn, come over; it's here again!" Mike was in complete ecstasy, like a little boy solving an Agatha Christie mystery. "Take a look!"

Jenn walked into the kitchen, tying her bathrobe, her hair still dripping from the shower. "What? What? I'm not even done taking my shower."

"Read this!" he said triumphantly and turned the screen to Jenn. She pulled the chair from under the table, sat, and leaned toward the computer. As she read, Mike could see her face tense up and her right leg start bobbing up and down—a clear signal that she was disturbed.

DOUBLE MURDER IN ORCHARD VALLEY

A man in his late thirties and his wife were found murdered in their house on Orchard Valley Street, close to Pine Mountain Boulevard. Both were shot by what seems to be an automatic weapon and were killed on the spot. Around noon, the shooting was reported by a passerby after he heard a loud argument coming from the victim's house, followed by a rapid fire that killed the victims. It is the second murder of an entire family in the span of three days. The police are investigating a possible connection between the two.

"You know it's here, a few blocks from my office," said Mike, pointing to an area on Google Maps where the alleged murder was supposed to happen. "We often go to lunch at the mall plaza nearby."

They sat silently, concurrently pinching the screen in and out.

"Do you have any doubts now that the killer published his intention to kill tomorrow?" Mike finally said.

"Why, for God's sake, would a killer want to do that? It doesn't make any sense, Mike!"

"No, it doesn't. Yet it's here."

"Should we call the police?"

"I don't think so. This would be the strangest call they ever received. Can you imagine their reaction?" He mocked their potential call: "*Hello, is this the police? Tomorrow, a serial killer will kill two people on Orchard Valley Street. Oh, no, I am not the killer myself, just learned of his intentions. Sorry, I cannot give you my name, but I know this is gonna happen, and please don't trace my call. I have nothing to do with tomorrow's murder, pinky promise!*"

"Yeah, they'll say you dialed the wrong number and need to call a psychiatrist instead…" Jenn scrolled back to the beginning of the page, but before she reached it, the screen went blank and then changed to a new one, completely blank with only one line of large green letters, all capitals: "NEXT UPDATE—APRIL 4, 12:01 AM."

After a few minutes of sitting in complete silence, Mike finally spoke in a low voice. "Do you believe now it's a serial killer? I think he initiated some sort of a game and is thrilled to walk on the edge of the potential to be caught."

Jenn did not reply but went to the front door to verify it was locked. When she spoke, her words were languid: "If this is a serial killer case, Mike, I am scared to death because we could find ourselves targeted too…"

"How come? What do we have to do with it? We were just browsing through the internet and reading some random stuff. How could we possibly be targets? Even if he is a serial killer, how in the world could he potentially think of us? Do you know how many millions can read this freaking page?"

"Can he get us if we talk to the police? Like somehow get our names and go after us?"

The idea gradually sank in, and for a moment, a mix of fear and confusion occupied Mike's thoughts.

"You are right, Jenn, he could make us his next targets. I need to take care of that," Mike said, and spent the next few minutes clicking on his laptop's keyboard.

"I installed the VPN, just in case, so he won't be able to track us here," he said when he finished, and then asked an obvious question: "So, why all the other articles? What purpose do they have?"

"Clues? Deception? I don't really know. Do you remember what they are about?"

"Frankly, I didn't pay that much attention to them; I went directly to the murder section. I recollect there was some politician giving testimony to Congress, something about a new movie release, some boring stuff. Oh, yes, there was something about the Miami Open sensation, but I really didn't focus on any of them, just scrolled down."

"Mike, don't you find it really"—Jenn searched for the right word—"ah, disturbing, that these murders happen around you, either where you live or where you work?"

Mike looked at her, and his eyes visibly widened. "Do you think he somehow is targeting *me*?"

"I don't know, but what is the probability that there is another person that reads this freaking website at midnight and spends his days near the murder sites? I am frightened to death." Jenn went to the window and closed the blinds. "Mike, tell me we are not in danger, please tell me!"

CHAPTER 2

The board meeting, which was scheduled for the next day, ran much longer than usual, well into the evening. But Mike's boss, Duke Houston, was happy: the board green-lit everything the company management asked.

"You did a good job, Mike," said the Duke, as he was called behind his back.

The Duke had a massive frame and, with his six-four height and athletic background, many found it challenging to keep pace with him when he was walking. Originally from Louisiana, Houston was known for his take-no-prisoners attitude toward everything in his life. He'd been a player on an Ivy League college football team with a promising future when two severe injuries impaired his ability to move forward with a professional career, and he put all his efforts into his studies. A few decades later, he was the same fierce competitor as he'd been in his youth, smashing his opponents like there was no tomorrow.

Knowing the Duke quite well, and now, after the board approved the project and Mike's hopes to be promoted began to finally materialize, he was pretty afraid to admit that he did some data massaging.

"You know, Mr. Houston, errhh, I redistributed revenues from all our product lines for the next two quarters. Overall, it's the same, but from the accounting perspective, the revenues will be different."

Houston gave Mike a small pat on his shoulder, like father to son. "Stop mumbling, boy, we got a budget and a go-ahead, so let's focus now on delivering on our promises." And with a slight push, he signaled that the conversation was over and said goodbye.

Mike bought a bottle of Coke to keep him alert on his drive home, as his veins, which were pumping him with adrenaline for the board meeting, suddenly stopped their supply after the meeting concluded, and his body was completely drained of energy, leaving him emotionally exhausted and uncharged.

Jenn had just returned from her work, too, and was quickly cutting a salad from whatever vegetables were in the fridge, an Ultimate All-In Salad, as Mike called such creations, which, depending on the previous few days of cooking, could be made from any combination of roughly cut tomatoes, cucumbers, beans, sprouts, onions, bell peppers, mushrooms, mint leaves, asparagus, lettuce, spinach, carrots, cabbage, or anything else that the grocery store down the street carried. She never bothered to keep any predefined proportions, as she believed that regardless of which ingredients were used and how much, with the right amount of salt, pepper, and olive oil, any salad was equally edible.

"How was the meeting?" asked Jenn, continuing chopping the leaves. "Did the board approve your requests?"

"Without any real challenge," replied Mike. "The Duke told me they finally realized we must diversify into a new product that I proposed, so they weren't grilling us. I think I might be given a shot to be in charge of the project."

"So proud of you, dear!" Jenn embraced Mike's neck with her knife-free hand and gave him a long kiss. "You so deserve it! So the Duke told you this?"

"Well, he didn't tell me explicitly, but I think he hinted after the meeting. What's up with you today? How was your work?" Mike asked, changing the subject.

"Nothing exciting. Instead of spending time with the kids, I needed to work on presentations to attract donations. Apparently, working with underprivileged children isn't as sexy as other philanthropies to the world's richest." Jenn was visibly upset.

"Of course. It's sexier to donate to medical research than to help troubled kids in their own city," Mike said. "A benefactor's name engraved with big silver letters on top of a cancer treatment center looks better than graffiti on the walls of a semi-demolished store."

"You gave me an idea for the presentation! I never looked at it from the perspective of what is in it for them! I'll redo my pitch tomorrow. Thanks, dear!" She gave Mike a peck on the cheek and added, "You know, I couldn't stop thinking about the murder. All day, I was scanning the local news, but nothing happened. I even drove to Orchard Valley Street, but everything was as usual. I think all this is unrelated; maybe we just let our imagination run wild and wound each other up."

"Thank God nothing happened! I couldn't check the news myself today, but I was thinking about it all the time too."

They continued to chat over the kitchen table about everything that happened that day, about tomorrow and the day after tomorrow, and after that day, too, until it was clear that it would be better to discuss the next themes in bed.

THE WALL CLOCK was making hissing sounds, its old mechanism tired of running day after day, even before both of them were born. Suddenly, Mike felt Jenn's nervous poke. "Mike, wake up. It is going to be today!"

"What's going to be today?"

"The murder at Pine and Orchard! Today *is* tomorrow!"

Mike slowly woke up. It was not unusual that Jenn had some unique ideas in the middle of the night and often asked him to participate in the discussion. Thankfully, he needed only to show initial interest, then peacefully fall asleep again next to Jenn's monotonic murmuring.

This time, Jenn's tone alerted Mike that her mind was on an urgent, important, and don't-even-dare-ignore topic. He raised himself up on his elbow. "Jenn, it didn't happen. All this was probably some sort of a cruel joke and strange coincidence."

"Mike," Jenn whispered as if she was afraid somebody was eavesdropping on their bedroom conversation, "Think about it—we read the news before we went to sleep yesterday, right?"

"Right, and there was nothing today—"

"But the news appeared *after* midnight," Jenn interrupted Mike, "so it was practically today, I mean, yesterday. So he intends to kill *today* at noon. That's why we haven't seen anything yet."

Jenn's logic was correct, Mike realized. They rarely went to sleep after midnight, so it did feel like they had confused the time frame. "Right, assuming there is a killer and he plays this sick game. Somehow I am less convinced now than I was two days ago."

"And if there is a killer, and if he kills again?"

"Then we should talk to the authorities and have them trace the maniac. But there are too many 'ifs' here. The whole thing is based on my memory about what I had read, and it might not even be connected to anything. Jenn, come here."

And with that, Mike pulled her toward him to lie on his shoulder, slightly patted her on the back, and within a minute, he was asleep, leaving her alone to morosely contemplate the perspective of a killer on the loose.

THE WHOLE NEXT morning, Mike was talking on the phone about his new software, but near noon, he was startled by Houston's shouts, which echoed across the entire floor.

"Boys, let's go, let's go, let's go!" Houston was in high spirits, pacing through the corridor and knocking on each door, closed or wide open, as he passed them on his way to the elevator. His loud, commanding voice did not require additional fortification, yet he never thought it would be overabundant to guarantee their attention. "Twelve o'clock at The Boat, boys." Houston got onto the elevator, and finally, his words faded.

Gee, doesn't he see that I am on a conference call? Mike had mixed feelings toward Houston; while he admired the man's business skills, he was too often intimidated by Houston's personality.

The Duke was often too brutal and treated his employees as his disciples, frequently roaring in meetings when somebody screwed up. But he had fantastic business instincts and excellent negotiation skills with his customers, which made him one of the leading CEOs in the industry. The media loved him, and he was second to none at spinning his story.

Houston was the son of a teenage drug-addict single mom who'd dropped out of the tenth grade to give birth and then spent her short life scuttling between jail terms and crack houses. On rare occasions, she'd crawled back to her parents' house to find out she was no longer welcome. She hardly ever acknowledged her son or showed any signs of connection or remorse, and when she was finally gone ten years later, he didn't shed even a single tear.

Mike finished his call, hung up the phone, and took an umbrella from the corner. It was a ten-minute walk to The Boat, enough time to check in on his mom and tell her about his engagement.

Mike's mother was fixing her washer when he called. His father had passed a couple of years ago, but she was still the same harried woman she'd been when she married his father. She didn't trust technicians to do their job in repairing anything in the house. She sincerely believed that their primary purpose was looking for ways to make money by replacing the most expensive parts. So when an unfortunate appliance showed even a slight sign of malfunction with a minor, easily repairable defect, in Mrs. Eaglewood's house, this meant a permanent death, as she would tear it apart, shake it or unscrew and screw back one piece to another, disconnect and reconnect wires from their plugs, and do many other different sadistic acts. More often than not, she was surprised to see spare parts left on the floor after the reassembly. (If there weere appliance priests, this was the right moment to pay a visit to the poor device prior to its final breath.)

"Hi, Mom, what's the noise?"

"Hi, Mikey!" She greeted him with his childhood nickname, which Mike had secretly hated his whole adult life, especially when Mrs. Eaglewood used it in public. "Can you imagine? This washer is barely three years old, and the timer stopped working."

"You need a new washer, Mom," replied Mike, saying a little quiet prayer for the soul of Mrs. Eaglewood's washer.

"Nah, I think I'll fix it."

"As I said, Mom, you need a new washer. How are you doing otherwise?"

"You wouldn't believe, Mikey, but we busted Jordan Schuller and his cronies from the board, and I've been voted in!"

Mrs. Eaglewood had spent the last three months campaigning in her gated senior living community to get rid of the undoubtedly corrupt association board, which was allegedly (but undoubtedly, mind you!) using their hard-earned monthly fees to definitely enrich themselves and their children. But now, when justice finally prevailed, no way anyone on the board would implement totally ridiculous rules and fine people each time when they slightly overused the public facilities or parked in a guest parking spot for more than five minutes, because now it would be on Mrs. Eaglewood's watch, and no one would dare get in trouble with her, she related in one long, unstoppable sentence.

"I am happy to hear that you made it right." Mike was finally able to squeeze a word in. "Listen, Mom, I want to share with you something. I proposed to Jenn."

"Oh, good, congratulations, Mikey. You know the most outrageous thing? You wouldn't believe it—Schuller brought his wife to the board, and they had two votes for their household. Two votes, would you believe it?"

Despite being used to the fact that his mother never dwelled too much on his news, Mike's heart squeezed from a pain that such a life-changing event didn't elicit a slightly more enthusiastic response. On the other side, however, he quickly attempted to reason to himself, the only thing that changed in his and Jenn's relationship from his mother's perspective, was a ring on a finger, merely a symbolic thing, so what's the fuss? He took a brief pause, forbidding his disappointment to cross the space between them, and before hanging up and entering the restaurant, replied with fake calmness:

"Glad you got rid of them, Mom. Good luck with the washer and the association. I gotta go, bye, kiss you!"

The Boat was one of the oldest diners in the city, located in a massive old building with huge columns and an arch at its entrance. The current owner renamed it The Boat, a name that couldn't conflict more with the building's exterior, which looked more like a bank than a restaurant, especially a seafood one. The new owner redesigned the interior and completely changed how the restaurant operated, focusing on modern eaters who were conscious about the environment, food, and processes. Nowadays, the restaurant featured large tables, bright ambient light, and a menu that changed daily, based on what fresh produce, fish, and seafood was available. The management betted that customers would agree to pay a premium for a guarantee of absolutely the freshest ingredients, and this premium would be enough to make up for the inefficiency of such an operation. So far, the last two years proved them right, and The Boat's constantly changing cuisine was in constant demand.

The Duke was towering over the central table with a glass of wine in his right hand and a piece of paper with some graphs and numbers in his left hand, his voice filling the whole venue. He spotted Mike entering the building, raised the glass again, and roared, concluding his toast:

"And to you, Mike, for your vision and guts in developing the next-generation solution. Cheers!"

"What did I miss, Andy?" Mike asked Andrezj Linowski, plopping down on a chair Linowski saved for him. Linowski was a short man with the biggest brain Mike had ever encountered, and the two had been close friends since they'd met, often spending entire nights and weekends in the office.

"Big bonus coming next week, as last year's numbers were much better than forecast," Linowski murmured, hiding his mouth behind the napkin like he was a middle-school student afraid to be reprimanded for talking during the teacher's lecture.

"Fantastic! Jenn would appreciate a nice wedding."

They hadn't set the date or finalized the details of their wedding yet, but Mike hoped it wouldn't be his headache to plan. A bigger budget meant fewer tradeoffs to discuss: venue, food, drinks, ribbons, amenities, candles, cards, glasses and plates, and thousands of other items, without each, as any bride planning her party would agree, no wedding would be complete.

"May I have your attention?" Steve Kwon rose from his chair, looking right and left and making eye contact with everybody around the table. Kwon waited a few moments to let people put down their forks and knives and stop talking. Kwon was their head of human resources, or head of talent, as he loved to call himself. He was a very valuable person in Houston's organization, for he was a wizard at extinguishing any fire.

Just as he was beginning to propose a toast, three or four sirens erupted in front of the building, forcing everybody to jump in their chairs. Moments later, two policemen entered the restaurant and stayed in the doorway, glancing over the dining floor. The maître d' approached the cops, and the three of them talked a bit about something, with the maître d' constantly raising his hands in a motion of shocked surprise and horror.

An unpleasant feeling filled the room, and an ominous silence abruptly ended every conversation. The maître d', taking charge over the situation, turned from the cops and addressed his patrons in a shaking voice, which sometimes broke from its regular pattern and moved to a high pitch for a word or two.

"Dear guests, there was a shooting near The Boat with several victims. The police blocked the nearby streets and ask that everyone remain in their seats until they've thoroughly assessed the situation and cleared the area. There is no danger to us, and the police are in full control. Please return to your lunch, and I hope it will be over soon."

Right, thought Mike, *like it's even possible to return to eat when there's a shooting outside and the doors are protected by the police. Who is he kidding?*

Indeed, nobody continued to eat, and everyone trapped inside tried to learn the news from each other and their phones. The two cops at the door either did not know all the details or decided to keep quiet and resorted to their single reply line: "Sorry, ma'am,

I have no more information to share." And with an impenetrable attitude, they didn't let people out, regardless of how urgent and vital they claimed their business elsewhere was.

The sirens continued roaming through the street and were dying far away, and the sounds of a commotion outside coming from the front door unsettled the nerves of the people locked inside the restaurant. It'd been more than an hour since the event occurred, and yet they were not allowed to leave, as if the man responsible for the shooting was still out there waiting for them to step into the street.

At last, another policeman entered the building, said something to the two cops at the entrance, and loudly announced, to the relief of the impatient people waiting: "Ladies and gentlemen, you can leave the venue now. I will direct you to a safe exit. Please follow me." And with that, he motioned in the air, inviting all to follow him.

When they finally got outside the building, which now reminded Mike more of a war zone than the shopping plaza of just a couple of hours ago, he caught up with Houston, who was striding with his giant steps and fast-talking with Kwon.

"Mr. Houston, I am sorry, sir, for the interruption, but I need to call it a day."

"Boy, it was a nuthouse!" Houston exclaimed. "What a mess! Of course, I think we all better call it a day. That's what I am talking about with Steve."

Mike shook hands with them both, turned, and rushed back to the restaurant.

CHAPTER 3

Rachel Sorrow was desperate to get any worthy information from police officers at the crime scene, but it looked like they were unwilling to share anything new, much to her annoyance. She was a young, promising investigative journalist at the local QQBC TV network in her early thirties, with a fantastic hunch for exciting news in the city. Her internal station ratings were up in the skies, as she always was the first to bring the story and spin it unpredictably. At her young age, she had held an unbreakable record of covering high-profile scandals in the city—from corrupt city hall officials to illegal sports gambling to drug and sex trafficking, and many more. Yet she did not succeed in securing a contract with a big cable news company, and so she stayed with a local television station, waiting for the right moment.

Even her biggest story wasn't enough to break through with major networks, despite shaking up the local political world. The report exposed a multiyear bribery scheme at the city municipality, bringing the whole chain of command and a couple of development corporations to their knees, resulting in thirteen indictments and two bankruptcies. As Rachel Sorrow showed in a series of five episodes aired on every weekday night at prime time, the scheme involved tens of millions of dollars paid to several city officials to get approvals for their multimillion-dollar projects on public lands. The money was laundered via different mechanisms, including donations to the election campaigns, and when the story was brought to life, not only did the involved officials pay the price with their freedom, but the whole party lost the next election, which changed the city politics for good.

It was pretty amazing how much Rachel knew of the scheme, the level of detail and all the transactions. Often, it felt like investigators learned more clues from her five episodes than via their investigative process. Once, in an interview, the defense attorney angrily remarked that there was no way Ms. Sorrow could unveil this unless she was capable of sneaking through the wall cracks and being present at the moment, which wasn't surprising at all, looking at her. That was no doubt a desperate attempt to diminish the validity of Rachel's accusation, and his sexist reference to her petite, almost boyish figure raised a lot of resentment in her viewers, who loved Rachel and were ready to give up watching a basketball game to devour the latest scoop she brought.

Rachel wasn't a popular figure in a police department, as her city story exposed a couple of their officers too, and whenever they saw her on a crime scene, they turned a deaf ear to her inquiries at any chance they had. And so this time at Orchard Valley, her efforts were unproductive—cops did not express any desire to cooperate or volunteer any significant details. After three more desperate attempts, Rachel sat on a curbstone and lit a cigarette, waiting for a new opportunity to emerge.

"Excuse me, Ms. Sorrow, I might have some information."

An unexpected voice from behind jolted her forward. She quickly turned: an average-built man with sunglasses and a raised jacket collar, hiding his lower jaw, stood in front of her, and without any pause, continued.

"I came to believe that the person responsible for the murder of this family is the same one who killed the family two days ago. I think it is not revealed yet, but the victims are husband and wife. He will kill again, I am positive." The man told Sorrow everything in a single breath, and without waiting for her reply, he turned and rushed back toward the corner.

"Hey, stop, how do you know this? What's your name? Who are the victims? What do you know about the killer? Who killed them? Why…? Hey, wait…" Rachel had shot millions of questions, trying to catch him, but she was incapable of matching his fast steps and shortly lost him as he disappeared around the corner.

Rachel rushed back to the scene and shouted to her cameraman: "Roll!"

"MIKE, WHERE HAVE you been?" Jenn was yelling on her car phone. "I called you thousands of times!"

"Sorry, I forgot to turn my phone on. The Duke invited us to The Boat, and it's been on silent mode since then. It happened, Jenn."

"I know. I just saw Rachel Sorrow's flash news. She announced that she received information from an anonymous source that the victims are husband and wife, and these two murders are connected. It fits the post we read, 100 percent matching."

"Jenn, it's me who told her about the victims…"

"What?" Jenn exclaimed and then suddenly swore: "Damn it! Gee!"

"Are you OK, Jenn? What happened?"

"Nothing! Because of you, I almost bumped into the minivan in front of me, not paying attention that the green light had already changed to red. I can't believe it, Mike, are you out of your mind? We discussed that talking to the police might be dangerous, but to Sorrow?" For the first time in their relationship, Jenn was furious, proving that no other language could compete with Russian in making a point with just two words.

"I know, Jenn, I took every precaution to stay anonymous…"

"I'll be home at six. See you there." With that, Jenn disconnected, leaving Mike to wonder whether her ancestors would be proud of her command of the Russian phrases.

JOHN AND SAM ambushed Mike outside of his garage, blocking the stairways to his apartment. Mike was disinclined to meet them, but it was impossible to sneak past them unnoticed.

"Evening, John, evening, Sam," said Mike, hoping his dry, businesslike tone of voice combined with not slowing his strides toward the stairs would indicate that he was in no mood and had no time to engage with them in gossip trading. John and Sam hadn't earned their reputation for no reason, and Mike's pitiable attempt to avoid a conversation had no effect.

"Hi, Mike! Glad you are home safe—they say it was a real mess at The Boat! How long have you been held there? Did you look at the scene? Did you hear what Rachel Sorrow reported?" John and Sam bombarded him with questions.

Mike abruptly stopped, as he did not expect John and Sam to know either about him being at The Boat or talking to Sorrow. Suddenly, a feeling of real fear squeezed his guts: if Sam and John knew his whereabouts and that he'd talked to the reporter, then the killer might learn it too.

"There were shootings there, and the police blocked the area, but I have no idea what it was; they did not tell us." Mike decided not to lie about him being close to the crime scene. "How do you know I was in The Boat?"

"We were watching TV, and then there was a breaking news segment with Rachel Sorrow. There was a murder on Orchard Valley, a husband and wife. You know, just near The Boat," started Sam.

"And I have a nephew, David, working as a waiter at the restaurant, so I called him right away to check on him, and he told me you guys had a celebration lunch there," added John. "You surely know David, right? He was at our twenty-fifth anniversary party. Remember him? Red shorts, yellow sneakers?"

"Sure, I remember him, but somehow didn't notice him there. Guess I was too focused on our group's discussions." Mike had no clue who David was, but he didn't want to hurt John's feelings.

"Of course, you couldn't see him—David said he wasn't waiting on your group's tables."

"Oh, yes, makes sense, as I would definitely say hello to him if he were…" Mike exhaled in relief.

"This girl knows her way around digging the news," continued Sam, visibly annoyed by John for getting sidetracked from the more important topic. "She said there is a serial killer over there, and he killed Martinez and these poor guys, same person, same motive. The police are now on full alert, as the situation is much more serious than they thought."

"Did the police say anything?"

"No, the detective refused to comment, but I am sure there will be a press conference later this evening or tomorrow, as they wouldn't be able to ignore her reporting for too long."

"Right, David told me she came to the restaurant and interviewed half of the staff—he said she's onto something." John gleamed with pride that his nephew had significant firsthand knowledge about the case, which raised John's position about the matter way above his partner in their never-ending contest.

They reached Mike's building, and, unable to hide his annoyance from Sam and John's spinning of the same story again and again, Mike, rather rudely, interrupted them and, bidding goodnight, climbed to his apartment, skipping every other stair on the way up.

Jenn was waiting in the living room, still fuming from the earlier call.

"Mike, didn't you think that this woman doesn't hold *anything* sacred? She would easily give up your identity for five minutes of glory on the screen. That's all she cares about—her ratings!"

"Jenn, she barely saw me, relax! I wore sunglasses, and mostly, she saw me from my back. The whole thing took maybe twenty seconds, and I was gone. I don't think she even registered me…"

"Don't tell me to relax!" Jenn yelled at him. "There is a killer out there, and once you have talked to Sorrow, he might find ways to get to us, in our very house! It even matches his pattern!"

"We aren't married yet for that." Mike tried to lighten the situation.

"Ha ha, *very* funny!" Jenn's look was anything but entertained.

"Jenn, I am very sorry. Please calm down. Nothing happened. Let's think about what's going on." Mike embraced Jenn around the shoulders and held her tight to his chest, not letting her get free despite her furious attempts. Slowly, Mike's hold had its effect, and she relaxed her tension.

"You know what, maybe talking to Sorrow might actually not be that bad of an idea," Jenn suddenly said.

"You gotta be kidding me." Mike was stunned, as he was not used to seeing his fiancée in an upset and argumentative mood and then suddenly switching her thesis to the complete opposite without any sign of discomfort. "After grilling me for half an hour, you now think that it was OK to talk to her?"

"I didn't say that, Mike! You definitely shouldn't be making an impulsive decision to talk to her. What if the killer is still around and was watching her? Going to talk to her in the light of the day, in the middle of her TV reporting, was at least"—Jenn was looking for a word not to insult Mike—"careless."

"Jenn"—Mike was very confused whether he did the right or the wrong thing by talking to Sorrow, but he decided to let it go—"I think we should recheck the freaking page. We also should dig into who the victims are and see what they had in common."

He brought a laptop and opened the browser on the book-marked page. Familiar big, ugly, flashing red letters appeared again on the screen: "NEXT UPDATE—APRIL 5, 12:01 A.M."

"I'm not going to sleep until I read it," said Jenn as she nervously began to prepare the dinner.

CHAPTER 4

The evening was slowly crawling, not willing to give in to the night and, with that, to the terrible revelations it might bring. Breaking News of Tomorrow promised a midnight update, and Jenn and Mike were glancing at the old wall clock every few minutes as if it would help the time to pass faster. The clock, however, decided not to cooperate, instead shifting the blame to its old mechanism, which every minute was making terrible sounds, resisting to move its arm and then suddenly dashing to the next dial. This struggle of time and progress was almost unbearable in an ominous silence of waiting and expectation.

"You should throw away this damn clock," said Jenn, for the first time showing signs of her annoyance at anything in the apartment with unhidden anger in her voice. "This old piece of junk is barely working."

"It's the only thing left from my grandfather. He got it from his grandfather, and I am certain it will outlive us to be passed on to our grandchildren." Mike tried hard to defuse the tension that hung in the air.

Jenn ignored the attempt, and they continued to search for any piece of information related to the two recent murders, but not much was available. Largely the same facts circulated between different local news outlets, without bringing anything fresh and relevant. From time to time, they reluctantly uttered a few words or traded a couple of ideas, but mainly were quietly lost in their thoughts, confused with an aftertaste of their first quarrel.

For every couple in the world, the first quarrel set a simple rule for the rest of their relationship: the first to give in in the argument and come with an apology was destined forever to be the one to ask for a truce. Some were born with this knowledge, some observed their parents, but the vast majority experienced the power of this law themselves.

"C'mon, Jenn." Mike belonged to the last group. "Stop being mad! I did not think the killer could be there; I thought he would flee the area right away. C'mon, let's have peace?" Mike moved his chair to Jenn's, embraced her, and tried to kiss her cheek.

"I am not sure you realize how stupid your actions were and how much you could endanger us," replied Jenn. And with that, she just followed the second important rule of relationship dynamics: an apology was a process that should be savored, and the first one should never be accepted. Finally, Jenn gave Mike's cheek a couple of pats, and from that very moment, each of them knew what would happen next time if, God forbid, they seriously disagreed again.

"It's almost time, Jenn. He should update any minute now."

Mike refreshed the page. A screen blinked, stayed black for a moment, and a new entry appeared in the same irritating letters, in a big, ugly, flashing red font: "Breaking News of Tomorrow."

The articles started to load in the same order as before: first some unrelated to each other—items about politics, culture, pharma, a fossil fuel company in Europe, tennis—and then the dreaded post appeared in front of their eyes, the last one on the page.

THIRD DOUBLE MURDER AT WASHINGTON SQUARE

The city is struck with the terror of a serial killer who enters the private residences of our citizens and kills entire families. Just moments ago, a new murder was reported close to the Washington Square area. According to Rachel Sorrow, who was the first person to report this horrific incident, it is the same person who meticulously planned and executed his terrible acts of assassination. Police did not reveal the identity of today's victims, but Rachel Sorrow told in her reportage that the killer targets middle-class couples in their mid-thirties. While this information is not confirmed by the police, based on Sorrow's impeccable track record in investigative journalism, we have all the reasons to not doubt the validity of her report.

Mike and Jenn finished reading this story and sat without saying a single word, rereading the same lines again and again, until the screen blinked, went black for a moment, and the text was replaced with a now-standard line: "NEXT UPDATE—APRIL 6, 12:01 A.M."

Finally, Mike broke the silence: "Jenn, it looks bad. We should do something. The killer plays some dangerous game—he literally tells us what he will do next."

"I think he is a real psycho. He is, like, sending invitations to the police to his homicide party."

"Only they didn't get them yet…"

Jenn took her tablet and looked at the map. "Washington Square is a pretty big place."

"You know, Jenn, it's close to where my mom lives, look, like two blocks away." Mike pointed to the map. For a second, his tone showed signs of concern, but after a quick look at Jenn's expression, he changed it to downplay the issue. "But it's not really her neighborhood." He zoomed in, and Mrs. Eaglewood's neighborhood looked much farther.

"Mike, I'm scared! We need to talk to the police. He kills close to where you might be: our apartment complex, your work, now your mom's neighborhood."

"I am not worried about my mom. This freaking site says he killed a couple in their mid-thirties. Besides, you said it yourself. Washington Square is a big place."

"Mike, it's only two blocks from your mom! I don't like that every murder is connected to you somehow! I am terrified! It's like he is watching you!"

Mike attempted to brush this off, but Jenn interrupted him: "Please don't tell me this is just a coincidence! We must do something!" She zoomed in to the Washington Square and added: "There are quite a lot of apartment complexes in the area, anyone can be targeted.

"He chooses apartments and not single-family homes…
Strange… It's more difficult to escape from an apartment building
and not be seen."

"Jenn, I don't understand what he's trying to accomplish by
updating us with his next steps, but I think I must notify the police."

"Not the police! You said yourself—the page is not preserved. No
way you would be able to explain anything. Better to tip off Sorrow."

MIKE STARED IN the mirror—the person in the reflection could
use a good shave and a good rest; dark bags under his eyes and
two-day-old stubble gave him a grim look, adding a few good
years to his biological age.

A plan, discussed and argued at length the whole sleepless
night, and finally agreed to by Jenn, was tricky, incomplete, and
dangerous, yet it seemed to be the only suitable option for them.
The undeniable reality of the killer loose, with four lives already
taken and at least two more at stake, heavily weighed on both of
them. They did not ask to participate, but it happened against
their wishes and desires. Often, a burden, shared with others,
becomes a responsibility, while a responsibility, shared with no
one, remains just a discomfort.

Deep in his heart, Mike felt sorry he had not shaken off the
first case as a coincidence; now he had no choice but to prove
his manhood and worthiness, both to his fiancée and, to his
great surprise, to himself as well. He again looked at himself in
a mirror before stepping out of the bathroom.

Jenn stood in a kitchen with two cups of coffee.

"Here is the money," she said, pointing to a fat white envelope on the table. "I withdrew only $1200, as I have a limit on each card."

"Should be enough," replied Mike. "Thanks for the coffee." He took a bagel from a bag Jenn had brought from the diner around the corner and started to spread cream cheese on it. "So let's go over again: at 12:15 p.m., you go to The Boat's plaza to this hamburger place. Then in about twenty to thirty minutes, buy something from a gift shop near my office. The PIN is 1394. Use it in both places." He handed her his debit card and left.

On his way to the office, Mike stopped at the convenience store and purchased a prepaid credit card. He drove a few more minutes, parked his car, and went on foot another couple of blocks until he reached a twenty-four-hour convenience store, where he purchased a prepaid cell phone and paid for it with his new Visa. He registered it under the name of Douglas Jordan, exited the store, turned on the phone, and dialed.

"QQBC, g-o-o-o-d morning! This is Amanda Lee. How can I help you?" The trained operator's voice radiated happiness to talk at this early hour.

"Good morning, Amanda. This is Doug Jordan. May I please speak with Rachel Sorrow?"

"Oh, Ms. Sorrow is not yet in, Mr. Jordan. I can leave a message for her if you wish."

"Do you know by chance when she would be coming?" Mike tried to speak as casually as possible. "I am her high-school friend, in town for one day. Rachel asked me to call when I arrive so we can have breakfast together, but I lost my phone on a plane, and all the numbers were gone."

"I am sorry, Mr. Jordan. I lost my phone myself a couple of years ago, and I felt like my whole life ceased to exist—I couldn't remember even my mom's number!"

"You bet! It's crazy how much we rely on electronics! So, when did you say Rachel is coming?"

"Oh, I never know, Mr. Jordan. She comes and goes whenever she wants. Sometimes she doesn't even show up in the office for days! It's all based on what story she is working on."

"How recognizable! Same ol' Rachel! Is there any way I can reach her?"

"Of course. I can transfer you to her desk, and you can leave a message on her answering machine. She regularly checks her messages no matter where she is."

"Fantastic! That would be great! Thank you very much, Amanda!"

Mike waited for the greeting message to finish, cleared his throat, and started to speak with a transformed voice: "Good morning, Miss Sorrow. I am the one who tipped you off two days ago about Orchard Valley Street and the murder details. I came to know about these killings. Please call me on this number. That is very important, as another couple is about to die."

Mike continued to walk toward his car with his hand clinging to the phone in this pocket. He started the car, and after driving for ten minutes, he stopped at a gas station, where he fueled his car and brought another prepaid cell phone; every transaction he made with cash. The phone didn't ring.

Mike anxiously checked the phone every now and then, which made him feel even more nervous than before. Finally convinced that it would take time for Sorrow to get the message and call him back, he reluctantly drove to his office. If she didn't call him within the next hour, Mike decided, he would abort his plan.

The phone in his pocket finally buzzed when Mike was only three blocks from his office. He looked at the screen and memorized the caller ID. Illegally stopped at the bus station, Mike cleared his throat and clicked the "Talk" button: "Hello."

"This is Rachel Sorrow. You left me a message."

"Thank you, Miss Sorrow, for calling me. You might hardly believe it, but I have very reliable information about the murders. I know where and when the next one is going to happen. But I cannot go to the police. Not that they will believe me anyway. "

"How did you get this information?"

"Miss Sorrow, can we meet? I will tell you everything I know."

"I am not sure this is a good idea, Mr.…"

"Douglas Jordan, you can call me Doug. Miss Sorrow, can we meet at 12:15 p.m. in the Palm Valley mall? I understand you are worried that I might be some maniac. But frankly, if I wanted to harm you, the last place I would do so is in the most populous city venue during lunchtime! Please go to Los Amigos in the food court, and after you get your food, find a table and wait for me there." And with that, Mike hung up.

CHAPTER 5

A scoop of such proportion came to Rachel Sorrow rather unexpectedly. Typically, it was the police who fed a reporter information about a murder case, not a reporter who tipped the police, especially in such a high-profile case that brought the nerves of the entire city to the verge. This could be her long-awaited breakthrough, her way into the world of investigative journalism with a big TV network.

She was pacing back and forth in the living room, still wearing an stretched-out, almost-down-to-her knees T-shirt, in which she'd slept, smoking her third cigarette since she woke up merely half an hour ago, not really paying attention that its ashes fell on the floor when she shook them off, missing the ashtray. She started to feel the adrenaline rush of believing that Douglas Jordan had a trustable story, and her intuition told her he meant no harm. And why should she doubt him? After all, it was Jordan who'd told her details of the previous case when the police were not willing to share anything, and everything he'd told was fully corroborated later! And boy, wasn't she delighted to piss off the detectives with her story! Next time they would be better to cooperate than play a "no comment" game with her!

Rachel smashed her half-finished cigarette and threw her sleeping T-shirt on the chair, which already housed yesterday's jeans, a few days' worth of worn blouses, a couple of bras, and some sandwich wraps from the last week or one before. She started a shower, cursed when discovered that she had run out of shampoo, and used a liquid hand soap as a reasonable alternative.

The contents of her fridge didn't include anything breakfast-able: three bottles of sparkling water, ketchup, two lemons, a quarter gallon of spoiled milk, mustard, several bags of pizza spices, some open, two cans of Coca Cola, and a few pickles in a big jar. That didn't discourage her, as a newly lit cigarette, washed down by a freshly brewed hot coffee, was a good substitute for breakfast. And anyway, in about two hours, she was supposed to meet Douglas Jordan over lunch, so no biggie.

Rachel opened her computer and decided to learn everything she could find out about Douglas Jordan. After about thirty minutes of searching, she picked up her phone and called the station.

"QQBC, g-o-o-o-d morning! This is Amanda Lee. How can I help you?" Amanda Lee sounded to be in her typical everlasting good mood.

"Hi, Amanda, Rachel Sorrow. Listen, did anyone call me today?"

"Morning, Miss Sorrow! Yes, a former classmate called. He told me you were supposed to meet for breakfast. Did you get his message? I transferred him to your desk phone."

"Doug Jordan, yes, I got it, thanks." Rachel hung up. She'd never had a classmate named Douglas Jordan, and it became clear to her that whomever she was meeting was not really named Douglas Jordan.

THE ONLY THING that occupied Mike's head was his upcoming meeting with Sorrow, and instead of working on the new Solutry software, he spent his entire morning researching her work. Around half past eleven, Mike turned off his computer and headed toward the exit. Luckily no one paid attention to him leaving, as everyone was finishing their last tasks before taking off for lunch. The drive to Palm Valley Mall took about fifteen minutes, and he would arrive before the big crowds started coming.

The mall parking was still empty, and Mike parked at the West Parking Garage entrance, assuming Rachel Sorrow would come through it, as it was the closest to the food court. Mike changed his jacket to a hoodie, his dress shoes to sneakers, and continued to sit in his car, carefully observing every vehicle passing the gate.

Precisely at noon, a hard-beaten gray Jeep Cherokee approached the gate, and its driver, a short-haired woman, wearing sunglasses and with a cigarette in her mouth, parked in front of the mall entrance in a disabled spot. Shopping malls, as it happened, rarely enforced parking rules, and field reporters, champions in receiving parking tickets, knew this intimately.

How nice of her! Mike thought sarcastically.

He got out of his car and followed Sorrow to the food court, leaving enough distance between them. Rachel went through the entire food court, throwing almost imperceptible glances at every passerby. Mike, disguised to his best ability, was confident she wouldn't recognize him among the crowd despite her trying to single out the man whom she was supposed to meet. Not finding anyone who rang familiar, she finally went to the line formed near the Los Amigos counter and waited.

Mike went to the line, stood behind Rachel, put a hand on her shoulder, and quietly said, in a low, altered voice: "Do not turn, Miss Sorrow. This is Doug Jordan."

Rachel jumped, but Mike's firm grip held her petite figure in place.

"At the end of the food court, there is an instant photo booth. Please enter it and close the curtain. I will talk to you from the other side of it. Please trust me and do not look."

"Jesus, Doug, you startled me!" replied Rachel, quickly subduing her tense anxiety. "You have a special way around girls! I will not turn, promise. You can let me go now."

Mike took his hand off her shoulder, and true to her word, Rachel went to the photo booth without turning around even once.

"Miss Sorrow," started Mike, "what I am going to tell you sounds crazy, but it is true."

"Call me Rachel. Don't worry, I have seen my share of outrageously insane things that turned out to be true."

"By pure chance, I stumbled upon the diary or planner of the murderer. Initially, I dismissed it as nonsense, but then I started to see that he means what he says. He is choosing married couples in their mid-thirties living in apartment buildings."

"That's all very interesting, but so far, everything you told me about him can be found in the news."

"Right, but the next time he's going to do it is tomorrow, early afternoon, at Washington Square."

"If you are positive that this is reliable information, why wouldn't you go to the police?"

"Two reasons. First, I do not have any way to prove it until it happens, and cannot reasonably explain my source of information. Which will inevitably make me either a prime suspect or accomplice, and I am not. And second, I'm afraid to be exposed and potentially become a target."

"And you are completely OK that it will be me who will go to the police and expose myself, right? Oh, boy, as I said, you have your way around the girls!"

"Actually, Miss Sorrow, arr…Rachel, I am not OK with that. But it is the killer himself who wants you to cover this case…" And with that, Mike disappeared in the lunchtime mall crowd that was roaming in a search of cheap food.

RACHEL WAITED A few more minutes in the booth before she decided to step out. As she expected, the area near the booth was clear, and there was no man nearby who could be identified as Doug Jordan. People continued walking in and out of the food court with bags and trays filled with their lunch, and nobody was paying any attention to a young woman standing alone and looking lost. She clicked the speed-dial button on her phone.

"Sorry, Rachel, I succeeded in taking only one shot from his back, when he was standing behind you in a line. But he wore a hoodie… Then you suddenly went somewhere, I lost you, and I couldn't see you because of the crowd between us. The next time I saw you was when you were leaving that booth."

"Damn it, Dick!" Rachel replied angrily, looking at her cameraman, Dick Newman, who stood at the other side of the court. "Is that usable at all?"

"Well, at least we can tell how he is built and how tall he is. I'm sorry, but you gave me no time to prepare."

RACHEL DROVE HOME in a deep thought, which made her drive slowly, uncharacteristically obeying every traffic rule. Too many things didn't make any sense. Presumably an innocent person, Doug Jordan somehow stumbled upon a serial killer's plan and knew exactly when and where the next two murders would happen. By itself, this was as outrageous as it sounded, and the fact that the killer wanted her personally to cover this case really frightened her. How in the world did Doug Jordan know that the killer wanted *her* to cover the case? And why her? What made *her* so important? Her heartbeat accelerated at this thought, as suddenly she felt like Clarice Starling from *The Silence of the Lambs*, and she didn't feel that brave at all.

An unwanted fear occupied her mind more than she was willing to admit even to herself. She looked at the clock; it was half past one, and, hoping that Josh Koppelman would be available, she dialed him.

CHAPTER 6

Josh Koppelman knew Rachel Sorrow better than anybody else. They first met at a party, and she was a free-spirited college freshman whose mesmerizing personality hid her nondescript looks. She behaved more like a boy than a girl, never cared about her appearance, but she was one of the brightest liberal minds on campus. Five years her senior, Josh fell in love with her, and they dated for three years.

They were an odd couple, different in almost every aspect of their personalities. He, always dressed to the highest standard, which he brought from home; she, always wearing the jeans and T-shirt that were the first to reveal themselves in the morning: sometimes from a closet, sometimes found on a shower floor from the night before or fished from a laundry basket that was waiting for an eventual trip to a laundromat. But despite their polar differences, after only five minutes in their company, it was not difficult to see why he was so enamored of her.

They broke up on the day of her graduation, as their relationship reached its natural end—she wasn't willing to be domesticated for him; he wasn't able to cope with her eccentric lifestyle. They maintained a close friendship and claimed no hard feelings. Both went to lead their lives separately and never looked back. At first, their friends didn't notice any significant differences in their moods or attitudes. With years, however, it became apparent to everyone that they hadn't succeeded in adjusting to life without each other. Rachel never let any other man into her life; Josh, on the other hand, had been married and divorced twice within just five years of their separation. She substituted chain-smoking for him; he became bald and, after his two miserable marriage failures, found solace in joining the FBI as a special agent.

Koppelman was at his desk when Rachel called.

"Hi, Rach, what's up?" He wasn't surprised to hear her voice, as he often was first on her dial list when she needed to dig something up.

"Hey, Josh, you're good, I hope?" replied Rachel, and without giving him a chance to answer, she continued. "Are you following the murder case of the apartment couples?"

"*Following?* The whole office is on its toes! You got anything?"

"I think I do. But I am not sure yet what I should make out of this." And with that, Rachel told Koppelman everything she'd learned in a couple of last days, including her bizarre meeting with Doug Jordan.

Koppelman carefully listened to Rachel and took notes while she was talking, never interrupting her, as he'd learned that she would lay out the story in an impeccable way, and stopping her with questions would be more counterproductive than just letting her cover all aspects by herself.

When she finally hung up, he looked at the page full of his writing. The case, which had shaken the whole city, was high profile. This serial killer already claimed four lives, and Koppelman knew that he needed to start showing some progress.

He buzzed his deputy, Samir Bashir: "Cancel all your plans, including going home today, Samir. We got a lead."

KOPPELMAN GATHERED ALL the papers with his notes and different printouts of case-related material into a single folder and looked at his wristwatch. It was well after midnight, and not much progress had been made. Samir stood in Koppelman's doorway with visible frustration on his face.

"What did you find, Samir?" asked Koppelman, feeling like they were running out of time if the murder indeed happened today at noon. If Rachel's intel was correct, the killer would strike shortly, and they had yet to narrow down the likely area. With less than a day of preparation, the mission was looking almost impossible.

"There are forty-six couples in a radius of ten blocks that match the criteria. But this area has a lot of private apartment buildings and some undocumented leases, so we are surely off by a factor of two, at least. Take a look at the map; I think we should focus on high-density places, but in any case, we will not be able to cover the whole area."

Koppelman looked at the map. A few of his men were already in the field, but he felt in the dark without knowing precisely where their disposition should be.

As if guessing what his boss was thinking, Samir added: "I have coordinated the spread with the police. The chief agreed to send two guys. He laughed at me when I told him about the information and its source. Especially when I mentioned Rachel."

"I know. If anybody else but Rachel had told me what they had on the case, I would have laughed my ass off as well. But you know her; she has this sixth sense. And it seems this is our only lead. Did you get any intel on the caller?"

"Not much. The call was made from a prepaid phone, and there is no way to trace it. Most probably, he discarded the device after the call. And Dick Newman's picture of him is mostly useless: we have the man from behind, and only the upper half body is visible, and he's wearing a gray hoodie. He is about six feet tall, average build. That's all we can tell so far."

"Hmm, get somebody to look after Rachel. I don't trust this 'Doug Jordan' guy, or whatever his real name is. Don't like the game he plays." Koppelman thought a bit and added, "And, Samir, she shouldn't know, or she'll go ballistic."

CLOSE TO NOON the next day, after spending a sleepless night working on different theories, Rachel was driving her Jeep on the streets near Washington Square, secretly hoping that the killer would walk in plain sight with a gun in his hands and a placard with the address of his next crime. Dick Newman, quite used to Rachel's style of work and unexpected missions, was trying to sleep in the passenger seat, his baseball cap covering his eyes, ready at immediate notice to start filming. Rachel wasn't fond of stopping on red, so every time she approached a junction and the light was about to change, she either suddenly sped up to get through during the remaining moments of yellow or, in the worst case, turned right. These sudden accelerations, stops, or turns caused Newman to bump his head against the window or the dashboard, which Rachel told him to consider an occupational hazard.

Today was not "reveal your identity" day, Rachel thought, and after driving down all the nearby streets at least several times in each direction, she abruptly stopped near a hot-dog food cart, recalling that she hadn't yet eaten today, and wasn't that sure about the night before.

She'd spent the last few days trying to establish even the thinnest connection between the victims. Nothing. The only resemblance was their demographics—married Hispanic couples in their mid-thirties. Her hope was that Koppelman would use his vast resources to dig much deeper than she could.

Rachel bought a couple hot dogs and two cans of Coke and gave half to Newman, who grimaced but took them. Using the Jeep's hood as an improvised table, Rachel stopped midbite, put the sandwich and the Coke on the car, and suddenly said, "Dick, I think it will be around here! I can feel it!"

Newman flung his half-eaten hot dog into the garbage bin on a corner, gulped a few sips of his Coke, and threw the rest of the can after the sandwich. "I'm ready."

Rachel froze in place, raised her nose as if she were a hound picking up the scent of game, and for some reason whispered, "If he's going to kill, it should be now."

She was just about to finish her sentence as, somewhere in the distance, from the direction of the buildings across the street, they heard four quick rounds of gunshots, followed by silence. Without a single word, in complete unison, they jumped into the car. Rachel pushed the ignition button, and disregarding the traffic lights, she hit the gas pedal and took off toward the sounds. Frightened by the Jeep, which looked as if it had recently returned from a war zone and wouldn't mind getting into another fight, every other driver pulled aside to let her pass.

She tossed her phone to Newman. "Call Koppelman."

He found Koppelman's number in her contacts and briefly described their location and what they had just heard. It was much more efficient than calling 911—Special Agent Joshua Koppelman would know what to do next.

It had been less than two minutes from the moment they heard the shots when she stopped the car in front of the building they thought the gunshots had come from. Both rushed toward the building in complete synchronization, ready for the broadcast, when multiple sirens erupted around them.

"OK?" asked Rachel and turned on her microphone, ignoring the commotion that had started to develop around them.

"Go," replied Newton simply and pressed the "Record" button.

"Just a moment ago, another terrible tragedy happened in this peaceful neighborhood, as the serial killer continues to terrorize our city. While it is not yet confirmed by law enforcement, based on my information, I believe it is the same killer who murdered another two married couples last week."

She continued talking until Koppelman and Samir arrived. After exchanging several words with a few other men on the ground, Koppelman approached Rachel, who paused her broadcast.

"Did Doug Jordan contact you yet?" asked Koppelman when Rachel turned off her mic.

"Nope, but basically everything he told me is true."

"Rach, I know you disagree with me, but from where I stand, Doug Jordan and the killer are the same person. And we will apprehend him when you two meet next time."

KOPPELMAN WAS WAITING for Rachel in the Night Angel bar in the same plaza as The Boat restaurant. *Should bring inspiration*, he thought, slowly sipping his beer. Recent events in the vicinity, combined with a reduced crowd in the city's business district during the middle of the week, meant the bar was almost empty at this hour. *Perfect for our discussion*, thought Koppelman.

Waiting for Rachel often required a lot of patience. It was not uncommon for her to suddenly recall something about the story she was working on and spend extra time on meticulous research, or interviews, or editing her piece, neglecting to keep track of her time. She always carried her khaki backpack, which Koppelman had given her during her last college year. It was irreplaceable, as it contained a great deal of precious items: small notebooks, block notes, Post-its, letters, keys to God knew which doors, small scissors, a Swiss Army knife, dried-out ink pens, broken pencils, chargers for several of her cell phones, cell phones themselves, headphones, and whatnot. The only thing that was always replaceable in her bag was the latest book because she read at least one or two of them a week.

For the tenth time, a waiter with an expression of deep disappointment approached Koppelman, who finally asked for a gin and tonic with a slice of lime and a refill for his beer.

Rachel entered the Night Angel and immediately located Koppelman in the almost deserted bar. She flopped down on a chair next to him and, skipping the usual pleasantries, said, "You already ordered for me, right?"

Koppelman nodded.

"I might have a lead," started Rachel. "I just spoke with Samuel Miller and his partner, John Courting. They are retirees in West Park, live in the apartment complex as the first murder. On the day before that killing, at around 12:15, they saw a man in a utility company uniform. They did not report this as suspicious, but I checked with the complex's management office. According to the administration, there was no utility service scheduled in the last ten days for any of their apartments. There was also no call to them—everything goes through the administration."

"So the first obvious conclusion is that our man scoped out the area disguised as a utility service person. Did Samuel and John give you a description of him?"

"Not really. It is not unusual for the complex to have service-men coming and going, so this did not raise any suspicions."

"We will contact the utility company and check if they have performed any services. Sometimes they schedule their own maintenance so the administration wouldn't know," said Koppelman. He thought a bit and added: "Can it be Doug Jordan?"

"It can. But I do not think Doug is the killer. It does not make sense to me. I think he's telling the truth, Josh."

"Rach, how many serial killers have you met in your life? They do not keep their killing diary public, so people can read it. Whoever this Doug Jordan is, he came to know the details well in advance and quite precisely." Koppelman sipped his beer, then finally added: "I cannot make anything from that other than he is the killer. And, Rach, I think he'd playing with you and plans to go after you."

CHAPTER 7

"Mike, got a minute? The Duke wants to talk to you." Steve Kwon stood at the doorway to Mike's office and waited for Mike to get up.

Mike suddenly felt a pain in his guts as if a wrench did a few turns inside him. A sign of an HR person at the end of the day asking to proceed to the manager's office was as ubiquitous and final in corporate life as a sign of the angel of death on one's threshold.

Kwon loudly laughed, somewhat insincerely but nevertheless calming.

"You should see your face, Mike! Don't worry—you aren't fired! The Duke just wants to discuss some aspects of the project!" Kwon was an experienced executive and known to recognize the gamut of feelings of his employees.

"Oh, sure, Steve, no problem, of course!" Mike was relieved but quite puzzled about Steve's role in this.

Houston was finishing a call and motioned Kwon and Mike to step in and close the door.

"Hi, Mike, how have you been doing?" Houston sounded friendly and casual.

"Very good, Mr. Houston, busy with the project. How are you doing?"

"Not bad at all! What a roller coaster we've been at for the last quarter! At some point, I thought we were running too fast to stay on the rails. That's a fantastic proposal you put together, well done, boy, well done!"

"Thank you, Mr. Houston. I appreciate your feedback! Andy and I were working on weekends to develop a prototype. It was really our common effort…"

"Yeah, Andy is a real whiz, no doubt," said Houston, pausing before moving to the actual point for this meeting. When talking to his team, Houston never beat around the bush. "Steve and I had a discussion about the project. We need to put somebody very bold in charge of execution. So Steve asked me who the best person to run all this is. You know, I have been thinking hard about this. No doubt, you are a great candidate for this position. You know more than anybody else—it's your brainchild, after all! And you will get credit for it. But…"

Mike was waiting for the "but," so he stopped breathing to hear the unavoidable verdict, which was the real reason for Kwon's presence.

"But," continued Houston, "I do not think you will succeed, as number one, you have no experience, and we have no time for trials. I hope you understand that. But you will be fantastic as second in charge for all the product features."

Houston continued to discuss the project in detail, but Mike had already tuned out and cursed himself for convincing himself that Houston would trust him to be the one to run the project. He felt robbed. It was true that he lacked the experience to handle such a high-stakes execution. Still, he believed he would compensate for any of his deficits with knowledge, passion, hard work, and a burning desire to succeed. The project was his creation, and seeing how it was taken away from him created a big void inside him and filled him with indignation. One of the biggest betrayals a person could feel was a betrayal in one's own beliefs, and Mike couldn't think of anything else now.

Back in his office, he stuffed the laptop into his backpack and headed home, ignoring multiple urgent emails that filled his inbox.

Mike realized that one glance at his face would tell Jenn that something bad happened, but he was unable to pretend that nothing had happened. After three years of living together, he thought she knew all of his insecurities. So when Mike told Jenn about being passed on for the project he'd invented, presented, and defended in front of the board, she didn't look surprised, which annoyed him more than he thought her reaction would.

"That's alright, Mike. It's not the end of the world, and it will let you work on the development, which you like, and not mundane daily management."

"Really, Jenn? *Really?* Just a couple of days ago, before the board meeting, The Duke let me believe that I might be the one to lead the project, and now he thwarted my chance, and all you have to say is that's alright?" He didn't notice that he'd raised his voice.

"Dear, you have a brilliant mind, creative thinking, and the ability to see the big picture. That's why you were the one to invent this new software! But to lead a big organization…you lack self-confidence. You have too many self-doubts. You need to work on that, and there will be another opportunity to make a name for yourself."

Jenn continued her efforts to analyze this turn of events more favorably than Mike felt, until she exhausted her all arguments, and she patted Mike's hand and changed the subject.

"We also need to talk about your discussion with Sorrow. I know it couldn't be worse timing for your meeting with Houston today, after everything that's going on with the murders."

"Right, I know, I didn't forget. Just—the Duke took me off guard. I guess I shouldn't be so emotionally invested at work."

"That's a wrong conclusion, Mike! You should be yourself at work. But enough about that. We just talked about Solutry for an hour—tell me how it went with Sorrow."

"Very short meeting, with me totally incognito. I couldn't reasonably explain how I came to see the Breaking News of Tomorrow website. It sounded ridiculous, so I told her that I stumbled upon some information and know that tomorrow there will be another murder."

"You didn't tell her about Breaking News of Tomorrow?"

"I just told you, didn't I?" Mike snapped, still fuming from the unfair development at his office.

"Sure, you did. I only wanted to make sure I understood you correctly." To Mike's relief, Jenn let his tone pass unnoticed.

"No, I didn't bring up the source of the knowledge, as a normal person wouldn't believe it, and I have no way to confirm the information. Remember, the site goes blank—what I can show? Nothing! There is no proof, so what's the point of even mentioning it?"

"You can take a screenshot before it goes blank and show it to her."

"The screenshot is just a picture that can be easily photo-shopped. It proves nothing, so there is no point in it."

"The point is that now you look very suspicious in her eyes," Jenn said in a tranquilized voice, trying to defuse his unjustified aggression with calmness. "And I am sure now in the eyes of police too. Can you explain how you got this knowledge, Mike, if they question you? Now they might implicate you in these murders."

Jenn's calm voice and reasoning had its effect, and Mike finally succeeded in controlling his nerves.

"She didn't see me, and I changed my voice when I talked to her and then disposed of the cell phone I called from. There is no way they will identify me."

"Let's pray this will be the case." Jenn's tone indicated that there was no point to continue arguing. "What do you think Sorrow will do now?"

"Contact the FBI to track down and stop this guy," replied Mike. "I don't like the alternative."

MIKE AND JENN sat glued to the laptop screen, expecting the page to update at any second. Somebody's tragedy was unveiled in front of their eyes, and they could not help but watch in real-time how the murderer's sick mind played with others' lives. It was as if they saw a news program about some faraway country's disaster, or war, and felt terrible for the people, wishing it would not happen yet continuing to watch with unquenchable interest. Only, this time, both Mike and Jenn felt they had some ability to intervene.

Exactly as it promised a day ago, right after midnight, the page uploaded, and Mike quickly scrolled toward the end. There was nothing about the murders. They scanned the page up and down and checked all the stories, and each one was entirely irrelevant to the case.

"That's the damn reason I didn't want to talk to the police and tell Sorrow about this website," said Mike, with clear triumph of his rightness. "If he stops broadcasting his intentions and I cannot prove anything, I would be grilled about the source of my knowledge, maybe even convicted of conspiracy. You see now why I was right?"

Jenn quickly looked at him and said nothing, clearly avoiding a pointless argument. Mike hit the reload button twice, knowing perfectly well that it would not change the result, and loudly swore, accusing the killer of not following through with his daily announcements, forgetting for a moment that they actually meant murders.

"Mike, that's OK. I hope he is done with the murders," said Jenn. She squeezed his hand lightly as if trying to subdue Mike's frustration at the lack of new information.

"I don't think so. He is a real maniac, a real psycho. He just thinks that he's giving too much of a hint, so I am afraid if he continues to do this without telling, it will be much harder to catch him."

He sat without speaking for a minute and then added, "You know, he might realize that the FBI is on him. It is clear that this guy is skillful, looks like a computer hacker. He surely knows how many times his page was viewed, and he can also more or less know who loaded the site based on the IPs."

"He can *know* that we saw it?" Jenn was genuinely terrified by the idea.

"Oh, don't you worry. Our IP is hidden now, I continue to use the VPN, just in case," replied Mike matter-of-factly, "but based on how his page is viewed, from where, he might think it's too hot for him and stop updating, or upload some irrelevant nonsense like today."

"So you think he will continue to kill?"

"What changed for him? He wanted a high-adrenaline game, and he got one. Maybe the police, the FBI, or who knows who else is on to him, and that's what he wanted. I don't understand him; it's like a tag game for him."

"So today's murder will happen, you think?"

"Most probably, unless Sorrow succeeded in convincing the police and they are lucky."

"Mike, this is the most terrible feeling I've ever had—think about it. Somebody is sleeping their last sleep in their bed, and within a few hours, they will be cruelly murdered, and we know about it, know where and when it will happen, and can do nothing!" Jenn's voice trembled.

"Jenn, without being cynical, what is the difference between that and any other disaster or war in any other place we read about and know that people there will die?"

"Mike, I cannot believe you! It's a huge difference, *huge*! When there is a war, or earthquake, or hurricane, I cannot make it disappear, I cannot help, I can do *nothing*! But now, now…" And with that, Jenn burst into tears, and Mike couldn't help but feel completely stupid because of his remark and his previous behavior toward her and, at the same time, somehow guilty and a little complicit in the murders himself.

CHAPTER 8

The whole next morning, surprisingly uninterrupted by his coworkers, Mike was fully immersed in reading the latest breaking news about the serial killer and what the police and the FBI had told the press when Steve Kwon unexpectedly appeared in Mike's doorway again and startled him.

"Mike, the Duke wants you to meet somebody in his office."

Kwon's visits annoyed Mike. Every time Kwon stepped into his office, it portended some unpleasant turn of events.

"Sure, Steve, I'll be there in a minute. You know who that is?" asked Mike, but Kwon was already on his way to Houston's office, visibly avoiding Mike's question.

Reluctantly, knowing something was up, Mike went to Houston's office on the other side of the corridor.

"Good morning, Mr. Houston, you wanted me to meet somebody?" asked Mike as he crossed the threshold. He noticed a woman sitting on the couch.

"Yes. Mike, please meet Keana O'Connor. I believe you know each other. You used to work together before, right?"

Mike stopped dead, seriously taken aback. Finally, he uttered, "Nice to see you again, Keana." He looked at Houston with a question in his eyes.

"Mike, yesterday, you and I discussed that we need to find a leader for your project. I talked to the board, and they had a perfect candidate for us—Keana. Keana has a history of impressive results, and I am sure she is what we need for this project! I wanted you and Keana to have a good discussion and see if you would be able to work together, so I told her that her offer is contingent on this discussion. Do you have time now to meet with Keana? I promised I'd call our chairman this evening." Houston wasn't exactly asking Mike's availability.

"Yes, definitely. Here?"

"Oh, no! Of course not here! You can do it in your office." Houston rose from the armchair, extended his hand to shake Keana's, and said, "Thank you, Keana, it was a great conversation!"

"Keana," said Mike, "I need to get something from the mailroom. Would you wait for me in my office—it's 902, at the end of the corridor, right before the elevators. I will be back in a few minutes." He showed her where she should go, turned around, and walked away in a different direction.

He entered the men's room at the end of the second corridor and washed his face, trying to wipe away his astonishment from the meeting with Keana. When he finally returned to his office, Keana stayed near the window, observing the city from the ninth floor.

"Great view you have from here," she said in a lovely voice.

Mike quietly closed the door, leaned on it with his back, and, not knowing what to do with his hands, stuffed them in his pockets.

"Keana, *why?*"

"Why what, Mike?"

"Why do you need to come here? Couldn't you find any other company to work at?"

"Because you don't have any choice, Mike! What do you think, it's only today that your chairman asked the Duke to call me? Don't be naive, Mike! The board wouldn't finance your project without a proven management team in place. The last board meeting you presented at was a formal review and approval: the decision was made beforehand."

"No way! I finalized the presentation just the night before. Even Houston saw the final version in the morning! Do you know how many things I needed to readjust to make it look right?"

"They didn't need the numbers. They needed to have a direction and a team to execute."

"Keana, this is wrong. We cannot work together after what happened. I must tell Steve Kwon about our history. He wouldn't allow it. It's a bad omen for the company."

"Mike, I gave full disclosure—that's why Steve was in the office when you joined. And they don't give a damn. There is no other way for the company to survive but to switch all their customers to your software and do it ASAP. So the Duke couldn't care less who you slept with in your previous life."

Blood flushed into Mike's face, both from the anger that they'd played him and from the disappointment of his own naivete, as he clenched his hands in his pockets.

"That explains why they need you. But why did *you* accept, knowing I am here?"

"Because, Mike, I need it too," Keana replied in a calm, low voice.

Mike took a chair and sat in silence for a few minutes, trying to digest all the information she'd dumped on him. He looked at her and slowly said, "Is it even possible for us to work together?"

"Mike, it's been five years since we broke up. You moved on. I moved on. I am married."

"Congratulations, I didn't know."

"Why should you? I am not on your radar anymore. I heard you are engaged to Jenn Zharkova."

"You apparently know about me more than I do about you."

"Don't flatter yourself, Mike, I learned about you and Jenn only after Houston asked me to look at this position and told me you are pioneering the product."

"Keana, do you *really* believe we can put the past behind us?"

She looked intently at him, weighed her words, and replied, "Mike, I know we will be able to work together as good colleagues. There are only a handful of people whom I trust. You are one of them."

She went to the door, half opened it, and, with the words, "I trust this interview is over, right, Mike?" stepped out.

HOUSTON WAS DRIVING home in an excellent mood. Every piece was falling into its place and was perfectly aligned. Keana proved to be very versatile in managing her relationships. And that was what Houston needed. He clicked on the dashboard screen and dialed his chairman.

"Hi, Bruce!" said Houston and continued straight to the point of his call. "It looks like we nailed O'Connor—the offer was irresistible, and I believe managing Mike won't be a problem for her."

"Good, will he stay?"

"I am sure he will. This is his baby. He would be an idiot to pass on it. O'Connor doesn't give a damn about him anymore. I saw their interaction, and I think, despite the initial shock, neither does he. I am confident they will be a great team, and she will cover for all his immaturity and diffidence."

"Good. I already spoke with Firetec. They are actually happy she moves out—this solves their problem too."

"What problem?" asked Houston, concerned about a potential issue from her current employer, but the line was already dead.

TO MIKE'S RELIEF, Jenn decided to visit her parents and wasn't home when he returned in a terrible mood, feeling at the lowest point in his career. Just a couple of days ago, he'd thought he was at the top, at the pinnacle of his life: his project was approved, he was a real candidate for a promotion, and Jenn had said yes to his proposal. And how fragile it all could be: a few days later, Jenn and he were thrown into a dangerous murder case, he was passed over for the proposal, and his new boss would be his ex-girlfriend, who, and Mike hated to admit it, looked more stunning than he remembered. And why on Earth did he deserve all these complications?

He was pacing between the kitchen and the living room, unable to shake off his thoughts and unwilling to face Jenn. He hated to feel discomfort and remorse, and he couldn't explain why these feelings occupied his mind and controlled his mood, defying any rationality.

Pacing back and forth, Mike dreaded the moment when Jenn would open the door and he raised the topic of Keana. He fleetingly considered forgetting to talk about this, but he quickly realized that not telling Jenn now would imply he had something to hide. But on the other hand, telling Jenn now would lead to… Well, better not to think about it! All this caused Mike to feel guilty, when he shouldn't.

He heard Jenn's voice coming from the open window. Unsurprisingly, Jenn was talking with Sam and John about the murder on Washington Square. Jenn had too good of a soul to listen to their meaningless reports on current events, and this quality raised her to the ranks of their most favorite neighbor, a title Mike secretly despised, especially when they got out or returned together. Now, however, he thanked them for their detailed reportage, as he needed more time to prepare to talk to Jenn.

When she finally received a complete account of the early events and began to climb the stairs, Mike opened the door for her and waited for Jenn to come.

"John and Sam just told me everything they saw on the TV about the murder. Did you hear anything else? Mike, it is awful what is happening here. We need to do something—I cannot believe there is nothing we can do to stop these murders!"

She quickly rinsed her hands over the kitchen sink and opened the refrigerator to hunt for something for her next culinary creation.

"Jenn, tell me what else we can do. We talked about this. The guy does not leave any trail, and they say he picks his victims randomly—they couldn't find any connection except the age and race… We need to wait until he posts on Breaking News of Tomorrow."

"But don't they already have sufficient information? How many such couples are in the city? Why can't they establish surveillance on them and catch this monster?" Jenn quickly chopped some vegetables, expertly balancing cutting, frying, and serving all at once.

"Jenn," interrupted Mike, trying to guess from the looks of her process what kind of plates and silverware he should put on the table. "First of all, there might be hundreds of such people, living all over the city. And even if they are all known, do you know when he will kill? Tomorrow? Next week? A month from now? They can't hide hundreds of cops at the next-door neighbors for an unspecified time. Unless they have some additional information, there is little to no chance of catching him."

"I can't believe nothing can be done!"

"Jenn, the only thing that we can do is to notify Sorrow when we read any updates. I am sorry, but we are more or less useless otherwise."

"Mike, how can you have such thick skin! People are dying, and you are mumbling 'we can do nothing.'"

"I don't have thick skin. I'm just less emotional than you, and thus more realistic," said Mike, letting her unusual mocking pass.

Jenn patted and disorganized his hair, as if she noticed that he'd disengaged from a needless argument, and simply said, "Let's eat, dear. Dinner is ready."

Whatever was ready did not yet have a name in any specific cuisine and was true in its inclusivity of modern times. Mike carefully probed each layer of Jenn's culinary creation with his fork, moving the dish around with the accuracy of a sapper on a minefield, and demonstrating enthusiasm with each bite.

Intuitively, Mike knew that the most critical argument in domestic disputes was the first sentence, and not the closing one, contrary to popular belief. And Mike was not ready with his opening statement to bring up the subject of Keana, and so he devoured his food much more slowly than usual.

Mike hardly paid any attention to what Jenn was saying after the dinner when they discussed the upcoming wedding party. From time to time, based on the tone of her voice, he replied "Aha" or "Yes" or "Sure," making an impression on Jenn that he was fully engaged in the conversation.

Music, venues, gifts, dresses, guests, dates, and other essential details about the wedding didn't mix well with a mention of an ex-girlfriend of five years who Mike was going to see every day from then on. When Jenn finished weighing in on pros and cons of small versus large parties, Mike said in his most normal and casual manner, "Ah, Jenn, forgot to tell you about an unbelievable coincidence in the office. They hired Keana to work on the project too."

The characteristic of deafening silence was that every word, even whispered in the lowest voice, exploded with a thunderous bang.

"Keana? You mean *your* Keana?"

Mike disliked that framing, as he immediately felt himself in a position that required a strong defense.

"She is not *mine*. I knew her many years ago, and besides, she is married."

Mike misjudged the effect of this information on Jenn: for him, it was an ultimate alibi, while for her, it clearly indicated his interest in Keana's marital status.

"So, she is *married*! How reassuring! Glad you checked!" Her voice, however, indicated anything but being reassured. "Did you tell them you two cannot work together? That this is inappropriate? That you veto her hiring?"

"I cannot, Jenn."

"Why not? This is your project. You can do anything!"

"Because the Duke hired her to be my boss."

The unexpected prospect of Mike spending time with Keana daily, actually spending much more time with Keana than with her, didn't sit well with Jenn, and her face showed every passing emotion caused by the thought of sharing him, even in the most professional setup.

Mike was quite prepared to see Jenn's reaction and decided to keep quiet to avoid infuriating her any further. The old clock, having been in the family's possession for a few generations and having witnessed quite a few family dramas, came to Mike's rescue and, with a loud hissing, moved both of its arms to twelve and, with a chime of celebration, announced midnight. Mike, clearly seeing his escape path, quickly changed the subject.

"Jenn, it's time! We should take a look at what this maniac wrote today!"

Without waiting for a reply, he opened his laptop and loaded the site. Several entries appeared on the screen one by one.

Jenn leaned toward Mike and watched him scroll through the irrelevant entries, which were just trying to distract their attention.

JAPANESE YEN PLUMMETED AGAIN

Economic troubles continue to hurt the Japanese economy. With the severe slowdown of worldwide exports, interest rates barely above 0 percent, and the stock market continuing to underperform, the yen plummeted today and reached its lowest in a decade.

14 CHILDREN SAVED FROM RUBBLE IN SOUTH ARMENIA

Frantic search-and-rescue efforts started in South Armenia following the destruction caused by an earthquake earlier last evening. The death toll is devastating—the 7.0 earthquake claimed 131 lives, more than a thousand are injured, and many are still missing. Rescuers managed to save 14 children that were trapped under the cement rubble of their day-care facility. To the huge joy of the nation, none of the children suffered any significant injuries.

SURPRISING WIN OF A BRAZILIAN TEENAGER

The last Miami Open kept its promise to be the most unprecedented tournament in series history, with most top-level players dispatched one after another in their first rounds. The unseeded Brazilian Carlos Gustavo, a seventeen-year-old player from São Paulo, shocked everyone with his surprising win of the title, a result that established Gustavo as the youngest player ever to win the tournament.

A NEW RECORD FOR SALE OF PAINTING

In a surprising bid, Georgio Galavatti, an eccentric billionaire from Italy, bought two paintings by Italian Renaissance artists totaling 892,329,000 USD in Sotheby's art auction.

Until they finally saw the one they were looking for:

THE SERIAL KILLER WHO TERRORIZED THE CITY IS FINALLY CAUGHT!

In a well-coordinated manhunt led by the FBI, a serial killer who terrorized the city and killed six people was finally caught at the Rincon Green Apartments complex. The killer was apprehended by the FBI when, disguised as utility personnel, he was on his way to execute another victim couple. During the course of capture, he opened fire on the law enforcement officers, and in a cross shooting, he was wounded, arrested, and taken to the Lincoln Cross Hospital, where he is undergoing surgery.

"This is a huge relief for the city," said QQBC's special correspondent Rachel Sorrow, who was instrumental in helping the FBI to investigate the case...

Mike was staring into the screen in disbelief, reading and rereading the story again and again, until the screen flashed and wiped all the stories from it.

"I don't understand, Jenn. I totally don't understand him. This is a seriously sick man."

"What do you think we should do?"

"I don't think we have too much of a choice—we need to talk to Sorrow. I still have a second prepaid phone. I want to call her, but don't want to do it from here, just in case. Mind taking a ride with me?" he asked but immediately knew the answer: few women would want to stay in an empty apartment in the middle of the night after reading about a serial killer at large in their city.

"I am going with you," said Jenn. She took her coat and was quickly at the door.

Mike hugged her in reassurance, grabbed his wallet, cell phone, and car keys from the kitchen table, put on his jacket, and they went out.

"I hope this will be the end of this nightmare," he said as he was starting his car.

After fifteen minutes of driving, Mike stopped the car, shut off the engine, and dialed Rachel's number. Jenn was quietly sitting in the passenger seat and listened intently to the conversation.

Rachel picked up the phone on the first ring as if she were waiting for Mike: "Rachel Sorrow."

"This is Doug Jordan, Miss Sorrow. I am sorry for the late call. Tomorrow, the killer will be at the Rincon Green Apartments. He will be wearing a utility company uniform." Mike did not let Rachel ask any questions but quickly disconnected and took out the battery. "Now it's in her hands," he added and drove back home.

A CAR'S HEADLIGHTS hit the first-floor windows when Mike parked it in his garage half an hour later. Sam sat on his bed, gave John a hefty shove, and said to him: "Did you see that Mike and Jenn went out in the middle of the night? Very strange. I told you Mike is bad news, didn't I? Don't think he's up to anything good." And with that, he looked at the clock. It was one a.m., not a time for decent people to wander around the city.

CHAPTER 9

The murders of the last week completely deprived Koppelman of any sleep, and he was still in the office preparing to leave when Rachel called after midnight. Their conversation changed his plans. He went to the restroom, turned on a faucet, and put his head under the cold water jet—there was a lot of ground to cover in the next twenty-four hours. He returned to his office, took a bottle of carbonated water and a lemon, which he always stocked in a small corner refrigerator, cut the citrus in two, and squeezed one half into the glass of water. Coffee was never his thing to keep him awake and alert for an extended period of time, but carbonated lemon water did the trick for him.

Koppelman phoned Samir, went to the whiteboard that he used for his brainstorming sessions, and started to write down everything he'd learned about the case: facts, assumptions, and action items. By the time Samir and three more agents came to the office some forty minutes later, the whiteboard was covered with a lot of ink.

"We have a huge amount of ground to cover," Koppelman said after he filled Samir in with details of the tip Rachel received, "and

I cannot guarantee it's all verified and solid. All our information is based on what Doug Jordan told Rachel, but unfortunately, this is our only lead."

After about an hour of brainstorming, going back and forth over various assignments and actions, the brightest minds of the country's investigative force went off determined to justify their reputation.

RACHEL SPENT THE whole night working on her end to decipher the case, looking for different connections and motives, and she didn't pay attention that it was already midday. She looked at the pile of notes spread across her table, hesitating to decide which one was her most promising direction. She'd barely slept and was already finishing her second pack of cigarettes since Doug's middle-of-the-night call.

Her line of work, dealing with and reporting about a lot of people on both sides of the law, taught her many things about human psychology, especially when it came to illegal activities, and everything in Doug's behavior was telling her of his innocence. Yet Koppelman was adamant that Doug Jordan was either a killer himself or at least an accomplice to the killer. She knew in her sixth sense that he wasn't the killer. But an accomplice…well, it was impossible to explain his explicit knowledge of the killer's moves. Except, she continued to think, how many serial killers in history worked with accomplices? The whole idea seemed challenging to comprehend; except…she thought again, except…this might be not a serial killer case but a meticulous execution of people who were somehow connected. That thought began to take center stage in her mind.

Rachel lit another cigarette and resumed pacing back and forth in the hope that the right answer would reveal itself. But it didn't. Instead, she realized that she was very far from understanding. She forced herself to recall all the moments when Doug Jordan had contacted her, and she tried again to fish for any new hints she previously missed. His first contact was at Orchard Valley Street when he told who was killed and claimed it was the same killer from the first murder. Then they met in the mall, and Doug Jordan told her about the upcoming murder. Now he'd told her the exact location. It seemed like he was narrowing it down with each contact. *What does this mean?* she continued to ask herself.

She returned to the notes, which were the results of the tedious work of Phil Matthew, her loyal private detective. Koppelman used to say that he envied her, as her detective was never overwhelmed with unnecessary legal formalities and protocols.

It was clear Doug knew about the planned murders. That was fact number one—she approached the table and wrote this on one of the clean notes. He wanted the killer to be caught. That was fact number two, she scribbled on the second note. She was still pacing when her phone buzzed with a message from Matthew. She looked at the screen, and then suddenly, a thought came to her like it always did when she got her mind into the right place. Initially, it was a very light, almost intangible idea, very fragile to be rushed out, and Rachel carefully nurtured it so it wouldn't flee. She sat down, mindlessly staring at the wall until her fleeting idea was conceived into clear action.

She jumped from the chair, ran to the bathroom to take a quick shower, rinsed her mouth with Listerine, threw herself into the first pair of jeans and sweater that was hanging on the bathroom doorknob, grabbed and shoved her notes into her backpack, and hurried out to her car. The apparent connection between all cases had clearly formed in her mind, and all she needed was to get to Koppelman quickly.

She jumped into her Jeep, sped off without using the turn signals, instead honking to guarantee an unobstructed change of lanes, which other drivers gladly obliged, unwilling to engage in a right-of-way fight.

"Josh, I have an idea!" Rachel was yelling into the speaker, navigating the early-afternoon traffic with one hand, the second hand trying to make some sense out of her still-wet hair. "I am driving to you now."

"Drive safe!" he said. "Let's talk over lunch. I haven't eaten in more than twenty-four hours, and I can't chase killers on an empty stomach."

KOPPELMAN PUT ON his jacket and headed out to a nearby diner, which he favored for the secluded dimly lit niches and a rather expensive lunch menu, which prevented cheap deal hunters from overcrowding the place. He realized how starved he was. He was shown a table, and when a waiter came, Koppelman was ready with an order: a Coke and a chicken salad for Rachel, as he knew she needed some protein, and sparkling water, steak, and a double portion of French fries for himself.

A single glance at Rachel when she tried to find him in a row of dim-lighted alcoves told Koppelman that she'd had as little sleep as him, with the only difference between them being her taking a shower. When she finally saw him in the farthest corner of the dining hall, a waiter had already brought their food, following Koppelman's request to not wait for her to arrive.

Rachel flopped down on the bench, pushed her backpack toward the wall, and ran her fingers into a big basket of fries, which Koppelman had elegantly placed in the middle of the table.

"Josh," she started talking after swallowing the first bunch of fries, "I believe we made a wrong assumption."

Koppelman looked at Rachel and refrained from asking questions, giving her the ability to tell the story the way she wanted.

"I know. It was me who first coined the killer as a serial. Now I believe I was absolutely wrong. When I think about the cases, they do not look to me like the work of a serial killer. You know what they look like?" Without waiting for an answer, she suggested it herself: "Executions!"

"So the killer wanted to execute each couple for some reason?"

"Not a couple—a person! The spouse, and I do not know whether it is men or women he is after, was just in the wrong place at the wrong time!" She started to be more and more excited and stopped eating.

"Rach, eat, we can talk while we eat. And in any case, I need to digest it all!" Koppelman said, playing with words.

"We all were focusing on how these couples are connected. It was too obvious—in each of the three murders, the victims are like clones: married, middle class, in their mid-thirties, living in apartment buildings, always killed around noon."

"These killings also happen within a couple of days of each other, an MO which is quite uncharacteristic for a serial killer."

"Exactly!" Rachel said with excitement. "So I thought that there is nothing 'serial' here. Then these can only be executions, carefully planned and implemented. And this Doug Jordan somehow knows about it—most probably, he is an accomplice, afraid of something. So what is he afraid of? Must be revenge. He wants to disclose his partner or whoever this might be, but he fears for his life. So I thought there must be some prison connection. And then my private investigator sent me some new info, and it occurred to me: there is a connection between the first killed couple and the last one." She paused and looked triumphantly at Koppelman, who himself stopped eating and listened to her every word with his full attention.

"What my PI discovered is that the sister-in-law of Martinez from West Park is married, and her husband has a cousin that served four years in prison some ten years ago. Juan Alvarez from Washington Square was a correction officer and was discharged five years ago—from the same prison. So that's the connection—it cannot be just a coincidence!"

Koppelman was staring at her in admiration.

"Rach, you are a genius!" he finally exclaimed. "It does look solid, and this is the first real promising lead we could follow. I will have my guys check it!" He pulled out his phone and dialed.

"Samir, Rachel has a lead." He quickly summarized their conversation. "Check the backgrounds of everybody in the Rincon Green. If you find somebody there who is connected to the same prison—this guy is the next target."

MIKE AND JENN sat in their kitchen after a long day with a feeling of huge moral relief. The whole story was very puzzling, but the worst was already behind them.

"It's ten o'clock," said Jenn when a wall clock notified them of the hour. "*City Night* is about to start." *City Night* was a weekday program on QQBC with Benjamin Wolf as its host and was one of the most-watched evening programs on cable, with Rachel Sorrow a frequent contributor.

"Good evening, ladies and gentlemen!" Wolf's voice was low and welcoming. "This is Ben Wolf with you this evening. It is the night of April 8, and for the first time in the last week, the city can finally sleep unworried—the notorious killer that terrorized lives of our community and killed six people in less than a week was finally caught during a massive manhunt organized by the police with reinforcement from the FBI. Rachel Sorrow brings the story."

"Good evening, Ben!" Rachel projected energy and confidence. "That's right! A terror that paralyzed our community is finally over, as Anthony Dowell, an alleged killer of six people, was taken into police custody. Earlier today, around noon, law enforcement identified Dowell as the person responsible for the murder of three families, following a solid lead from one of their informants. In an attempt to escape, Dowell opened fire and wounded two officers. The FBI arrested Dowell after shooting him down. Dowell was admitted to the Lincoln Cross Hospital and is currently undergoing surgery. Fortunately, the wounded officers are stable."

"Thank you, Rachel! We all pray for their quick and full recovery! Can you tell us what is known about Dowell?"

"Yes, Ben, from what law enforcement has disclosed, Anthony Dowell is a known hit man. Apparently, he was on the FBI's Most Wanted list for multiple murders across the country over the last few years. His capture not only ends the nightmare we all have been in recently, but will also help to solve many unresolved cases."

"That's excellent news indeed! We cannot be happier with the results of the swift operation of our law enforcement agencies. These tragedies shook us all! Do you have any information about the motives of the crimes?"

"The FBI is carrying on an investigation of connections between the victims and is waiting for Dowell to sufficiently recover from his surgery. I will continue to follow this development and will report when new information is available."

"Thank you very much, Rachel, for your relentless work as always!"

"Thank you, Ben, and back to you."

JENN POURED MORE wine and clinked her glass with Mike's. "I am so glad it's over and we can return to normal life!"

Mike nodded and sipped his wine.

"And now to the sports news," continued Wolf's voice in the background. "James Cobalt has some exciting updates from the arenas. James—to you."

"Good evening, Ben! It's been a sensational night in the sports world, truly sensational! A young unknown tennis player from Brazil won the Miami Open tennis tournament in unprecedented victorious matches, easily beating all his titled opponents, none of whom could win even a single set against him. Remember his name, guys, Carlos Gustavo, a seventeen-year-old teenager from São Paulo, as he is going to be the next big tennis star in the years to come!"

A series of short clips from the Miami Open played one after another, showing Gustavo effortlessly winning his matches against much older and more experienced opponents, each of whom had more titles under their belts than strings on Gustavo's racquet.

"Carlos Gustavo, why do I think I have heard about him?" asked Jenn, who generally didn't follow any sports news. "I think I recognize this name from somewhere." She looked at Mike, who was listening to the program very intently, his face showing complete bewilderment.

"Jenn," he finally said, looking back at her from the TV set. "Do you remember the content of the Breaking News of Tomorrow?"

"Of course I do! It said that the killer was captured at the Rincon Green apartment complex."

"Right, what else?"

"That it was a report from Sorrow…"

"No, not that. Do you remember any other item from the news, not about the killer?"

"There was an earthquake somewhere in Asia or Europe, something about an art auction, something about…" She stopped and her eyes widened in realization. "There was an article about the surprise win of a teenager in a tennis tournament. But I thought all these stories were gibberish to serve as camouflage for the killer story…"

"I thought this too and quickly skimmed through them without giving them too much attention. But I remember a few." Mike took a deep breath. "There was an article about fourteen kids saved in Armenia, about Japanese currency plummeting, about this Gustavo, and about the record-breaking sale for an art piece at some auction."

"Right, I vaguely remember something like that," Jenn agreed with him.

Mike rose from his seat, went to the kitchen table, and brought his laptop to the sofa.

"OK, yen, art, saved kids," he repeated again, as if to cement them in his memory.

His fingers quickly typed respective queries in the browser search bar, and one by one, recent daily news articles appeared on his screen. He quietly read them several times, and finally turned his screen to Jenn, who was silently watching him.

"It's much bigger than we thought, Jenn. Something completely different and way bigger."

CHAPTER 10

Mike learned everything there was to learn about the three topics he remembered from yesterday's postings of the Breaking News of Tomorrow. He knew exactly where the earthquake in Armenia happened, what it destroyed, how fourteen children were saved, how many more people were missing, what humanitarian help the Armenians got, and who was providing it. He learned the names of the paintings and why they were so outrageously expensive, who Georgio Galavatti was, and what he did, why he was interested in art, and how much money he spent on his collection.

But that was not what occupied Mike's mind the most. Up to that point, he was certain that the serial killer, referred to by the name of Anthony Dowell, played a game with law enforcement. He couldn't understand what Dowell's motive was when he believed the Breaking News of Tomorrow was Dowell's own making, but he'd at least had some reasonable explanation. Now, he was utterly puzzled. The site did not make any sense anymore, and the accuracy of its predictions shocked the very foundations of Mike's knowledge about how the web technology worked. If before Mike had created a theory that explained the site and made himself believe in it and see every midnight update as confirmation to that theory, now he felt a huge disappointment in himself for even contemplating this theory, which from where he was standing was looking very naive and wrong. And he hated being naive and wrong when it came to technology. The Breaking News of Tomorrow site played him for a fool.

"Mike, don't you think this might be a smart prediction or some sort of insider knowledge?" asked Jenn, not hiding that she, too, was disturbed by unexplainable coincidence and trying to find some logic. "I just checked—apparently the Miami Open is a big international tennis tournament with high-ranked players that runs for two weeks. This Carlos Gustavo was a surprise discovery on the first day of the tournament, and then with each round, all eyes were on him as he continued his winning streak. Check the sports news about him for the last two weeks. I think it was a no-brainer to predict he'd be a winner based on the earlier rounds and how easily he won them."

"That's possible," agreed Mike, "but how do you explain the other three—yen, art piece price, and the earthquake?"

"Could this have already happened in Europe or Asia, but as it is midnight for us, we are tricked to think it's tomorrow?"

"Nope, even in Japan, our midnight is still today, and I checked every major news network: they all reported one day later."

"So how did Dowell know about them? I mean, how was he able to predict them?"

"That's a whole new assumption now, Jenn, about who wrote it. It was bizarre from the beginning that the killer would put his plans online, but we went along with that because all these plans correlated with what really happened. Now, as I think of it, I am not really sure Dowell is the author. Jenn, I feel so stupid thinking it's the killer, so stupid!"

"But there must be an author!" exclaimed Jenn impatiently, clenching her fists. "Who else if not Dowell?"

She thought for a moment and, slowly probing her theory, suggested, "Sorrow said that Dowell is an FBI's Most Wanted fugitive, and he is a known hitman. It looks like he was hired to kill all these poor couples for some reason. Maybe a person who hired him wanted to get rid of Dowell and published his killing itinerary?"

"There might be something here," said Mike, "but why didn't they publish more precise locations? Why not his name?"

"I don't know. There might be so many reasons: they didn't want him to be caught right away, they still needed him to carry on his mission, who knows. Maybe he is a hitman for some syndicate and they needed to kill their enemies and then get rid of their hitman. Or they thought that Dowell would try to escape and would be killed by the police during the chase. Maybe they assumed there would be a SWAT team to go after Dowell and he would not have a chance to stay alive?"

"Well, these definitely are the more probable explanations than what we initially had," agreed Mike, "but they do not explain at all the whole thing about other news entries, and I do not get it yet."

At this moment, the old wall clock coughed and, loudly cursing his destiny, moved both its arms to the twelve-hour mark, announcing the start of the new day. Jenn took her tablet, clicked on the link Mike previously sent her, and stopped breathing, as if afraid to spook the latest update. In the deathly silence of the house, only three sounds were heard: the clock's angry fight with its own mechanism and the fast beating of two hearts. The tablet screen blinked, and familiar, ugly, flashing big red letters appeared on it.

She quickly ran through the entire contents of the webpage, taking a screenshot every time she scrolled down, and just as she completed the whole pass-through, the screen blinked, and a new caption appeared, like every time before: "Breaking News of Tomorrow—Next Update April 10, 12:01 A.M."

"Mike, there's nothing here about these goddamn murders or even about the city."

"I see it. Strange. You know what, I am going to catalog and follow this BNOT every day. I just want to get to the bottom of it."

"What is 'be not?'" asked Jenn.

"Oh, I just abbreviated it—'Breaking News of Tomorrow,' or BNOT. I will check tomorrow evening to see whether any of this is going to happen. It is the most bizarre thing that I have ever seen, and there is a reason behind it. Somebody does this for some unexplained reason. Right now, I do not have even the slightest idea why they do it and most importantly how they do it. I want to know who they are, I want to know how they do it, and I want to know why."

"Mike, let me say something… I don't want to sound naive or immature…"

"Why would you? Shoot!"

"OK, but don't judge me. The truth is that now I am terrified. With Dowell out there, it was clear—there was a killer on the loose, and it was scary. But I was mostly worried about you getting involved with Sorrow and whether you took all the right precautions and kept your identity out of this mess. I was not that worried about the killer himself."

"What the…"

"Don't get me wrong. He did terrible things, really terrible, to kill all these people… He is an animal… But…but somehow I knew that the police would catch him."

"Oh, darling, I am with you. But what are you scared of now?" Mike hugged Jenn and pressed her to his chest. "Nothing to be scared of now! They caught Dowell, they have no idea who Doug Jordan is, and there is not even a single trace of him in the world, so nothing can really happen! This BNOT site, I think this is a work of some genius who hacked many different systems. There are a lot of things to understand, but that's what I believe this site really is."

"Mike, you don't understand. This"—Jenn waved toward the tablet—"this all feels…ah…satanic to me."

KOPPELMAN AND SAMIR were standing against the whiteboard that still had all their drawings from a few days ago.

"So we know now that Anthony Dowell is not the same person as Doug Jordan, which is obviously an alias Jordan uses. There are only two options that I see: either this Jordan is a rogue accomplice or a handler who wanted to eliminate Dowell and use the FBI to keep his hands clean. Any other hypotheses?" Koppelman looked at his colleague, who shook his head in reply.

"Dowell is not yet in a condition to talk. The hospital will call me when he's capable," Samir said. "It looks like Doug Jordan disappeared into thin air afterward. Unless Dowell talks, chances of finding him are slim."

"What do we know about the second killed pair, Juan Alvarez and Martha Benito? Did we find any connection between them and the first killed couple, Adrian Martinez and his wife?" Koppelman inquired.

"Not yet. I interrogated Enrico Diaz, husband of Martinez's sister-in-law. He admitted that when he was an inmate, he saw Juan Alvarez among the prison guards. Diaz claims he did not have any contact with Alvarez, neither in the prison nor later. We, of course, will verify if they had a post-prison relationship," Samir replied.

"Keep an eye on Diaz. I am sure he's hiding something. There must be a reason Dowell was hired. What do we know about the relationship between Diaz and Martinez?"

"Diaz claims that they had met only at family gatherings. He said he was genuinely shocked when he heard that Martinez and his wife were murdered at their own home, but he has nobody to suspect."

"He is lying," replied Koppelman. "Do we have anything from any of the security cameras in each complex? Can we conclusively implicate Dowell in all these killings?"

"We have quite a lot of overall footage. So far, we did not see anything that jumps out as a clue. And Dowell does not appear to be in any of them, but I wouldn't expect him to be so careless and pose for a camera, so no surprise there. We are working on mapping all people on these films with tenants, their guests, administration, and service providers. This will take us a few days."

"Yeah." Koppelman sighed. "The mayor and the police are happy with capturing Dowell, and they consider the case solved. Not for us. There is something going on, something big, if somebody hired a hitman to eliminate at least eight people, with six killed. Dowell, Diaz, and Jordan are keys to this. Dowell is in our custody, and I hope he recovers fast and starts talking. We have nothing on Diaz, so we need to follow him carefully, and Jordan vanished without a trace. The case, as far as I am concerned, is wide open."

RACHEL OPENED HER eyes and, as usual, lit up a cigarette, took bottled water from the nightstand on the right side of her bed, and checked her voice messages, both on her cell phone and on the office landline. After each successful story, the number of messages was insurmountable. She was hoping to receive two calls: one from any of the executives of the major TV network, congratulating her on a fantastic story and inviting her for lunch, and another from Doug Jordan. Neither of the calls came.

She felt a lot of disappointment. Time after time, she believed she produced high-level reportage that should land her a gig on a national scene, but yet again, it went unnoticed for unexplained reasons. Or worse, they noticed it; after all, six murder cases in the same week by a serial killer was not a story these network executives would miss, no matter where in the country it happened, but apparently, they weren't impressed with her investigative journalistic work.

The lack of the call from Doug Jordan upset her more than disappointed her. She disagreed with Koppelman's assessment of the informant: everything in Doug's behavior suggested he was a good man. Koppelman made his point: Doug knew too many details to rule out his relationship with the hitman. Doug's knowledge of the killer's next moves was almost an indictment of himself. That, most probably, was the reason he hadn't contacted Rachel again. Yet Koppelman did not interact with Doug, while Rachel had, and in such matters, she often relied on her feelings and intuition. And her instincts told that Doug was telling the truth, and he was innocent. But intuition, as she discovered many times, could play nasty tricks.

She mentally went over every tiny detail she could recall from her communication with Doug. A general picture loomed in front of her eyes, and she created a narrative that seemed very reasonable to her:

Some sort of gang was formed in the prison ten or so years ago, a gang of both prisoners and guards, dealing with drugs, as most gangs did. For ten years, their operation went smoothly, and then things changed, bad enough for their opponents to hire an assassin.

That was a very rough story outline, Rachel continued to think, with too many missing links. Enrico Diaz was alive, *still* alive, she mentally noted, and those who hired Dowell were out there too. And, of course, Doug Jordan, whom she couldn't place into this picture at all. She realized that the story was far from being completed.

The city had already closed the case. Dowell had been caught and was in custody—no more murders, no more terror. But as a real journalist, she wasn't satisfied with the outcome. And that meant she needed to get to the root of the whole thing, to uncover and expose the organization, if there was such, to bring all others to justice.

She knew these guys were dangerous; after all, they'd gone to the extent of hiring a shooter who killed six people and would continue killing if Doug had not tipped her off. But the thrill of the big story pumped enough adrenaline into her veins that it clogged her mind like a fog, and she wanted nothing more than to dive into work. Her heartbeat accelerated in anticipation of something big, maybe even bigger than her city corruption story. And maybe she would get a serious nod from the big networks afterward.

The cigarette burned her fingers, and she pushed its butt inside the water bottle, where it died with angry hissing. Then Rachel stood up and went to the bathroom to prepare herself for the day.

CHAPTER 11

Mike was slicing a watermelon to snack on during the long-awaited final episode of the first season of a popular Netflix show he and Jenn watched every Sunday night, when Jenn suddenly asked, "Does Keana start at Solutry in a week?"

"Yeah, I think so. Why?"

"Mike, it's been hanging above us since you told me about Keana. We must set it straight. I believe in you, and I don't think Keana would join the company if she wouldn't put everything behind, for real and for good. But"—she looked at him without blinking—"but your past will continue to loom, and we all will feel awkward. It's inevitable. So let's cut to the chase from the beginning. Invite Keana and her husband to dine with us next weekend."

Mike accidentally avoided cutting off his finger with the knife, flinching in surprise at such an unexpected suggestion. He couldn't imagine this turn of events, and he felt completely unable to formulate any reasonable response. He did not even know what would be a reasonable response to that. He looked at Jenn in bewilderment, but her face showed that she was absolutely content with that. She smiled, patted his hair, which felt to him like a wordless warning, and added,

"And besides, I need to know who I will be against."

THE MORE MIKE tried to hide his nervousness, the more it showed. He selected a bottle of wine to open, then put it back untouched, rearranged silverware on the table to then realize the previous setup was better, and then he redid it again, turned on the music but then decided the genre was wrong, and did many other small things that were supposed to help with his anxiety but actually proved to be counterproductive. From time to time, he took a sneak peek through the window at the sound of every passing car.

Jenn, on the other hand, was in a perfect mood and oblivious to Mike's state, much to his envy. She said she would dress quite casually for this home party, but it actually amplified how beautiful she was—tight jeans, sneakers, white blouse, loose hair, and just the right amount of makeup to force you to hold your breath but not lose consciousness. She did exactly the same things as Mike: fixed the silverware, opened the curtains, cut the lemons. But unlike Mike's Pinocchio stiffness, she had the elegance of a white-swan ballerina.

"They're here!" Mike suddenly exclaimed when a black Porsche Cayenne parked in the visitors' parking across the stairs, sounding like he'd been preparing the whole day for that moment. He dove to the back of the room to avoid being spotted.

"Excellent!" said Jenn. "Very nice of them to be on time."

She opened the door and stayed in the doorway waiting for Keana and her husband to climb the stairs.

"Hello!" she greeted her guests as their heads appeared on the stairs, with the warmth of a longtime friend. "I saw you when you parked. Come on in! Hi, Keana!" Jenn gave her a slight kiss on the cheek and extended her hand to Keana's husband. "I am Jenn. This is Mike." She pointed to Mike, who was still thinking about the first thing he should say and to whom.

"Nice meeting you, Jenn, Mike. I'm Robert."

They shook hands.

"So great you came! I told Mike since he has a new boss I must bribe her with a nice dinner." Jenn laughed. "I took some risks today with the cooking. Hope it will be successful. Otherwise my whole bribing plot fails!"

"Judging how everything looks and smells, it seems your risks have paid off. I can hardly wait to be bribed!" Keana radiated great pleasure to start this visit.

Finally, Mike succeeded to join the conversation: "I don't remember a single time when Jenn didn't take risks in her cooking, and it always tastes fantastic."

"We would love to try everything!" said Robert. "I hope this bottle of wine would be a good complement to the dinner. This twelve-year-old Antinori Marchese Chianti Classico Riserva goes well with almost any meat. Do you have an aerator, Mike?"

"Is this twelve-year-old Antinori-whatever drinkable without an aerator, or are we doomed to drink our regular red wine?"

"Oh, no, that's OK, it just gets a fuller body," Robert said, either not hearing the sarcasm or ignoring it.

"Let's eat before it becomes cold. That risk was not accounted for." Jenn waved to the table and nodded to Mike to pour everybody wine, secretly throwing at him an angry look for trying to mock Robert, in which Mike took a hidden pleasure.

"So, Robert," started Jenn, "I know all about what these guys are doing, but what about you? You are also in tech?"

"Oh, these guys do cool stuff. I work in a very boring area—corporate law. You know, my most exciting activity yesterday was reviewing a 200-page license agreement. I had caffeine poisoning from the amount of coffee I consumed."

"Well, dear, you forgot to mention that these 200 pages have a price tag of $10 million attached to them. That's why your chief bought you an espresso machine." Keana patted Robert on the shoulder, demonstrating her admiration for Robert's achievements.

"Unfortunately, in the modern world, it's impossible to get along without these boring agreements!" said Mike, noticing that Keana's attempt was a bit too superficial. Surprisingly, it brought Mike a sense of satisfaction, even though it was unclear why he even cared as if he was in competition with Robert.

"I read somewhere that the Japanese don't have written contracts at all," added Jenn.

"That's because prior to the contract, they golf and dine together for months or years, so when it's time to close the deal, they are friends," Robert explained.

"Then that would be my favorite job, closing the contracts with the Japanese!" exclaimed Jenn, finding an elegant way to change the subject. "When we just moved to the US, my father's first job was a golf course operator, and every day, he taught me how to play golf. I remember swinging for hours as a child. I hated it then, and started to appreciate it only when I got to college."

"That's an unusual sport for a Russian girl, isn't it?" said Keana half jokingly. "I thought most of them are doing ballet, gymnastics, or figure skating."

"Indeed! But all these cost money, and the golf was free for me," replied Jenn. "And what sport do American girls like you usually do in their childhood, Keana?"

"I don't think I was a typical American girl. I was raised in a very traditional rural family, with four brothers and two sisters, and sports were for boys. We girls needed to learn quilting. Unfortunately, there were no Division I quilting schools, so I was admitted to college only because in the radius of 10,000 miles from where we lived, there was no girl in the last five generations who got into college. I think the admission officer went crazy from the excitement when he saw my application."

"I propose to raise a toast to you girls, for your achievements against all odds!" said Mike, filling everybody's glass with another round of twelve-year-old Antinori Marchese Chianti Classico Riserva.

When Keana and Robert left their apartment three hours later, Mike exhaled with colossal relief, embraced Jenn, and with a warm kiss, he raised her in his arms and carried her to the bedroom.

"Mike, you are going to miss your Breaking News of Tomorrow update!" Jenn slapped his back, pretending to protest.

"The killer has been captured, and the rest of the world will tell me tomorrow what happened," Mike said, ignoring her not-too-adamant objection.

CHAPTER 12

Rachel was reviewing her Dowell case notes, as she now referred to them, for the hundredth time in the last month when her phone buzzed, and the name "Josh" appeared on its screen.

Rachel picked up the phone on its second ring. "Hey, Josh, morning!"

"Good afternoon, Rach, the world woke up some six hours ago!" Based on Koppelman's voice, Rachel knew he was calling with some news. They all—meaning she and the FBI, as the police considered the case to be closed—were missing an important clue, and Koppelman calling her in the middle of the day sounded like he had information to share. Typically, Koppelman would call her once a week on weekend evenings to check on her.

"The world woke up that early because it did not work until three thirty in the morning working on some stupid story that will lose its relevance shortly after the broadcast."

"So it looks like nobody will be arrested as a result. What's happened, Rach, did you lower your bar?" Koppelman tried to joke.

"A girl needs to eat, doesn't she?"

"She definitely does! Speaking of which—I just ordered takeaway sushi. The weather is great, so brush your teeth and I'll meet you at the park bench in thirty minutes."

"Ciao," Rachel said and went to take a shower.

She loved her park—it was just two blocks from her town house, and since it did not have a playground or a running trail for joggers, it was always empty during the daytime on weekdays. A perfect place to talk.

RACHEL SPOTTED KOPPELMAN immediately after she turned the corner of her house. She noticed that, as he watched her, he carefully looked at every passing car, a habit acquired with his profession. Rachel was marching fast, holding a cigarette between her fingers, and every few steps, she blew out white smoke that slowly dissipated in the windless air.

"You should stop contributing to the air pollution!" Koppelman said when she reached the park a few minutes later.

"Oh, I heavily contributed today: I walked here!" Rachel replied. "Besides, it neutralized the street stench."

"Well, cannot argue here." He gave her a quick kiss on the cheek, which mostly was in the air rather than on the cheek itself. "That's yours." He handed her a plastic lunch bag and proceeded to the bench at the entrance.

They ate in silence for a while, and then Koppelman said, "Rach, the Bureau sees it as pointless to continue the investigation."

"How so?" she asked, but her voice suggested that she wasn't really surprised. She herself was running in circles, and there wasn't any new information or even a slight hint.

"Dowell doesn't know anything. He was hired by an intermediary whom he never met and from whom he received the job and 50 percent of the payment via a drop location. It took him three weeks to plan the operation, during which time he did not have any contact with the intermediary."

"Can this person be Jordan?"

"Potentially. Your Doug Jordan disappeared like he never existed."

"Was there anybody else on Dowell's hit list?"

"No, there wasn't. The Bureau thinks that it was revenge for some old deeds, and so they do not want to spend any more taxpayer money on chasing the wind. Besides, we have other cases to work on and our resources are spread too thin, so they want to wrap up the investigation."

"I see. What do *you* think?" Rachel looked into Koppelman's eyes.

"I don't know, frankly. I think there may be something else beneath the surface. I find it highly implausible that somebody would wait for five or more years to settle an old prison score. Unless…"

"Unless he was just recently released from jail," Rachel finished for him.

RACHEL LOOKED AT her buzzing phone: Phil Matthews, her most effective and most expensive private investigator. Following her park meeting with Koppelman, Rachel instructed Matthews to find out anything he could about this jail and its recently released inmates. She was certain there was a real connection to Diaz and Alvarez, and she was determined to find it, whatever it would cost her.

When she was starting her investigative reporter career, Rachel felt some twinges to her conscience about the legalities of Matthews's methods. From time to time, these concerns accumulated and tormented her, but with experience, a sense of accomplishment and pride for bringing justice numbed her.

"Yes?" Rachel said to her phone.

"I am in the park," Matthews said and hung up.

Rachel put on sunglasses and a baseball cap with a visor on her neck. Wearing jeans and a jacket, she could easily pass for a short teenage boy. She jumped into her beaten-up Jeep and drove to the park two blocks away, where just a week ago, she'd met Koppelman. She stopped at the entrance, and a middle-aged man with an absolutely inconspicuous appearance got into her car. She drove off, periodically looking in the rearview mirror.

They passed a few interchanges, got on a highway, and then suddenly she took the next exit, and went to a small side street. When it became clear that nobody had followed them, Matthews said, "I found the connection. There is this guy, Jesus Juarez, he was released on December 14. His older brother, Miguel Juarez, lives in Mexico and is engaged in drug trafficking. He is sought after by the DEA, but no success. Last November, Juarez was here, in the city, and he met none other than Enrico Diaz—remember this name? He is the husband of Martinez's sister-in-law. The purpose of this visit was to establish additional local operations, but something went wrong. Miguel Juarez left the country very pissed off. The timing of his trip, of two weeks prior to his younger brother's release, cannot be coincidental, as his brother was supposed to play a central role in the new operation. When Jesus Juarez got out, he learned that his old friends from the prison were stealing from them, and did not like it. He and his brother hired a hitman."

Not asking how Matthews got this information, Rachel stopped the car on a corner of a small street with no traffic at this early afternoon hour, and Matthews got out. Rachel drove for a few blocks and then called Koppelman. The intel Matthews passed her was a bombshell, and she was confident Koppelman would act upon it. And she would finally have her breakthrough story.

RACHEL'S PHONE WAS continuously ringing in the early morning hours four days after the meeting with Matthews. With fully draped windows, the room was as dark as midnight, and it took the caller several attempts to wake Rachel up. She was sleeping on her stomach, fully covered by a blanket, and if not for that annoyingly loud ringtone, she would have continued to sleep at least until noon. Without raising her head and opening her eyes, Rachel pulled her hand out from under the blanket and blindly fumbled on the nightstand, searching for her phone.

She answered the phone, not opening her eyes and hoping to return back to sleep. "Yes?"

"Jesus and Miguel Juarez were shot to death today by Enrico Diaz in his apartment. He fled the scene, and the police are chasing him." Phil Matthew's voice was as calm as if he were announcing the latest weather forecast. "Diaz's wife is in custody. She was there when everything happened."

In a moment, all Rachel's desire to return to her sleep disappeared without a single trace. She abruptly sat up in bed, put Matthews on speakerphone, and said, "Go on?" She went to the bathroom and listened to Matthews's report while brushing her teeth and getting dressed.

"On my way," Rachel said. "Text me the address."

Rachel finished dressing, which wasn't that complicated, given she'd put on the same jeans as yesterday, a blouse from a clean laundry basket, and ignored any cosmetics, counting on the fact that at this heavy-traffic hour, there would be enough slow intervals to apply it while driving. She put her feet into sneakers that she found lying near the entrance door, and rushed out. She made two calls as she started to navigate the morning craziness of the streets—to Dick Newman, her trusted cameraman, and to Josh Koppelman. Her hunch regarding last month's killings was correct—they were all connected.

When she arrived at the Diaz's house twenty-two minutes later, it was as busy as any homicide scene—tons of flashing lights coming from the police cars, yellow tape, people in uniforms and civilian clothes running in and out, a crowd of fascinated onlookers sharing and then magnifying every rumor. Her phone buzzed. She took it out of her jeans pocket and read two words from Koppelman: "Diaz's taken."

With the expertise of a surgeon, Rachel dissected the crowd into relevant and not, talked to witnesses, ignored the hearsay, and found those who personally knew Diaz or his wife and could provide information about them. Newman followed Rachel while he talked to the network about Sorrow's soon-to-be-aired news report from the live crime scene.

"We're about to start!" Newman yelled to Rachel, and he showed her the best spot to stand. "Three, two, one—live!"

"The horrific murder of two people that concluded a series of three homicides in the last two months just happened in the Rosemary Gardens apartment complex north of the Westmont neighborhood. This is Rachel Sorrow in a QQBC exclusive live coverage report from the crime scene."

MIKE SAW JOHN and Sam from the corner right when he turned onto his street returning from the office late that evening. Usually, he succeeded in avoiding too-long discussions with them. A quick hello, hope you are all fine, same here, greeting to Jenn, was his typical conversation with them, and he never slowed down his stride from the garage to his second-floor apartment. This time, Mike realized it was impossible to avoid them entirely, as John blocked the stairway, and Sam was ambushing him near the garage door.

Mike put on his friendly neighbor face, which he needed to wear more often, as Jenn repeatedly suggested, and got out of the car, delicately trying to bypass Sam. To no avail. Sam blocked Mike from moving forward and victoriously looked at John, who was already trotting toward them. Sam triumphantly announced, as if the matter were his own personal achievement: "They caught the killer and solved the whole case!"

"What killer? What case?" Mike asked, not understanding what Sam was talking about.

"The one that killed all these couples in the city a month ago, including Martinez here!"

"But I thought they got their guy, what was his name…?"

"Anthony Dowell!" John exclaimed, breathing heavily from his run across the small street from the stairway to the garage. "He was an infamous hitman, hired to kill the whole gang, but the man behind all this was Enrico Diaz!"

"Enrico Diaz? Who's that?" asked Mike, stopping in place. This was the first time he was hearing this name.

"Oh, it was all over the news today." Sam preempted John's reply. "Rachel Sorrow cracked the story, totally on her own. It turned out that several inmates from the state prison, including a couple of guards, organized a drug ring outside of the prison. They sold drugs that originated in Mexico from a brother of one of the inmates."

"Right," said John. "The guy in Mexico was like a cartel boss. He was the head of the entire operation, very powerful. Remember his name, Sam?"

"Yes, Juarez somethin'," replied Sam. "So, these guys, they got out of prison and started to steal from this Juarez, like millions of dollars' worth of stuff, all while pretending the business was good and keeping Juarez happy."

"Remember our Martinez?" John said. "He was killed first—apparently, he was also an ex-inmate, from the same gang! I don't know why Management let him into this complex!"

"Exactly!" Sam said. "We definitely should talk to Management tomorrow about how they could have anyone with a prior conviction live in our complex! See what happens to the neighborhood when such a person moves in! It becomes a crime scene!"

"What happened with this gang?" Mike brought the topic back.

"So this Diaz apparently was the boss outside of the prison and the main man to work with Juarez. He was the brains here, all the money went to him, and he was channeling part to Mexico and keeping another part here," Sam continued. "Only he ran out of luck—the brother of this big cartel boss was released, and he found out that Diaz was stealing their money. The brothers hired a hit man, this Dowell, and he was supposed to kill everybody in this gang, but got caught."

"It turns out he did not plan to kill the wives. They just happened to be home at the time," John intervened, to Sam's visible displeasure. "You know, with so much money from the drugs, their wives didn't need to work."

"The Juarezes wanted to get their money back and came to talk to Diaz. Only he had a different idea, shot them, and ran away. And the police chased and got him. It all happened today, and Rachel Sorrow was the one on top of everything!" Sam concluded the story, stealing the grand finale from John.

"Who could have imagined we had an operating drug gang in our backyard!" said John. "Right here, among us, and Martinez was such a nice person. But I always told Sam he was too nice, didn't I, Sam?"

"Yes, and I told you that it is because he's hiding something. From the day he moved in, I thought he looked suspicious, just too polite all the time."

"Of course he was too polite—he didn't want us to suspect him of any criminal activity!" John added knowingly. "But that's exactly why we suspected him!"

"If he hadn't been killed, I would have gone to Management the next day and asked them to look into his past! He was too nice to be innocent!" Sam summed up his imaginary plan with determination.

"I see," Mike said politely. "Glad the police solved this case. Goodnight, guys!" He waved to them and ran upstairs, taking the steps two at a time.

Jenn was waiting for him in the living room, reading the same story on her tablet.

"You know what really bothers me, Jenn?" he said after kissing her hello.

"Tell me, Mike."

"Why wasn't this story in the Breaking News of Tomorrow? I read everything daily, trying to analyze the site and crack it, but there was not a word about these Diazes and Juarezes. I don't understand what to make from it."

He looked at the old wall clock. There were a few more hours before the midnight update, and he hoped to get some answers.

PART 2
A NEW DAWN

CHAPTER 13

Wakeups before dawn turned out to be a very productive routine in the last two months, and it was the only time Mike could guarantee he would be uninterrupted, as there was nothing that Jenn hated more than getting up early. A freshly brewed coffee in a large personalized mug that Jenn gifted him on their first Valentine's Day was all it took for Mike to keep going regardless of how late he'd gone to sleep the night before.

He started his early morning with the latest issue of his favorite biweekly newsletter, authored by a famous physician Professor Jeremiah Eliah Jeremei, who, for Mike, was an embodiment of everything Mike was not: a brave scientist who was unafraid to debunk theories he formulated only a few months before, who was taking risks and was unconcerned about public opinion or rejection. Mike never missed an opportunity to look for any flaws intentionally hidden in Jeremei's theories and took it as a personal intellectual challenge to find one. He knew there was always something, as it was the whole idea of Jeremei's blog—put a presumably scientifically solid theory out there, big enough to create significant changes in modern society if they were true, and prompt leading experts to initiate a dialog. While most of the science was beyond Mike's field of expertise to fully understand, what drew him to the newsletter was the wide range of daily implications. Mike quickly commented on the blog and closed out of his email application.

There was a lot of work ahead of him in his BNOT research, as he called his moonlighting project. Mike loved diligent work and wasn't afraid to enter a new field. Having majored in math and computer science, he believed that almost everything could be learned once you understood the underlying logic behind the subject. His main weakness, however, was a complete inability to adequately capitalize on his abilities, and Houston and Kwon, and many before them, quickly learned to leverage this.

Mike opened a spreadsheet and began to write some formulas, and soon, the whole screen was covered with different numbers highlighted with green or red. When the coffee in his mug got cold, he quickly finished it off in a few large gulps and brewed another cup. He stopped working only when it was time to wake up Jenn and depart to Solutry.

He went to the bathroom for a quick shower and woke Jenn up for breakfast. His research would need to wait till the evening, and he had high hopes for it.

IF THE LAST month was any indication of how their life together would look in the future, Jenn would be a very unhappy woman. Mike was hardly with her this whole time—his work at Solutry demanded long hours, and when he returned home late in the evenings, instead of spending time with her and talking about important daily matters, including their wedding planning, he was obsessed with following the latest news and spent all the remaining evening, often well past one or two o'clock, on his laptop.

His yearly bonus, $32,542.11 on top of his salary, was the only nice thing that happened last month. This definitely was a huge amount of money suddenly disbursed into his checking account, more than enough to cover the wedding Jenn envisioned, but recently, she'd complained that Mike wasn't helping her plan the wedding. If before it was so heartwarming to cuddle on the sofa and chat about all the little details, now he wasn't there for her anymore.

"But, dear," Mike said in his defense after Jenn once again expressed her sadness about Mike's disappearance. "What has changed? Did I ever before argue with you about any of the preparation ideas? It's exactly the same now: whatever you think we need for the wedding, as long as it fits into the budget—go for it. What's the difference?"

"Mike, that's totally different! Before, you were listening to me. I could talk to you. Preparing for the wedding was fun. *Our* fun. Now you have dropped everything on me like the wedding is not interesting for you anymore, and it's like I am the only one here who needs it!"

Here it comes again! Mike thought and audibly replied, "I need this party too, Jenn, and I want this day to be the best in my life! It's just that you are so much better than I am with all these details, so I don't see any point in my suggestions: anything I can think of is quite inferior to your ideas!"

"It's absolutely not! I can't do it alone if you are not partici-pating. It just doesn't work that way!"

"Of course, dear, I'm here with you!"

This meant that for the rest of the evening and the next day, Mike would do his research in stealth mode, trying his best to show active interest and participation in whatever wedding-related stuff Jenn deemed important to talk about. This was a reasonable compromise to keep their relationship healthy.

When finally Jenn disappeared into the bathroom for her nighttime routine, Mike impatiently opened his computer, trying to squeeze all his evening plans into a thirty-minute window of alone time.

He could hardly wait for the next morning's dawn when an idea finally hit him.

WHEN JENN ENTERED the kitchen in the morning, Mike was already there, sitting with his back to her and with keen interest typing something on his laptop, not noticing her until Jenn hugged him from behind.

"Good morning, dear!" Mike said, returning a kiss. "How did you sleep?"

"Like a child," replied Jenn. "How is it going, your research?" She refused to look at the Breaking News of Tomorrow website since the killer was captured, and did not really understand what kind of research Mike was conducting.

"Very good, Jenn, very good! I have a crazy idea and want to talk to you about it tonight."

"Do you know what day it is today?" Jenn asked, making it obvious that Mike should know the answer.

He searched for any clue in his memory, quickly recalled all significant dates, birthdays of her family members, or whether a few days ago she mentioned a wedding-related activity, such as going to see a venue or meeting with somebody for something utterly important—but nothing rang a bell.

Jenn watched his inner struggle, an unspoken expression of criticism in her half-sarcastic, half-innocent smile, torturing and annoying him with yet another example of his ignorance and a clear demonstration that she was entitled to be offended by it.

"Well, today is June 9, our Meeting Anniversary Day!" Jenn victoriously announced. "And we are invited to my parents' at seven, remember?"

"Oh, right, congratulations. Of course, I remember!" Mike lied, embracing her around the waist. "I just didn't realize it was the ninth already."

"Of course, dear, I'm sure with all your work and your BNOT research, you don't feel the days change. Why bother with all these nuances, such as weddings, my family..." Jenn wasn't letting him off easily. "Speaking of which, you will finally meet my half brother, Anton."

"Really? That's great. I would love to meet him—I had no idea he's coming!" Mike decided to turn a deaf ear to Jenn's sarcasm.

"Neither did I, but he texted me yesterday that he's arrived. I last saw him when I was still at school on our visit to Russia. My father divorced his mom when Anton was little. He is five years older than me, and unfortunately, we rarely see each other. But Anton has a fantastic quality—whenever we talk, I am always very comfortable with him. We can pick up a conversation and resume our relationship like there was no gap. He is here for a few days' visit—he said it's a business trip—and it's your chance to meet more of my family."

"Does he speak English?"

"I assume he does—otherwise, how can he conduct any business here?" replied Jenn and finally poured herself a cup of fresh coffee.

"Great, looking forward to meeting him. I'll pick you up at six thirty, then. Be ready by then—your dad doesn't like when we are late, and until we are married, I need to maintain a good reputation with him." Mike stood up to leave and closed his laptop.

"Right." She sighed with pity before the door behind him closed. "And before you worry about maintaining a good relationship with my dad, you should do it with me, with all your obsession over this freaking BNOT."

Mike ran downstairs, pretending not to hear this remark.

MIKE CLIMBED FIVE steps to the entrance of Jenn's parents' house, waited for her to fix her hair and straighten her blouse, and then rang the bell.

Sergei and Maria Zharkov lived on the other side of the city in a tiny two-bedroom town house that they'd finally bought after fifteen years of being in America. They took all their savings, borrowed some additional money from their friends, and were able to come up with just enough for a down payment to purchase their dream house. Their mortgage interest rate was terrible, as they hardly had a credit line, and their best asset, as Sergei unsuccessfully tried to joke with the loan officer, was their daughter. This hard-earned apartment was their highest financial achievement and a subject of their pride, and they loved hosting family gatherings.

Mike warmly greeted Jenn's parents, looked at the new person in the room, who must be Anton, and extended his hand. "Good evening, I'm Mike."

"Nice to meet you, Mike! I'm Anton, Jenn's brother." Anton's English was surprisingly decent.

Jenn threw her arms around Anton's neck, warmly kissing him on both cheeks. "So happy to see you after all these years! You haven't changed a bit!"

"I cannot say this about you, Jenn! When I saw you last time, you were still an ugly duckling. Now you are the most beautiful woman I ever saw!"

"She never was an ugly duckling!" Jenn's father, Sergei, intervened with a very thick accent, worthy of Hollywood movies, finally taking hold of Jenn after all family hugs were exchanged. "She was born the most beautiful girl in the world!"

The apartment was filled with the smell of freshly cooked Russian cuisine. Mike demonstratively raised his nose and loudly inhaled the air. "Masha, this smells amazing! I skipped lunch today for your dinner! Oh, I see you prepared my favorite Kyiv's cutlets!"

Unlike her daughter, Maria, or Masha as her friends and family called her in short, never improvised with the food. Her cooking was very predictable and clearly of the Russian style—from salads to the main course to desserts. You could dine with them once, and the next time everything would be exactly the same, with rare changes to the table arrangement. Masha cooked well, but every time they hosted a party, she worried and reinvented her grocery list over and over again, ending with a meal identical to the previous times and firmly convinced of her originality.

"Yes, yes, let's go to the table!" Masha always fussed over her food. "Let's sit down, shall we? Anton—you are our guest of honor today. Why don't you sit down here?" She showed Anton his chair, which was raised to the status of an honorary chair for the occasion.

"Thank you, Masha!" Anton replied pleasantly. "I remember your cooking as culinarily divine."

With these pleasantries toward each other, they all moved to the table. The conversation was about everything families talk about—Anton's work in Russian machinery company's import/exports department; his life in Moscow and his wife; Jenn and Mike's wedding plans, which Jenn was happy to share in detail, some of which Mike heard for the first time but was smart enough to pretend to have an intimate knowledge of the matter; the latest from Sergei's golf club, which was the only workplace Sergei had ever had since coming to America; and, of course, a favorite topic for all parents, deprecating the youth, commenting on how their lives were different from the current generation, which possessed half the values the glorified previous generation had, or even less.

"You see, Mike, back in Russia, we did not have all the infinite number of goods at the extension of a hand. We needed to work hard—harder than you can imagine!" No topic was sweeter for Sergei than comparing spoiled Americans to his ascetic Soviet friends.

"Of course, we had free education and free medicine, but we also needed to pay it back to the country with additional work."

"What do you mean, 'with additional work?'" Mike was confused. "You mean overtime?"

"Mike, let me tell you a story. When Anton was about two years old, there was a drought in Russia—nothing was growing.

We had no food, no bread, no potatoes. You go to the store and all shelves—nothing! It was really bad in Russia. But in Latvia— you know Latvia, back then, it was a Soviet republic. They had rain, they had sun, beautiful! Everything was growing. They had excellent wheat, and our factory sent all its engineers to gather straw that was left in the fields after the harvest, and to ship it back to Russia to feed cows."

"Engineers were sent to gather straw?" Mike was genuinely surprised. "Isn't this a big waste of resources?"

"Big waste? Are you crazy? Having all this good straw rot in the fields when cows in Russia had nothing to eat, that's a big waste!

"For two months, we were working in the fields—you know how much straw we shipped? Every day, several trains were going to Russia with our straw. And in Latvia, they had a lot of potatoes. Because of rain. We had nothing. They had a lot. So I bought ten bags of potatoes, each a hundred pounds, and it cost me only five rubles each, and I found a train going back home and loaded the last car with all the bags. And then when I came home, I was hunting for that train for a whole week until it arrived, and I sneaked out at night to the last car and offloaded the potatoes and brought them home. You know, I paid in Latvia five rubles for the whole bag, and at home it cost ten times more! I gave potatoes to everybody—my parents; my ex-wife's parents, God bless their souls; her sister's family; and my friends. One bag I left to us. We had only Anton back then, small family, so we did not need more potatoes. It lasted the whole winter, and we weren't hungry! Now try sending any American engineer to a farm during the harvest, what will they say? Will they go? Will *you* go, Mike?"

"Papa"—Anton laughed—"nowadays, Russian engineers will not go either! Not because they are spoiled. This was just a completely different regime."

"It's called character, boys, character, not a regime. That's what I am talking about—this generation is different: everybody demands; nobody is giving back!"

They continued to chat more, in a lovely family gathering, listening to the same stories again and again, and enjoying them anew as it was only possible to enjoy the same old stories in warm and loving families. Despite the difference in cultures, and in language, Mike felt himself at home, a warmth he'd never had in his own all-American family.

"Very nice man, your half brother," Mike told Jenn as they drove back from her parents. "And his English is good, much better than your parents'. If I didn't know, I would assume he lives here."

"Yes," replied Jenn, "his English is fantastic. Thanks for being so nice with my family."

Mike looked at the dashboard clock: eleven o'clock. There was no chance for him to sneak out of bed for the Breaking News of Tomorrow without infuriating Jenn. After the recent quarrel and such a nice family gathering, he didn't have the guts to check on the BNOT. A light shadow of sadness fell over his face. The most beautiful woman in the world was driving home by his side, and all he felt was sorry for being unable to read tomorrow's news. He glanced at Jenn, who shone with happiness and joy after such a nice family dinner and meeting with her brother, and forced himself to stop thinking of the site.

CHAPTER 14

To Rachel's unpleasant surprise, there was no big fanfare at QQBC, and her phone didn't ring even once with an invitation for lunch from one of the major networks' executives. Several of her colleagues discreetly congratulated her on the good work, the chairman wrote nice emails—one to her personally and another to the entire editorial staff—and that was it. Really? All her discovery, all her investigative work, all her sleepless nights, all that brought her was only a nod? Dowell's capture, all her investigation regarding Diaz and Juarez, all this was insignificant in their eyes? Really?

How often did a journalist break a story of such proportion? Why did everybody else—for much less, significantly less!—receive all accolades and celebrations, and she got nothing? Why was she treated so unfairly? What was wrong with her? What was she missing?

Rachel lit another cigarette and went to the kitchen. The contents of the fridge didn't surprise her: as usual, there was nothing to eat, and its drawers revealed two bags of already rotten vegetables. The odor that came from the fridge succeeded in penetrating the curtain of the cigarette's smoke. Rachel grimaced and began to throw everything out of the refrigerator. That gave her unexpected gratification. She put out her cigarette under the kitchen faucet, where it instantly died; took a small bucket, detergent, and a scrub sponge from under the sink; and for the next hour, she relentlessly cleaned the refrigerator and the entire kitchen, releasing her anger via physical labor.

When she finished, and there was nothing else to clean to take her mind off her disappointment in life's fairness, she sat on the floor, leaning against the wall, and gave her nerves the freedom to bring as many tears as her eyes could muster.

SHE DIDN'T NOTICE how long she was sitting there when her phone rang and its screen identified the caller. Rachel took two large gulps of air to stabilize her voice to sound normal, and answered the call.

"Hi, Josh, what's up?"

"We need to talk about the case with all that has recently happened. I have a few unanswered questions about Doug Jordan, wanna brainstorm together with you. Your choice—dinner tonight or lunch tomorrow."

"Dinner, I haven't eaten yet."

"Ah, let's make it an early dinner, then. How about five thirty at The Boat?"

"Sure, no problem. Why The Boat, Josh?"

"Kinda closes the circle."

"Didn't know about this sentimental side of yours." Rachel attempted to sound casual, fully aware of the stiffness in her voice and suspecting Koppelman picked up on it.

"It developed with age. So we are set. See you in a bit."

"Yep," she replied to the already disconnected line, then stood up, stopping herself from breaking into maudlin crying again, and went to the bathroom to take a shower, pulling off her overstretched T-shirt and throwing it on her bed.

RACHEL WAS THE only guest in the restaurant at this hour, which most people considered too early for dinner. That served her well, as she had plenty of time to look at her old notes before Koppelman entered the venue.

"Rach," said Koppelman after they ordered, "I am really puzzled by this Doug Jordan."

"Did you get anything from Dowell or Diaz?"

"Absolutely nothing! They have no idea who he is. Of course, it is a phony name, but there is nobody they know in the entire organization that fits the profile. Are you sure he is not Mexican? He knew too much about this gang to be an outsider."

"As sure as I am sure you are a white Caucasian male," Rachel replied. "I briefly saw him fully disguised here, near The Boat when he first contacted me, and then only heard his voice, but he is white, alright?"

"Alright, alright! I have a theory that he is a member of a rival gang and had an informant in the Juarez/Diaz ring. But this has yet to lead to anything. We continue to dig, but nothing so far."

"My clock is ticking, Josh," Rachel said suddenly, totally out of the blue. She looked at Koppelman's eyes, which were filled with a mix of terror, bewilderment, and disbelief, and painfully laughed. "Come on, Josh, I am not talking about children and you fathering one!" She saw his expression change. "I am talking about my career."

"What do you mean, Rach? You are making me worry. You have a fantastic career, you are a highly respected journalist, your name is well known…"

"I am talking about becoming too old for a successful career on a major TV network, not QQBC! I am talking about hating myself every single day and blaming my parents for that."

"What are you talking about? Are you thinking clearly, Rach?"

"Josh, year after year, I break new huge stories that shake everything up. How many such stories does an average journalist bring? You know, they all go to work for these big networks, bringing less than half of the stories I do! But I am still at QQBC. Wanna know why? Because other networks hire only six-foot-tall blondes with long hair and large boobs, not this midget. I'll be here forever, Josh, forever! So why bother?"

She got up from the chair and went to the restroom to wash her face. When she returned, the waiter was arranging their food on the table. She sat down and looked at the worried Koppelman, who silently continued watching her with a great concern. Then she said, "I'll get this son of a bitch, Josh, I'll get him! Whoever this Doug Jordan is, I'll get him. You have my word! They'll have their story."

CHAPTER 15

Mike rushed home and, driving against the traffic, arrived half an hour before Jenn. That didn't surprise him much, as he vaguely remembered that Jenn mentioned she would be meeting with a potential benefactor to her project. He didn't remember exactly what project it was supposed to be, something involving adoptions, he recalled, or whatever. Good stuff, as he told her last time they talked about it, really good stuff. And frankly, why bother? Soon it would all become irrelevant. If—and there was a big if here—he succeeded in convincing Jenn to trust him with his plan. If only she would think logically and not emotionally. If she could agree to accept his mathematical explanation and detach herself from her unsubstantiated fears. If she would only listen to reason and understand what great things could be achieved, and not face all his ideas combatively, which, he expected, would be an uphill battle with Jenn, pun intended.

When Jenn finally returned home, Mike was already on pins and needles waiting to talk to her.

"OK, Mike," said Jenn, detecting his excitement, "before we talk, let me fix something really quick."

Within just a few minutes, she prepared their dinner, all while Mike was finishing the last few calculations he wanted to show her.

"So," started Mike, more nervous than he'd been pitching to Solutry's board of directors. "So, Jenn, since they caught the killer, I have been monitoring the BNOT daily. I didn't miss a single day."

"Yes, I noticed this," Jenn replied quite sarcastically, which fell on Mike's deaf ears.

"Right, so I was puzzled by what it is. I cannot clearly tell you what it is for sure, but I'm starting to get an idea."

"So, tell me, Mike, what is that?"

"I will, promise, but first, let me tell you what I want to do with that and what I can do with that."

"You already did, Mike. You helped to catch the killer. What, now you want to become a private detective and chase all the criminals?"

Mike ignored her sarcasm again, perfectly knowing the reason for it, as lately, he was spending more time with the Breaking News of Tomorrow than with Jenn, to the point that she was growing impatient about his new hobby, especially in light of the preparations for their wedding, and she was not shy to show it.

"No, Jenn, of course not. That's the job of the police. But I learned that there is so much more here. I believe we can make a huge profit from the site. And when I say huge, I mean it." Mike was so excited with his pitch that he missed that Jenn uncomfortably shifted in her chair on the word "profit."

"I correlated every article of the Breaking News of Tomorrow with actual events the next day. Jenn, they all happened, one by one." Mike's voice was now in a much higher pitch than his usual tone. The food on his plate was still untouched, and it was unclear whether he even paid any attention to it.

"Every day, I researched every item mentioned in BNOT in depth. I noticed their typical structure and identified several patterns. I started to look at some major events and major trends that followed the news, and if I can be bold enough, I believe we could make some money."

Mike rubbed his hands together, and Jenn shifted in her chair again.

"Mike, we do need money, of course, especially as we are going to be married and need to think about the future, but…but since when have you been so excited about money?" she asked.

"It is not money—it is about something bigger. Something much bigger than money, Jenn. The money will be a side effect, sort of a by-product."

"I beg your pardon?"

"You see, there is some organization—I don't know which one, but somehow it 'predicts' tomorrow." He made air quotes around the word "predicts." "I think that, in reality, they use very sophisticated algorithms and a lot of search data to make estimations. Very powerful. Very accurate. Mind-blowing stuff. That's what I am excited about. But I also want to build algorithms that will leverage data and eventually replicate it and then improve it further. Some money can be made, too, as I go."

"Mike, go slow with me. I am not sure I follow you. But I cannot understand how anyone can predict the killer's moves, or the saved kids from the natural catastrophe that did not happen yet, or that art collection sale. You say they are doing algorithms and data to 'predict,' or rather 'estimate' some events, but how come? I don't buy it."

"OK, Jenn, I know it is hard to grasp. I fight with it too. But let's just focus only on the easy part now."

"Which is what, Mike?"

"How to make money from this."

"I am not sure how you can make money from knowing about art collection or saved kids…"

"There are a lot of other items there that are monetizable…"

Jenn's eyes went blank, and he proceeded to explain: "There are a lot of major events that affect the world. Wars, climate change, and many others of that nature can affect many areas of the economy…"

"I still do not follow, Mike." Jenn grimaced like he was talking about an extremely dull and irrelevant subject.

"Think about this. In August 1990, Iraq invaded Kuwait, and a lot of oil fields were set on fire. This war adversely affected oil prices, and the gas in the United States jumped in price. What happens locally here when gas is much more expensive? Say twice as expensive as it was just a couple of weeks before?"

Seeing Jenn look at him without responding to such a trivial question, Mike continued. "People start driving less. Suddenly, big-engine cars, like pickups or SUVs, which suck a lot of fuel, become unpopular, and Japanese fuel-efficient vehicles become a hit. So stocks of big car manufacturers drop. Follow me so far?" Mike looked at Jenn and decided that she was following enough to continue. "All this leads to one simple thing—if I know that tomorrow a war starts between Iraq and Kuwait, I can bet that Ford's and GM's stocks go down, Toyota goes up, and I can make some money from this advanced knowledge."

"Mike, you are teaching me a history lesson!" By now, Jenn sounded totally confused and annoyed at the same time. "History is history because you learn what happened afterward, but here you are looking at things that have not happened yet. There is no war that starts between Iraq and Kuwait tomorrow. It is all past!"

Mike saw that she was having a hard time grasping the concept, which he thought was pretty easy to understand, so he continued to provide a simple explanation, despite an urge to just reply, "Why can't you understand what I am trying to say!"

"Jenn, let me explain all this to you in more straightforward terms. Suppose I know what tomorrow's lottery draw is. If I go and buy a ticket and pick all the winning numbers, I would win the whole pot. Right?"

"So we are playing the lottery now?"

"No, for God's sake! That's only an example! Please try to understand!" Mike cried, losing his patience.

"Why are you yelling at me, Mike? Why do I deserve to be yelled at?"

"Sorry, dear, I apologize for that!" Mike quickly pulled himself together. "I just got too carried away. Of course it's a difficult concept to grasp right away: I have spent a few good weeks thinking about it and shouldn't expect you to digest everything in two minutes. Sorry! I am trying to say that if I know exactly what happens tomorrow, I can make smart decisions today, since I already know the outcome. Exactly like with the lottery or cheating on an exam: if I know the correct answer and take away all the guesswork and uncertainty, I can win big-time.

"So, for the last month, I've looked at some of the events mentioned in the BNOT. And I tried to understand their connection to other events and the markets. Until two days ago, I was merely looking at this from the algorithmic perspective, but then it occurred to me to check how my predictions correlated to reality. You know what I found?"

"What?" Jenn asked in a tired voice, not hiding her dislike of this conversation. "What did you find?"

"I found that my predictions were about 63 percent accurate. Here, take a look." He turned his laptop toward her, which displayed a spreadsheet with multiple rows and columns, filled with numbers, highlighted in red or green, with green visibly dominating. "Greens are my correct estimates, and reds are mistakes, so 62.7 percent of greens. But more importantly, even my mistakes aren't that far off from reality."

"Mike." Jenn closed the lid of his laptop. "You know I don't understand all these numbers and formulas. I got a C in math, and since I started to pay in stores with a credit card, I don't even need to count the change. I believe your formulas are great, but I still don't get where you are going."

"Actually, Jenn, it's all about formulas in my algorithm. I input some parameters, I get some estimations, and based on that, I can decide what to do. That means, if I invest money in what I estimate will rise with time, I will make some profit. That's the ABC of investment."

Jenn looked at him in astonishment.

"You base your algorithm on a site that knows tomorrow's lottery and the war in Kuwait, and you want to say to me that you are fine with that?"

"Why shouldn't I be?"

"For one, Mike, who can know this stuff that even didn't happen yet?"

"I told you, there are these guys—or most probably this organization, hackers, I guess—who developed a system of very advanced algorithms that, with high precision, estimate the course of tomorrow's events—" Mike started to reply but was immediately interrupted by Jenn, who was almost shouting at him.

"Mike, these guys, or this organization, whoever they are, track down serial killers and hitmen and bring them to justice! Imagine what they will do to *you*, to *us*, once they realize that you're stealing their data to make a profit from it!"

"I am not stealing their data! I am just using it to calibrate my algorithm! The data is mine! It's from *my* algorithm!" Mike shouted back.

Jenn looked at him and said in a very calm, quiet voice: "Right, that I understand, but you omit one important point here."

"What do I omit, Jenn, what do I omit? And anyway, I can always improve my algorithms…"

"You omit how you got your initial data. Your formulas and spreadsheets—all this is math."

"Exactly! That's exactly what I am talking about!" Mike exclaimed, thinking for a second that Jenn finally comprehended everything.

"But your starting point is not based on math. Your starting point is based on this freaking site. Or even worse. And I am not comfortable with that at all, Mike, not at all!"

She stood up and with a cold "goodnight" went to the bedroom, where soon enough the lights turned off, indicating her real mood. For the first time in their relationship, Jenn did not wait for Mike to join.

FOR THE NEXT few days, Mike tried to hide his obsession with the Breaking News of Tomorrow and his formulas, painfully remembering the argument with Jenn. He suspected that she understood that he snuck to his laptop in every "Jenn-free" moment, but they both pretended that everything was normal.

One Saturday night, having returned late from going out with their friends, Jenn sat down in front of the TV in the living room, not willing to go to sleep right away, cuddling on the sofa under a plaid blanket and sipping a warm black tea with honey and lemon, when Mike suddenly shouted to her.

"Jenn, come over, quickly!"

If there were women in this world who loved to jump out of their warm blanket into the chilling air of a late night, following a sudden yell of their spouse, Jenn definitely wasn't among their ranks. Especially as she spilled the tea in the process.

"You scared me, Mike!" she said and muttered something in Russian. "Can I change my shirt first?"

"Later, please, come over!"

Mike feverishly printed his laptop screen to capture every new page: "Read!"

Jenn leaned toward his computer and started to read the text under the big ugly green title:

FIRETEC TO ACQUIRE DYMANICK TECHNOLOGIES

Firetec Corporation and Dymanick Technologies on Wednesday announced they have entered into a definitive agreement under which Firetec will acquire Dymanick Technologies for $24.6 per share in an all-cash transaction valued at $862.8 million, inclusive of Dymanick's net cash. The transaction is expected to close this calendar year.

"Jenn, do you understand what this means?" Mike was overly excited and anxious to share this news with her.

"Isn't Firetec the company Keana came from?"

"Yes, yes, but that's not what's important," Mike said impatiently. "Dymanick is Firetec's major competitor. Together, they control about 65 percent of the market. As a single company, they will be able to really dominate the market. Take a look—Firetec today closed with $134 per share price, and Dymanick with $14.1. That's before the market learns of this merger. This news will drive the share up on Wednesday, way up!"

"So what do you want, Mike?" asked Jenn.

"Jenn, this is not a history lesson. These are two real companies we know. I want to buy $10,000 worth of Firetec shares and $10,000 dollars of Dymanick, tomorrow, before they announce. It's a no-lose strategy."

"So you want to invest $20,000, right?"

"Yes, but this is risk-free."

"$20,000, risk-free. Just like that," echoed Jenn, sitting on a chair that she'd pulled from under the kitchen table. She sipped whatever was left of her tea.

"Risk-free. Think about that. Firetec acquires Dymanick. Right off the bat, Dymanick costs about $10.5 more. So if I purchase around 700 shares based on today's price for a total of $10,000 and sell right after the announcement, I get $10.5 multiplied by 700, which is about $7,000 of net profit. I do not know how much Firetec will be worth. Surely, it will increase over time, but even if not—the profit is huge."

"Mike, we have $37,000 in savings—barely enough for our wedding. You want to take $20,000 and play with it on the stock market. Haven't you heard stories about people losing their money?"

"Jenn, my investment strategy is different. I am not going to make a long-term investment. I only plan to make a single sure bet based on the news only I know. I must try it. There must be a reason why I received this Breaking News of Tomorrow!"

"Mike, I see I cannot convince you to back off with this idea. Do it if you feel the urge. After all, this is your bonus money. We could have even not received it." Jenn patted Mike's shoulder and left the kitchen.

Mike sat a little longer, looked at the charts of both companies, and the plan of what to do next shaped in his head. He logged into his online stock brokerage account, which, without Jenn's knowledge, he'd opened two weeks ago and funded with all his bonus money, and with a few keystrokes, he sent the computer instructions to purchase both companies' stock.

CHAPTER 16

For the first time in his life, Mike experienced the real thrill of betting. He woke up early on Monday morning, as he'd become used to, and was constantly checking the market news. His first investment had not lost any monetary value, as both stocks enjoyed a day of relative inactivity and weren't traded that much. This was pretty much expected—no big news was coming from either of the companies.

So far, the Breaking News of Tomorrow site did not disappoint Mike with its prediction. Nevertheless, he was nervous, as he'd invested $20,000. That was a lot of money, and it would be embarrassing and excruciating if his first transaction was a losing one. It was easy to follow any number on his spreadsheet, watch stocks going up or down, and compare the actual values at closing with what his algorithm had calculated. There was no sentiment, no nerves, no skin in the game. With a cold mind, he could improve his algorithm and readjust the assumptions. But now, he had $20,000 vested in the game, more than half of all their money bet on his wild theory. Well, the good thing was that he was here not for the long term but a short one. Just one transaction, to see how it goes.

Close to the afternoon, he started to feel a chill, and his forehead was covered with sweat, despite the air conditioning in the office. Some of the Firetec investors decided to dump its stock, and suddenly, it went down, which wiped a few hundred dollars from Mike's investment. *Be rational*, he thought. *This is a typical daily fluctuation in the market, nothing to worry about, and I should definitely ignore such minuscule changes.* Which, of course, was correct, unless your almost entire net worth was invested in two stocks following some speculation.

His heart sank even lower when Dymanick's stock curve also changed direction and moved down. Mike rose from his chair, unable to think about work, and went to the restroom, where he washed his face with cold water in the hope it would stop his sweating. It didn't. Instead, he became even more worried about his investment status and rushed back to his office to check on the latest numbers. It did not provide any confidence. Quite the opposite; now both stocks were racing to drop faster, and a few hundred dollars more were wiped from Mike's account.

I cannot monitor every slightest change, he tried to convince himself. *It's maddening, it's irresponsible, it's irrational.* Despite his understanding of how the stock market worked, all he was seeing in front of his eyes was value erosion.

A nasty feeling of shame arose inside, an admission that Jenn was right, that he shouldn't even entertain the idea of doing any speculation based on some dubious site, with its unclear agenda and unsubstantiated data. She told him that he was basing his faith on something totally wrong, something inhuman, something satanic, even. How right she was! More dollars evaporated from his stocks. *Should I pull off now?* A panic overwhelmed his mind. *Should I get out before it's too late and I will lose even more? Should I hold a bit more, and hopefully, it will gain everything that was lost?*

Following the shame came the guilt, first as a fleeting uncertain feeling, faintly touching his mind and heart, leaving a slight uneasiness, and then, moments later, hatching a full-fledged attack upon every thought. The guilt of not investing his time into the only real thing that earned him money—his work. He just realized that he literally wasted tens, no, hundreds, of hours researching some nonsense. He allowed himself to go after some sick dudes and convinced himself to spend his time learning their algorithms. If he would instead put this time into Solutry, into his project, which he'd completely neglected recently, the project would be in much better shape. His work was the only thing that brought him a salary, an honest salary. And he let himself be sidetracked by some fantasy. Like building a business plan based on the revenues from the winnings in Vegas slot machines.

A rapid knock on his office door woke him up from these thoughts, and he took his eyes off the red graph. Keana. She stuck her head into the room and said, "Mike, you are not answering your emails! The London guys sent two messages asking where the simulation stands. They lined up meetings with three potential customers early next week, and they must know the results."

"I haven't completed it yet, Keana," Mike said, glancing again at his monitor. Now the whole index was going down.

"You told me yesterday that by noon, you'd send them the numbers." Keana's voice started to show a sign of displeasure.

"I know, but I told you—I was busy and did not do it yet."

"Mike, what have you been busy with?" Keana did not even try to conceal that she was clearly annoyed with Mike's unresponsiveness.

"I am sorry. They'll get their numbers tomorrow. It's not that big of a deal—it's already evening there."

Keana stepped inside and closed the door behind her.

"Mike, you are worrying me. I don't know what is going on with you, but your head is not here. Spill it—what's happening? Can I help with anything?"

"Everything is OK, Keana. I am just a bit tired. Don't worry. I will send the data by tomorrow. Promise. Anything else?" Mike rose from his chair, showing Keana that he wanted her to leave.

Keana hesitated, took a deep breath, and, staring into Mike's eyes, said, "No, that's all. Let me know if you change your mind, I am here to support you." She opened the door and stepped out. "I mean it, Mike."

Mike waited until her steps faded down the corridor, looked one last time at the hugely disappointing trends of today's market, and angrily closed all the tabs in his browser.

It was already past four p.m., and he didn't have much time left to run the simulation and produce performance analysis results. Solutry really needed them. Goddamn it.

JENN WAS SITTING with her tablet absently skimming through the news when she heard Mike's voice outside greeting John and Sam, and she dashed to open the door. $20,000 was a lot of money, more than she'd ever had, and putting it into the stock market was very stressful for her. She didn't fully understand the mechanics of the investment, but one thing was clear to her—the acquisition news was a key to them making some money and, most importantly, to them not losing $20,000. She had spent her entire day reading market news with bland titles. Jenn impatiently waited for Mike to finally come upstairs to their apartment.

A single look at this face told her that his day wasn't that good. But, as her mom had told her many times, "Don't ask your husband how his day was before you feed him. An empty stomach sucks a man's emotions," Masha used to say. And so Jenn simply greeted Mike, kissed him like usual, and said, "I made a simple dinner today, but you'll like it. It is just ready now."

They ate their dinner mostly in silence, with Mike thinking about when it would be a good time to tell Jenn she was right and he was wrong, and, as a result, almost 10 percent of the money he'd put in was lost. Jenn, on the other hand, patiently waited until Mike was ready to talk, as she could tell something obviously bothered his mind.

"How was your day at the office? Did you do these tests for your sales? You told me yesterday they are important for winning some customers over," Jenn probed Mike.

"Yes, I finished it all. That's why I stayed late at work," Mike replied, chewing his last bite.

"Oh, then you probably didn't see the news," Jenn said in a matter-of-fact way, hiding her excitement.

"No, what news?" Mike asked, now fully alert.

"Firetec announced today that they are acquiring Dymanick," started Jenn, but Mike was already dashing to his backpack, taking out his laptop, and opening the browser.

The news was all over the place; every outlet was reposting Dymanick's acquisition press release. Mike opened his broker account, looked at the aftermarket stock prices, and froze: investors loved the news.

Jenn looked at his broad smile and the gleam in his eyes from looking at the computer screen as if they mirrored the dollar signs of his earnings. He was gasping for the air to say something, but it wasn't necessary; his face said it all. Jenn realized that for the first time in his life, Mike was really experiencing the thrill of betting, and she was convinced now that he would love this feeling. The game was on, and she wasn't sure she wanted to be a part of it.

CHAPTER 17

Armed with a second glass of wine to commemorate their first investment success, purchased for $40 at the liquor store on the corner of their street a few minutes before they closed, Mike tried hard to convince Jenn how their lives would be different from now on.

"You see, Jenn, I was able to make $7,000. With taxes, we still net $5,000. In the last four weeks, there were three news reports that could lead me to guaranteed investments that could make another $11,000 post taxes. So, in total, we could earn $15,000 in just one month! Let's take a conservative approach—assume only $10K. Still, it is more than $100,000 in a year!"

Mike's mind was spinning fast with prospects, and he wasn't quite sure what held Jenn back from being as festive as him.

"Think about paying off all the loans, think about putting down a sizable amount of a down payment for our house—hey, we can even afford a three-bedroom house in the suburbs! We can get you a new car!" he continued.

Jenn quietly sipped her wine, letting Mike do all the talking for both of them. Suddenly, she asked, "Is this even legal, Mike?"

"Is what legal?"

"This, what you're trying to convince me to do—buying shares and then selling them when they rise."

"Why wouldn't it be legal?" Mike was genuinely surprised.

"When you went to buy wine, I read a couple of articles on trading, and one of them brought me to Wikipedia's 'Insider Trading' article, and then I read a bit more on the topic. I think this might qualify as insider trading, which is illegal."

"But how does this qualify as insider trading, for God's sake? What do I have to do with either Firetec or Dymanick?"

"Mike, let me play the devil's advocate. You learned about the merger a few days before the announcement and purchased their shares only because you wanted to profit off of it. If I understand correctly, you cannot use this internal knowledge as your deciding factor. I am afraid it might look illegal to the authorities."

Mike did not expect any of this to come. He put down his glass of wine, which had acquired a bitter taste for the unjustifiable $40 price, and sat for a few moments staring at Jenn, then opened his laptop to read about insider trading. As he continued to read, his face became grimmer with every minute.

"I'm not a lawyer that can fully judge this, but I think you have a point. It might look illegal," Mike slowly said. "But I don't want to argue about this either with investigators or with a court."

"Gee, Mike, I told you this is a bad omen, didn't I? This Breaking News of Tomorrow site frightens the hell out of me, and now you might be complicit in a crime!" Jenn's voice was trembling. "Can you quickly sell these stocks and get rid of them?" she asked.

"Jenn, calm down, please. You don't need to worry now," Mike replied as composedly as he could manage. "They say that inside traders profit from the knowledge. What triggers the authorities is a sale with unusual profits. If I hold on to these stocks for now, it will become no issue."

"How long do you need to hold them?" Jenn asked.

"I don't know. I guess until this merger news is not news anymore. In any case, the money I invested is too minuscule for the Feds to even bother," Mike replied.

Jenn rose from her chair and poured the remaining wine from her glass into the kitchen sink.

"I'm going to take a shower and then go to sleep," she said with a metallic tone in her voice and left the kitchen without saying anything more.

Mike sat alone in the kitchen contemplating his new realization that maybe, just maybe, what he wanted to do, and almost had done, was illegal. This unpleasant thought began to nag his mind with obsession, and he made every effort to shake it off. Going to bed was out of the question. Personal failure had the most bitter taste.

The wall clock announced the arrival of midnight as loudly as it could manage in the complete silence of the house, causing Mike to jump from his self-imposed misery. He looked at the clock absentmindedly, and suddenly, a thought came into focus, first fleetingly, and then seizing his entire essence with forced presence, awakening a whole gamut of emotions—regret and hope, shame and curiosity, anger and belief. Mike's mind rushed between these thoughts and feelings, and he cursed himself for his weakness. With shaking hands, he unlocked his laptop screen, and with the words "Just one last time," he clicked on the saved bookmark in his browser. Familiar, fateful big ugly flashing red letters appeared on the screen.

IT WAS DIFFICULT for Mike to accept his defeat. The feeling that he'd done nothing wrong by trading Dymanick's stocks was humming in his head and with untiring importunity urged him to look into the matter in depth. There was no way he could be accused of anything illegal; it was just illogical.

With a mindset ready to accept any justification, he entered "Insider Trade Cases" into a search field and started to read through tons of pages of information, each leading to new links and resources, sometimes to the SEC pages, sometimes to newspapers, and sometimes to opinion pieces by legal advisers. The closest Mike ever came to the field of legal matters was signing a rental agreement several years ago or clicking on the "Agree" button on the legal terms and conditions of some online services he subscribed to, without reading through more than the first sentence. And now he found himself building a legal defense of his actions via internet articles.

The more he read, the better his mood became. But the new, unexpected challenge, much more difficult, in his opinion, than securities laws and regulations, was looming in front of him: convincing Jenn that his plans were both legal and moral.

MIKE SPENT THE whole next day learning everything he could on the topic, and he was waiting for the right moment during dinner to initiate a discussion. He watched Jenn happily milling around the kitchen like nothing had happened the day before. He pretended to listen to her story about the two boys who were saved from juvenile prison a while ago and how they found a new path and everyone was happy. He missed the reason for them almost getting into prison and how they were saved, but his exclamations said in the right moment with the right tone made enough of an impression of active engagement in the discussion.

"I am so proud of you, dear!" Mike said when Jenn completed her story, and with a kiss on her cheek, he sealed the happy boys topic. Now it seemed to be a good time to talk about the BNOT, the best opportunity, given Jenn's elevated spirit. "Listen, I have been reading a lot about insider trading today."

"Really? Did you stop working, Mike? What about your job? This Breaking News of Tomorrow site will get you fired if you spend all your time at work on it," she said rather angrily, but Mike ignored it.

"Oh, don't worry. I got it all under control. I completed a code integration today and couldn't progress too much anyway since they needed to test the whole release first. Besides, only I fully know the architecture and functionality, so they will never dare to fire me, not now, anyway."

"Well, it's compelling to know that you are irreplaceable, but you know what they say about irreplaceable people?"

"What?" Mike didn't notice the sarcasm in Jenn's voice.

"That a cemetery is full of irreplaceable people."

"That's your Russian humor, Jenn. I am not irreplaceable, but it's too risky to fire me now."

"Maybe, but I think it is unfair to Solutry that you spend your time at work not working on their product."

"Jenn, how many nights, weekends, and holidays have I stayed in the office to work for them? Was it fair to me? You never asked then!"

"That is your job, Mike, and for that, you got both a bonus and now a promotion."

"*Promotion?* That's hardly any promotion! I do the same job I did before. I just have a different title and report to Keana. She is calling all the shots and has convinced the Duke to give her more people and broader authority. I am getting tired of Solutry, to tell you the truth!"

"Are you getting tired of Solutry, or are you too engaged with this Breaking News site?" asked Jenn.

"I think it's both, but maybe without the Breaking News, I would not realize it yet, would continue to let inertia pull my plow."

"This plow brings food to the table," Jenn said quietly, primarily to herself, but Mike heard it and decided to ignore it again. As passionate as Jenn was for her cause, and as much satisfaction as her work brought to her, it was clear to both of them that the major income contributor would be Mike. "So, tell me what you learned today about insider trading? I know that if you are fixated on something, you'll get it anyway."

"I learned that doing trades based on the information provided by the Breaking News of Tomorrow site does not constitute an insider trade in any way, not even remotely."

Jenn looked at him with a question in her eyes, prompting Mike to continue. "Let's take a look at an example. Suppose I am standing in a Starbucks line behind the CEOs of Firetec and Dymanick and overhear them talking about their merger. Now I know all the details to the last penny of the transaction. I rush home and buy their shares prior to their announcement. Does it make it an insider trade?"

"You wanna say it's not?"

"Exactly! It's not because I came to know about it without them intending or knowing about that, and I have no duty to not act on it. Me reading about a potential merger on a strange website and then acting on it is even less insider than me over-hearing the CEO talking in line for the coffee."

"So, you are absolutely certain that this is completely legal?"

"Yes, absolutely certain! There is nothing illegal about it. But this does not mean that once the sums are large, the Feds won't probe me."

"*Once the sums are large?* It sounds like you plan to continue doing these speculative trades. I thought we already talked about that!" Jenn was genuinely upset about Mike continuing to make these shady investments, as she classified them.

"Well, that's what I wanted to talk about," he calmly replied. "I told you I started to work on an algorithm that takes the parameters from the Breaking News predictions and calculates various stock movements. I compared the results of my algorithm with actual market values. My algorithm is very accurate, astoundingly accurate, and it is only a draft version, a prototype. And I have tons of ideas on how to make it broader and faster and even more precise."

"Mike, I am not comfortable with anything that comes from this site! Doesn't it bother you that you're basing all your calculations on some maniacal site with unclear intentions and ulterior motives, and have no idea who is behind this site?"

"I don't think there is any hidden agenda; after all, it plainly reports the news of tomorrow."

"There is only one entity that can report news of tomorrow."

"Which one?" Mike asked, not catching the irony in Jenn's voice.

She looked at Mike without blinking and said, "It's in the books on theology. So, what's your plan?"

"I want to open a company. And do all the trades as a company, based on my algorithm. If I am right and I will be able to improve its accuracy, I believe this company will be positioned to make a lot of money, and I can quit my job at Solutry."

He saw bewilderment and fear in Jenn's eyes and continued with enthusiasm, interspersed with resentment: "I've been thinking about this a lot. I can do more than they think I can. I know it. But they don't give me the opportunity, and they'll never will. The Duke just doesn't believe in my abilities, and he makes this point again and again. I might be inexperienced in management and strategy, but I am a fast learner. But no, he will never give me a chance. Never! How much more should I take? This is my chance, Jenn. This is my perfect opportunity to prove to them that I am worth it. And to show you that I can."

Mike abruptly fell silent, surprised at his own frankness. He opened his laptop and pulled up a set of windows. Numbers with dollar signs in front of them started to change one after another, continuously increasing.

"This algorithm that I began to develop and which already shows auspicious signs is a breakthrough because it was built on a different set of assumptions than anything else on Earth. It is based on what we know will happen tomorrow and then self-calibrated." He pointed to the revenue columns. "This is what a company can make based on the initial amount I invested, the bonus money, $30,000. See the potential growth in one month, one quarter, one year? It is unbelievable how much someone can profit when he knows what will happen tomorrow."

Jenn stared at Mike in silence. In front of her sat a completely transformed man, with a quality that hadn't been there before: a determination to pursue his course despite objections.

CHAPTER 18

With the satisfaction of a writer who just typed "The End" after completing a long novel, Mike shut down his laptop, exhausted from the development marathon of the last three months. He closed his eyes and sat for a few minutes in total silence, feeling sudden emptiness, tired of the rat race at Solutry. He continued to sit with closed eyes and thought about a good day to quit. He opened his eyes, stuck the laptop into his bag, and went toward the elevators, stopping for a second in Keana's room, who didn't show even the slightest hint that the day was almost over.

"Done, I submitted everything," Mike said to Keana. "After the last few months, I need to relax. So, I am taking three days off, remember?"

"Of course. By the way, next month I am going to London. I want you to go with me."

"London, next month? It's October, their most rainy season."

"Bring an umbrella."

"Sure. Do we fly first class at least?"

"Better, private jet and a stay at Buckingham Palace."

"Sweet, I look forward to it. But first, need to order a passport. Never been abroad. Au revoir!"

"Don't waste your time learning French," Keana said to Mike. "They speak English. Well, sort of." But he was already at the elevators.

London was the last place he wanted to be next month. And not because of the rain.

JENN WAS FIXING dinner when Mike came home.

"Finally!" he exclaimed. "I thought work would never end. I took three days off."

"Great, so now you can relax, and I will see you in the daylight," Jenn said, resting her hands on his shoulders, kissing his forehead, and staring into his face. "I am starting to forget what you look like."

"To tell you the truth, with all the latest work at Solutry and my fifteen-hour days, there is nothing that I want more than to spend time with you! Do you know how much I miss it too?"

"Really? I thought you were pretty happy with your Breaking News of Tomorrow."

"Jenn, stop worrying! This is my work, but you are my life, dear!" He gave her a firm squeeze around the shoulders, held it for a few seconds, and then released as if indicating that the romantic part of the conversation was over. "Speaking of which, by the way, I ran two scenarios this morning in my algorithm. First—with the predictions from the site from last month, and second—without any. My algorithm gave 63 percent without relying on the breaking news parameters and 87.5 percent with them.”

“So, Breaking News improves your algorithm by 25 percent. Cool.” Jenn’s tone didn’t hide her disappointment that even at the start of his short vacation, Mike wasn’t ready to let go of this topic.

“That’s not the point, Jenn. The point is it is still very positive, and if I restrict my trades to only using the version of the algorithm without any inputs from the Breaking News, I am still making a huge profit.”

“So, you can finally stop using it?” asked Jenn with a clear indication in her voice that this would be the right course of action.

“Well, not yet. But, as a matter of fact, Jenn, I doubled my April bonus: now we have $70,000.”

“Wow, holy cow!” was all she said. “So we have $70,000 now?”

“Well, it’s all in stocks, but yes. Firetec grew nicely—after they announced Dymanick acquisition, their stock became investment’s holy grail.”

“Great, I’m glad.” Jenn’s tone didn’t really match her words, despite the growing money in the trading account. “Let’s eat. I made something special.” She unveiled her new masterpiece in a Dutch oven on the stove. “And, Mike, can we talk about the wedding? There are some things I would like to discuss with you, and I need your input to decide.”

“Of course, dear, I would love to!” Mike said as he helped Jenn set the table.

He looked at the wall clock—there were less than five hours till midnight, and so he was eager to dive right into the wedding party discussion.

MIKE HARDLY BELIEVED his eyes. It was impossible to miss or make a mistake; the text did not leave any chance for a different interpretation.

"Jenn, come over!" he shouted from the kitchen. "Take a look, please!"

Jenn came from the living room and leaned on the back of Mike's chair, looking at his laptop from behind his shoulder. Beneath, familiar ugly letters showed the latest breaking news.

FIRETEC'S CEO IS ACCUSED OF SEXUAL HARASSMENT AND HUSH-MONEY PAYMENTS TO SEVERAL FEMALE COWORKERS

Renowned CEO of Firetec Corporation, Howard Waterman, used his corporate power to promote young female employees to senior roles with high salaries and hefty bonuses in exchange for sexual relationships with these women. When these women failed to execute in their roles, Mr. Waterman terminated them and paid hundreds of thousands of dollars to settle any potential future allegations. Megan McCarty, Angela Pwesold, and Jessica Stewards are among the women who stepped forward with these allegations. Firetec recently announced intentions to acquire its primary rival, Dymanick, in an all-cash transaction, a deal that still awaits the approval of Dymanick's shareholders and regulatory authorities.

"Gee," Jenn said, sitting on a chair near Mike. "That's very shocking news. I don't even know what to say."

"Do you understand what this means?" he asked.

"At a minimum, they will kick him out, and it will be the end of his career too. Then he'll publish a memoir called *Unzipping My Downfall*," Jenn replied.

"Ha!" Mike appreciated her humor. "Dymanick will pull out of the deal, and some key customers will switch from Firetec to them. Which means Dymanick's stock will go up."

"You say this because you have already decided to invest in them."

"That's exactly what I want to do, Jenn. Look, this is a perfect example of a case to settle our previous argument about insider trading. Do you think this qualifies as such?"

"Of course not! But I think we're not arguing about insider trading. My concern is the source of this breaking news site. It's very unsettling to me. I already told you—"

"Yes, you did. But now it's different, don't you agree? It looks like these guys behind the breaking news got some advanced intel and dug this up. Anyway, this is clearly not a company secret, like new technology, a merger, or something like that…"

"Right…"

"So, I can do whatever I want with that, right?"

"I guess," Jenn replied. "If this weren't coming from the Breaking News site, I would say go ahead. This bastard had it coming. But I'm terrified of this site, Mike. I always was, and I always will be: it feels nonhuman."

Mike let her last sentence pass without saying anything. They talked more about Firetec and Waterman and how he was famous and had it all, and why he couldn't refrain from harassing women at work, and how stupid it all was, until Jenn stood up and went to take a shower.

Mike opened his trading account, looked at the aftermarket closure of the Firetec stock, and whistled in pleasant surprise. With a few strokes on the keyboard, he sent an instruction to sell his Firetec stock and to acquire Dymanick stock.

Then he opened the algorithm's interface and entered some parameters. "Time to run—five hours, thirty-two minutes," the algorithm prompted on the screen. Mike looked at the clock—almost one in the morning. The adrenaline of the last hour evaporated from his veins, and unbearable tiredness took possession of him. He turned off the lights, set his alarm clock to six thirty, and left the kitchen.

MIKE WASN'T LYING to Jenn when he said he missed her. She was fun, loving and caring, smart and passionate about many things, and Mike loved being with her. She had her shortcomings too, mostly her obsession with the wedding party details, which Mike had a hard time contemplating, but these were insignificant and easily ignored. Overall, he really cherished the time they spent together, and so he was genuinely looking forward to the next three evenings. And as a bonus, he had at least ten hours each day to devote to his algorithm, and he hoped that without any distractions, he would be able to make substantial progress.

He opened his email as Jenn left for work early the next morning, and read the latest newsletter from Professor Jeremei. "A Thousand Reasons to Decide," was the subject of the newsletter, in which the famously controversial professor made a claim that he'd developed a theory of predicting human decisions. There were one thousand parameters that characterized any human society, from entire nations to local communities, stated Jeremei, and based on these parameters, one could gauge how society would feel about any common topic. The mathematical models that the professor developed were too complex to be published in the newsletter, and he urged advanced readers to check them out on his personal website. But in the newsletter, he gave a few examples of his theory in many controversial cases, from the Russian Communist Revolution of 1917 to the Nazis coming to power in Germany in 1930s to the Vietnam War and then some local elections in the United States.

This newsletter couldn't have come at a better time, thought Mike. He impatiently poured himself a new cup of coffee and clicked on the link to Jeremei's website. The model was described in so much detail that Mike realized that it would take him at least a day to fully understand it, and with regret, he closed the page. "A Thousand Reasons to Decide" would need to wait a bit, despite resonating well with his own algorithmic development, hopefully just a few days, until he got back to work and would be able to devote his time to professor's theory during his lunch breaks. Now, he wanted to embrace the luxury of being on vacation and spend three uninterrupted days on his own research.

Mike launched his algorithm and excitedly rubbed his hands together. In the last few months working diligently but sporadically on his algorithm, he'd developed many ideas and directions worth exploring, and while he recognized the sadness in Jenn's voice every time the topic of the BNOT came up, the creative inkling of the software artist inside of him was unable to ignore the task at hand. He looked at the screen and froze in disbelief: his $70,000 was estimated to grow to more than $300,000.

A niggling thought began to drill Mike's mind with the insistence of a woodpecker hitting a tree. He was puzzled since he didn't know whether the hitman Anthony Dowell was caught because he had tipped off Rachel Sorrow, or if she would have obtained the same information regardless of his help. He never contacted her to ask. Similar doubt about Firetec now relentlessly pounded his brain. He wanted to wait and see, but the prospect of risking $300,000 didn't quite appeal to him.

He dressed up, poured his untouched coffee into a travel thermos cup, and headed to the car. He'd already made this trip before, and a sense of déjà vu occupied him. After three brief stops, armed with prepaid cellular phones bought in cash, Mike parked in the lot of the Dartmouth Mall Plaza, between Peet's and Starbucks, the only popular places at the otherwise still-dormant shopping plaza at this morning hour.

He killed the engine and, without getting out of the car, dialed a number. The first several attempts went to voicemail. Mike waited for two minutes and then dialed again. A sleepy voice, which clearly had been screening previous calls, answered, "Hello?"

"Miss Sorrow, good morning, sorry for the early call. This is Doug Jordan." Mike tried his best to disguise his voice.

"Doug?" Any hint of sleepiness in Rachel's voice evaporated in an instant. Within a split second, she'd transformed to all business. "Doug, we must meet! There are a lot of things I need to ask you…and, please, call me Rachel."

"Miss Sorrow, uhh, Rachel, I will not be able to talk to you about Anthony Dowell more than we already did."

"Why not, Doug? You are a good man, and your info was invaluable in catching him."

"Thank you, Rachel, but as I said, I cannot help you with that case anymore. But I have other information that you might find interesting, not related to that case."

"I am listening," Rachel said and clicked the record button.

"Do you know Howard Waterman, the CEO of Firetec?"

"I don't know him, but I've heard a lot about him. He is a visionary and a very unorthodox tech executive."

"Yes, very unorthodox. It turns out that he harassed his female employees, and part of the deal was they'd get promotions with big salaries and perks, and when it did not work out, he paid them hefty sums to shut them up. I know of three women: Megan McCarty, Angela Pwesold, and Jessica Stewards. Goodbye, Ms. Sorrow, uhh, Rachel!" Mike hung up without giving Rachel any chance to reply or ask anything.

Satisfied, he started the car and drove home. Three uninterrupted days of algorithm development beckoned him with all their luring power.

CHAPTER 19

Utterly bewildered, Rachel lit a cigarette and entered "Howard Waterman" into the web browser. His name was all over, and the common sentiment was that he was an exceptional technical visionary, a prodigy of the tech sector, a person that inspired a generation of programmers. Not even a single time was there any subtle clue of a scandal. His reputation looked immaculate, and if valid, the information that Doug Jordan dumped on her would ruin it.

She lit another cigarette, boiled some water, and mixed an instant coffee drink, a palatable substitution to ground coffee, which she'd run out of. Then she dialed her private investigator.

Phil Matthew picked up the phone right away as if he were waiting for her call.

"Phil, please check whether there were any private payments coming from Howard Waterman to Megan McCarty, Angela Pwesold, and Jessica Stewards." No hello or any other form of greeting, no small chat.

"Howard Waterman of Firetec?" Matthew was never surprised by Rachel's peculiar requests.

"The one and only. These women also worked there," Rachel replied and hung up.

She returned to the living room's table, which was overloaded with numerous kitchen items, pieces of clothing, beverages, and garbage, each competing for the privilege to stay at the top of the pile, but losing their strategic advantage due to Rachel's unpredictability with the placement of the next piece. She pushed one pile toward the middle of the table, freeing some space for her laptop and notebook, and immersed herself in research on Waterman and Firetec.

It was not yet lunchtime when her phone buzzed and Phil Matthew's name identified the caller.

"Yes?" she answered.

"This was the easiest assignment you've ever given me. All it took was a little digging. I feel I did not deserve my honorarium for such a little amount of work." Matthew was in a very festive mood.

"Then you should refund me," Rachel replied.

"You bet! Didn't you read the small letters in the contract— no refunds." Matthew laughed. "Anyway, each of these ladies founded their own consulting company when they left Firetec. Guess who their registered agent was? Cowald, Dreichman, Miller and Waterman, a big legal and accounting firm in downtown."

"…and Waterman. Are they related to Firetec?"

"Oh, absolutely, Waterman here is Johan Waterman, Howard's older brother. I smell a little bit of nepotism here, but that's not the most interesting thing. The most interesting thing is that these ladies each had only one client, Firetec, and each got paid about $300,000 in one lump sum for a consulting in the area of executive coaching. All these consulting companies ceased to exist after the payment was processed, by the way."

"Fascinating. What do these women do now?"

"Two are employed. Angela Pwesold is on maternity leave. Do you want to get their addresses and phone numbers?"

"Writing…" Rachel answered and scribbled after Matthew in her notepad.

"Rachel, I forgot to mention. Angela Pwesold isn't married and lives alone…"

After an uneventful summer, a much-needed break had finally come, Rachel thought, thanks, again, to Doug Jordan.

THE WOMAN STOOD on her porch and was fiddling with her keys. She fixed the blanket in a baby's stroller and smiled at a sleeping child as only a mom can smile, melting from the peaceful expression on the baby's face, then sent him an air kiss for the hundredth time that morning and started to head toward the community park, carefully pushing the stroller so as not to wake up her three-month-old son.

Rachel watched the woman from a distance, waiting for her to enter the park and walk toward the other end of the alley to join the group of young moms exchanging the secrets of successful motherhood.

When the woman stopped to find a pacifier that fell out of her baby's mouth, Rachel reached her.

"Hello, Miss Pwesold, my name is Rachel Sorrow. I am a reporter from QQBC."

Angela Pwesold jumped in surprise but immediately calmed down and smiled nicely, recognizing the familiar face of the TV journalist.

"Good day, Miss Sorrow. I've seen your program. How can I help you?"

"May I call you Angela? You can call me Rachel."

"Yes, sure, of course."

"Angela, I am investigating Howard Waterman from Firetec. I believe you know him from your days at Firetec, right?"

Angela's face turned stiff. "I am not sure I can help you, Miss Sorrow. I know who Howard Waterman is, as he is the CEO of the company, but I was several levels lower than him and didn't really know him."

"Well, Angela, that's not exactly what my sources told me. I believe you had a very close relationship with Mr. Waterman, intimately close, and I know that when you quit Firetec, you were paid hundreds of thousands of dollars to keep quiet."

"Miss Sorrow, I have nothing to discuss with you. I need to attend to my son. Sorry for not being able to help you. Goodbye!" Angela quickly placed the pacifier in her son's mouth and began to stride away.

"Miss Pwesold." Rachel made her tone more official, sending her metallic words to the back of the walking-away woman. "You were paid for a nonexistent consultancy in the area of executive coaching as a hush-money payoff for your silence. You are not alone in this. Howard Waterman targeted many women in the company. You can either talk to me as a victim of workplace sexual harassment, or you can talk to the FBI as a complicit party in a criminal scheme. Your choice."

Angela abruptly stopped, and her shoulders dropped as if Rachel's words put a massive weight on her. She turned back to Rachel, and her previously happy, beautiful face changed its expression. Now in front of Rachel was a frightened woman who looked ten years older, unsure of her future and not capable of making a decision.

"I did nothing wrong." Angela suddenly started to weep. "I thought he loved me and would divorce his wife, whom he hated. They don't even sleep together anymore! But he didn't. He was courting me from my first day in the company until I…" She continued to cry.

"It's OK, Angela." Rachel patted her shoulder. "It's OK. You don't need to share all the details now. Tell me about this consultancy company."

"I just signed a few papers and gave my bank account information. Martin Joyce organized everything."

"Who is Martin Joyce?" Rachel asked.

"He is VP of human resources. He contacted Howard's brother in some big law firm, and they did everything. I just received the money in my bank account."

When Rachel left Angela one hour later, she had all the pieces of Angela's story and felt really sorry for the woman. She didn't ask who the father of her child was, but she knew the answer.

She left Angela crying in the park and looked at her notes. Next to speak with was Megan McCarty. Now understanding the whole payment scheme, Rachel was pretty confident she would easily crack both her and Jessica Stewards into a confession. The story was born, and it would cause turmoil in the highest ranks of Firetec. As she drove to her next victim, she took her phone out.

"Josh," she said when Koppelman answered. "Doug Jordan called me this morning."

"Who?"

"Doug Jordan, you heard it right." And she told Koppelman everything that she had learned in the last several hours.

"Jesus, Rach," Koppelman said after Rachel finished. "That's quite a story. I will ask my guys to look deeper into it. You know what puzzles me the most?"

"Why don't you tell me? I myself have a long list here."

"What puzzles me the most, Rach, is who is Doug Jordan? A Nostradamus?"

MIKE DEVOTED THE last day of his short three-day vacation entirely to Jenn. He spent as much time with her as she needed, attending to numerous tasks concerning the upcoming wedding, and he rediscovered the almost lost pleasure of being together completely unconnected from everything else. Late in the evening, Mike sat down on the couch and embraced Jenn. A familiar music theme preempted the late-night TV program they were watching, and then the enthusiastic host appeared on the screen.

"Good evening, ladies and gentlemen! This is Benjamin Wolf with our daily evening program, *City Night*. Today we will open the night with a rather shocking breaking-news story brought to you by Rachel Sorrow. Rachel, good evening."

"Good evening, Ben. You are right. The story I have to share today is very shocking and disturbing. It's about systemic sexual harassment and hush-money payment of millions of corporate dollars to cover up a scandal at one of the biggest tech companies in the city, Firetec, and by none other than Howard Waterman, their renowned CEO, and Martin Joyce, the VP of human resources."

Mike and Jenn listened to how masterfully and methodically Rachel told the story with enough details to accuse Waterman and some of his executives while still preserving the dignity of the involved women and positioning them as actual victims.

"Mike," Jenn asked, turning down the volume when the program finished, "didn't Keana used to work at Firetec?"

"She did indeed!" Mike said quietly and looked at Jenn. "Do you think she was a victim too?"

"I don't know, but she is too beautiful to not be noticed."

"ARE YOU BUSY?" Mike asked, sticking his neck through the doorway of Keana's office the next morning.

"Hi, Mike," she replied. "Come on in. How was your time off? I told everybody to not disturb you on your vacation. But now expect to be bombarded with bugs."

"Thank you for that! It was surprisingly refreshing not to get any support calls." He hesitated, a bit afraid to intrude on too private a topic, but finally went for it. "I guess you've been bombarded with questions about your former boss at Firetec. Since Rachel Sorrow exposed him on TV, the internet is full of more stories accusing him."

"He had it coming," Keana replied. Mike took this as an invitation to continue this discussion.

"So you knew about this?"

Keana put her hands on the table and looked straight into Mike's eyes.

"What do you think, Mike, it was my dream to join Solutry and work with my ex-boyfriend?"

"I thought we were cool with that…" Mike started to say.

"We are *now* cool with that, Mike, but not when I was still at Firetec and thought about the prospect of seeing you daily. It is just that, at some point, I didn't have any choice. I think I told you then."

"So he harassed you too?" Mike hesitantly asked.

"He tried to, and when it was impossible to deflect anymore, I quit."

"But why didn't you file a complaint against him? It is not the 1950s anymore!"

"Mike, I am a woman and an executive. How many positions are out there for me, do you think? Do you believe there is any right-minded CEO willing to hire a female VP who filed a sexual harassment complaint against her previous boss?"

Mike stood silent and then said, "If this means anything to you, Keana, I am glad you moved here. You are doing one hell of a job!" And with that, he left the room.

He unlocked his office and opened his laptop. The trade was already in full steam, and he looked at the latest market charts. The next chapter of Firetec and Howard Waterman's life was developing in front of his eyes.

CHAPTER 20

Mike never experienced such tiresome jet lag as he did when he crossed the Atlantic Ocean. He had yet to figure out how to get used to the time difference. Failing to fight his unexpected insomnia, a novel and uncharted state of his body, he stood up, brewed a cheap hotel coffee, and opened his computer.

He did not know how long he'd been working when his phone's alarm chimed: midnight back at home. Mike put aside his algorithm and opened a web browser. He missed yesterday's update of Breaking News of Tomorrow, as he was 30,000 feet above the ground and two feet left of Keana's aisle seat on the flight to London. This saddened him, and the whole flight, it was the only thing he thought about, experiencing the same body and brain reaction as any heavy smoker gets on commercial flights—anxiety, shakiness, and inability to focus on anything but the time until the destination. The alarm he had set was his savior from that mental fever.

Familiar ugly letters displayed something unexpected: "Next update: October 22, 12:01 A.M." Mike was puzzled for a moment and, just in case, calculated the time difference again—all was correct. It was 12:01 a.m. back home. *Something is wrong*, he thought. *It cannot be.* He clicked the refresh button again and again, but it was no good: the page was still displaying the same maddening text.

He paced back and forth around his hotel room, his first instinct being to call Jenn and ask her to check the page. It was midnight there, and most probably, Jenn would be asleep, and of course, she would be mad to get a call asking her to read the breaking news, knowing her attitude about the site. But this was a matter of data integrity, validity of daily inputs, and refining his algorithm structure. She surely would understand that. Jenn knew how important it was for him to develop a perfect solution, and with all his Solutry obligations and this damn trip to London, he really needed to invest all his free time into the algorithm development, especially since who knew when these guys would realize that they were giving all this information for free and would shut down access to the breaking news? Jenn knew this. Yes, she hated the site and preferred not to be reminded of it. Still, he rarely asked her for anything—really, almost never. It was always one-sided requests from her to him—do this, go there, pick this up, send that. He never said anything, so he didn't understand why she wouldn't support him with the algorithm, just once, compared to all her unending requests to look at pictures and choose between two identical silverware options or bands or whatever else she needed for the wedding. He secretly alternated between the right-side and left-side choices without really looking. So far, he always made the right choice, as she always thought the same. If he could support her all the time, why couldn't she support him only once, just once, just today? Of course she would, even at midnight, even if the unexpected call woke her up.

Convinced, he picked up the phone and dialed Jenn. She answered on a third ring: "Mike, is everything OK with you? It's midnight here. Are you alright?"

"Hi, dear, everything is OK. I just wanted…" Mike stopped in the middle of the sentence. "I just wanted to hear your voice. I miss you so much, Jenn!"

"I miss you too, love!" Jenn didn't sound mad at all for his call. He heard her arranging the pillows on the bed more comfortably. "Tell me how your first day in London was? Did you have a chance to see the city?"

"Mostly just walked a few blocks around the hotel, Jenn, but it is close to the city center, so we kind of breathed in the city atmosphere. It feels bizarre—everything moves on the other side of the street. When you see it in the movies, it looks OK, but experiencing it is totally different! I am afraid to be run over by a bus, but for dummies like me, they have a curb sign that says 'Look Right.'"

"Mike, why don't you stay a few more days and do some sightseeing! It's your first time in Europe. Take advantage of this opportunity!"

"Oh, Jenn, you are so sweet! I don't want to travel without you, not the slightest fun! So I'll come home as planned, and then we will need to decide where to spend our honeymoon. OK? How was *your* day?"

"The usual, you know, to the office, back home, and then I went to my parents, and when I returned home, I looked at the catalogs. I'll save a couple of final options I want you to see."

"Sure, dear, I would love to. But if the timing is critical, don't wait for my input. I trust your judgment!"

"Thanks, Mike, but it can wait for your return. OK, dear, rock it tomorrow! Kisses and hugs, darling! Love you!"

"Love you too!"

Mike hung up and went back to his algorithm, unhappy with his cowardice but at the same time satisfied with his restraint. He'd pressed his luck with Jenn enough times already, so doing it again in the middle of her night would be just way too much for their relationship, which he felt needed more work on his side. Instead, he would need to figure out how to make the system more resilient to missing parameters and be able to self-calibrate better. There were rarely real problems; most of the time, there were tasks that just didn't have solutions at the moment.

THE DINNER WITH customers was boring and a waste of time, and Mike hated that he was forced to give in to Keana's insistence that he join.

"It's relationship building," she said. "They need to trust us on a personal level. They need to see who the person is on the other side of the line when they have a problem."

He was right, and she was wrong, it turned out. How connected were they now with him if he hardly exchanged a few words with them during dinner? It was Keana who did most of the talking and laughing and socializing!

"Happy?" Mike asked her on their way back to the hotel. "You see, you could have excused me from the dinner—they were hardly interested in me!"

"Mike!" Keana exclaimed. "What are you talking about? They were interested in talking to you. You are the major architect of their solution—they wanted to establish a good relationship with you. But it was you who decided to be surly today, so I needed to save the situation."

Mike swallowed hard. It now occurred to him that if it hadn't been for Keana, the dinner would have been a complete bust because of him. This unexpected revelation left a bitter taste in this mouth, an unpleasant mix of resentment and unappreciation, and without hesitation, he answered, slightly pursing his lips like a capricious child: "I wasn't surly at all. I was my regular self."

"Of course you were. I just forgot how you are."

"You weren't complaining then."

"Nope, because you were hilarious when you were in the mood, and luckily for me, you were always in the mood then. Hope you make Jenn laugh too. Don't ever forget to keep it that way, Mike. Women need this."

He resisted the urge to reply that he did. Instead, he tried to remember when the last time was that he was funny with Jenn. In the past, she told him that he was the funniest person she knew and could make any situation hilarious, but now, walking alongside Keana a few thousand miles away from Jenn, he was unable to recall when he'd last made a joke. They walked toward the hotel without saying anything else, each lost in their own thoughts.

"OK, let's go to sleep. I feel exhausted from the time difference. Meet you downstairs at seven thirty?" Keana said when they entered the hotel.

They parted ways in the lobby, and finally, Mike returned to his room to continue working on his algorithm. He opened his computer to launch the algorithm's interface and immediately forgot about the annoyance of the customer dinner.

The next time he raised his eyes from the computer, Mike noticed that the clock on the nightstand showed midnight. He was about to close the laptop lid when he saw an icon in his browser had changed the color as if a page on it had just been updated. He opened the browser tab, and to his surprise, big red ugly flashing letters appeared on the screen: "Breaking News of Tomorrow—October 22."

Confused, Mike skimmed through the articles, one by one, and with each passing entry, his bewilderment grew. Most of the news items were related to Great Britain.

Going to sleep was out of the question. Mike checked his computer settings. The VPN he usually used was tuned to his city, as always, using the zip code of the central library, so he was puzzled by the Breaking News of Tomorrow site recognizing his actual location. He continued to check, but couldn't find a satisfactory answer. Baffled, he finally fell asleep.

At five a.m., a strange force pushed him out of bed. He sat, disoriented at first about where he was, and it took a few moments to recognize his whereabouts. He brewed a cup of coffee, sat in an armchair facing the window, and started to think, watching the big city awakening to a new day.

CHAPTER 21

Andy Linowski was standing near the whiteboard in Mike's office drawing a diagram when the desk phone rang. Without taking his attention from the board and not looking at who was calling, Mike reached his arm backward, groped for the phone, and pressed the speakerphone button: "Hello, Mike Eaglewood speaking."

"Good morning, Mr. Eaglewood!" said a friendly but official voice. "My name is Eugene Stoltz, and I am a special agent with the Federal Bureau of Investigation. Do you have a minute? I have a couple of questions I would like to ask you."

Mike saw how Andy's face stretched and thought that he himself probably had a similar expression. Only he'd been expecting this call sooner or later. He picked up the telephone receiver: "Good morning, Agent Stoltz, please give me a second." Mike covered the receiver with his palm and said to Andy, "Andy, do you mind? Let's continue later.

"Yes, Agent Stoltz, I can talk now," Mike said after Andy had stepped out.

"Thank you, Mr. Eaglewood. As I said, my name is Eugene Stoltz, and I am here with Special Agent Samir Bashir and with my supervising agent Joshua Koppelman. This conversation is being recorded."

"No problem, good morning, gentlemen," Mike said.

"Good morning, Mr. Eaglewood," Samir said too. Koppelman kept quiet.

"Mr. Eaglewood, I am calling on behalf of the Securities and Exchange Commission of the United States in regard to the recent transactions you made."

"Of course, no problem. I am more than happy to answer any of your questions."

"Very well, Mr. Eaglewood. The reason for this inquiry is the number of suspicious transactions that earned you a significant amount of profit. They were flagged for potential insider trading violations."

"I understand they might look suspicious, Agent Stolz, but I assure you nothing illegal is going on here. As far as I understand, insider trading, when illegal, is purchasing or selling securities while in possession of material nonpublic information, received from tips of such information from a person breaching a fiduciary duty. Is my understanding correct, Agent Stoltz?"

"Excellent one, Mr. Eaglewood. Looks like you did your homework."

"I assure you I never talked with any person regarding any of the companies, their stock, or their rivals. But there is a simple answer to your question, Agent Stoltz. I developed an algorithm that provides trading recommendations with a high level of accuracy."

"Mr. Eaglewood," Stoltz said after carefully listening to Mike's explanation. "I am sure you are a very talented scientist, but I doubt there is an algorithm that is capable of producing your level of earnings based on what stocks you traded."

"Oh, then you are very wrong, Agent Stoltz! The difference between my algorithm and anything else in the world is how well it can speculate about tomorrow and self-improve from correlated events. But it all must sound like gibberish to you, so why don't I prove it to you?"

"Prove what, Mr. Eaglewood?" Stoltz was confused.

"Oh, of course, the strength of the algorithm."

"Sure, Mr. Eaglewood, that would be interesting to see. But how can you demonstrate it?"

"Can you give me your email address, Agent Stolz? I will do the following: In about ten minutes, I'll send you a list of twenty-six stocks and their projected price tomorrow, calculated by my algorithm. To make it entertaining, each ticker will represent one letter, and you'll get them all from A to Z. You are welcome to make any trade based on my recommendations, and I am sure you wouldn't consider these deals insider trading. Please send an email to Michael Eaglewood at Solutry.com and I will reply with that list. You can thank me later for the tip. I hope that's all, gentlemen. I must return to my work. You know where to find me if you need further clarification. Meanwhile, goodbye!" And without waiting for any reply from the dumbfounded federal agents, Mike hung up.

He looked at his hands—they had started to shake. He couldn't understand where his bravado had come from. This wasn't like him; typically, he would try to avoid any sort of argument and would back off when confronted by authorities. He took few tissues from the box on his table and wiped big sweat drops off his forehead, still trembling. He stood up and leaned on the windowsill, trying to slow his heartbeat, stabilize his sudden labored breathing, and fight the desire to throw up. He hadn't expected the call to go the way it went, and he realized that his desire to quit Solutry and to form his own company, which until this call was still on his theoretical wish list, materialized into a set of strict cannot-walk-back deadlines.

KOPPELMAN, SAMIR, AND Stoltz sat around the phone, astonished by the unpredictable turn this routine conversation had taken.

"Did he just mock us?" Koppelman finally said, still not believing what had actually happened.

"He sure did!" Stoltz replied. "I can see only two options here: he is either a cold-blooded criminal or an ego-inflated genius."

"Or both, cold-blooded and ego-inflated criminal genius, Gene," Samir said. "He talked to us like we were first-grade students. I think he bluffed about his algorithm to get us off his back. I don't believe there is such a thing, and frankly, I don't think it's even theoretically possible."

"Well, Samir, we can easily check. Gene, send him an email; I want to see what this mad scientist comes up with," Koppelman said.

Stoltz typed a boring, official-looking message and hit send. Instinctively, he looked at his watch. They waited for about five minutes; then a new email appeared in Stoltz's inbox. Stoltz clicked on it and opened a table with twenty-six rows, each with a ticker name corresponding to each letter of the English alphabet and their respective target price labeled, "November 22, close of the market."

Under the table, Mike had added a paragraph of text. Stoltz read it aloud:

Dear Agent Stolz (and I am sorry—I forgot the names of the other two gentleman),

Below you will find the recommendations produced by my algorithm. Three stocks (highlighted) are projected to increase by 12 percent, 13 percent, and 16 percent respectively. That's where I would put my money. As you represent the highest law enforcement agency in the USA, I trust the information about my algorithm will be kept within the agency's walls.

With utmost respect,
Mike Eaglewood.

Koppelman looked at the A-to-Z list of tickers and said, "That's the boldest and craziest discussion I ever had with a suspected inside trader. Let's start watching him. Gene, if you need any warrants, let me know." And he left Stoltz's office.

MIKE'S DOOR WAS ajar again when Andy poked his head inside. "Are you ready for lunch?"

"Yes, sure, let's go."

They took the stairs down, all nine floors, their daily exercise, and made the brief trip to the shopping plaza, where they got food and found a table to sit down.

"So, what was it, the Feds call?" Andy finally asked the question he'd wanted to ask for the last two hours.

"You know, these were Feds. So if I tell you, I'll need to kill you." Mike tried to make a joke, but it died without reaching Andy, whose sense of humor usually relied on seeing the smileys in the text. Not getting a reaction, Mike continued. "You would be shocked by what I'll tell you. I made tons of money from trading in the stock market, and the Feds suspected me of an insider trading violation. They called to probe whether there were any grounds to their suspicions."

As he predicted, Andy was speechless and even stopped eating.

"Before you ask me what tons of money means and whether I am guilty of any insider trading, the answer is hundreds of thousands in net profits, and no, I didn't engage in insider trading."

"Hundreds of thousands?" Andy sounded baffled. "Really? How?"

"I designed an algorithm that makes very accurate market predictions. There are a lot of things in this algorithm, but the main thing is that it operates on a number of wide market parameters, including those unrelated to any specific sector inputs, and it correlates its calculated output with the actual market conditions by recalibrating the core logic itself. Part of the algorithm's output is redistribution to my daily portfolio of stocks."

"You have a daily portfolio of stocks, Mike?" The more Andy listened, the more puzzled his expression became. For many years, Mike had been significantly underpaid and often earned less than a new grad, only because he felt awkward displaying his worth. "I see that Jenn finally succeeded to graft some common sense about money into you."

"I made my first investment when we received our bonuses," Mike replied. "And the algorithm has multiplied it several times since then."

"Sweet." Andy whistled. "So, what about the Feds thing?"

"I got them off my back. I just told them I developed an algorithm and as proof sent them a list of my predictions for tomorrow. This clearly shows that I have no knowledge of insider trading and they should leave me alone. No case."

"Mike, that's crazy!"

"What's crazy about that?"

"You telling the Feds you have an algorithm! You sending them proof of it! I don't even know how to explain how insane that is!"

"Andy, I plan to resign from Solutry and start my own firm. Anyway, the Feds will know that I have proprietary software, as I am going to make big trades. Millions of dollars' worth of trades. So no reason to hide something that will become obvious."

"You are leaving?" Andy pushed his tray away, looking at Mike in astonishment.

"It's time. I couldn't do it before; I wanted to see Solutry dig itself out of the hole. And besides, I already left Keana once, and didn't want to leave her so vulnerable again. I hold a warm and soft spot for her in my heart. I would never want to hurt her. Anyway, after Thanksgiving, I will be moving on from Solutry, and I'm going to establish Eaglewood Solutions, Inc."

Andy finished his drink in a single unstoppable gulp, then chewed on his straw, contemplating Mike's announcement.

"So, we are going to part after what, eleven, twelve years of working together?" Andy's tone didn't succeed in hiding his sadness.

"Andy, I want you to come and work with me. This is the most interesting and challenging software I've ever worked on. You would love it! Even as a prototype, it is impressive. And I have developed it in my spare time. I can only imagine what we both could do working on it full-time! I want you to be my partner."

Andy sat silently, deep in thought. He finished sipping his drink from a straw and said, "Thanks for the offer, Mike. I am flattered. I'll tell you what bothers me. You are my closest friend. What I am afraid of is what working in your company might do to our friendship."

Mike stood and emptied their two trays of leftovers into the garbage bin. They walked back to the office in silence. When they reached the building, Mike held the entrance handle and, before he pulled the door open, said, "I need somebody whom I fully trust with my deepest trade secrets. Up until recently, I thought I would be able to isolate the core of my algorithm and have only an abstract interface to the rest of the software. However, during my trip to London, I discovered something that requires me to have a trusted person who shares this core with me. Andy, you are the only person I can trust wholeheartedly."

"STILL WORKING, GUYS?" Koppelman was already in his jacket and ready to head home.

Stoltz raised his eyes from his monitor and replied, "Yeah, this report is taking more time than I estimated. But I'll get it done tonight. Samir is helping me."

"Great, thanks!" Koppelman replied. "Gene, by the way, did you check the stocks Eaglewood sent us?"

"Frankly, no, I was occupied with this report."

"Well, out of curiosity, let's check."

With the rare exception of two stocks, the twenty-four others were identical to Mike's predictions. The three men looked at each other, then back to Stoltz's monitor. Then Koppelman said, "This smells like a big scam to me. Something really stinks here. Gene, I want full surveillance on this Eaglewood."

CHAPTER 22

Mike stood in the bedroom doorway, holding a glass of cold water with a squeezed lemon, her favorite first-thing-in-a-day drink, and looked at his beautiful fiancé peacefully sleeping on Thanksgiving morning. The smell of fried eggs, toast, and freshly brewed coffee finally woke Jenn up. Mike approached the bed and leaned down to kiss her a good morning.

Jenn lightly kissed him on the cheek, avoiding his lips, then took a glass and said to Mike: "Morning, dear, thanks for letting me sleep in! If you haven't thought about my Christmas gift, I have a wish list. I want a little device that does my hair, brushes my teeth, and puts my makeup on while I sleep so I can wake up for you like they do in movies—fully presentable!"

"But where will the surprise be in that?" Mike asked, sitting on the edge of her side of the bed.

"Oh, believe me, you will be surprised!"

"Ha ha, Jenn, I meant surprise in getting the gift if you know what it will be?"

"Oh, that! Wrap it in a gift box, attach a handwritten note, and I will be as thrilled and curious as I am when opening Amazon boxes with yesterday's order. Even more because of the note," she said, kissing him on the cheek again and slightly pushing on his shoulder. "Now, go and wait for me in the kitchen."

As she sat to enjoy the breakfast Mike had prepared for them, Jenn said, "By the way, Mom just texted me that Anton arrived. His business is picking up. It looks like he will be coming every few months."

"It would be great to have him at the dinner table today. What time should we be there?"

"Mom told me to arrive at five."

"Good. Listen, I wanted to finalize my plans with you. You know it's time for me to move on. So I would like to give Solutry my notice next week." He decided not to tell her about the call with the FBI and how it had expedited his decision.

Jenn listened without asking a question, and Mike continued. "As I told you, all the trading decisions I make are based on the output of my algorithm. I am very confident about everything."

"You know what you need to do?" Jenn finally asked.

"More or less. I mean, I know that I need to register the company, open a bank account, things like that. It's not rocket science. I talked to Andy, and he agreed to join my new company. Imagine how much the two of us can accomplish together, Jenn!"

"Then, Mike, we should raise a toast for your success today," Jenn said without too much enthusiasm.

Mike came around her chair and hugged her from behind, pressing his cheek to hers. "Thanks, dear!"

She nodded and smiled weakly. Mike didn't fail to note that the only reason she'd agreed was that she knew she'd exhausted all her arguments and realized that further contradiction would not be healthy for their union. This wasn't the best reason, and her agreement didn't bring him immense pleasure, but at this stage, Mike was willing to take anything.

ALL THE GUESTS were already there when Mike and Jenn arrived at Jenn's parents' house. Masha, Jenn's mom, as usual, was worried about the dinner, which had courses identical to those in all her previous family gatherings, with the exception of American-style stuffed turkey replacing her typical beef Stroganoff. For the hundredth time, she ran a mental checklist of all dishes, and everybody noticed her disquieted clucking when she nervously passed them on her run from the kitchen to the dining room. Finally, she called all the guests to sit at the table and start the feast.

"Michelle," Sergei, Jenn's father, loudly said to Mrs. Eaglewood, continuing their previous discussion, "you are wrong about the Soviet medical system. Many times, doctors did not care about their patients at all! I remember one case when a doctor simply wanted to cut my dad's penis because of a small pimple!"

"Sergei, what are you talking about! Be ashamed. We are eating. That's not a story for the table!" Masha cried.

"No, Masha, please don't stop him." Mike laughed. "We are totally OK. Let's hear this story!"

"Papa, maybe next time?" Jenn asked, clearly pretending to support her mom but, in truth, curious herself to hear a family story she'd never heard before.

"Oh, that's a great story, Papa. I remember it. Please do tell," Anton encouraged Sergei.

"How old was my papa then, Masha, like, what, seventy, seventy-two?" Sergei asked his wife.

"No, it was later. Jenn was already born. He was at least seventy-five!" replied Masha, giving up on objecting to the story.

"Right, seventy-five and in excellent health! One day, he had something on his manhood, a little pimple, right in the middle!" On his left middle finger, Sergei demonstrated the whereabouts of said pimple. "And my papa, even at his age, wasn't a man who could tolerate any pimples on his manhood, not even a little one. You know, he was that kind of a man. So I took him to the family doctor. She was a woman. And she said to Papa: 'You're old, you don't need it, let's cut to the root. No penis, no pimple.'" Sergei's right palm made a sawing motion at the base of his left middle finger. "So, what does my papa do? Of course, he does not agree. He asks me to take him to a doctor who understands penis pimples. I took him to the hospital, and another doctor looked at the problem and simply prescribed putting fish oil on the pimple daily."

"Sergei, you forgot the most important part!" Masha said. "Before the hospital, they treated the pimple with radiation, and it was all burned after that. This doctor in the hospital gave him fish oil to treat the burns, not the pimple."

"Does not matter, burned first and then treated with fish oil. He did not cut the penis! And it was a good thing because he used it wildly for the next five years, my papa, that was the kind of man he was!"

"I love your stories!" Mike could hardly talk from laughing, "Even if Jenn ever decides to leave me, I will still come to your dinners to hear them!"

"I'm going to leave you?" Jenn asked. "Are you crazy? I am about to fulfill the dream of any Russian girl to marry a rich American man!"

"Who is a rich American man here—my Mickey?" Mrs. Eaglewood intervened. "Mickey will never be rich. From his early days, everybody took advantage of him, all of them—in school, college, work, everybody made money off his ideas but him! Give up your fantasies, girl. Run away if you still can and find a real rich American man!" She laughed and pinched Mike's cheek as if he were still her five-year-old boy.

"Oh, you are so wrong, Michelle! Mike is leaving Solutry to establish his own company, Eaglewood Solutions, Inc."

"Congratulations, Mike!" boasted Sergei, grabbing a new bottle of wine. "Let's raise a toast to your success!"

Mrs. Eaglewood almost choked at the news. "Mickey, entre-preneur? Are you sure, darling, you're dating *my* son?"

"Oh, absolutely, Michelle! He has changed since he left home. Mike, do you want me to tell everyone about your idea, or do you want to do it yourself?" she asked.

"No, go ahead, Jenn. I'm curious to hear your presentation!"

"Sure! So Mike developed a super-smart stock trading algo-rithm and has already earned a lot of money while doing it only part-time. He's going to bring his best friend, Andy, with him."

"How much do you make, Mike?" Sergei asked straightforwardly.

"Sergei, how can you ask this question?" Masha cried again. "That's personal!"

"He is family, Masha! He is soon to be my son-in-law," Sergei replied. "So what's wrong with this question?"

"People just don't ask such straightforward questions, Sergei. Maybe Mike does not want to answer."

"No, I am totally OK to answer, Masha. We are family," Mike replied, to Jenn's complete astonishment over his unexpected openness. "I made $784,000 net profit based on my algorithm's suggestions."

Silence had several levels of volume. Many thought the lowest was when you could hear heartbeats. It was not. The lowest volume was when you could hear each other's thoughts.

"OK"—Anton broke the awkwardness of the moment, raising his glass—"let's drink to Mike's success!"

"YOU KNOW, ANDY, this is the most significant step I've ever taken in my life," Mike said at the building's threshold, on top of which, above the fifth floor, a signage company was erecting a giant neon sign with a strange combination of red and green letters, which read, "Eaglewood Solutions."

"It's weird to sit in that huge building alone," Linowski said, looking up. "Are you sure we will be able to afford it?"

"Andy, not only will we be able to afford it, but soon we will need to rent the rest of the building. I've put a provision for the first right of refusal in the contract," Mike replied.

"You are a crazy dude, Mike," Andy said, taking his eyes off the sign and looking at Mike. "I am used to this from when we discussed your product ideas, but to tell you the truth, I wouldn't expect that same level of craziness from you in business."

"Andy, it's not craziness. It's all data-driven. No magic. If I see that I can multiply our earnings in a short time, even with the most conservative approach, then nothing is crazy here. All we need to do is to guarantee that we have the right infrastructure to support this operation."

"Well, you talk about infrastructure. I can tell you what kind of machines we need, what type of network configuration they require, what level of redundancy and reliability we should have. That's what I understand. But all this requires people to support it, contracts, salaries, regulations, lawyers, stuff that I have no damn idea about and don't want to know. My mind is bogged down just thinking about all this."

"I have no freaking idea myself, Andy, about all of this. Heck, I've never even hired anybody in my life! But I know people who did."

"Who do you have in mind?"

"Houston."

"*What?*" Linowski almost shouted. "The Duke nearly smashed my head when I told him I was going to resign and work with you! Do you want to hear all the names he called you? He was rather colorful."

"What did you expect—the Duke is a footballer; that's what they do. But I have something to offer he couldn't resist."

"What?"

"World power."

CHAPTER 23

"This Mike Eaglewood looks legitimate, Josh," Agent Stoltz said. "We checked every angle, and there is not even the slightest hint to any of the potential illegalities when it comes to the insider trading."

"So what have you learned, Gene?" Koppelman asked, coming to the whiteboard to doodle his Eaglewood ideas in the hope something would come up.

"Well, this guy is very boring, to start with." Stoltz sat on the chair near Koppelman's desk, which he turned toward the whiteboard. "He doesn't go anywhere for fun. His regular route is home to work and back home. Sometimes, mostly on weekends, his fiancée Jenn Zharkova takes him to some wedding-related shopping or tasting, and they have visited her parents twice, once for Thanksgiving, and that pretty much sums up his social life."

Stoltz stood up, went to a mini-fridge, and without asking, as it was customary in their group, took a bottle of sparkling water from it, sipped a bit, and continued. "But it seems that he was swamped lately. I am starting to believe he was telling the truth about his algorithm. A few weeks ago, on December 1, he quit Solutry and registered a company named Eaglewood Solutions, Inc., with his partner, Andrezj Linowski. The company description says it deals with financial solutions and investments. Its website is still under construction with no information on it."

"Anything about this Linowski guy?" Koppelman asked.

"Your typical software genius. Nothing exciting, nothing illegal, no membership anywhere except several software standards committees, all clean with the only violation being two speeding tickets in the last ten years."

Koppelman wrote a few items on a board, preparing a visual playground for their brainstorming.

"I don't share your opinion, Gene," he said. "The SEC guys called me several times—all the transactions Eaglewood does are spot on, every damn time. They cannot believe this is a stroke of luck or an algorithm. These guys have seen millions of algorithms in their lives, and none of them has even come close to the level of performance of Eaglewood's 'algorithm.'" Koppelman made air quotes around the word. "However, they saw thousands of insider trading transactions, and all of them look the same, exactly like Eaglewood's dealings. Now add one plus one."

"I agree with you on how it looks," Stoltz said. "I am puzzled too. But I did not find any evidence of potential insider contact. Not via phone or meetings anyway. Besides, most of his latest transactions were unrelated to any public announcement of mergers. But they were spot on. You cannot explain them as insider trading. Anyway, Samir compiled all available information on Eaglewood's company." Stoltz nodded to Samir, who was not saying a word and leaning on Koppelman's doorframe.

"Go ahead, Samir." Koppelman was stuck unable to put a new chart on the whiteboard and was eager to add a few blocks to it: the lack of charts was an indication for the lack of crime, a conclusion Koppelman was not yet ready to make.

Samir approached the whiteboard and grabbed a marker.

"Eaglewood sold all his holdings and netted $1,054,243. His initial investment was slightly over $20,000. That, by itself, is what flags the SEC guys. He opened a Chase account for the corporation and wired all the money to it.

"He rented a big office space downtown. We have a detailed building plan. It was an IT company, but they moved out of downtown last summer and put the building up for lease. Eaglewood leases the first two floors, and three more floors are still unoccupied. The ground floor was a server farm. It has all the electrical and cooling infrastructure, and the second is an office space for at least fifty people. Currently, there are only two of them—him and Linowski. So Eaglewood is poised for rapid expansion."

Koppelman whistled. "This guy is bold. He is not taking half measures. Did they move in already?"

"Not yet, the lease starts on January 1. But it looks like they are going to grow fast," Samir said.

"A clear sign that points to the existence of this algorithm is this server farm, where he wants to install computers to run his software. But this insider trader theory does not hold up when you look at everything he does and his plans."

"Nope, it doesn't," Koppelman hesitantly said. "But something smells rotten here, guys. I do not believe in any software algorithm that makes such accurate estimations. I just don't buy it. He must have a crystal ball for that."

"Do you want us to do anything about it?" Samir asked. "The building is still unoccupied. It will be a piece of cake now."

"No, we don't have any legal grounds. Let's keep an eye on him for now. I'm sure he will stumble one day."

RACHEL WAS LATE, as usual, and Koppelman entertained himself by listening to yesterday's late-night show via his earbuds. They made it a tradition to meet on Christmas Eve in a bar, a ritual neither of them intended to break. They talked about everything that happened the year before, summing it up, from books to politics to different stories they found worth talking about to theater and movies to common friends and not-so-common enemies. Finally, the year was behind him, and Koppelman felt that even federal agents needed some recharging.

The bar was busy, and he was glad that he'd arrived earlier to get his own table at the window, and he comfortably shifted in his seat to observe the street and all passersby, a habit that came with the territory of his profession. Waiting for Rachel seldom bothered him.

"Five min." A laconic, Rachel-style message lit up the screen of his phone, which he'd placed on the table. Koppelman raised his hand, and when a waiter came, he ordered gin with tonic and lime, her favorite cocktail on a night out. Shortly after, before the waiter returned with the drink, Rachel appeared in a doorway, killing a cigarette at the entrance.

She sank into a chair, throwing her backpack onto the table, and managed to give a quick friendly hug on her way.

"Here, this is for you, Rach, Merry Christmas!" Koppelman said, putting a small, book-sized red paper parcel on a table and pushing it toward Rachel, whose face began to gleam with absolute joy as she unwrapped it.

With her rise in the media company, and as a result, in pay grade, Koppelman found it more and more challenging to think about appropriate gifts for Rachel. From one hand, she couldn't care less about any material possessions—a quick glimpse at her house, car, or clothes confirmed that. On the other hand, the fact that she did not care about anything material made gifting her quite challenging. But today, he was happy and believed she would appreciate her gift as nobody else he knew—it was a rare edition of *A Tale of Two Cities* by Dickens, which he'd acquired by chance in a small thrift store in Germany last summer, precisely for this occasion.

"So, when you are flying?" Rachel asked after managing to subdue her excitement.

"First flight in the morning," he replied.

Every year, Koppelman visited his parents for Christmas and stayed with them till the end of the year. "A Yearly Calibration of Manners," Rachel called these holiday family reunions. To all their friends' amusement, Koppelman's parents really loved Rachel, and despite being the complete opposite of Koppelman's family, Rachel loved them back. Koppelman joked that with their inability to follow his career, they most probably kept clippings about Rachel's much more visible public life. Knowing that Rachel and Koppelman had stayed good friends, each not married, his parents continued to invite her to join him on these holiday trips, secretly hoping this would bring them back together, as Koppelman suspected, and every year, she respectfully denied their invitation.

The end of the year was as calm for both of them as it possibly could be. Big scandal stories, which Rachel thrived at covering, gave way to holiday themes, and the federal criminal investigations, the type Koppelman was mainly involved with, also calmed down. So, for a change, they did not talk about anything work-related until Koppelman suddenly said, "Rach, some weird case bothers me, and I want to talk it out. The SEC guys asked us to investigate a potential insider trading violation. There is this guy who used to work in Solutry, Michael Eaglewood, who a few months ago decided to start stock trading. But unlike most newbies, he did not invest in different funds or indices and didn't ask for professional investment help. Instead, he purchased specific stocks directly by himself. What triggered the SEC is that his trades were spot on, all of them—he bought at the lowest and sold at the highest like he was a Fed with insider information."

"Did you find anything?" Rachel asked unenthusiastically, as if this type of white-collar crime story wasn't really appealing to her.

"Nope, nothing. But I have an itching feeling that something is wrong here. Eaglewood made more than a million-dollar profit on the initial investment of about $20,000—all in about six months. We talked to him, and he claims he invented an algorithm that makes very accurate predictions. Almost 100 percent precision, he bragged, and he demonstrated this to us. He just opened a firm, Eaglewood Solutions, Inc., downtown, rented a huge place for him and his partner, and moved all his earned money to the company's account. On the surface, all looks legit."

"So, case closed, then, Josh," Rachel replied. "If his algorithm can calculate stock movements, I think this does not qualify as insider trading. What is there to investigate?"

"That's what my guys tell me too. But I don't buy it. There is no algorithm capable of such precision. Think about what would happen to the world if so."

"That sounds like your private opinion, Josh, but nothing of what you told me looks illegal."

"I know," Koppelman said, "and it bothers me. A lot. But I cannot let it go. Something is wrong here. I just cannot put my finger on it yet."

He sat a minute or two without saying anything else, looking at his drink, and then raised his eyes and locked on Rachel.

"Rach, his first trade was buying Firetec and Dymanick stocks a day or two before their merger announcement. Then he sold all of Firetec and bought all Dymanick's stocks two days before you broke the Howard Waterman hush-money payments story. Did you talk to anybody when you were working on it?"

"No, I did not talk to anyone, Josh," Rachel replied with certainty. Then she suddenly went quiet and said, "But somebody talked to me about this, Josh. Remember, it was Doug Jordan who tipped me off about this story."

Koppelman looked at her, a fleeting smile touching his lips, and he asked, "Do you think you will recognize Doug Jordan if you see him?"

"I don't know, Josh, but I really, really want to."

"MERRY CHRISTMAS!" PHIL Matthew said in greeting. "I am surprised you called today. Did you decide to run a piece on Santa Claus and need some dirt on his operations?"

"Merry Christmas to you too!" Rachel was always in a gloomy

mood on the day before Christmas. "That sounds like a good idea. Next year, maybe. I want you to find anything on Michael Eaglewood. He used to work at Solutry, recently quit and established his own firm, Eaglewood Solutions, Inc."

Matthew registered the name and asked, "How urgent? It's the holidays, you know. Things are slow now."

"Don't worry, not urgent. I just have a reason to believe that Michael Eaglewood and Doug Jordan are the same person."

"Really? Got it, will see what to do. So, talk to you next year, unless you want that piece on Santa."

"No, we're good. Have a nice holiday." She hung up.

Yesterday's morning promised the holidays would be boring, but the drink with Koppelman had opened her up to a new perspective on how to spend them usefully. She lit a cigarette, opened her laptop, and entered "Michael Eaglewood" into a search bar. A vaguely familiar face appeared on the screen.

CHAPTER 24

Rachel's version of a lunch meeting was a hot dog and a Coke consumed on a remote bench in the city park, where she could neutralize the taste of a cheap street-cart sausage with the flavor of expensive cigarettes. Matthew, opting only for a bottle of water, always preferred to talk in an unexpected and unplanned place with little foot traffic in the middle of the day. Covered by a baseball cup and large sunglasses, with a raised collar on his coat and a neck scarf reaching his nose, which looked weather-appropriate on this cold January day, it was almost impossible to identify his facial features.

He passed Rachel a small manila folder containing photos and a printed dossier.

"Everything about Eaglewood and his fiancé, Jenn Zharkova, AKA Zheniya, whom he is marrying on February 21, is there. I also included a good measure of detail on Linowski.

"There are two facts that reinforce your assumption that Eaglewood and Jordan are the same person. First, he lives in the apartment complex where the killing of Martinez happened.

Second, his ex-girlfriend, Keana O'Connor, used to work at Firetec and fits the same visual profile as all other pretty women who accused Howard Waterman of harassment."

"What's your theory, Phil?" Rachel asked, glancing at the photos.

"Firetec's case is easier to explain. He talked to O'Connor, and she confessed that she was harassed too and told them about other cases she knew. Then Eaglewood called you, to avenge the hurt feelings of his ex-girlfriend and profit from Waterman's downfall as well. Two birds with one stone. Looks highly plausible to me."

"It does," Rachel agreed. "What about the case of the killings?"

"I dunno," Matthew replied. "Everything I thought about this case is too far-fetched. Somehow it should be connected to Martinez. Other than them living in the same apartment complex, I wasn't able to find any other connections. All money Eaglewood made was from his stock trading, and his first investment was from his bonus money. I couldn't find any connection with this prison gang. It also looks improbable—Eaglewood is a computer scientist, published several papers in technical journals, some theory of predictions and algorithms on advanced heuristic search. You know, he is a bright but quite unremarkable guy. So why would he get himself involved in drug crimes?"

"This unremarkable guy, as you said, just leased huge office space, only for the two of them. How much will he pay—$40K, $50K a month, at least? He's cooking up something."

"Maybe he *is* connected to the gang, and his firm is a front for money laundering. With the volumes of his trading, he can move tons of money for them. I will keep a close eye on him."

Rachel nodded, and Matthew stood up and walked toward the exit. She watched until his figure disappeared at the gate.

IT WAS JOHN who spotted Rachel parking her Jeep in the slot marked "Visitor" on the side of Building A. Rachel exited the car, shut the door, and started to walk between the buildings on the lovely small alleys of the neighborhood.

"Sam, Sam, hurry up!" John's voice was ecstatic. "Hurry up!"

"Good morning, gentlemen!" Rachel said warmly, greeting them like her old friends. She thrived during discussions with a neighborhood watch, as these two nice old men certainly were, and as she'd learned from experience, such men were an unending depository of information about everything. One just had to have patience and conversation skills, both of which Rachel possessed with a vengeance.

"You are exactly the ones I was hoping to meet here again. I cannot believe my luck! I was passing by and wanted to check on you. How have you been coping with everything since then?"

"Of course, Miss Sorrow, we are always here to help! This was a shocking experience in the neighborhood, tragic, really! I told John how irresponsible it was of Management to allow an ex-convict to rent here!"

"Oh, absolutely, there should be a rule to do a thorough background check for every applicant," Rachel readily agreed. "Did you notice anything suspicious about him? Any unusual guests, odd hours when he came or went? I am sure in such a nice and quiet complex, such behavior will be very noticeable."

"Of course, our neighbors are all nice people," John started, only to be immediately interrupted by Sam.

"All our neighbors are nice? Are you kidding me? Martinez was a very nice person when he was alive, and before we discovered he was an ex-con. You can call Jenn nice, but definitely not Mike!"

"Who are Mike and Jenn?" Rachel innocently asked. "Friends of Martinez?"

"No! I don't think Mike even knew who Martinez was until he was killed! Mike is an arrogant snob, hardly says hello when he sees us, always pretends he is busy, but we know he is not. But Jenn, his girlfriend, they are gonna get married next month. She is such a sweet girl, very gregarious. I don't understand how she can stand that schmuck," Sam said.

"So Mike and Jenn live here in the complex?"

"Just above us. Can you imagine how rude it is for such close neighbors to behave with Mike's superciliousness? If it were not for Jenn, I would complain to Management that they drive late at night and disturb neighbors in their sleep. Such ignorance toward people who work hard and want to sleep at night, and Mike doesn't have any sensible consideration!"

"That does sound like very unneighborly behavior," Rachel agreed with compassion. "Going back and forth every night is hugely disrespectful toward the neighbors! I bet in such a quiet and peaceful place, when a car ignites in the middle of the night, it wakes up everybody!"

"Thank God Mike did it only once!" John said. "Otherwise, it would drive us nuts! But it was strange—they both sneaked outside at midnight, drove somewhere, and then returned in about an hour, waking us up again the second time."

"Very irresponsible!" Sam intervened. "John acts like it's no big deal, but mind you—we all had our nerves shaken by the killings, and the first one had just happened a few days before, right here, in our very complex! I told John that I am afraid to sleep—who knows, maybe the killer decided to come back—and you see, we live on the first floor. You know how easy it is to break in? So my blood pressure is up, my sugar has had the worst levels in years, and then suddenly, in the middle of the night, Mike starts his car and goes out. I almost had a stroke and couldn't sleep at all. He frightened me so much. I wanted to talk to him about it, but you know, as I said, he is an unapologetic schmuck! If he were to repeat this, no way would I keep quiet anymore and not talk to Management; they should discuss norms of behavior with their tenants."

"I am so sorry, gentlemen, I can only imagine what you went through, so much stress!" Rachel was Mother Teresa in jeans and sneakers. "Do you remember exactly when Mike wandered out in the middle of the night, by any chance?"

"Of course I remember! How can I not?" Sam said with triumph. "They caught the killer the next day. I was so relieved to see your reportage on that! Just hearing the news from you that day stabilized my blood sugar."

"You cannot imagine how stressed I was that day! It all happened so fast, but the FBI did a superior job. I think it was the happiest report I ever did. So many people were on edge!"

"They were!" John added, inserting himself into the conversation. "My nephew David was working a shift at The Boat that day, and he said that when the second killing happened, the police kept them locked in the restaurant for half a day. Remember, Sam, Mike was also at the restaurant?" John smiled, proud that he'd had a chance to insert his relative into the story.

"How is David relevant to Martinez and our neighborhood discussion?" Sam said with an irritation in his voice for hijacking his conversation about Mike just as he'd finally found somebody he could talk to who understood his feelings toward his impolite neighbor.

"Directly!" John exclaimed. "Don't you find it odd that the first killing happened where Mike lives, and the second happened where Mike dines?"

"I am sure it's a coincidence," Rachel said. "Happens all the time. But I would definitely love to talk to David about what happened at The Boat. I am sure he remembers things if they were strange. Such traumatic events aren't easily forgettable."

"You can be certain of that!" John said. "David is such a sensitive soul. He always works morning shifts during the weekdays, so the poor boy was there when it all happened."

"Thank you, Sam and John, I hope this terrible experience is behind us forever. So glad to see you are in good health! I must go now, thanks again!" She climbed into her car, ignited it, and looked at the dashboard clock: David's shift would finish soon.

"YOU GOT THE nerve, boy!" Houston exclaimed, squeezing Mike's hand with his full force as if he were practicing with a hand grip strengthener.

The maître d' showed them their table, and Houston immediately asked for sparkling water without waiting for their waiter.

"So, boy, if I were not curious about why you wanted to meet, I would smash your head against the wall right away. I figured you would leave, but you had the guts to take Andy with you! Luckily, we have Keana to keep everything afloat."

"I know, Mr. Houston. It was hard for me too—I gave Solutry my best efforts, and I couldn't fully express how I valued my time with the company, but it was time for me to go." Mike always felt very inferior when he talked to Houston. "But I didn't want to meet to apologize for my leaving."

"OK, boy, shoot, I am all ears."

"Yes, Mr. Houston, ahh, I am sure you have heard that I've founded my own company," Mike started.

"Heard? I drive by the damn sign twice a day. Ugly letters, if you ask me."

"I don't, Mr. Houston," said Mike, and as if frightened by his own impudence, he quickly added, "but I wanted to talk to you about my firm."

"Sure, I told you I am curious to hear. I was told you are the only occupant in the building. Is that so? I am totally puzzled. I haven't heard about any venture deal of that scale in the last two months, so you must have raised some serious angel money, right under my nose, all while working at Solutry. Correct?"

"Well, let me explain. I founded the company with a big initial investment, seed money, if you wish, of $1 million. It was my own money, no outside investment."

"You got an inheritance or won the lottery?" Houston asked. "That's for sure not from your salary at Solutry."

"No, it is not, Mr. Houston. In my free time, I developed a stock trading algorithm. In about six months, I had more than thirty times return on investment."

"Wow, boy, you got my attention! Maybe I should also invest in your firm if you have such a high ROI!"

"We don't take outside investments, Mr. Houston," Mike replied in all seriousness, not hearing sarcasm in Houston's voice.

"I got that. If you can generate thirty times in six months, you don't need anybody's money."

"Right, but I need more than my algorithm to have real success. I need an organization that can support the algorithm. Mr. Houston, when you bypassed me last year and brought in Keana, I was pissed off that you didn't trust me. Looking back, I believe it was the right decision. She is fantastic; she is a real asset to the company. But you know what else I realized?"

"Nope, why don't you tell me?"

"I realized that I don't have it in me. I can build a great algorithm, I can improve it from initial thirty times to forty times and then fifty times and more, but I cannot build an organization, I cannot build all the teams and solve all their problems, I cannot make everyone work together smoothly. I realized my own limitations."

"That's a very mature self-assessment, I must admit. It is not easy to understand and internalize, and I appreciate you telling me this. Yes, you wouldn't be able to do what Keana did, and I am certain that your own creation would fail in your hands if you were to lead it. Now, however, even after you left and took the best damn engineer with you, she will still be able to carry on without you two bastards as if nothing happened. That's the power of the organization."

"Right," Mike agreed and continued. "Anyway, the algorithm that I created deals with short-term market predictions and is astonishingly accurate—above 60 percent, but most often in the range of 85 percent. I had a dilemma—either to speculate on a small scale, you know, from the comfort of my couch and earn millions of dollars here and there, or to do something significant, something that would change the world. I have chosen the latter. But to do that—I need an organization that can support and protect this growth."

"You are saying that your algorithm increases your investment by a probability of 60 to 85 percent? What about failures?"

"It is always successful, statistically, thus the growth."

"But this means that if you continue that level of growth, pretty soon the whole market will be yours. It is impossible! There is a flaw somewhere here." Houston was skeptical.

"There are some caveats here, for sure, Mr. Houston, and I will explain them to you later. But now I have a proposal for you."

"You do? What's that?"

"Mr. Houston, I want to invite you to take this journey with me, as a president and COO of Eaglewood Solutions, Inc. Here is what I have in mind." Mike took a piece of folded paper from his chest pocket and gave it to Houston.

Houston unfolded the list and carefully and at length read the content, several times recounting the zeroes.

"Boy, if it weren't you, I would laugh in the face of the person who told me about his fantasy. But I have seen your crazy ideas take shape. Gee. Tell me more about your algorithm," he finally said.

"I will in a minute," Mike said, then waited a bit, looked into Houston's eyes, and said, slowly and quietly: "And, Duke, ehhh, please call me Mike."

RACHEL PARKED IN front of The Boat and quickly climbed the steps, hoping the restaurant would still be open.

"Good afternoon, ma'am!" the mâitre d' said, faking a smile. "Hope you are well. Unfortunately, our kitchen is closed until five p.m., so we cannot serve you lunch, but we have a nice selection of homemade pastries if you fancy a dessert. I can recommend some delicious options for you."

"Oh, thank you, dessert is all I want!" Rachel said. "May I come in?"

"Of course, ma'am," he replied. "Please sit wherever you want." The mâitre d' made a gesture at the almost empty dining hall.

Rachel looked around the venue, spotted a pair of men having some intense and engaging conversation, and went to sit on the opposite side of the room.

"Excuse me," she asked the mâitre d', who walked with her to the table. "Is David around, one of your waiters?"

"Yes, he is," the mâitre d' replied. "Do you want me to call him?"

"If it would not be a lot of trouble. My friend told me he works here, and I wanted to talk to him. Is it possible that he's the one to serve me"

"No problem at all, I'll tell him. Here's the dessert menu, ma'am. David will be here shortly." The mâitre d' put a menu on the table and disappeared into the kitchen.

Rachel looked at the men across from her. She recognized Duke Houston, as he was a frequent guest on her programs, talking to somebody she did not recognize from his back. Typical business lunch discussion, thought Rachel, as The Boat was famous for its catering to the business people in the district.

A waiter approached the table, and Rachel read "David Courting" on his name tag.

"Good afternoon, ma'am, you wanted to talk to me?" David asked.

"Good afternoon, David, my name is Rachel Sorrow. I am a reporter with QQBC." Rachel introduced herself.

"Yes, Miss Sorrow, I know, I am a big fan of yours! How can I help you?" David asked.

"Thanks! I just met with John Courting and Sam Miller near their house, and John told me you were working here when the killing on Orchard Valley happened."

"Right, the police did not allow us to leave for several hours. We were all trapped inside, as they were worried that the killer was out there, I think."

"John told me that Michael Eaglewood was also here with you that day."

"Miss Sorrow, he was here at the restaurant, but not with me. He was with his company celebrating something. I am sure he has no idea of my existence."

"Really? I thought he knew you from the neighborhood and John."

"We met only once, a few years ago, at the twentieth anniversary of my uncle and Sam."

"You saw him once a few years ago and recognized him? Is he so remarkable?"

"Remarkable? The opposite—he is very unremarkable. The only remarkable thing about him is his girlfriend. She is a real beauty and really a great gal, very lovely, charming. I remember wondering what she saw in that man. She could have anyone. That dude is weird, I think."

"Weird? In what sense?" Rachel asked.

"He behaves really weird. For example, when the police finally let us go, you know, everybody wanted to run from this place as soon as possible. I was standing at the entrance, as the manager had asked us to wait until everybody left. Suddenly, I saw that he turned around and ran toward the place where the shooting was. I was curious about what happened. He stood at the corner, like he was watching somebody, then dove into the crime scene, was there for a few minutes—I think he talked to somebody—and/ then he ran away. Weird dude, I'm telling you!"

Rachel was listening intensely to David when suddenly he said, "Speaking of the devil, Miss Sorrow, here he is, with Duke Houston, the CEO of Solutry, across the hall."

Rachel turned her head again toward Houston's table, and a slight shiver ran down her spine.

CHAPTER 25

The astonishing discovery Rachel made about Michael Eagle-wood shuttered all her assumptions about the man behind Doug Jordan's pseudonym. Working on the serial killer story back in April, she'd rationalized that Doug Jordan's motive was good. Now seeing the rise of the Eaglewood empire, and she couldn't call it anything else, she realized that her previous beliefs had completely changed, evaporated. Michael Eaglewood was anything but a good-hearted person. His every step was ruthless, carefully calculated, and executed with cold boldness. The real villain in her story was not Anthony Dowell, Diaz, or the brothers Juarez. The real villain was Michael Eaglewood. And she *would* expose him.

Rachel had been sitting in the living room on her sofa for the last two hours drawing in her notebook different stick figures, each figure representing Mike Eaglewood, AKA Doug Jordan, as she was absolutely certain was the same person by now; Keana O'Connor; Howard Waterman and his company; Anthony Dowell and his cronies, living or dead; Jenn Zharkova; and a few others, still unnamed. She drew lines between the figures with potential connections or transactions, writing a word or two for a motive. She looked at her schematics and highlighted the line between Mike and Keana, but the line between Mike and Dowell did not want to stay solid, even on a sketchy drawing. She turned the pencil to the eraser side and changed it to the dotted line.

She was clearly stuck. Even Phil Matthew failed to expose anything or bring in any new information valuable to the case, not a single iota of it. She received his daily "briefings," as she called them, a file describing everything about Eaglewood. Initially, Matthew also provided material on Jenn, but after a few days, he ceased doing this—Jenn's entire life revolved around preparations for her wedding.

Eaglewood, however, was a different case. His days were full of new developments and almost free of wedding worries, with rare exceptions on weekends, when he reluctantly, judging from photos, followed his beautiful girlfriend to different appointments. His days were occupied by the rapid establishment of his corporation. Every day, truckloads of computers, routers, cables, switches, disks, printers, and monitors were unloaded in front of his building with its big red-and-green sign illuminated twenty-four seven; computer engineers, from new graduates to seasoned industry veterans, were coming to be interviewed for an advertised highly classified position with pay significantly above the average. In his first three reports, Matthew was trying to guess how many people had been hired. He counted eleven total, basing his estimations on facial expressions on their way out, but then he lost the count.

Neither Matthew nor even Koppelman could estimate the current transaction volume of Eaglewood Solutions, Inc. Mike's every transaction was made with surgical precision, buying at the lowest and selling at the highest, like he was reading tomorrow's charts. Eaglewood's trading drove SEC guys and the FBI nuts because they couldn't find anything incriminating about them. Mike was still too small for Wall Street to fully notice him, but Rachel was confident that they would be taken by storm, and she believed it would happen pretty soon.

Rachel lit a cigarette, the last one in the pack she'd opened earlier in the morning, and below a stick figure with Eaglewood's name written above its head, she drew a box, inside which she put "W.S." in capital letters. She stood up and started to pace around the living room, not paying attention to the ashes falling to the floor. And then it occurred to her. She returned to her notebook and drew a bolt of lightning coming from Eaglewood and striking the Wall Street drawing. A new story had been unveiled in front of her eyes, a story that, as her intuition whispered to her, would be much bigger and scarier than anything she'd exposed before.

She pulled out Eaglewood's picture from the manila envelope Matthew had given her a few weeks before and added two sharp little horns and a narrow beard to it. The face from the photo smiled at her, and its cold, penetrating eyes gave her an eerie feeling. She turned the photo upside down and called the only person who would always be on her side.

THE PARK WAS abandoned due to the heavy rain, with not even a single soul wandering its paths on this cold, late January day. From time to time, a strong gust of wind was blowing past the trees to the central grass field, raising a curtain of water and leaves. Rachel gave up trying to cover herself with an umbrella—the wind, often changing directions, laughed at her attempts to stay dry and continuously sprayed her small figure with fountains of water at every turn. What had been a nice shower only two hours before had quickly developed into a full-fledged storm. Rachel ran toward the exit and jumped into her Jeep, shivering from the cold as she tried to start the car and light a soaked cigarette. The former was designed to work in such weather conditions, but the latter refused to cooperate. She cursed, smashing the cigarette and pushing it into the overflown ashtray, and realized that she'd forgotten to replenish her untouchable stash in the glove compartment.

With shaking and wet hands, she unlocked her phone and called Koppelman.

"Change of plans, Josh," she told him without a greeting. "I am as wet as a fish from this rain and going home. No way am I going out for the rest of the year. If you still have time, come over. I am ordering Chinese for lunch with a bottle of Grey Goose."

"No problem, Rach," Koppelman replied. "Why didn't you check the weather forecast? I rely on my weather app on the phone, but you have direct access to your weather anchor!"

"And how do you think he predicts the weather?" She laughed and sped away. "The door will be unlocked: I need to warm up in the shower."

JUDGING BY THE sound of running water, Rachel was still in the shower when Koppelman arrived. He looked around the room and instinctually started to clean up her mess, first taking care of the table, collecting two trash bags of casual residue that had piled up since he was here last. Finally, Rachel stepped out of the bedroom with a towel wrapped about her head, and with a "Hi, Josh," she gave him a quick, friendly kiss on the cheek, on her way to the kitchen, where, she said, she had seen her hairbrush last.

"My mom used to tell me when I was little and got wet in the rain that I would grow tall from all this watering. I remember every rainy season up to high school, I deliberately tried to wallow under the rain. Apparently, it didn't help," Rachel said, climbing onto the sofa and taking a cup of hot lemon tea that Koppelman had made while she was in the shower. "Thanks, Josh, you are a savior. I feel like a ten-year-old girl coming home to Mom's tea!"

"You are welcome, Rach. I hope you returned home before you got too cold," he replied, sitting on a dining chair, only to immediately stand up at the sound of a doorbell chiming. "Our food has arrived," he said and took $3 from his wallet for the tip.

"So, nothing that can be hung on Eaglewood except your vague memory and testimonies from his neighbors and The Boat's waiter. Right?" Koppelman asked rhetorically, picking noodles from the cup.

"But I know for sure it's him, Josh! I do not understand how he is connected to all these murders, but I swear it is him!"

"I am sure you are certain it was him, but without any proof with substantial evidence, this is just a theory, Rach."

"What if your guys question him about this?" she asked.

"You know better, Rach, that this is useless. What can we do, waterboard him?"

"What about his connection to Firetec? Eaglewood was the only one to benefit from the situation with Waterman. He was able to make a huge upside from selling his shares and avenged his ex-girlfriend O'Connor at the same time. This whole situation with O'Connor is bizarre. I don't buy he can work with her normally after they broke up."

"Are you serious, Rach?" Koppelman was quite surprised at her remark.

"Come on, Josh, it's different with us! I am not as attractive as she is!"

"Hmm," he replied. "Says who?"

"Stop it, Josh! Don't break my self-image as a tough girl." She sighed and returned to their initial conversation: "Any way you can continue to investigate him?"

"I don't like this guy, Rach. I don't trust him a bit. He is full of himself, an arrogant bastard, bold and self-assured, and he mocks everyone. Look at how he talks to people, gee—you should hear him talking to us! *Us*—the FBI! People usually wet their pants when they hear 'FBI special agent.' This Eaglewood—he laughed in our faces, for Christ's sake!"

Koppelman ate a bit more and continued, "But, all this doesn't matter. We couldn't find anything, nothing at all. And believe me, we looked hard! I hate to admit it, but he is either smarter than all of us and can cover his tracks really well, or he's a genius and really developed his freaking algorithm. The last month's development with his damn company says to me it is the second option. And even if he was the one who tipped you off about all this sexual misconduct and profited from it, where's the crime? And other than your calls with this mystical Doug Jordan, there is nothing that can connect Eaglewood to the killings in the spring. So let it go, Rach, just let it go."

Rachel pushed away from her barely touched food, lit a cigarette, and sat in silence, contemplating Koppelman's words.

Two puffs later, she quietly said, "I thought Doug Jordan was a good man. And then he became Michael Eaglewood. And it's Eaglewood we should be afraid of, Josh."

THEY MOVED TO Houston's office, the three of them, the first company management team, to discuss their initial strategic moves. It was the largest office on the floor; granted, it was only one-third of the size of the space Houston occupied at Solutry, but it was the largest among all offices in Eaglewood Solutions, Inc. Mike knew that Houston was very sensitive about his regalia, and it was important for Mike that Houston was well aware of it.

A big mahogany desk, similar to the one Houston had at Solutry but smaller in size to fit the room, declared its presence with a pleasant odor, and there was a single object standing on it, a basketball-size globe.

"I guess it was left by the previous company," said Houston as he disposed of it in the garbage bin.

Mike approached the table, retrieved the globe from the bin, pressed his finger on the equator line, and quickly spun it.

"This, gentlemen, is our playground," he said, looking at Andy and Houston. "And we should be able to turn it at will."

He placed the globe back on the desk, and it continued its ominous rotation amid the complete silence. Only now Houston noticed a red-and-green engraving on the globe's gold base: "Eaglewood Solutions, Inc."

MATTHEW ALWAYS CALLED during the late-morning hours, respecting Rachel's sleeping habits. Only today it was unnecessary: she'd woken up at seven in the morning after barely sleeping for four hours.

"Yes," she replied, answering Matthew's call on the first ring.

"I have his full itinerary," Matthew replied. "Ceremony and the party—on February 21, it's four days from today. There are about 200 guests on the list. The newlyweds are spending the wedding night at the venue's hotel—he booked the presidential suite on the upper floor. They fly to Europe on the twenty-third, starting with London, and plan to travel to a few countries after that."

"Got it. Anything else?"

"Not about Eaglewood. Not sure if this is relevant, but just in case—Keana O'Connor has been named the CEO of Solutry. I know she was invited to the wedding too, but I am not sure whether she'll go."

"Why not?"

"She was his girlfriend in the past. Wouldn't it be weird?"

"I think nothing is weird anymore with Eaglewood for me," Rachel replied and hung up.

MIKE DID NOT PAY attention to the woman who sat at a corner table in the hotel restaurant and watched him place his order.

"It will take us about thirty minutes to get the order prepared, sir," the cashier said to Mike. "We will bring it to your room."

"I'll take it myself," Mike replied. "My wife is still sleeping. Can I have a coffee in the meantime?"

"Of course, sir, no problem. Please sit anywhere and we will bring it to your table. Any room for cream?" The cashier clicked a few buttons on his monitor.

"No, thanks, just plain black," Mike said and went to sit near a window facing the garden, which was covered in puddles.

He took out his phone and logged in to his emails, skimmed through a couple, decided against replying, and put the phone back in his pocket. A forgotten desire of media- and work-free time descended on him, and to his own amusement, he didn't want to think about his algorithm or the Breaking News of Tomorrow site, not even about trading in the next two weeks. Instead, images of the wedding party and Jenn, who looked more beautiful than ever in her wedding dress, with her long dark-blonde hair falling on her naked shoulders, pushed out any other thought.

His enjoyable thinking was abruptly interrupted when from the corner of his eyes he spotted a woman at the far end of the cafeteria shamelessly staring at him. He immediately recognized her. He didn't show any signs of anxiety, successfully fighting an initial flight reflex, realizing her presence was not a coincidence. He continued to sit at his table, focusing on watching the rain falling in the outside garden and listening to its monotonic sounds. Gradually, he calmed down, enough to regain his voice, which had disappeared at the sight of the woman.

The waiter brought him coffee with two French cookies, and Mike used this short interaction to legitimately turn his head and look at the woman. When the waiter left, he managed to bring a grimace of recognition to his face, stood up with a cup in his hand, and approached the woman.

"Good morning, Miss Sorrow! My name is Mike Eaglewood. My wife and I are huge fans of your work!"

"Good morning, Mr. Eaglewood, thanks."

"I believe that with all your exposés last year, all your contributions, you should win a Pulitzer Prize, no doubt!" Mike continued, unceremoniously sitting in a chair across Rachel. "And please, call me Mike. It feels like we have known each other for a long time. But that, of course, is because I have watched your program for years!" He laughed.

His initial anxiety was gone, giving way to curiosity mixed with a gentle touch of adrenaline. He read in her eyes that she recognized his voice, despite him trying to disguise it during their every communication. He was surprised by how calm he was while on the verge of his pseudonym being exposed, which surprisingly didn't bother him; instead, he actually welcomed the unexpected desire to tease Rachel.

"Thanks, Mike," Rachel replied. "It was a team effort with all these stories. Doug Jordan was helping me with crucial information. You might know him, I think."

"Who is Doug Jordan?" Mike asked. "Never heard this name, Miss Sorrow."

"Call me Rachel, Mike—as you said, it feels like we are old acquaintances indeed."

"OK, tell me, Rachel," Mike said, forcing himself to call her by the first name. "What brings you here?"

"You," she replied directly, looking at him without blinking.

Mike smiled, knowing exactly what she meant. He playfully raised his eyebrows, pretending to show genuine surprise, and let her continue.

"I never know, Mike, what I could stumble upon today that I will report tomorrow," Rachel said.

"You wouldn't believe, Rachel, how similar our business principles are," Mike replied.

"Right, your recent unexpected success brings a lot of attention to you."

"Thanks, Rachel, we are growing nicely indeed. So, that's what brings you here? You seem to have quite a good grasp of what we do. Do you want to write a story about Eaglewood Solutions? You could just call our office directly and avoid a two-hour drive in the rain."

"You know, Mike, it will be fascinating for me to write the real story of Michael Eaglewood. Everybody is talking about your rise, but I can clearly see your fall. And I want to be here when it begins."

"Well, Rachel"—Mike looked at her sternly—"I have big plans for the world, but falling isn't one of them."

"Until you stumble, Mike, only until you stumble," Rachel said, rising from her chair and leaving a tip on the table. "It was nice talking to you. Goodbye for now." She started to walk toward the exit, then stopped, turned on her heels, and said to Mike: "And, by the way, when you happen to meet Doug Jordan, tell him I know who he is."

And with that, she left.

PART 3
UNQUENCHABLE THIRST

SEVEN YEARS LATER

CHAPTER 26

Mike was sitting at his office desk when Jenn burst into the room. A quick look at her face was sufficient for Mike to realize that his quiet evening work was gone. He closed his laptop lid and, as calmly as he could manage, asked, "Well, what's it this time, Jenn?"

"You are seriously asking me that question, Mike? Haven't you seen what the kids did in the kitchen?"

Preferring to see by himself instead of listening to a colorful description from his wife, which would be a de facto depiction of the damage without any real resemblance to the actual deed, Mike hurried to the kitchen. It looked like a room after a thorough search, with all cabinets and drawers opened and their contents thrown out and pantry items mixed up on the floor, creating an abstract art piece with pasta of different sizes and shapes. A typical playground for bored kids, but nothing that warranted such an angry outburst.

"What is that?" he sternly asked his two crying kids, who were confined to the far corner of the kitchen, hoping the distance would save them from punishment. "I just left you two for ten minutes to watch cartoons. Why did you do this?"

"It finished a long time ago, Mike!" Jenn replied on behalf of her children. "What could you expect three- and five-year-olds to do when their father is so busy with his work? Sit down and nicely doodle?"

"They could tell me the cartoon had ended! And yes, I do expect Anastasia to take her brother and play peacefully and not to create a pogrom in the kitchen!"

"They did play peacefully, Mike!" Jenn was almost yelling at her husband now. "But they cannot be by themselves for hours!"

She picked up little Alexander, took Anastasia's hand, and, on her way to the bathroom, said, "Please clean up. And I want to talk after they go to sleep. I don't think I can carry on like this any longer."

MIKE STOPPED HIMSELF from calling the housekeeper to help with the cleaning, which would only infuriate Jenn more. She insisted on having no support personnel at the house after six p.m., and no logical arguments could convince her: her decision was indisputable. His wife's stubbornness was driving him crazy, as it was always a huge waste of time (not only his, but their time together!) to do mundane tasks that could have easily been done by others. Like cleaning up now.

Finally finished, he opened the refrigerator and fixed himself a sandwich, patiently waiting for Jenn to put the kids to sleep. Going back to work was definitely out of the question given the circumstances, and Mike quietly sat in anticipation of the storm that was about to hit the fan.

He couldn't understand why they spent more time arguing than talking normally lately. He was worried that they were growing apart, and more often than not, Jenn went to sleep in the kids' room.

Jenn entered the kitchen an hour later, after bathing the kids, putting them to sleep, and taking a shower herself. Without saying a word, which Mike took as a sign of a hostile mood, she boiled water and brewed herself tea. Holding a cup in her hand, she sat at the table across from Mike, and said with determination: "We must talk. I can't live like this anymore."

"What do you mean by 'like this?'"

"I mean that your family is not important to you anymore. That you consider us to be a distraction from your work, that the only thing you want is for us to leave you alone."

"That's not true!" Mike cried in resistance. "I absolutely don't think that! You are my family, and I love you all!"

"Do you, Mike? You didn't even go to kiss your children goodnight! You love us in theory, as an abstract thought about your wife and kids when you look at a family photo album, but you don't do things with us!"

"I didn't go to kiss them goodnight because you were furious, and I didn't want to create drama in front of the kids!" Mike tried to find an excuse, but he knew it wouldn't move the needle.

"Yeah, right," Jenn said. "I don't want to rehash this discussion again. It costs me too much. So let me just tell you how I feel and then you can tell me whatever you want, but please try to listen."

Mike leaned forward attentively.

Jenn gathered her thoughts and continued. "I feel, Mike, that we are just household partners. We rarely spend time together anymore, you are hardly home, you act like the kids are an annoyance, and every free minute, you rush to open your laptop. There are three things that you are interested in: your company, this freaking Breaking News of Tomorrow site, and that bitch Sorrow, with whom you are obsessed. Tell me I am wrong, Mike!"

"Anything else, Jenn?"

"That isn't enough?"

"Well, that is definitely a huge accusation, but it's not entirely correct."

"So, tell me where I am wrong, then! One by one, so you don't miss anything. You can start with us if you wish."

"Jenn, everything I do is for this family. You know I love you—I always have, more than anything! And I love my kids too! You are not a distraction or annoyance. I love spending time with you. Maybe it does not always look like that, but please, please, please believe me! I am not blind to the fact that I often disappear and leave you and the kids alone, and I know how you must feel about that.

"Remember where we came from? We could hardly go any-where, had more loans than income to pay them off. Remember how many times we ate out or where we went for vacation? Take a look at what our life is like now, what we can do."

"Mike, it's not about money! I was the happiest woman back then, despite living in a tiny one-bedroom apartment on the second floor of a shabby old building. Now we have more money than some countries, and I feel lonely. I feel I've lost you."

Mike came to her and embraced her. "C'mon, Jenn, you know I love you so much!" He pressed her head to his belly, patting her long, slightly wet hair. "Please, dear, trust me, please! It's not because I don't want to be with you. It's just that the burden to run the company takes its toll. I know I need to offload more tasks, and I promise I will!"

"You don't miss a day without going to this site, Mike! It's like a daily dose of a drug for you," she continued, her words now muffled, as she was still pressed against Mike's body. "You know how much I hate it? I feel like it takes my family from me! Why can't you stop? How much more power do you need? You already have everything! And everybody in the world hates you!"

"It's not about wealth or power."

"What is it about, then?"

"It's about a mission, Jenn."

"Mission, mission, mission!" Jenn's voice took on a sudden high pitch. "I've heard about this mission for so many years! And I feel that with this mission, you are losing your family. This damn site drains our blood, Mike, don't you feel that? Don't you see you are a slave to it? Why can't you stop? Why can't you use your algorithms, which you claim can work independently of this site, and just continue your investments?"

"I can't stop now. Please, Jenn, give me a little time, and you will see your old Mike who never stopped loving you, not for a second!"

"Why, for Christ's sake! Why can't you stop? Why can't we return to living our normal lives?"

"Because I am about to crack the Breaking News of Tomorrow."

CHAPTER 27

The European headquarters of Eaglewood Solutions, Inc., in London, managed by Jeffrey Rogers, was divided into two parts. The first floor was accessible to the public—it featured a gigantic lobby in a modern design, and behind the reception desk on both sides were elevators to the upper floors. The entrance resembled a Las Vegas hotel more than an investment firm. With multiple coffee tables scattered around, with armchairs and tablets mounted on each table, the lobby served as a quick meeting place, from informal interviews to initial meetings with customers.

The rest of the building was accessible only to the employees, and there were several levels of clearance to access different parts of the building. Technical support resided on the second floor; their job was to ensure the machines in the basement and the computers of the investment professionals on the third floor were running like Swiss clocks, but better.

The third floor was occupied by investment professionals, whose ranks ranged from first-year clerks to the real sharks in their field, and the more teeth they had, the better they performed. There was only one rule—whatever you cannot chew, swallow.

The fourth floor was internally nicknamed Dracula Cave, and only five people from the entire company could reach it: Jeffrey Rogers, Andy Linowski, Duke Houston, and Michael Eaglewood himself, and the fifth person was a mystery man. He came to the office once a day, except Saturdays, around eleven p.m.; spent about one hour on the fourth floor; and then left after midnight. Few people knew his name, met or talked to him, and due to the mystical nature of the fourth floor and this man himself, people called him Dracula. Nobody knew what he was doing up there every midnight or why it was important, and in the first year since the establishment of the European headquarters, rumors were spreading around the office, but eventually, they faded due to the lack of any new information.

Dracula's real name was Brandon C. Leland, and he was an ideal candidate for the job, personally approved by Michael Eaglewood himself. Brandon C. Leland was fifty-nine years old, previously an entry-level clerk in a small local bank, where he worked for the last twenty years, single, with very few friends and even fewer relatives, and as insignificant a person as one could be. He did not even know that he would be interviewing for a new job—his ideal way of life was changing nothing as long as the bank continued to employ him, which the bank indeed intended to do, thanks to how low-maintenance Leland was and his lack of any ambition for a promotion or increased compensation.

For two months before he was approached by Jeffrey Rogers, a private investigator, hired by Rogers specifically for the job, gathered all possible information: from the man's grocery shopping list to an exact schedule of all Leland's activities, his routes on weekdays and weekends, all his meetings, and even the TV programs, newspapers, books, and journals he preferred. Once a week, on Fridays at six p.m., he met with the same group of friends for a long, usually uneventful bridge game, which typically lasted till ten p.m., when after one pint of beer, he went home. This was the only time he had a beer during the week. Sundays was church day, and Saturdays he was either fishing with two of his bridge friends when the weather or laws allowed or he was playing another round of bridge with the same group of friends or, in the worst case, spending the entire day watching TV and reading newspapers with hot tea and cookies. Once a year, during summer, he went on vacation and drove to the countryside for a weeklong fishing trip. In short, he led a happy life.

This lifestyle brought him to his current position in Eaglewood Solutions five years ago. On the last Sunday before Christmas, a middle-aged man, nicely dressed as a real gentleman, sat next to him in his pew, and right after the service ended, he addressed Leland by name ("good day, Mr. Leland") and asked for permission to quickly chat at Margaret's Pastry House next to the church, where Leland had been a regular customer on Sundays for as long as he could remember. The man identified himself as Mr. Jeffrey Rogers, an executive vice president in London's headquarters of Eaglewood Solutions, and he said that he'd approached Mr. Leland following Mr. Edward Clark's personal recommendation.

Mr. Edward Clark was a director of the bank where Leland worked, and three years before, Leland actually met him at the entrance, and they had exchanged a very heartfelt conversation about the weather. As Mr. Rogers explained to Leland, Mr. Clark had personally vouched for Mr. Leland, praising his dedication, attention to detail, and loyalty, which had been proven by more than two decades of work at the bank. Leland was pleasantly flattered that Mr. Clark personally recommended that Mr. Rogers talk to him, and he confirmed that these traits were of extreme importance in his line of work and that he was delighted that the highest ranks of the bank management had noticed and valued these qualities in him.

"Absolutely," replied Mr. Rogers. These qualities were so rare nowadays that when Ms. Clark, a long-time friend of Mr. Rogers's, described Mr. Leland's virtues in a casual discussion, Mr. Rogers immediately knew that Mr. Leland was the right person for one of the most critical jobs in the entire Eaglewood Solutions organization. Due to such a close personal relationship between Mr. Clark and Mr. Rogers, the former reluctantly agreed to let go of Mr. Leland and personally wished him the best of luck in his new endeavor.

After a short negotiation—or to be more precise, a presentation—Mr. Leland agreed to join Eaglewood Solutions, Inc., in one of the most critical positions in the company, besides Mr. Rogers's himself, as a new daily communication orders officer. The position, as Mr. Rogers explained clearly and in great detail, required special attention to the protocol. Once a day, excluding Thursdays and Saturdays, Mr. Leland was supposed to report to headquarters around eleven p.m. and perform daily communications of orders with the rest of the world, from his personal office. As London's time was a central world time that synchronized all other countries, London's midnight was literally the start of all Eaglewood Solutions activities around the world, as Mr. Rogers explained, and even a single hiccup in execution might disturb the pulse of their harmonic operation, and that's why only a person with such an impeccable reputation as Mr. Leland would be able to perform such an important job.

Because of its importance, Mr. Rogers said, and his inability to find an adequate candidate until now, the company was willing to generously compensate Mr. Leland if he would agree to accept the position after careful consideration. His compensation would be 5,000 pounds a month, he would be provided with a corporate car because the reliability of transportation would be vital for the job, and, of course, insurance, tolls, and petrol would be fully reimbursed. He would need to always carry his corporate cell phone in case something happened and he was needed, and, for the same reason, he must always drive his corporate car unless there were reasons beyond his control.

Only thanks to many years of bridge experience did Leland not share his honest thoughts about that offer; instead, he gently inquired, because the nature of the job required such a great deal of attention, whether it wouldn't be more appropriate to have a salary of 5,500 pounds, to which Mr. Rogers agreed that indeed the uniqueness of the position and Mr. Leland's qualifications would dictate a higher compensation, and also, he, Mr. Rogers, totally forgot to share that Mr. Leland was entitled to two weeks of paid vacation during the summer, exactly when the trout was at its prime in the rivers, as Mr. Clark had mentioned that Mr. Leland was an avid enthusiast of fishing.

Mr. Leland was not to discuss the details of his job with anyone, Mr. Rogers added, due to growing concerns about industrial espionage, but he had no doubts about Mr. Leland's integrity, as

Mr. Clark himself had vouched for Mr. Leland, and Mr. Clark was not a man to offer baseless compliments.

On his first day on the job, Leland learned his main routine, and it did not change even once in five years. As easy as the job was, it was one of the most essential jobs in the entire company, and Mr. Rogers himself was Leland's direct supervisor, a clear sign of great responsibility. Leland was very proud that such an esteemed businessman as Mr. Rogers, whose name often appeared in the newsreels of almost every media outlet Leland consumed, was personally taking care of all Leland's needs when they arose.

Every day around eleven at night, Leland drove to the corporate parking lot, and using his badge, he took an elevator to the fourth floor. The building was almost abandoned at that hour, and whenever he met anyone, it mainly was security personnel with whom he exchanged a quick greeting before hurrying away. Upon exiting the elevator, Leland went to the first room, which he called Room Number One and which had a few shelves stocked with office supplies, a small table with a computer, and a shredder underneath. The room led to the second room also accessible by his badge, which Leland unpretentiously called Room Number Two. In that second room, which looked more like a bank vault than an investment company office, there was a booth in the middle and a printer. At midnight, Leland needed to step inside the booth and press a red button while looking at the mirror in front of him. Five minutes later, he was supposed to collect printouts and leave the room. He typed the numbers from these pages into the computer in Room Number One, twice for validation, and then shredded the papers.

Leland was never late for work and never failed an assignment. The sixth year of Leland's employment with Eaglewood Solutions, Inc., started as uneventfully as the five previous ones, and, parking his corporate Ford Fiesta in the underground garage of the corporate headquarters, Leland was even happier with his life now than he had been when he was employed by the bank, and much richer.

MIKE ARRIVED IN London unannounced, right on the first working day of the new year, when the world was reluctant to return to the daily working routine after their winter celebrations. Something big was about to happen, his unusual excitement revealed, and he spent the whole day impatiently reviewing different reports and financial data, waiting for night to come and forcing Rogers to stay with him.

"Well, Jeff, all looks good for tomorrow. I am happy. It is going to be one of the biggest days in Europe," Eaglewood said, closing all his files.

"That's great news, Michael," Rogers replied. "We finally did something right if you are happy."

"You always do things right, Jeff. I just want you to do them better!" Eaglewood smiled. He was in a good mood today, for a change, and Rogers noticed it and smiled back.

"OK, almost midnight. I need to go upstairs." Mike closed his laptop and stood up.

There was only one destination upstairs—the Dracula Cave, or Communication Room, as this mystical place was officially named. Roger had no idea what was behind the button Leland was pushing or what numbers the computer printed. He vaguely understood the concept—the whole company had been founded on the premises of a robust prediction algorithm that Eaglewood had developed a few years ago, which helped him acquire unbelievable wealth and control over so many companies. The core of this algorithm, the real brains that controlled everything in the investment decision-making process, was a secret guarded more than the Coca-Cola formula, and there were only two people in the company who were developing the algorithm and its interfaces: Eaglewood himself and Andy Linowski.

The Communication Room, Rogers speculated, was most probably a single isolated computer doing some algorithmic calculations and relied on being in the Greenwich time zone and at the appropriate latitude to make the correct calculations, and perhaps at midnight, it must be recalibrated and the data sent to the rest of Eaglewood's offices in the world. And because Eaglewood was very paranoid about the core algorithm, the computer in the Communication Room was disconnected from the rest of the network, and it was Leland's job to manually enter the data it calculated into the main network. Satisfied with his own reasoning, long ago, Rogers had stopped dwelling on what happened in the Communications Room. The only thing that initially bothered him was Eaglewood's request to personally handle, without any delegation, Brandon C. Leland, a man of such low position that Rogers's first impulse was to be insulted and vocally express this, but then he rationalized that he was paid enough not to be.

They went to the elevators and reached the fourth floor, where, as expected for this hour, Leland was waiting in the first room.

"Good evening, Brandon!" Rogers said to Leland when they entered the room. "Please meet Michael Eaglewood, our CEO and chairman!"

"Good evening, Brandon!" Eaglewood said in an amiable voice and was the first to extend his hand to shake. "I am so impressed by everything Mr. Rogers told me about you! He told me there is nobody in the company that performs his duties better than you: your precision, accuracy, and dedication are not left unnoticed. As a matter of fact, earlier today, Mr. Rogers recommended you for a sizable yearly bonus and salary increase, but I am sure he will talk about this with you himself next week, right, Mr. Rogers?"

"Of course, Mr. Eaglewood!" Rogers replied, despite the fact that he was hearing about this for the first time. "Brandon performs his duties to the best of his abilities, and we are thrilled with that. As we discussed, a bonus is due indeed!"

"You see, Brandon, that's what the European management thinks of you!" Eaglewood said and continued. "Mr. Rogers also told me that you love fishing. I'll be sure next summer to free myself for a day to go with you to your sacred fishing place—I've heard nothing can beat English countryside angling!"

"Of course, Mr. Eaglewood." This was all Leland succeeded to utter.

"Brandon, since I am here today, why don't you take the day off—I will take it from here," Eaglewood said. "It was so great talking to you, Brandon. I am looking forward to our fishing date. I am sure it will be fantastic!" He shook Brandon's hand. The man was still unable to speak, and Mike went inside the second room, pressing his badge against the card reader.

"Thanks, Brandon!" Rogers said. "You can go home now. I will call you next week to talk about your bonus and a raise."

Dumbfounded, Leland left the fourth floor, and on his trip to his car, he thought about the remarkable things he must have done if the directors of his last two companies, the bank and Eaglewood Solutions, went above and beyond to personally recognize his contributions. Whatever it was, Leland told himself, he was determined to continue impressing his bosses.

LELAND'S ROLE WAS the only step Mike did not succeed in automating: the site always required a person to open it. It was cumbersome. Mike hated such ineffectiveness, and he and Linowski had spent a lot of time developing a computer interface capable of reading the news without human intervention, but all in vain. And so the Lelands of the world were born—dumb and dedicated operators of a single button, looking into a one-way mirror with a computer monitor hidden behind, and being paid and treated as company royalty to secure their loyalty and discretion. It also didn't hurt that they drove a corporate car and used a corporate cell phone, and could be secretly surveilled to ensure their full compliance with the requirements.

In the second room behind closed doors, Mike again appreciated its design and opened the computer. He didn't need to. He could read the news in his office, but he couldn't resist the urge—it was pretty symbolic to do it here.

Mike opened a browser on the computer and entered the URL. The familiar ugly flashing red letters of the Breaking News of Tomorrow site appeared on the screen. Mike skimmed the news, ignored what he thought irrelevant for now, and went directly to the entry he'd come for.

EUROPE WOKE UP TO A NEW REALITY

Starting today, most of the European airlines will have one major shareholder—Eaglewood Solutions, Inc., the largest American investment and holding company. The only European country that avoided selling off their stocks to Eaglewood Solutions is Russia, where all transport and infrastructure companies maintain their original ownership.

Mike reread the news and stayed there long after the news disappeared. There were two messages in it—his European transactions succeeded, but Russia did not fold. Four Russian oligarchs, Alexander Dubrov, Dmirty Atamanov, Evgeniy Suzhdenko and Sergei Sharkov, had divided between themselves almost the entire field of Russian transportation, and it looked as if they'd coordinated between themselves, unlike their European counterparts.

Mike closed the laptop and left the room. Rogers was still in the first room, patiently waiting for Mike to complete his task.

"Well, Jeff, I am done here," Mike said. "Let's go back to the office—we have work to do."

THE PHONE RANG nonstop, finally waking Rachel up. She'd left it in the kitchen yesterday, not expecting anybody to call in the morning, or maybe secretly hoping nobody would call that early. Barely opening her eyes, Rachel shuffled to the kitchen and, without looking at the caller ID, answered, "Yes?"

"Rach, looks like I woke you up. Turn on the TV!" Koppelman said harshly as if it were Rachel's fault for what the news channel was reporting. "See what your friend is up to."

Rachel clicked on her remote and listened without saying a word.

"Breaking News: New Transportation Tsar in Europe" was all over the news items. The anchors gave the same report again and again and invited different contributors to weigh in.

Rachel muted the TV.

"I knew it, Josh," she quietly said. "But I never imagined that it would happen so fast and be that scary. I told you ages ago. Eaglewood is the most powerful and dangerous man in the world now. We must bring him down!"

"*We*, Rach?" asked Koppelman sarcastically. "We can't do anything. You know this. He does nothing illegal, as far as I am concerned. It's all up to you, Rach. But I will help you with that. I, too, want to see this son of a bitch down."

"I will. He will make a mistake, and I'll get him."

CHAPTER 28

It had already been a month since the European Union approved all the acquisitions, and Eaglewood Solutions could move forward with completing their multistage plan. Running their operations in complete secrecy was challenging but essential, and so far, everything was happening according to plan. Mike looked at the time on his screen. It was midnight, and he opened the Breaking News of Tomorrow site. The very first entry, which appeared under the big ugly letters, shocked him so much that he was incapable of moving on to the next one until the text was replaced with a never-ending promise: "NEXT UPDATE: MAY 5, 12:01 A.M."

Mike furiously slammed the lid of his computer shut. *They are all morons*, he thought. *Why can't they see the bigger picture!* He hesitated and then opted to dial despite the very late hour. After all, it was in Rachel's best interest to get the facts straight.

Rachel picked up the phone on the third ring: "Hello, Mike."

"Good evening, Rachel. It's a long-forgotten feeling when somebody outside my closest circuit calls me Mike. Lately, it's been only Mr. Eaglewood. How did you know it's me calling you?"

"Aren't we old acquaintances, Mike? Call it a hunch." She seemed to take pleasure in teasing him. "I just assumed you are the only person from Eaglewood Solutions to call me."

"Hmm." This added to Mike's already irritated mood, but she'd unintentionally admitted his suspicions. He succeeded in keeping himself calm, and said, more to himself than to her, "I thought this specific phone line masks the caller ID."

"Well, well, well! Finally, I found an imperfection in Almighty Michael Eaglewood's empire!" Rachel teased him again. "Why don't you fire your phone infrastructure guys, like you usually do?"

Mike ignored her cynical remark. "Speaking of firing, Rachel, you got facts wrong in the piece you plan to air tomorrow. You describe me as a monster, but you missed the fundamental economic principle of my company, which is to improve performance and efficiency. Yes, the profits are maximized, of course, but the savings are passed on to the customers, so shareholders aren't the only ones who enjoy it. In a broader view, the world is the real winner."

Rachel grinned and said with sarcasm: "Is that so? Everything you do is for the sake of the world, I see."

Mike was quite annoyed that she was playing games with him. He knew what she was planning to do and was pissed off by how she'd portrayed him.

"Rachel," he said. "I am surprised to see your cynical side, but yes, the layoffs are going to create a better world, and I want you to see the big picture, even if right now it looks like the monstrous Eaglewood cares about nothing but profits, as you think. That cannot be further from the truth—I care about making the world better, and its current ineffectiveness must be repaired. Any angle you look at it, this is a win for the world—efficiency in operations drives better prices for customers and, by the way, decreases the carbon dioxide footprint. I can give you a whole lecture about all of this, but I am sure you don't need me lecturing you about that. I just wanted you to really understand that when you report tomorrow about the layoffs, you shouldn't forget to present the full view."

Rachel listened attentively and replied, showing no sign of being impressed, "All this sounds very noble, in theory, but think of the lives of the people who are severely affected by the layoff; they rely on their abilities to honestly provide for their families. Your high-level economic view does not put food on their tables."

"Rachel, you're thinking very small and very local, and you need to think big and global. For these 50,000 people, it is a big deal indeed, but I am sure they will be OK down the road. They always find alternatives, and we gave them a great severance package. When I look at my obligations, I must weigh the other eight billion people in the world who benefit long term. And I am telling you, Rachel, all my actions are to improve the world by making it more efficient, even if locally and in small resolution, they sometimes look brutal."

"Thanks, Mike, for your input. I surely will present your comments."

"Very good, Rachel," Mike replied, "very good, I always valued you for your unbiased journalism."

Rachel hesitated and then asked, "I wonder, how did you know that I planned to report about your layoffs tomorrow?"

Mike smiled to himself and clenched his hand in excitement. He was hoping for this question—no, actually, he'd anticipated it! Years ago, he'd told Rachel that he would always be one step ahead of her, and he experienced a deep satisfaction now that he could demonstrate it to her. It so often happened that a little win, incomparable with any other significant achievements, and otherwise having no real value, but bearing only a personal meaning, became a real driver of one's motivation.

"Remember, Rachel, our last conversation? I told you I will always be one step ahead of you. Anyway, I apologize for the late call and wish you a good night!" Mike hung up the phone.

He was happy for this small personal triumph. Of course, he did not expect Rachel to report anything positive about him. He knew she was constantly watching him and would take a personal interest in any of his miscalculations. But today, today, he'd showed her, loud and clear, that he had the upper hand in their private game. And that brought him profound satisfaction, beyond the level he thought it would.

He forgot how furious he'd been just ten minutes ago, and now he was back to business. He opened his computer and started to type an email:

To: Houston, Duke
Subject: URGENT: Mole in the company

Duke, Some SOB told QQBC about planned layoffs, before the announcement. Pls. find who.

—M.E.

ON THE OTHER side of the phone line, Rachel sat utterly bewildered by Mike's call. She lit a cigarette and searched online for any information about upcoming layoffs in one or several portfolio companies of Eaglewood Solutions. 50,000 people laid off in one swoop would have a significant impact on the country. Something must be out there. She did not find anything, despite all her sophisticated online queries. It was late, almost one in the morning, and she was confused about what to do next. She sighed and dialed Phil Matthew.

"Sorry for the midnight call, Phil," she said when he picked up.

"Yeah, what's up?" Matthew was unhappy with the late call, but thankfully, Rachel did not overuse her privilege too often.

"Phil, Eaglewood is preparing for massive layoffs in some of his companies, about 50,000 people." She heard Matthew whistle in astonishment. "Please find whatever you can."

Her second call was to Jonathan Choi, QQBC's young and brilliant economics expert. At this hour, he most probably was already sleeping, but the scale of the news and the impact on the entire country's economy would be enormous and definitely warranted the late call. She knew Choi would not want to miss this opportunity and would not rest until they aired the story.

Her last call for the night was to Koppelman. He picked up almost immediately: "Yes, Rach, is everything OK?"

"Josh," she said, "Eaglewood just called me with the most bizarre message. He notified me that he plans to lay off 50,000 people."

"Why?"

"He said he wants to reach world efficiency and contribute to the planet by reducing emissions."

"I mean why did he call you?"

"I don't know. That's the strangest thing. Remember the Firetec scandal seven years ago, Josh?"

"The one about sexual harassment that brought their CEO down?"

"That one. Back then, he called me pretending to be Doug Jordan. He made me investigate this harassment case. If you remember, he earned tons of money leveraging that scoop, and that started his company. I think he called me today for a reason too."

"How can I forget that son of a bitch? Do you know what his reason might be?"

"No, Josh, I don't understand. Why would he want to give me a scoop about himself? What game is he is playing?"

"Can you reproduce your conversation with him word for word?"

"I think so," Rachel replied and proceeded to describe her conversation with Mike.

"Did you plan to write about the layoffs, Rach?"

"No! That's the strangest thing. He talked to me like I was already preparing the airing, but this was the first time I'd ever heard about upcoming layoffs."

"All these years, Rach, I've had a feeling this dude has a crystal ball and knows our every move. Now it looks like the crystal ball has turned against him."

"Do you think he called me by mistake?" asked Rachel, hoping Koppelman would not lose his train of thought.

"I do, Rach, I do. And that's the first failure. I need to sleep on it and think about how we can get him. Good night." He hung up.

She knew Koppelman would not go back to sleep that night.

CHAPTER 29

Andy Linowski sat on a far end of the sofa watching Houston and Mike discussing their strategy. *Their strategy*, thought Andy, *theirs, not mine, definitely not mine.* His thoughts drifted away from the conversation right from its beginning, and neither Houston nor Mike paid any attention to him, as he was quietly sitting in the corner.

For a long time, he had trouble understanding Mike. Initially, Mike made brilliant investment deals, but very quickly, it had turned into more than just smart investments, and Mike shortly became the richest man in the world. Andy and Houston themselves were rich beyond imagination, enough for each of them to buy a small country.

And that bothered Andy a lot. He couldn't understand the whole idea of that wealth, when obviously it was impossible to spend even a fraction of it, especially given that the source of the money was unquenchable. He himself gave little thought to his money; his lifestyle hadn't changed significantly beyond obvious upgrades, and if anything, all this money made him more miserable than before. All of a sudden, he'd become more in demand, more lovable and desired, and women found him very attractive. His real friends, the ones that he cared about, gave way to new ones, and during the first three years, he enjoyed the new company, the parties, and the women.

Four years before, he'd woken up on a Christmas morning and seen faces he didn't recognize, faces that looked foreign and greedy, faces that expressed a lust for his money and allurement toward his position. They were all new faces, some he met no more than a few weeks ago, but they all swore their undying affinity. To his horror, his old friends were reluctant to accept him back, as the gap between them had grown to an immense size over the years, and they didn't believe it could be repairable. And so he lived in a big secluded mansion, surrounded only by his bodyguards, who Mike insisted were necessary since the day they'd received the first threatening message.

He couldn't understand why his life and his feelings were so different from the Duke's and Mike's. The Duke was enjoying every bit of his wealth and his new life, with his new expensive toys, his ability to meet with any powerful person in the world on short notice, and visiting Eaglewood Solutions' offices anywhere in the world and being treated like royalty.

Mike was different, Andy thought. Unlike the Duke, he did not enjoy the spotlight as much, and whenever it was possible, he always preferred the Duke to be on the front lines. While, for the Duke, his wealth meant a bigger jet, a yacht, a crazy gathering on some island with other rich people, or a new wife, Mike never used his money in such a tangible way. Of course, he lived in a vast estate, but this was mainly because he needed to employ a small army of security rather than enjoy the amenities. His motivation, his drive, was in something else, something that Andy could not understand.

The work was the only thing that brought Andy satisfaction: the complexity of the software systems, encompassing the whole world and every area of the company, was beyond a dream job for him. If not for that, he would have left the company long ago. It was his magic, his salutary escape, and, most important, his grip on normalcy and his only pride.

But even that had started to fizzle out lately, and each new development added to the considerable weight that was already on his shoulders. Without noticing, he began to drink, trying to kill his thoughts, first a little, and only on weekends, then on weekday evenings, and in recent months, it had turned into an addiction, much to Mike's concern.

Andy tried to focus on what Mike and Houston were talking about. But it didn't make any difference. It never did. Andy cared only for the software; all their strategy was irrelevant to him, and the more he heard about it, the more he was frightened by it, so it was better to focus on the system. He looked at his two partners, as different as they could be yet similar in their ambitions. The meeting concluded, and Houston left the office, leaving Mike and him alone.

"You're worrying me, Andy," Mike said, leaning on his tabletop and looking into Andy's eyes as if trying to read his thoughts.

"Don't be worried, Mike. I am fine."

"You don't look fine at all. Have you heard even a single damn word of what we were talking about?" Mike was sounding reprimanding all of a sudden.

"Didn't I tell you this gives me a headache and I do not see any value in my participation?" Andy barked back.

Mike sat without uttering a word. Then he said quietly: "Andy, it's not about you not seeing any value. It is about something else. You were vital to these discussions not that long ago, and then something changed. Tell me what happened, Andy. Don't look at me as the company CEO. Talk to me as your best friend."

Andy hesitated to engage in this conversation. He hadn't planned on a confrontation; he never was a person to fight, not a single time. He always took any authority as a given and was focused on his work. He never sought a managerial position—he knew he didn't have it in him—but here, it had just happened. He hated his official title and instead introduced himself as lead architect. And now Mike wanted to talk to him as his best friend. Where had he been the last two years? Had he ever talked to him and asked Andy how he felt? What bothered him? Mike's sole interest was growth, growth, growth, and it was never enough. How could Mike call him his best friend any longer? How could Andy himself call Mike such as well? Andy fought his urge to spill all this out and replied, "Mike, I really lost the reason we are doing this. And I don't have any justification for what happens around us."

"We are creating a better world, Andy. Much better than before," Mike calmly replied.

"Is that so? You don't need to feed me all that BS, Mike. You insult my intelligence. A better world? How? We lay off thousands of people, hardworking people, for God's sake! We acquire companies and kick out their management. For what—higher profits? Mike, I don't know what to do with all this money. I don't need it! Money, money, money, I am sick of it! Really sick!

I hate it! Hate it, you hear? I lost all my friends, I am paranoid about starting a new relationship, I cannot go anywhere without people wanting something from me!"

Andy started to cry from the overwhelming emotions and continued. "And what is all this misery for? Tell me, just give me one freaking idea what all of this is for? Tell me how it can make *me* happy, *me*, Andy Linowski, *me* personally, not a big corporation with an ambition to take over the world. How can I sleep well at night when I know that my software showed that if we freaking close one of the companies we just happened to acquire two weeks ago, our profits will be increased? I sometimes feel that the world is a big chessboard for you, Mike, and everybody is just a pawn on it. If you need to sacrifice somebody, you'll do it without blinking an eye. Did you see all these demonstrations by the people you laid off? Did you watch the news about the crying single mother who was the only provider for her two kids and who lost her insurance? Did you see what they write about us, what they call us? For God's sake, do you really care about anything, Mike? Tell me, what is this all for?"

Mike let Andy finish his whining uninterrupted, giving him as much time to vent it out as needed. When he finally stopped, Mike slowly said, "What do you think, Andy, I really need all this money for myself? Come on, you know me better. You see how we live! Jenn and I can be happy with a tiny fraction of what I earn! What do you think, I am happy with everything I do? Do you think I take personal satisfaction in any of the layoffs or restructuring? Do you think I enjoy watching this single mom you mentioned crying on live TV? Do you think I like the way my life suddenly turned and how I lost any ability to be invisible, to simply go where I want with Jenn? For God's sake, I cannot even pee without a security guard standing behind the door!"

Mike stopped, calmed down his emotions, and continued. "The world is a stupid place, Andy. They think that I hurt them, but I hurt them no more than a surgeon performing an operation. It looks scary, the surgeon holding a knife, and it might even hurt for a while after he is done, but it's an inevitable part of the healing process. All these companies, when they are independent, they are selfish. They care only about themselves, their own profits. Think about that, Andy, in a simple example: two airlines sending a plane from New York to San Francisco, exactly at the same time. Both planes are half empty. Why such stupid inefficiency? I'll tell you why. Because they don't care about cooperation. They care only about profits. They belong to two competing airlines, and they do not talk to each other. They compete with each other. And so to pay off their half-empty plane, they charge double for the ticket. And think about all the climate effects of operating two planes! And who pays in the end? We all do! And the world is doomed with irrevocable damage. And nobody gives a damn about that. They will fight for better deals, but they will never look at how to make everybody's lives better. Nobody cares about anybody else. They all live their short eighty years on Earth, and for all they care, they must have everything now. And there is nobody who can fix that."

"And you can? Why can't you, like other luminaries, work on some other ways to be good, to look good, and to have all us look good? Like all these billionaires—donate to the homeless, fight inequality or create vaccines against viruses, clean water, send space shuttles, do millions of good things. Why can't you do charity like them?"

"Andy, you are naive! Donating money to clean the water? Don't contaminate it in the first place! It is impossible to change the world if it works the same way! The only way to fix it is to come in with a surgical knife and cut it hard. And nobody can make it happen, nobody but me."

"So you are playing God now, Mike?"

"Nope, I'm a fixer. I want to leave the world in harmony with itself and not in constant competition. And to achieve that, I don't care what they think of me now. It will take them time to understand and realize that everything is for their own good, and I will be long gone by then. But we cannot waste time on the useless defense of our image now. Anyway, they will never see it until long after we finish."

"I cannot believe you don't care what they call you, how the media perceives you."

"Oh, I do, trust me, I really do! But I will not be able to change their perspective. Just to experiment, yesterday, I talked to Rachel Sorrow from the QQBC. Let's see whether it worked out," Mike replied.

"I don't know, Mike," Andy said. "I simply don't know. I feel terrible with my life now, and as much as I try, I cannot see the big picture you're describing. You sound like a megalomaniac to me, full of lunacy. Mike, I am telling you this as your best friend, at least I once was. I cannot see how one man can fix the world, even one as ambitious and smart as you are."

"You know, Andy, when I first started to invest, my only goal was to become rich. I didn't think about anything else. My whole life, I earned less than I was worth. I knew it, but I didn't have the guts to talk about it, to ask for what I was worth. Never. And then suddenly I could make a lot of money. I could buy a nice house, a sporty car. Then I reached a point when I could also quit working forever, and Jenn and I could travel the world together for as long as we wanted. But I couldn't stop playing. I just couldn't stop. I thought a lot about that. There must be a reason why I have this knowledge, and it is not to make me the richest person in the world. And then I knew. And once it occurred to me, I could not undo it. I can't stand how the world works, and I cannot bring myself to stop thinking about changing it. I became a shark. I must move to live. And you are a shark too, Andy, without realizing it. Once you stop, you are dead. Think about this and pull yourself together."

"Is that a threat, Mike?"

"It's a prediction, Andy."

CHAPTER 30

Oleg Kolobkov immediately recognized the voice of Natalia Serebrennikova, an assistant to Mikhail Vasilyevich Artemov, the director of the Russian Foreign Intelligence Service or, as they called it in Russia, SVR. Bad news, Kolobkov realized, as Artemov's office called him only when something went wrong. For any regular communication, they would use the deputies.

"Oleg Petrovich, good morning!"

"Good morning, Natalia Ivanovna. Hope everything is good with you?" Kolobkov answered, waiting for the message.

"All is good! Mikhail Vasilyevich requested your presence at a ten o'clock briefing with him."

That was it, no advance schedule, no questions about feasibility. *Must be really bad, then*, Kolobkov thought, looking at the clock on his Audi A6 dashboard, and replied, "Understood. Coming."

Time was short, and being late wasn't an option with Artemov. Kolobkov made a sharp U-turn and parked in front of the Metro station. He would take care of his towed car later; now his thoughts were occupied with getting to Artemov on time, and the Metro was his only option. He ran down the escalator, pushing away everyone who was too slow for him, and jumped onto the train, which fortunately arrived at the station just as he reached the platform: these ninety seconds were crucial.

Serebrennikova greeted Kolobkov with a nod—the wall clock with the "Moscow" label showed "9:58."

"He awaits you," she said simply and guided Kolobkov in.

One look at Artemov's face was enough to confirm Kolobkov's fears.

"The president talked to me, Oleg," Artemov said, skipping any pleasantries. "You know what he asked me?"

"I believe he wanted to know the status of the Eaglewood case, Mikhail Vasilyevich," Kolobkov replied, guessing what this would be about, but without a clear understanding of why the president wanted to inquire about the American billionaire.

"Exactly!" Artemov was almost yelling. "And all I could tell him is, 'We are working on it!' Do you want to know how the president looks at you when he thinks you are an idiot?"

"No, Mikhail Vasilyevich, I don't," Kolobkov replied, knowing that it did not matter how the president looked at his boss when he thought that Artemov was an idiot; the only thing that mattered now was how the intensity of how this presidential look would be propagated down. And the torrent coming from Artemov promised an incredible power.

"Pity, because I cannot tell him that I need to work with morons who cannot execute a simple task! Because all the imbeciles that work for you, and you included, cannot get any damn results!"

"Mikhail Vasilyevich, I understand your frustration. I am also highly frustrated, but Eaglewood Solutions' systems are guarded better than the American Department of Defense. We cannot penetrate them. But we are working on that."

"Of course they would be better guarded, you idiot; he pays his engineers top dollar—he can buy the best! So if you cannot hack them, send an agent there! Why should I have to tell you how to do your damn job?"

"You don't need to tell me, Mikhail Vasilyevich. I just didn't realize that this matter was so important to the president. I will make this a priority right away," Kolobkov replied, knowing that it did not matter what he said, his screwup now evident.

"I just didn't realize that this matter was so important to the president!" Artemov mocked him. His face was flushed with anger. "Are you indeed such an idiot, or do you just pretend to be? This is a matter of national security! Do you understand what would happen if Eaglewood implemented their plan to own Russian companies?"

"It would be a disaster. We cannot let it happen, Mikhail Vasilyevich."

"Finally! Finally, I hear something intelligent from you, Oleg. Hallelujah!" Artemov exclaimed. "Yes, we cannot compromise national security! He gets it! Now, do you finally get why the president of Russia is taking a personal interest in Eaglewood Solutions? Or you still need me to spell it out for you?"

"I clearly understand this, Mikhail Vasilyevich."

"So, move your butt! I want to see the results in three months. Not a day more!"

"But, Mikhail Vasilyevich…" Kolobkov started to protest. "To put an agent there requires years of preparation. This is an impossible task!"

Artemov pressed a button on his desk phone. "Natasha, could you please call the president and tell him Kolobkov said it is an impossible task?"

"Right on, Mikhail Vasilyevich!" replied Serebrennikova, then hung up and resumed typing her document.

"I understand," Kolobkov said. "Can I go, Mikhail Vasilyevich?"

Artemov stood up from his desk, came across to closely face Kolobkov, who was half a head taller than him, put his hand on Kolobkov's shoulder, and quietly said, emphasizing each word: "Oleg, when Russia meddles in American affairs, the world accepts it as normal. But letting America meddle in ours is not. And I don't want our president to be pissed off because of that. You have three months. Are we in sync?"

"Absolutely!" Kolobkov replied, then he turned on his heels, and off he went. The countdown for him started.

UNLIKE HIS BOSS, Kolobkov was always calm after being scrutinized by his seniors. A quickly assembled team of his two most trusted deputies sat solemnly around the conference table, each preparing the latest report on Eaglewood Solutions and its key personnel.

"Colleagues." Kolobkov looked around and for two seconds fixated his eyes on each person. "The Eaglewood case is bumped in urgency as the highest priority. The president became interested in our progress, concerned that they're aiming for a massive acquisition of Russian companies. This is, of course, a security and economic threat to the country and we must find ways to counter it."

The group exchanged glances among each other as Kolobkov continued. "So far, our mode of operation had been trying to electronically infiltrate the company, but as I understand it, with no success. Right, Yuriy?" He looked at Yuriy Zverev, head of Kolobkov's cyber-intelligence group.

"Nothing so far, unfortunately. We targeted every branch of Eaglewood Solutions around the world, but they are impenetrable. My guys are looking for alternative methods." Zverev's report was not very encouraging.

"We've got three months to crack the company and learn their intentions. They are notoriously famous for conducting their business in stealth mode. We must infiltrate them and know ahead of time their game plan with Russia. As I said, three months." Kolobkov looked at his watch and added, "Three months, minus two hours."

"I collected material on every key person in the company. There are two promising routes we should explore," said Pavel Uvarov, Kolobkov's field operative.

"Talk," Kolobkov said.

"The first one is that in every office outside the US, there is one person reporting directly to the director of this office. Nobody knows what this person does, their job description is 'communication officer,' and they all look like twin brothers. Each around sixty, single with little social life, drives a corporate car and reports to work around midnight and only for an hour or two. Based on their profile, they might have direct knowledge of corporate operations. In the UK, the guy's name is Brandon C. Leland; he reports directly to Jeffrey Rogers himself, and I believe Leland is a person we have a chance to hook up with—he is an avid fisherman and spends his Saturdays and summer vacations fishing. It is now the allowed fishing season in England."

A series of Leland's and Rogers's photos flashed on the screen of the conference room.

"Excellent." Kolobkov made a mark in his notebook. "Let's explore this angle. Do we have anybody in England around Leland's age?"

"We have an agent who is forty," Uvarov replied. "So we can make it work."

"Great, let's make sure Leland acquires a new best friend soon."

"Right, I am on it," Uvarov said, typing something on his laptop. "The second route looks even more promising. As it is known, Michael Eaglewood's wife, Jenn Eaglewood, was born in Moscow as Evgeniya Zharkova. She is a single daughter of Sergei and Maria Zharkovs. However, this is Sergei's second marriage, and he had a son, Anton Zharkov, with his first wife, Nadezhda Semenyuk. Apparently, Anton has a good relationship with his half sister and used to visit them during his business trips several years ago. He worked in a battery company that developed and sold special-purpose batteries for industrial machineries, such as forklifts, small specialized tractors, and things like that. Seven years ago, right around when Eaglewood Solutions was founded, he left his job and established his own business, which has not been very successful so far. The last time he saw Zharkova was at her wedding; afterward, he didn't visit the US and didn't see her. He lives here, in Khimki."

"That's a fantastic direction!" Kolobkov said, and for the first time that day, his barometer of optimism changed direction. "I want a full dossier on Anton Zharkov, his family, friends, interests, all his flaws, habits—I want to know him better than he knows himself. Find everything you can by the end of today. I don't want to wait. Pavel, this is going to be your task. We are all to your disposal. End of day today—first brief here. Adjourned."

A SILVER AUDI A6 stopped in front of Anton's Honda Civic, which was parked near his Khimki apartment, and the man inside it watched as Anton walked toward his car. When Anton approached his vehicle, the man stepped out of the Audi and said, "Anton Sergeevich, good morning. My name is Oleg Kolobkov, and I am a security officer in SVR." Kolobkov showed his ID to a very shocked Anton. "Don't worry, Anton Sergeevich. You are not in trouble, but there are several things that I want to talk to you about."

"Good morning," Anton replied. "Has something happened? I mean, SVR is not an organization I usually deal with."

"Understandable, most people don't," Kolobkov replied. "Anton, may I call you by your first name?"

"Yes, of course."

"Thank you. Can we go somewhere where we can talk without being interrupted? Please get into the car. I'll drive."

That wasn't a question, and without showing any hesitation, Anton obeyed and got in the car.

"I recommend that you contact your secretary and call in sick," Kolobkov said. "It will take us a whole day."

"Am I arrested for something?" Anton asked with a trembling voice.

"Should you be?" Kolobkov asked.

"No, of course not, but it feels like a story from a different era. Can you tell me please what's going on? Where are we going?"

"We are going to the SVR offices in Moscow, Anton. You see, I usually don't do field talks myself—there are better men than me—but in your case, this is a matter of national security, and the president himself is interested in our progress. So enjoy my escort. Why don't we chat a bit until we arrive? With the traffic, it might take us quite some time."

"OK," Anton replied.

He sent a text to his team that he would be out today and unable to reply to calls or emails until the evening. Kolobkov waited for Anton to send the message, then asked, "Anton, tell me about your sister, Zheniya Zharkova."

"She is my half sister, the daughter of my father, who immigrated with his family when she was young. Initially, we had a remote relationship—you know, I am in Moscow, my father and his family are in the US. Mostly phone calls, emails, and Skype for birthday wishes. Then later, I got a job in marketing, and my company sent me to the US to work on a few business development projects. That was when I saw her again, now a grown-up woman. I was in the States, I think, about six or seven times back then to close all these deals, and on my trips, we had family gatherings. The last time I saw her was at her wedding, but we hardly talked—she was, obviously, preoccupied with the ceremony and the party. I hardly know her, to tell you the truth. We live completely different lives and have little connection."

"Very well, Anton, thanks, that's useful. So you know her husband, Michael Eaglewood?"

"Oh, that's the reason you are questioning me," Anton replied. "I'm sure you want to know more about Eaglewood than about Zheniya."

"Yes, Anton, you got it right. I do not want to play games with you. There is very little time for that, so I'll tell you this straightforwardly so you understand the level of our interest. Eaglewood Solutions is working on making some business deals involving Russian markets, and we need to be able to better prepare to defend Russian economic interests."

"I understand, but I'm afraid I will not be able to help you that much. I hardly know Mike at all," Anton replied.

A smile similar to that of a python playing with his prey fleetingly crossed Kolobkov's lips, indicating that there was no way for Anton to get out of it, whatever it was. Especially since Kolobkov had mentioned the president. The SVR officer would not mention the president in vain.

"Oh, that's where you are mistaken, Anton. You are able to help us, and you will. But let's continue our discussion inside. We have arrived." Kolobkov stopped in front of the SVR building in Yasenevo, stepped out of the car, and gave his keys to a man who'd materialized out of thin air near them. He showed Anton the way in.

They entered the building and went to the first room right after the security check, inside which two men were already waiting for them.

"Come on in, Anton," Kolobkov said. "Let me introduce you to two of my colleagues: Pavel Andreevich Uvarov and Yuriy Semyonovich Zverev."

"Nice to meet you," Anton said but refrained from shaking hands. The two men did not extend their hands either.

"Anton, please sit down. We have a long day today," Kolobkov said and added, "Anton, this is not an interrogation—you have done nothing wrong. But we need your help, and this meeting is a request for cooperation. And I trust you will be willing to help us, right?"

"I don't know what we are talking about," Anton replied, "but I will help if I can."

"Very good. So why don't we start with you telling us about Eaglewood."

"As I told you on our way here," Anton stated, "I hardly know the man. I met him only a few times at family gatherings, and it was just a nice family dinner with my father telling stories from his glorious Soviet youth years. Back when I met him, there was no Eaglewood Solutions yet. He founded it around when he and Zheniya got married."

"I see. Anyway, tell us what you think of him and what you know about him," Kolobkov insisted.

"OK, when we met at my father's apartment, he was just a regular guy. You know, nothing special. Mostly, he listened to our conversations and said something here and there, but not much. Zhenya and Mike are the opposite of each other: she is quite gullible, and he is a bit taciturn. When I met him and Zheniya the first time, I was pretty surprised they were together: I couldn't imagine them fitting with each other. But apparently, she knew something about him I didn't.

"He loved stories of my father—I think, for Americans, they sound very bizarre, and my father is quite a storyteller, and he always makes them very entertaining. But as I said, most of the time, Mike was listening to us and did little talking himself. The only time I was really surprised was when he announced that he'd created a super-smart investment algorithm and had privately made almost $1 million in profit. I was shocked—everybody was, of course, except Zheniya, who obviously knew about it. Two days later, I returned home—I think it was Thanksgiving weekend, and then the following February, they got married. It was the last time I saw both of them, but as I mentioned, we hardly talked that day. You know, you never have a chance to speak with the groom or the bride at their wedding. They left for the honeymoon after the wedding, so I didn't see them after the party either."

Anton finished talking and took a sip of water from a bottle on the table in front of him.

"As I told you, I don't really know him. The truth is, I hardly know Zheniya. When I married my second wife four years ago, I didn't invite Zheniya or Mike to the wedding."

"Why not?" Kolobkov asked.

"He was already a big magnate. I couldn't think of how I would do it, and I did not want all that attention on my wedding. I don't want my life to be influenced by him in any way, and I thought that if I invited them and they came, my name would be all over the place here, and I will be only a brother-in-law of the great Michael Eaglewood. I called Zheniya and explained to her what I was thinking, and she understood. We had a nice conversation—she told me that this was her price to pay for her wealth, losing family and friends."

Kolobkov exchanged glances with his colleagues and asked, "So, you think she is not very happy now?"

"I didn't say that!" Anton quickly replied. "I think she meant that because of their fame, her social activities have changed. I don't know whether she is happy or not, but as I said, I didn't talk to her much. This was the only real conversation we had in all these years since her wedding, with the exception of exchanges of birthday wishes."

"OK, Anton, here is how you are going to help us. We want you to return to America for a few months and get back in touch with the Eaglewoods, with a really warm family connection, and help us get information on Michael."

"And what if I don't want to?" he asked. "I am not a spy, and I don't want to become one."

"Anton, dear, do you really believe that the SVR would waste its time talking to you if we thought there was a chance you'd refuse to help us?" Kolobkov smiled and looked at Uvarov and Zverev, who until this moment had not uttered a word, and now, as if they were synchronized by an inaudible order, they both grinned widely.

"You owe help to the motherland, Anton. This is your basic obligation as a citizen."

"I don't owe anything to anyone!" Anton firmly said. "I pay my taxes, I vote, I park only in designated areas, I pick up after my dog. I think I've paid my dues to the country."

"Here is where you are mistaken, Anton," Kolobkov calmly replied. "These are duties to your government, but not to your country. And the country is in great distress from the impact of the economic machinations of Eaglewood Solutions. You have two children, if I am not mistaken? What are their names, Valera and Vitalik? I saw their mom yesterday playing with them on a playground. Such sweet kids and such a beautiful wife! Lena, right? Can you imagine what their future will look like if you don't help the country avoid this distress?"

Anton swallowed hard, and tears came to his eyes. Stuttering, he asked, "Is that a threat?"

Kolobkov looked directly at his eyes, smiled with the edges of his lips, and said in a very metallic voice, which didn't sound cheerful at all: "Anton, the threat is from Eaglewood Solutions. We at SVR are just very concerned for the lives of our exemplary citizens, such as your family, who pick up after their dog, if we do not prevent this imminent danger from the American imperialist. I'm sure you share this concern too, don't you?"

Anton sat in complete silence, unable to speak. Kolobkov continued to gaze into his eyes without blinking, and with every passing second, Anton sank deeper and deeper into the chair. Finally, he said, "I understand."

"Excellent!" Kolobkov's voice was a bit playful now as if nothing had happened just two minutes ago.

"So, here is the plan, Anton. You are going to make a short two-month trip to the US to work on the business development of your company. There are several deals that you will need to close, and thus your full attention will be required there. We will take care of all the necessary paperwork and arrangements; it is entirely in line with your work at your company. Don't worry. Your task will be effortless, Anton. All you need to do is to install a few cameras inside the study of Eaglewood's house. Should be a piece of cake."

"Piece of cake?" Anton exclaimed, resting his palms on the table as if about to get up. "I have read on the internet that their estate is guarded by a small army of security and it is easier to get close to the US president than to them! And also I have no idea how to do all this spy stuff."

"Anton, calm down, please!" said Kolobkov, putting his heavy hand on Anton's shoulder and nailing him back to the chair. "For the next month, starting tomorrow, Yuriy Semyonovich and Pavel Andreevich will take you through a rush course on how to deal with all these things. It's not rocket science. You will be able to learn all this in no time, I guarantee: they employ the best teachers for that 'spy stuff,' as you call it!" He winked at Zverev and Uvarov. "And a security detail will be irrelevant for you—after all, you are the only brother of Jenn Eaglewood. What a great reunion it will be, especially since it seems she is craving to be with her family. Didn't she herself say that to you?"

"Uhh…" was all Anton was able to say. His hands fell from the table to his knees, leaving sweaty streaks on the polished surface.

Fear that life would never return to normal had a distinctive smell, and Kolobkov coldly smiled, clearly detecting it.

CHAPTER 31

Jenn climbed with both her legs onto the sofa and comfortably shifted between two pillows, with a TV serving as her only companion for tonight. Her two kids, five-year-old Anastasia and her little three-year-old brother, Alexander, were long since sleeping, and the evening with them, which, from the very first day, she'd vowed would be their exclusive family, with no nannies around, and it was the highlight of her day. She was tired of the never-ending cycle of small and big tasks every mom was doing. She realized that her daily routine was a significantly thinned-down version of almost everyone else in the world, with a small army of house servants, from nannies to cooks to cleaning and laundry helpers. Yet it was tiring nevertheless, as she insisted that from six p.m. until the kids fell asleep would be her own time with them—dinner, bath time, bedtime stories, and the Russian lullabies she'd grown up with, all these were her sole prerogative in an otherwise overcrowded house.

With the birth of Alexander, they moved to a vast estate full of security and help. She thought this was when her life spiraled downward. From that turning point, she saw Mike's face more on TV than in person, and his coverage had rarely been positive. Used to accepting the never-ending criticism coming from every media coverage, she expected to see a torrent of condemnation for everything Mike did on tonight's TV program, and by association, it applied to her as well.

"Good evening, ladies and gentlemen," an enthusiastic female voice sounded from the TV, suddenly grabbing Jenn's attention. "This is a special evening program with Rachel Sorrow. Today, we will be talking about the new phenomenon of our time, Michael Eaglewood, and discuss whether he is a Messiah or a threat to American democracy and the world's economy."

Here it comes, Jenn thought, attuning to the screen and turning the volume up. The way Sorrow presented the topic revealed her biased opinion, despite a presumable attempt to maintain objectivity. It was impossible to inoculate against a constant negative public opinion, and it got under her skin on a deeper and more profound level each time. Mike, despite preserving his cool in public, was often infuriated at unfavorable descriptions of his business decisions at home, and there was rarely a month when Jenn and Mike didn't have a heated argument about his company and their lives as a result.

The first really big quarrel happened after they moved to this house. Gee, how much she hated the place! The constant surveillance, the eternal presence of people, security running the ground of the property, the inability to be alone and do such trivial everyday things such as going to a coffee shop or to a park with the kids or to a mall to shop like a regular woman. She hadn't signed up for this.

She tried to remember what it had been like before, and she missed that time. She missed when she would come from work and fixed a quick dinner and Mike would hilariously name her new culinary creations; she missed going out to a movie, or a pub, or with their friends or even walking in the park. She remembered how Mike made her feel back then, how funny he was, his light ironic remarks, his humor, and his love. And now? Well, it was different now. Everything was different. He didn't joke anymore, he rarely made any humorous remarks, and all the cooking was done by Martha, their cook. And friends, well, having real friends just gave way to official parties and meetings and spending time with people they must meet. It turned out that their money opened doors but closed hearts.

Jenn's rambling thoughts returned to the program, and she focused back on the screen.

"A big question that is on everybody's mind is how Michael Eaglewood succeeded in flying under the radar for so many years." Rachel was clearly on a roll. "For many years, Eaglewood was mostly doing stock speculations. He is a real wizard when it comes to betting on the right investments. All his trades were unbelievably on point, to the extent that the SEC and the FBI opened numerous insider trading inquiries, but each of them led to nothing.

"As Eaglewood accumulated wealth, he started to acquire stakes in a completely horizontal way—acquiring entire industries. The most visible is the airline industry. Take a look at what happened—Eaglewood is by far the largest shareholder of major airlines, and his votes are basically decisive in every company. And due to differences in corporate structures and different countries' laws, Eaglewood succeeded in flying under the radar of the Securities and Exchange Commission, or SEC, as it is often called.

"But why does it matter who owns an airline, for example? Why does it matter more when the owner is Eaglewood?"

Rachel continued her program, playing multiple video clips of airlines layoffs and strikes across the world and the US.

"The answer to this question is rather simple: because Eaglewood owns most of these companies, and he can make quite unorthodox decisions that could never happen in a competitive market!

"Let me give you a recent example. Suppose two airline companies he owns operate between New York and San Francisco. When they are independent, they compete for the customers. When two airlines want to merge, there is a process of approval and regulatory review, and this transaction will be put under severe antitrust scrutiny.

"By being a major stakeholder, Eaglewood effectively created a sole monopoly in that industry. No regulatory scrutiny, no approval. He is now a czar of the industry. He can retire half the fleet in each company on each shared route, and he basically has the temerity to do whatever he wants—there is no competition!"

Rachel played a set of grim images, with sad stories of personal tragedies replacing each other on the screen.

"And that, of course, means significant layoffs, thousands of people finding themselves out of jobs. And who got the most profit now? Eaglewood, of course! So the world's richest man just enriched himself even more.

"Next week, there will be a hearing in the Senate regarding Eaglewood. And our lawmakers must answer one question: Do we want America to be held hostage by one corrupt oligarch, Michael Eaglewood, similar to what happened in Russia?"

JENN COULD NOT bear to continue listening to the program. As she reached for the remote, her phone rang. She did not recognize the number, but she picked it up. A familiar voice happily greeted her on the other end of the line: "Zheniya, good evening! This is Anton. Sorry for the late hour; I could not resist calling."

"Anton, what a surprise! Are you here in town?"

"Yes, I just landed! I will take a car and head to a hotel, but wanted to say hello first! How are you doing, sister?"

"I am fine. All is good. Anton, cancel the hotel and come over—there is no way I'll let you stay in the hotel tonight!"

"Don't worry, Zheniya. I am OK. I don't want to bother you—" Anton began to resist, but Jenn interrupted him.

"I don't want to hear this, Anton! You are coming here. I am waiting for you and meanwhile will prepare your room. See you soon—at this hour, it will take you less than thirty minutes to arrive."

"Are you sure? It's late…" Anton sounded hesitant.

"Absolutely! Don't even worry! I am not going to sleep, and Mike is in Washington for next week's congressional hearing."

"OK, then, Zheniya, I am coming. Do you think it is too late to call Papa?"

"Mom is already sleeping, I believe, but Papa should be watching Rachel Sorrow's show. He never misses anything about Mike; you can call him. I am so glad you arrived, so unexpected, but so on time. Enough—go call Papa, and I need to make a few things before you come. How hungry are you?"

"Starving!"

"Then you are about to get my signature late-night dinner. Bye for now!" Jenn said, then jumped to her feet. For the first time in the last few years, she was so excited to see the beloved face of a person from her past.

"MRS. EAGLEWOOD, SORRY for the late disturbance. There is a man at the entrance who says he is your brother, Anton." The guard spoke in an apologetic voice. "I would not let anyone disturb you, but if he is indeed your brother…"

"Oh, it's me who should be sorry, James!" Jenn replied. "This is my brother, Anton—he just came from Moscow! Please let him in. I totally forgot to notify you when he called an hour ago."

"Of course, ma'am, thank you for the clarification!"

Jenn opened the door and watched Anton's car approaching the inner gates and then entering their driveway.

"Anton! Come on in, so happy to see you!" she exclaimed and gave him a tight hug with kisses on both cheeks, receiving the same back.

"Zheniya, after all these years, you are even more beautiful than before!" Anton said when he finally entered the house.

"Stop it, Anton. I will be forty in ten days, and every reminder of my age gives me shivers. Are you here on September 16? Mom and Dad are coming over, and we will do a small birthday dinner here."

"Yes, Zheniya, I am here for a few weeks, still figuring out my entire itinerary, but I will make sure not to miss it!"

"Great, it will be family only—I hate my birthday, but Mike insisted this time. Says it's too important an anniversary to miss."

"Yes, I just talked to Papa. He also was happy that I will be here to celebrate his little girl," Anton said and added, awkwardly laughing, "but he forgot to mention that this little girl is the queen of this huge castle!"

"Funny you called it a castle, Anton. I say the same thing when Mike and I argue. I hate this estate—it's too big and too impersonal. This is not me. I feel like I am trapped here. But what am I talking about? Go and wash your hands. I will feed you, and we can talk then!"

Anton proceeded to the guest bathroom and then came to the kitchen, where Jenn had set up her promised signature late-night dinner.

"That's a great house," Anton said, looking around. "I like the design—very clean, and I would say…ah…quite minimalistic."

Jenn looked at him. Somehow, he seemed smaller than she remembered. His shoulders pointed down like he was carrying an invisible weight, and he stood in the middle of the kitchen not daring to sit and shifting from foot to foot. *Must be an effect of the house*, thought Jenn, accustomed to people changing their behavior around their wealth.

"Yes, I love the European style with clean straight lines," Jenn replied casually, not showing she noticed any uneasiness in Anton. "Our part of the house adheres to it. But the rest of the house, I have no idea."

"What do you mean by the rest of the house? Isn't this all your house?"

"Technically, yes, but the south wing is occupied by the support personnel. I never go there. Anton, this house is like Mike's empire. It lives its own life, and I have little say in how it is managed."

"You sound a little depressed, sister." Anton put his hand on her shoulder and relaxed his own. "I feel it. Tell me what's happening?"

"Nothing, actually, you just called right when I was watching this nasty program where they accused Mike of all possible sins. I guess I took it hard and still haven't recovered from it. Don't pay attention to it," Jenn replied. And quickly, a bit too quickly, she added: "Enough about me. Tell me how you are doing. How are Lena and the boys?"

"They are good, thanks! Lena sends her greetings. And the boys, the boys, they are growing so fast! Here, take a look." He took his cell phone out of the pocket and scrolled through his family photos.

When he reached the end of his camera reel, he stopped and looked at his feet, not knowing what to do next, and Jenn felt a strange sensation of something bothering her about Anton. She shook it off and took a tablet from a drawer. After a few clicks, a screen on the wall came to life, bringing up her family album with the latest kids' pictures. Mike was in none of them.

WITH A LOUD screeching sound, the old clock on the kitchen wall announced two o'clock in the morning, startling Jenn, who was in the middle of telling a story.

"It's so late!" she exclaimed, rising from her chair and putting her glass of wine back on the table. "Let me show you your room, Anton. I bet you are tired from the flight and just too polite to let me know."

"Oh, Zheniya, not at all, I wasn't even paying attention to the time. I am sorry to keep you up so late. I am sure the kids wake up early in the morning."

"No worries about the kids," Jenn said with a slight note of sadness. "One of the privileges of being Jenn Eaglewood is there are people around who will take care of everything."

They went from the kitchen to the guest room on the other side of the estate's living quarters, and Jenn showed Anton different rooms as they passed.

"OK, you can stay here, Anton. The bathroom is on the right. The towels are in the closet. Good night, dear!"

"Good night, Zheniya! Thanks for inviting me tonight. It's so great to see you and catch up. I will move to the hotel tomorrow, to not overextend your patience."

"No way, Anton! Mike is coming back next week on Wednesday morning, after the congressional hearing, so why don't you stay here until he comes? Keep me company, please! And I really enjoyed talking to you when nobody was around. I had a long-forgotten feeling. I insist!" Jenn did not let him resist, kissed him good night, and left the room, closing the door behind her.

Anton put his bags into the closet, sat on the chair in the corner of the room, and silently cried.

"OLEG, GOOD NEWS!" Zverev and Uvarov were in the doorway of Kolobkov's office, both smiling as they entered the room. "Anton Zharkov stayed the night in Eaglewood's house and sent photos of its interior."

"You gotta be kidding me!" Kolobkov replied. "Already? What do we have?"

"His sister was alone and insisted that Zharkov stay at their house. He used this opportunity to make detailed photos of all rooms. Apparently, there is little security inside the house, as she does not allow any violation of her privacy." Uvarov approached the projector and turned it on. He entered several commands on his tablet, and a series of images appeared on the white wall.

The three men sat around the table and looked at the photos of different rooms, the details of the walls and the shelves, the tables and chairs, and every other piece of furniture in the house. As he scrolled through the images, Uvarov made short comments about the room, reading from the notes he'd received with the transmission from Anton.

"Well," Kolobkov said when they reached the last image. "This is faster than we were hoping for and gives us more time to prepare. Still, we are very short on time."

"But now we aren't in the dark anymore. We can make it perfect," Uvarov replied.

"So, what's the plan?"

"Build the mockup model of the rooms." Uvarov displayed the images of the kitchen, living room, and Eaglewood's office. "Here are different angles. We can build almost exact life-size models. When we finalize a working procedure, our guys over there will train Zharkov."

"How long will all this take?" Kolobkov asked.

"From start to finish, including Zharkov's training, it could take at least two weeks. But we must finish everything by September 16, when Jenn celebrates her birthday. It's in nine days. This is our best window, and Eaglewood will be off guard, if he ever is. After that, I don't know when the next good opportunity will come," Uvarov responded. "The biggest task is to build these mockups and train Zharkov so he can do it with closed eyes and very fast."

"Well, friends," Kolobkov said and rose from his chair. "Let's get to work."

The two operatives rose from their chairs, too, and started to walk toward the door when Kolobkov stopped Uvarov: "Pasha, how stable is Zharkov?"

"Well, Oleg, he is under a huge amount of stress, but I believe he will carry it through. He is worried about his family and will not flip because of them. I am certain of that. But he cried last night when he thought he was alone."

"I see," Kolobkov replied, appreciating that his operatives did not leave any opening for Anton to go rogue. "Let's make sure he talks with his family before Jenn's birthday party. A little boost in motivation never hurts."

CHAPTER 32

Mike did not expect to receive this call. He looked again on the phone screen displaying the caller ID prior to answering—the name did not change. He was hesitant to answer and continued to look at the screen until the phone stopped ringing. A minute later, it buzzed, notifying him of a new voicemail, and Mike listened to the message. Now knowing what the call was about, he called back.

"Hello, Mike, good evening! Thanks for calling back!"

An electrical shock went through Mike's spine, a sensation he hadn't experienced for many years and the existence of which he'd completely forgotten about. A sensation that now confused him.

"Good evening, Keana, how are you doing?"

"Quite well, thanks for asking. Mike, I've got a problem at Solutry that we need to discuss."

"OK, sure, want to do it over the phone? I'm in DC for tomorrow's congressional hearing."

"I know. I am here too."

"Oh, you are? Then why don't we meet today and discuss? Is that OK with you?"

"You don't need to get ready for the hearing, Mike?"

"My team tries to prepare me for it, but it goes nowhere, and I canceled it for today: they cannot tell me what I already know about tomorrow."

"I see. How about lunch together, then?" Keana asked with a bit of hesitation in her voice.

"Sure, sounds good. If you don't mind, I will text you the place," Mike said.

"Not at all. Let me know. I can go with anything. See you at noon, then, Mike. Bye for now."

STILL HOLDING A phone in her hand, Keana looked at herself in the mirror of her hotel room. She had not talked to Mike in what, six, seven, years? A small, initially unidentifiable pinch unexpectedly materialized in her stomach, intensifying with each passing minute. She sat on the edge of her bed, unable to stand as this pinch transformed to a real pain crawling inside her intestines. She didn't doubt the source of this pain but was surprised by its manifestation. Her first instinct was to call the meeting off, but that would be admitting her own weakness, and that wasn't an impression Keana O'Connor wanted to make on Michael Eaglewood. She felt trapped in her own mistakes and found this feeling to be identical to the one she'd had many years ago.

She closed her eyes and lay back on the bed. The pain celebrated its freedom and started to twist her stomach at its whim. Keana kicked her high heels off, turned on her side, and brought her knees to her chest, lying in the fetal position in the hope of returning to tranquility. It didn't help. Instead, tears formed at the corner of her eyes and ran down her nose, dripping onto the bed's cover. Her mascara was gone. She stood up, pulled a tissue from the bedside drawer, wiped the tears and blew her nose, took off all her clothes, and then went to the bathroom, where she opened the hot water faucet and lay in the bathtub for an hour, forcing herself to think about anything but the upcoming lunch meeting.

AS KEANA WAS calming herself in a hot bath with Epsom salts, driving away any thoughts of Mike, he was doing precisely the opposite. He called off all his meetings for the day, creating a frenzy among his team of lawyers, who were anxious to chime in before tomorrow's hearings and were disappointed at the lack of opportunity to justify their fees by showcasing their preparation wits. He took off his shoes and jumped onto the bed, leaning on the headboard. He opened his laptop and logged into a cloud service that stored all his digital images. A young version of himself with beautiful Keana appeared on the screen, and Mike savored the memories until it was time to go and meet her for lunch.

KEANA ENTERED THE restaurant precisely at noon and immediately saw Mike, who rose from his chair. They hugged and quickly kissed each other on a cheek, like old friends who frequently meet. All their early discomfort instantly evaporated, leaving no trace and freeing room for the familiar feeling of comfort coming from an old place of intimate friendship.

"Let me go directly to the reason I wanted to meet," Keana said after a few minutes of exchanging memories.

"Sure, it's better to finish all pending business and then enjoy the rest of the lunch," Mike agreed. "Shoot."

"Mike," Keana said, "initially, I didn't see it coming, unfortunately, as I did not understand your real intentions. Well, me and the rest of the world, I guess. I am sure you are very aware that you are slowly destroying Solutry."

"Why wouldn't you elaborate on this before you accuse me of such deeds?" Mike said, but his expression did not show that he denied her accusation or was even surprised by it.

"Well, here are the numbers: Solutry's software is installed in about 60 percent of the companies you own. My salesmen report about 'strategic change' in their accounts: all of them plan to switch to our competitors. These talks already sent our stock down, and soon, we will be done, unable to recover." Keana's face expressed the seriousness of the situation better than her words. She paused for a moment and continued. "Tell me why, Mike, why are you doing this? You know Solutry is much better than anything out there. For God's sake, it was *you* who designed this software. I cannot find any technical, operational, or business reason why in the world you want to replace everything. The only explanation I found is that it looks to me like a personal vendetta. But I don't understand why." Keana continued looking directly into his eyes. "Why, Mike?"

Mike listened to her without interrupting. He took a long sip of Coke and said, "Don't you think that you might point to the reason in your very own fiery speech?"

Keana bent her head in bewilderment. "I am not sure I follow you."

"You said it yourself. The rumors that Solutry has been dropped caused its stock to plummet, so Solutry could be picked up for pennies, right?"

"You did all these machinations in order to acquire Solutry for a good price?" she angrily asked.

"I didn't admit to anything. I merely explored possibilities based on the story *you* told me," Mike replied. He straightened in his chair. "I do not plan to acquire Solutry. But I think we should make a better deal than the one we have now. That's what I thought you wanted to discuss."

Keana swallowed hard and was relieved when the waiter came with their food, so she could take a moment to subdue her mixed emotions. After the waiter left their table, she said, "I am ready to negotiate a new deal."

"Excellent, that's what I hoped we could accomplish today! So here's where I stand. I think that the Solutry system should power all our companies, exclusively. Of course, the terms must be renegotiated, but I believe we can come to a mutually beneficial solution."

Keana took her first bite, thinking about Mike's suggestion. She quickly weighed the pros and cons in her head and felt trapped.

As if sensing her inner struggle, Mike added, "You shouldn't be worried about me influencing your company decisions. I will not be able to work at such a level of details. But I know I can trust you."

Keana looked into Mike's eyes and slowly said, "You are a son of a bitch, Mike, but you know that, right?"

He laughed. "Somehow that sounds like a compliment coming from you."

"Take it as you wish. I assume it would be up to me and the Duke to tie up all the loose ends of this deal?"

"Right. And this leaves us the whole rest of the day without a need to talk business. Why don't we spend it as friends?"

"Are you sure that's what you want to do?" Keana asked, feeling trapped again, but this time, it was between her head and her heart.

"Remember we loved to hike and walk in parks? You know what I miss the most? Some regular recreational activity. Since I founded Eaglewood Solutions, I've never really taken a normal walk in a park. Do you know how many times I've visited DC? Would you believe I haven't been to most of the places any eighth-grader visits on their school trip here? Let's just spend the day exploring Washington, like we did when we were young."

That was totally unexpected, Keana thought, and despite the advice from her inner voice, she said, "Mike, it's sweltering outside."

"You see, that just proves the point of how disconnected I am from reality." Mike laughed. "I don't have the slightest idea what the weather is outside. It's always cool in my habitats."

Keana smiled. "Last week, Rachel Sorrow said in her special on you that it's gonna be scorching for you tomorrow on Capitol Hill."

"She has no idea what she is talking about. Believe me, nobody knows better than me what will happen tomorrow," Mike replied. "So, if the weather does not cooperate, then let's hit the indoor cultural heritage of the capital."

"And by hitting the indoor cultural heritage of the capital, you don't mean the White House, right?"

"Nope, I don't plan on visiting the White House," Mike said, and after a short pause, he added with a smile: "Not yet, anyway."

They quickly finished their lunch and stood up. Mike's knees were trembling as they had many years ago when he first met Keana. He looked at her and forced himself to chase the thought away.

"I WANTED TO ask you something," Keana said, standing in front of works of European impressionists in the National Gallery of Art.

"Anything," Mike replied.

"Tell me your end goal. I don't believe all you do is for money's sake. I also don't believe it is to acquire power. There's something else, but I cannot pinpoint it."

"Do you remember the names of any European king when van Gogh died? Or who our president was? Who the richest man at the time was?" Mike asked, pointing to the picture of the Dutch artist.

"The last one, I think, is easy to guess. Rothschild? The king's and the president's names I don't know off the top of my head, but I could search online. It wouldn't be too difficult."

"No, it wouldn't be. You know why you can hardly remember these almighty men from that era?"

"Why don't you answer this question yourself?" Keana said, refusing to play this game.

"We don't remember most of them because they are insignificant. We don't remember what they did, why they did it, and they left little impact on the world. But you know whose names are forever in history? Great leaders who changed the world, scientists, writers, and artists. Alexander the Great, Caesar,

Genghis Khan, van Gogh, Beethoven, Newton, Einstein. But how many industrialists or rich men can you name as having the same impact? Five? Ten? Twenty at most?"

"Are you comparing yourself to these people? To Caesar or Genghis Khan? Obviously not to Newton or Shakespeare," Keana mocked him a bit.

"You know, the modern world cannot produce Caesars or Genghis Khans. Weapons don't rule the world—trade does."

He continued to look at van Gogh's painting and then suddenly asked, "What will be left after me?"

"And do you think that living your life in a decent way, that having a positive impact on your family and friends, isn't enough? Does it make you happy to solve all the world's problems at the expense of your own little private happiness?"

"You sound an awful lot like Jenn," Mike said with a barely palpable sadness in his voice.

"She is a very unhappy woman, then," said Keana.

"What I love about you," Mike replied, "is that you've always held a mirror up to me. I always needed this, and probably do more now than ever. Anyway, remember how I told you about the greatness of Genghis Khan? He is my favorite. Do you think when he burned down a city, its citizens had a sense of love for him? But nowadays, historians agree that the modern world would be impossible without him."

"You are not Genghis Khan, Mike! You cannot even compare yourself to him!"

"No, I am not—he killed those who hated him."

"I don't like this remark, Mike, not even a bit!" Keana snarled.

"Relax, I'm not implying anything. In the business world, you don't need an arrow and a bow to kill. A spreadsheet will do," Mike said and paused as if his mind had caught a thread of thought.

"You know," he finally said, looking at her and not at the paintings for the first time since they'd started their conversation, "this discussion has given me an idea."

"I am not sure I understand."

"I told you—in my world, you kill your opponents with a spreadsheet, and that's exactly what I will do," he replied, and an evil smile twisted his face, the kind of smile that made you want to turn on your heels and run away.

BACK IN HIS hotel room, Mike opened the staff page of the QQBC website. Rachel Sorrow looked directly into his eyes.

"You should have let it go, Rachel!" he said to her portrait. He opened his email, hit the "New" button, and spent the next fifteen minutes drafting an order. Once done, he read his text, fixed it in a few places, and, satisfied, hit the "Send" button. The wheels had been set in motion.

CHAPTER 33

"**W**ell, well, well, I see somebody found my best spot!" Leland exclaimed in surprise, seeing a new man on a sandbank. "I am Brandon, Brandon Leland," he said, lowering his rod and a basket with all the fishing bits and bobs to the ground.

"Good morning, Mr. Leland!" replied the man, standing up and extending his hand for a handshake. "I am Kevin Phelan. I live in London but am visiting my aunt here. A friend of mine told me this bank has the best places to fish, and it's worth coming here. I couldn't resist the temptation."

"Wise fellow, your friend! This is by far the best place in miles. I often come here. This is my favorite spot—I can pull them out with my bare hands if I wish!"

"You know your business, then!" Phelan replied. "I scouted the whole bank and thought this must be absolutely the best spot to catch game. I am glad that you confirm this. Do you mind if I stay here or would you prefer that I give this spot back to you and find a place somewhere else?"

"Oh, by all means, please stay! What fun is it to fish alone? I hoped Howard, my good lad, would join me today, but he got sick two days ago and was hospitalized, poor bloke. And Jefferson said that he ate something and has a stomach disorder. Poor lad too, Jefferson, I mean. I am glad you found this spot, so yes, please stay, keep me company!"

"You are very kind. You know, I always said that fishing is the most social sport—what could be better than spending the morning with your best friends, talking about life, catching some game, sipping tea? What else does an old fellow like me need? Since my wife passed away, I try to spend my days fishing."

"I am so sorry to hear it, so sorry, but I hope that her soul rests in peace and she is happy seeing you continue your life's joy."

"Thank you, it's been a couple of years already. Here, I have a very nice tea in a thermos—very special, I must add. I use it only on my fishing days. Why don't we drink it? It's a bit chilly now."

"I would be delighted! And I am happy to find a person who is as enthusiastic about fishing as I am!"

"Ah, Mr. Leland, it is so rare to find a fellow who shares the same hobbies!" He poured tea in two red cups. "Here, take a sip. Try it. Please tell me whether you've ever had such tea."

Leland took the cup from Phelan's hands and felt very excited about having met such a nice person. "That's an excellent tea indeed!" Leland took another sip. "Superb, just splendid! By the way, Mr. Phelan, do you happen to play bridge?"

"Do I play bridge? Are you serious? Is there anything better after fishing than a game of bridge over a pint of beer?"

Leland smiled and raised his cup of steaming tea, toasting their new friendship.

LELAND HAD FORGOTTEN what it felt like to have such a close friend. In two short weeks, Phelan entered his life as nobody had since Leland was twelve years old, when he met his best friend Calvin something (he forgot his last name already, but the feeling stayed), and they spent the whole summer together, playing, nonstop talking, and dreaming about the future, separating only for a few short hours at night. Leland could hardly believe his luck to meet Phelan and experience the same thrill as he had when he met Calvin. Only now there was no parent who would take his friend and move overseas. Never since his childhood had Leland made such a friend, and it had taken almost forty years to meet one. He wasn't going to let his friendship be hurt again.

Phelan became more than a friend. He was Leland's real soulmate. A bit too active for his years, but that was a minor drawback, even more so since Leland was too idle for too long. And actually, it felt terrific to get excited again for wild ideas. The latest of them was driving up north for a seashore fishing trip.

"TAKE A LOOK at this beauty!" Phelan pulled out his phone and flipped through a series of photos he'd taken as Leland pulled out an enormous eleven-pound halibut.

"He is wonderful, isn't he?" Leland said, indulging in great moments with his new friend.

"I especially love this one!" he said, showing the photo of the fish looking at him with its big bulging eyes in disbelief at its own stupidity for being caught. "I appreciate your insistence on going to the South Shields, Kevin. I wouldn't have come this long way all by myself, and neither Howard nor

Jefferson would agree to the inconvenience of coming here for just two days."

"I feel so fortunate myself, Brandon, that you agreed to my rather unconventional idea!" replied Phelan. "For I wanted for so long to try the shore fishing here myself, but driving without a good companion wasn't an attractive option for me either! You know, I believe this is the largest halibut ever caught on these shores. Why wouldn't you send the photos to the *Angling Times*? It is easily the British record!"

"Oh, you surely exaggerate, Kevin. I am certain there are many others who caught even bigger game than me. You know, I am not an expert in seashore angling, always preferred freshwater fishing, especially with all that drive and all."

"I'm exaggerating? Absolutely not! I just searched the British records, and there is no official record of a halibut caught offshore of such magnificent size, absolutely nothing! I have the video and photos of you getting him out of the water—this is just fabulous footage! He is huge! Your name should be in every newspaper and magazine—you made British history! It is absolutely magnificent, absolutely!" There was no end to Phelan's enthusiasm.

"Oh, you are such a nice person, Kevin, but if not for you, I would never even have thought about going this far for seashore angling. Not in a hundred years, especially given I need to be at work today at eleven."

"Take a look, Brandon, this should be in every fishing manual!" Phelan scrolled to the video of Leland's triumph on what was presumably the biggest British halibut catch. "You should write an article on the subject! I am telling you—this material must find its way into seashore fishing manuals! Do you have a bottle of scotch? We must raise a toast in your honor!"

"Oh, no, no, no, you really are exaggerating!" said Leland, but the warmth from Phelan's compliments to his mastery nicely spread in his chest and eventually in his entire body, catching up with his eyes, which watered from a sincere realization of the meaningfulness of today's achievement, so precisely noticed and acknowledged by his friend. "I can't drink today, need to go to work soon. But let's have tea with biscuits. I will put a kettle on."

"Of course, let's have tea today, but we must raise a toast for you next Friday."

Phelan proceeded with Leland to his tiny kitchen, where Leland put a kettle on and took biscuits, sugar, and chocolate candies from the drawers. Helping his friend to organize a small table for an impromptu late-evening tea party, Phelan enthusiastically continued. "If you don't mind, I will write a little article to send to the newspaper along with the photos. I don't want them to miss all the details of your catch. I'll start with a description of the rods and baits—I think your equipment deserves a special review. Then I'll describe what you told me about choosing the right spot. That was absolutely the key to success. I still cannot quite believe you did it. If I weren't witnessing this with my own eyes and then catching it on video, I would say that this is yet another old angler's story." He exploded with a contagious laugh that passed to Leland, who happily joined his trusted friend.

They sat around the table and continued exchanging the details of this glorious day, destined forever to enter the British sport with its unprecedented accomplishment. The tea and biscuits did not commemorate the achievement as much as scotch would have, but one of Leland's best qualities was his reliability, a trait his current management at Eaglewood Solutions valued beyond anything else, and which he would not jeopardize even in light of today's events, as magnificent as they were.

They continued the discussion, periodically interrupting each other with additional details of the early-morning process, successfully fished from their memory and undoubtedly complementing the story with precise descriptions, of the right moment feeling, of bravery in front of the unknown, if you wish, of embracing opportunity and following one's heart, to the point that if a third party, unfamiliar with the events of today, was present in this truthful recollection of today's events, this person would imagine a small blue whale at the end of the line whom Leland succeeded in bringing ashore while bravely risking his own life.

It was at that moment that Leland felt a churn in his stomach, a churn that suddenly twisted his intestines and left no mistake to its meaning.

"I am sorry, Kevin, will be right back," said Leland and then he ran to the toilet.

A very audible sound came from inside, followed by a cry: "Sorry!" and then another loud sound.

Phelan, as a very polite English gentleman, had chosen to ignore his friend's sudden urge, and instead busied himself with his own phone, quickly typing something.

Five minutes later, Leland exited the toilet and rejoined Phelan, who had his phone lying on the table and was scrolling through photos again.

"I agree with you. The photo you loved is indeed the most descriptive one for the newspaper. I think we should send it as bait and say if they are interested in the story we can give them others and the video, but if they are not, we should hint that we will send the material to *Sea Angling*," started Phelan.

"Sounds like a good idea." Leland's face was pale and his voice much less enthusiastic than it had been just ten minutes before. "What's going on!" he suddenly exclaimed and retreated to the toilet again, this time for a whole fifteen minutes.

When he reemerged, he was half bent over from the abdominal pain, his face was all white, and large drops of sweat beaded on his forehead.

"What did we eat?" he asked Phelan. "I must have eaten something."

"Hmm," replied Phelan, looking very concerned. He helped Leland to reach the sofa in the living room. "When we last stopped, you had fish and chips, and I ate a sandwich. As I told you before, I don't like eating fish and chips at roadside restaurants. You never know their freshness."

"That's it!" Leland cried. "It's the fish and chips! I knew it!" And with those words, he jumped from the sofa and ran again to the toilet.

Sounds coming from within caused great concern to his friend, who stood outside the toilet door and asked Leland: "Do you want me to make you fresh tea? I think it will help soothe the pain. I believe you have food poisoning from that fish."

"Yes, please," Leland replied, and a round of new sounds exploded in the toilet, this time accompanied by his groaning from excruciating pain caused by the heavy vomiting and diarrhea, which both had already emptied his body of fluids.

Phelan heard a loud thud and pushed the toilet door open, which thankfully Leland had not locked. Leland was lying on the floor heavily breathing and twisting from the pain, his trousers unzipped and half down. Phelan quickly flushed the toilet and attempted to lift Leland to his feet, trying to carry him to the living room. When he finally succeeded in bringing Leland to the sofa, Phelan rushed to the kitchen, filled a glass with tap water, and brought it to Leland. Holding his friend's head, he placed the glass near Leland's lips.

"Drink this water, Brandon. You should feel better if you drink it!"

Leland took a few shallow gulps, but the water immediately came back up, soaking the rug and Phelan's clothes.

"No worries!" Phelan uttered, then went to the toilet, where he took a towel, wiped himself with it, and dumped it on a small puddle on the rug. "Brandon, maybe I should drive you to the emergency room? I don't like it a bit that you feel so awful, my friend. Let me see where the closest one is." He rushed to the kitchen to fetch his phone from the table and looked at the map. "It is only a twenty-minute drive."

"No, no emergency, I will be late to work," Leland said in a feeble voice. "I cannot be late. It's impossible to be late. Let me lie down for ten minutes and I will be back to normal."

His stomach, however, disagreed with that assessment and, to prove its superiority in knowing the matter better, forced Leland to roll on his side and heavily vomit again, this time into a big shopping basket that Phelan had prudently brought a minute earlier, just in case.

"What time is it?" Leland asked between a series of unstoppable attacks.

"Half past ten," replied Phelan.

"What?" Leland cried and forced himself to sit up on the sofa. "I must go. It's time for me to go!" He stood up, but the sudden movement caused another round of vomiting and twisting, and exhausted, he fell back on the sofa.

"You cannot go," said Phelan. "You must call in sick."

"No, I cannot call in sick!" Leland replied, crying. "They rely on me. They trust me. It's so unfair!"

Another round of sickness followed this outcry. Lying on his side, Leland suddenly looked into the face of his trusted friend, took his hand, and haltingly said, "You go, Kevin, you go instead of me. It is really nothing. It's very straightforward. The most important thing is to remember the sequence."

"You want me to go and do your job, Brandon. Are you out of your mind! I have no idea what to do and how to do it! Call your boss and explain the situation."

"I will teach you! It just needs to be on time, that's all. The job in itself is very uncomplicated. I will teach you in a minute. And you also look like me—same height and size. Nobody will even notice. Please do me this favor! I must be at work today—or they will stop trusting me!"

"Yes, but what if I run into someone? What will I say?"

"Nobody will be there at this time, only security, but they know my car. Please, Kevin, please do me this favor!"

"Of course, Brandon, if this is so important to you and you cannot just call in sick, I will help you. But please explain to me in detail what I should do."

For a moment, Leland felt relief from his pain. His inner voice praised his cleverness and subdued a new urge to vomit, much to Leland's satisfaction.

He pointed to his working shirt and jacket, and a badge clipped on the front pocket, and gave Phelan a full explanation of his routine and responsibilities at Eaglewood Solutions. True to his habit of paying attention to details, he requested that Phelan repeat everything to ensure nothing would be missed and Leland's responsibility toward the company would be uncompromised, and to his utmost satisfaction, Phelan remembered everything correctly, down to the last detail.

"Let me make you tea before I go," said Phelan, showing his concern for Leland's condition. "If I need anything, I will call you on your home phone, OK?"

"Yes, of course, Kevin, but I think you will be OK. It's really not that complicated, just very important for the company!"

"I don't understand why it is important if it is not complicated?" Phelan asked, ready to depart.

"Mr. Rogers said that a single, reliable performed function serves as a foundation for the successful operation of the entire company," Leland explained. "I am that function, and that's why I cannot fail them today. Go, my friend, go. Please don't fail to remember all the steps." He waved to Phelan, who was dressed in Leland's working uniform and closely resembled Leland himself.

"I never fail, Brandon. I will be back soon. Hopefully, you will feel better by that time!"

PHELAN LEFT LELAND'S flat and proceeded to his friend's corporate car, where he sat in the driver's seat and looked at his own reflection in the mirror. He was wearing a gray wig, had glued a small mustache above his upper lip, put blue contact lenses in his eyes, and applied several touches of makeup on his face. Phelan looked one last time into the mirror and was satisfied with the results—the familiar face of Brandon C. Leland looked back at him.

CHAPTER 34

Twenty-six-year old George Johnson considered himself to be lucky—he was the youngest among the security personnel of the Eaglewood Solutions' European headquarters, a position he'd obtained thanks to Morgan Griffith, his former army commander and now the head of an on-premises security group, which earned him the enormous amount of 40,000 pounds a year plus benefits, an amount Johnson wouldn't dream of having in the first dozen years after his discharge, and definitely not right after his return to British soil. As his training sergeant used to say when he'd just joined the army, giving them what always seemed like humanly unmanageable tasks, "Boys, work hard and the army will open up a sea of possibilities." Which, back in Nairobi's heat, it was impossible to believe. Yet here he was, in his new uniform, earning more than any of his friends, even those who'd graduated from college, to their parents' envy and to the pride of his own folks, and employed by the world's most powerful business corporation.

New to the job, Johnson was eager to learn the ins and outs of his responsibilities, which many people unfamiliar with the security profession considered quite an easy task, but for true professionals, it was a world full of complications and careful considerations. Sitting in a control room at the entry to the building, he studied the operational manual, comparing it with the footage shown on dozens of monitors installed on the wall in front of him. James Callaway, Johnson's shift manager, twenty-five years older than him and three years into his current position, was already very fluent in all things security, so he was able to spend his night shift doing crosswords while his junior colleague scribbled notes in a security journal following standard events on monitors. Johnson's eagerness was rather annoying, as from time to time, he would exclaim some trivial observations, interrupting Callaway's train of thought just as he was almost guessing the right word.

"A black Ford Fiesta entered the garage," Johnson suddenly said, yet again disturbing Callaway. "The monitor says Brandon C. Leland."

"We call him Dracula," replied Callaway without raising his eyes from his crossword. "A bit late today."

"Late?" Johnson was surprised. "What, he starts his job at this hour?" Obviously, his previous security detail briefing had not included this fact.

"Yes, he comes around this time, does something on the fourth floor, and you never see him again until the same time the next day. They say he gets tons of money for that."

"How much?" Johnson naively asked.

"Dunno, but you can retire on his salary."

"So what does he do?"

"Nobody knows. He reports to Rogers himself, so it must be something very important. He also has a company car. This fella is a big shot, a really big shot."

"He doesn't look like a big shot to me, looks like a pretty regular old fella." Johnson watched Leland's car parked near the ground-level entrance, and a man of sixty and some years emerged from the vehicle and proceeded to the lift.

"Don't let looks deceive you, George," Callaway said, moralizing. "Everybody in the company stays away from him, so you better too, just in case. Not for nothing they call him Dracula. Better not to cross paths with such people."

UNAWARE HE WAS a subject of conversation, Phelan, looking like Leland and walking exactly like him, with his slow, slightly uneven, and wobbly gait, entered the lift, positioned his badge against the card reader, and pressed the number four on the keypad. The lift took him directly to the fourth floor, which was abandoned, as expected. Phelan waited until the lift doors closed, registered a single overhead camera, and entered the room.

Everything matched Leland's description, which made Phelan's job easier. He looked around, as casually as he could manage, in search of a security camera, and to his satisfaction, found none. The company obviously did not want to monitor Room Number One, as Leland called it. The interior was simple—a small table with a computer, a shredder, a chair, a wastebasket, and a simple shelf mounted to the wall, containing piles of printer paper and cartridges. Leland told him that among his responsibilities was to maintain the printer and feed it with paper and cartridges if the need arose, as nobody except Mr. Rogers and himself could access Room Number Two. How the supplies found their way to Room Number One, Leland couldn't tell, but this question never bothered him, as it had nothing to do with his responsibilities—from Leland's perspective, the supplies were always supposed to be there.

Phelan drew out his camera and captured everything that was of interest, which wasn't a lot. He looked at his watch and approached the door leading to Room Number Two. Pressing his badge against the card reader, he heard a buzz and the door unlocked. Without any hesitation, he pushed the door open and stepped inside. With a soft thud, the door locked behind him. Still maintaining Leland's gait, Phelan walked toward the printer to check the level of ink and paper, caring less about either of them, but carefully looking for any sign of security cameras and, to his relief, finding none.

There were still ten minutes to midnight, and Phelan rapidly photographed everything in the room, giving most of his attention to the booth in the middle of the room. From a careful examination of the booth, it was clear to Phelan what its function was—all Leland did was press a single button, which, Phelan assumed, was connected to the "Enter" key on a computer hidden under a stand in the middle, closed on all sides, with a mirrored upper surface. Certainly, a one-sided mirror, thought Phelan, avoiding approaching it unnecessarily, concerned that there might be a camera underneath. He got on all fours and quietly entered the booth, avoiding the potential line of sight of an undersurface camera, if there was such, attempting to find a way to penetrate the stand and retrieve the computer.

His inner sense of time was impeccable, and two minutes before midnight, he crawled out of the booth, not finding any way to crack the stand without applying brute force. Outside, he stood up, resumed Leland's gait, and reentered the booth precisely at midnight. As required, he pressed the button and waited for the printer to start printing, which was his sign that he could leave the booth. Leland said it usually took five minutes, and these five minutes were the most concerning, as Phelan knew he was standing in front of the camera in full view. As much as his resemblance to Leland was very close, to the human eye, he realized that he could not deceive a computer algorithm.

These five minutes were the most vulnerable part of his plan and could mean a forced exit from the premises. His team outside was ready to retrieve him upon receiving a disturbance signal from him if things went awry. Phelan nervously patted a gun in his left pocket, waiting for those long five minutes to pass, but his expression remained as calm as it had when he'd entered the building.

Four minutes, four minutes and thirty seconds, four minutes and forty-five seconds, five minutes—Phelan's mind automatically counted the time, increasing his tension and alertness with each passing second. Whatever came next, he knew his decisions needed to be lightning fast. A printer came to life, and Phelan exited the booth. There was little time to waste—whatever he could do here was done, not a lot by his standards, but he'd exhausted his abilities. He took a printed list from the printer, opened its paper tray, and took out a blank sheet. He looked again at the booth and the stand inside with one last hope of finding a creative solution to crack it, but nothing new revealed itself, so he proceeded to Room Number One, entered the printed numbers to the computer, folded this printed sheet, put it into his pocket, and shredded the blank one he'd taken from the printer.

Mimicking Leland's gait, he exited Room Number One, placed his badge against the card reader, and called the lift. The doors immediately opened, as all this time, the cart had stayed on the fourth floor. He entered the lift and began his descent to the garage. So far, there had been no complications in this operation, and he assumed that if withing the ten minutes from the moment he entered the booth, security did not try to stop him, most probably it meant his exchange with Leland had gone unnoticed.

The lift stopped on the garage floor, and when the doors opened to the lift's lobby, to Phelan's unpleasant realization, there stood a very tall and powerfully built young security officer. A series of possible outcomes flashed through Phelan's mind, converging to the only acceptable scenario—a fast blow to the guard's right temple with the gun's butt to knock him out and a quick strangling to finish him. Phelan stepped out of the lift to get closer to the guard and measured the best angle to hit him, as the guard was a good four inches taller than Phelan.

"Good evening, Mr. Leland!" the security guard said pleasantly. "Such nice weather we have at the beginning of autumn! I hope you enjoyed it!" The young guard showed a lot of enthusiasm to engage in the conversation. "My name is Johnson, George Johnson, sir. I am new here, doing my regular security rounds."

"Uhh," Phelan uttered.

This didn't seem to bother Johnson; instead, he took it as an invitation to keep talking.

"I was just discharged after my second tour in Africa, and Morgan Griffith, my captain five years ago, was looking for a security guard, and here I am. I feel so lucky to work at such a great company, Mr. Leland! I am sure my army experience will help me in my role." Johnson continued to talk, dumping all his qualifications on Phelan, trying to make sure that such a high-level person as Mr. Leland received their good account.

"Anyway, it was nice talking to you, sir. I don't want to take any more of your time. Please let me know if you have any security concerns, and I will be happy to address them." Johnson saluted, more out of army habit than because of etiquette, and pressed the lift call button. "Good night, Mr. Leland! Nice meeting you!"

It was this moment that Phelan thought was right for the strike, but the naivety of Johnson and his evident ignorance of who was in front of him held Phelan back from exercising his fatal blow, as the risks of exposure outweighed the benefits of preserving his identity. Johnson was too oblivious to who Leland genuinely was and thus not dangerous, for now.

"Enjoy your day!" he replied, knowing that it would be Johnson's last one, and then he went to his car and drove out to the street.

He slowly rode back to Leland's apartments, following the traffic rules on already empty London roads. After ten minutes of driving, he stopped at the traffic light of a large intersection, having caught up with a red BMW M4 sports car, which was already at the same intersection in the lane to the right of Leland's Ford. Phelan rolled his window, tossed the BMW's driver a manila envelope, containing a printed sheet of paper and a camera, and turned left, driving away.

He parked at the same spot that Leland's car was parked before and typed on his phone: "Package delivered. Complication—sec guard George Johnson. Will take care. Suggest keeping the subject intact."

Within five minutes, he received a two-word reply: "Your judgment."

Phelan knew that the level of intelligence he provided would be inadequate for his mission, but having discovered what exactly Leland's responsibilities entailed, he had little confidence in acquiring anything else. Yet two fatalities from the same company in the span of one day would be too much to be a coincidence, and an unnecessary investigation would commence. With hard feelings, Phelan decided that Leland would live, at least for now.

He locked the car and went up to Leland's flat.

CHAPTER 35

"Happy birthday, dear!" Masha said, kissing her daughter and turning to warmly embrace her grandchildren as they ran toward their grandmother, who always carried a small gift for them. "Did you see what's going on at the entrance to your estate?"

"You are spoiling them, Mom!" Jenn exclaimed, returning kisses and hugs to her parents. "They cannot eat so much chocolate!"

"Yes, we can!" both Alexander and Anastasia simultaneously said. "We can eat millions of chocolates! No, even a hundred million!"

"It's my responsibility to spoil them," said Masha, divvying up her stash of dentist-forbidden candies. "Don't you know that grandmas are born to spoil?"

"Yes, Mama." Anastasia took the candies from Masha and shoved them into her pockets. "Grandma Masha is born to spoil!"

"Of course, she and your dad were born to spoil you, and I guess I was born to serve you."

"Born to serve! Born to serve!" Anastasia ran off to her room to hide the chocolates before the candy police had a chance for a raid.

"Not every grandma is born to spoil, Masha," Mrs. Eagle-wood said, patting Alexander on his head. "Some have a clear understanding that candy is bad for teeth." She smiled with her perfect Hollywood smile toward Masha and missed Jenn rolling her eyes behind her back.

"So what is this all about?" Sergei asked his daughter, refer-ring to the commotion outside the entrance to the enormous Eaglewood abode.

"People protesting my reforms and restructuring," Mike said as he joined Jenn to greet the guests. "As long as they do not start looting, I couldn't care less. We cannot even hear them from here."

"So you don't care that people are protesting against you in front of your property?" Sergei asked in bewilderment. "There is even a news truck here!"

"Why should I listen to a bunch of morons who don't under-stand a thing?"

"It's not just a bunch of people," Masha said. "There are hundreds of them. Driving here, we felt like we were going through a war zone."

"Well, this is a good example of when quantity does not translate to quality. Hundreds of morons gathered together do not become either smarter or more right. Just more dangerous."

"Wow, that was quite a ride!" Anton entered the house with a clear expression of unrest on his face. "Jesus Christ, these guys are nuts! I hope they did not ding my car—I will need to return it soon to the rental. Congratulations, dear sister!" He embraced Jenn and gave Alexander a small gift bag, searching for Anastasia.

"I am here, Uncle Anton," the girl yelled from the end of the corridor, running toward the newcomer to receive her portion of goodies as well. She'd met him for the first time only a week ago but quickly learned that Uncle Anton never came empty-handed.

"So, we're all here. Why don't we go to the dining table?" Mike said, ignoring Anton's remarks, and looked at Jenn, who felt quite uncomfortable about everybody's comments about the protesters.

They all sat around the table, with the kids strategically taking the chairs between Grandma Masha and Grandpa Sergei, ignoring Mrs. Eaglewood completely, to her satisfaction, as taking care of her little grandkids wasn't her primary source of enjoyment, as opposed to Jenn's parents. Mike filled everybody's glasses and raised a standard, bland toast for his wife, praising her dedication to family and kids and wishing for her long life and health.

With a kiss accompanied by clinking glasses, Jenn thought that Mike's toast sounded like a random toast generator had written it, one where you input program words you want to use and receive a legitimate toast built from these words. Words such as "Jenn," "dear wife," "family values," "dedication," "love," "devotion to the kids," "raising kids," "support," "me," "health," "prosperity" and "good life" would be fantastic input words for this toast algorithm, she chuckled to herself, continuously keeping her smile and looking at Mike during his toast. It became clear to her that even her last sanctuary, a family gathering, was no longer a shield from the outside world, as the cold was created from within. She lost the thread of the conversation around the table and focused on the do's and don'ts of the kids' table etiquette to hide her current mood.

She quietly thanked her dad, who, knowing his daughter better than anybody else and reading her thoughts in her eyes, took the lead around the table, telling countless stories of his glorious

Soviet-era youth and avoiding any further mention of the pro-testers, allowing Jenn to escape into her own quiet introspection.

She navigated the trivial tasks of changing the dinner course, sending the kids to their bedrooms at eight o'clock, thanking the toasters for their warm wishes, and countless other things a woman could do while letting her mind be somewhere else undetected.

"You know, Mike, efficiency is a matter of perspective." Jenn's attention finally returned to the room, and she heard her father arguing with Mike: "I read that when the Japanese replaced human kiosks with soft-drink-dispensing machines, people thought it would increase unemployment. Instead, it created more jobs—you know, to maintain the machines, to refill the drinks, to collect the coins. So, Mike, do you call this more efficient or less?"

"That was probably intentional," Mike argued. "However, what you had in the Soviet Union could hardly be called effi-ciency! You worked at the military equipment factory, and I remember your stories—they are all about how inefficient your management was!"

"Mike, dear, your point of view is very American, so I know that what you think about the world is how it is viewed by an American. But the world is different. If an American looks at Japanese dispensers, he sees waste—more people working the machine, more salaries to pay, plus the cost of making all the machines. You see a huge waste. But when the Japanese look at them, they see the benefit for their society. More salaries? Yes, but more people work."

"So your government did not make stupid and wasteful decisions?" Mike asked.

"Of course they did. I'll tell you a story. I was working as an engineer, and we were making spying devices, you know, to spy on enemy sputniks. So we had this great device that could trace every sputnik very well. Full of electronics that my factory manufactured. So one day the KGB brought in a small device, the size of a soccer ball. I don't know where they got it. But you know, the KGB is very efficient. They can get everything. So they bring in this device that does exactly the same thing our device does. But the Japanese thing, it was from Japan, was soccer-ball sized, and our was like a huge coffin, maybe even bigger. So we get an order—find how it works, and make the same."

"How do you know it was Japanese? What, they had a 'Made in Japan' engraving?" Jenn asked, her first time engaging in the conversation.

"Dear, back then, ours were the size of a coffin, but America's was the size of a sarcophagus! Only the Japanese did small things. Anyway, they told us we had two weeks to understand how to make the same. The KGB did not like to waste time. Very efficient organization, mind you.

"For one week, we tried to understand how this thing works, but couldn't. So our director called his friends from another military factory, and the chief constructor came right away. We looked together, and he said it was impossible to understand how this thing was made when we are sober. So he sent boys to buy a few bottles of vodka. We sat, drank a bit, like three bottles for six people, and then a genius idea came to our minds—we decided to cut the device in half and look inside."

"And then you learned how it was built?" Mike asked with disbelief in his voice.

"No, of course not. But we enjoyed the process." Sergei laughed heartily, and others joined him.

The old wall clock in the kitchen announced that the hour was now ten with an audible creak, and Masha discreetly looked at Sergei, hinting it was time to depart. Suddenly, Anton turned white and loudly burped. Embarrassed, he said sorry and rushed to the restroom in the corridor. But he failed to reach it before the sickness caught up with him, and he threw up just outside the door.

Jenn and Sergei were the first to realize what had happened and ran to him, Sergei bringing a bottle of water from the table and a bunch of napkins. The view that greeted them was somber—Anton sitting on the floor unable to stop throwing up, his pants and shirt covered in stomach liquid, weak and embarrassed at the same time.

Eventually, the vomiting stopped, and Anton leaned back against the wall.

"I am sorry," he said in a weak voice. "Let me clean everything up."

"Don't even worry about it!" Mike said. "I called our household service to help. What happened?"

"I think I ate something."

"Everything was absolutely fresh and my own cooking!" Jenn said, feeling terrible that it might be something from dinner that had caused Anton's nausea.

"Yes, we all ate the same thing," Masha said, unconsciously protecting Jenn, who noticed that Mrs. Eaglewood was looking at the dinner table with suspicion.

"No, it's not from dinner," Anton said. "I had lunch today from a street cart, and when I came over, I already had some unrest in my stomach, which increased during the evening. I should have refrained from eating, but who could resist your cooking, Jenn?" he said, trying to keep everybody's spirit up. "I am feeling a bit better, so sorry, guys, for ruining the evening!"

"Come on, it's we who are sorry you got food poisoning!" Jenn said. "Take a sip." She took a bottle from Sergei and passed it to Anton, which proved to be a big mistake.

For half an hour, Anton continued to sit on the floor, hugging a big bucket and leaning on pillows Jenn carefully arranged for his comfort. She did not imagine such a conclusion for her already despised birthday party, but on the other hand, she thought it was pretty symbolic.

After sitting for another half hour, Anton weakly stood and said, "Guys, I am so sorry, I feel so bad for ruining the party! I will go now and hope you soon forget about this! I am much better now, thanks a lot!"

"There is no way I am letting you go to your hotel now! You are staying here tonight!" Jenn said, and quickly added, "Don't even argue with me. I will not let you go!"

She bade goodbye to her parents and Mrs. Eaglewood, who were ready to depart, and went off to prepare the guest room for Anton. In a few minutes, she brought a set of clean clothes to Anton, borrowed from Mike's wardrobe, and after he changed, they went to sit in a break room next to Mike's office. Jenn brewed a green tea, claiming it would soothe any stomach disorder, and the three of them laughed as they recalled Sergei's stories.

The old wall clock loudly announced midnight, and Mike stood up, excused himself, and entered his study without closing the door behind him. He sat at his desk, logged into his laptop, and for the next twenty minutes immersed himself in some work, not paying attention that, from time to time from the sofa, Anton watched him with interest. After Mike returned, they continued to talk a bit more, and finally, well after one in the morning, and after Jenn was convinced that Anton's condition had finally improved, they said good night and went to their bedrooms.

LYING IN HIS bed, Anton listened to the sounds of the ancient kitchen clock, an old mechanism Jenn said should have been retired long ago but which proved to be a great help now, thanks to its creaking notifications of the time. The time was crawling slowly and continued to torture Anton with the prospect of unavoidable ramifications: physical if he failed to execute his task, or conscience-related if he succeeded. Either one would be a terrible outcome with consequences he knew that he would live with for the rest of his life.

The old clock struck three times, and Anton quietly rose from the bed, grabbed his laptop bag, hung it on his shoulder, and, without making any sound, tiptoed to Mike's study. The training in Moscow and especially last week's extensive training on an almost accurate mockup of Eaglewood's office had taught him to execute his next task with the utmost speed, precision, and stealth. And despite the unbearable weight of the real crime he was committing now, his hands completed the installations precisely as he'd been taught. He retreated back to his room and lay on the bed, but sleep did not come. Anton did not know whether he would ever dare to look in the eyes of his sister or her husband ever again, and then another thought terrified him even more—if he would be able to look in the eyes of his own wife and sons again with a clear conscience. Tears came to his eyes, and fear of a fatal and indefinite mental trap conquered all his other feelings.

WHILE ANTON WAS lying in bed thinking about his brutal future, two men at the back of the news van were silently sleeping when a soft beep woke them up. They jumped to their feet and looked at the monitor that emitted this beep.

"The system is on," one of the men said. "But the signal is too weak."

"Well, then tomorrow the protests should continue, and we will be there to provide twenty-four-hour news coverage. This should be close enough to the house to get a good signal," said the second man.

"Sure," replied the first man, as if whipping up a mob of protestors was an easy task for him. He turned the monitor off, and both returned to sleep.

CHAPTER 36

"So, Oleg, what do you have to report?" asked Artemov, sitting at his office desk and staring at Kolobkov with an expression which meant only one thing—you better bring good news, or else. After working for twenty years in the system, and reporting directly to the director of the Russian Foreign Intelligence Service for the last decade, Kolobkov knew better than to inquire about the true meaning of "or else."

"Good morning, Mikhail Vasilyevich," replied Kolobkov, standing in front of the director's desk. "We have a positive development on two fronts and believe that we figured out the source of Eaglewood's tactics."

Artemov showed Kolobkov to the chair, continuing to wear a mask of deep concern.

"The most important development," said Kolobkov, sitting down, "I would say, a key development, is with Anton Zharkov, half brother of Michael Eaglewood's wife, Jenn Eaglewood, born as Evgeniya Zharkova. Anton was at Eaglewood's estate last week visiting his sister on her birthday and stayed there overnight, securing continuous video feed. A week ago, we succeeded in capturing valuable information, and my team worked relentlessly to decipher it."

"Good," said Artemov. "Go on."

"There is this deep website, called Breaking News of Tomorrow, that every day at midnight provides a forecast for the next day's events. We are working to identify its source—so far, no definite results. But we have an initial lead. It seems that this is a multinational effort led by an MIT professor. We also do not yet understand the motivations behind this group. This Breaking News of Tomorrow site provides quite an accurate picture of tomorrow's events, and we believe that Eaglewood built his investment strategy on it. Whether Eaglewood himself is part of this group we do not know, but he is an active user of the site. It is also unclear yet who else is aware of this site."

"I am confused, Oleg, by your explanation."

"Yes, Mikhail Vasilyevich. Here is the screenshot of yesterday's information from this site. It's updated every day at midnight. These are all the events that the site predicted to happen. Yesterday, the site published twelve events, and some we will be able to easily verify today. One of the events is this evening's football match—an unprecedented upset of Zenit by Spartak, one to six."

"That's nonsense!" Artemov exclaimed. Having been born in Leningrad, he was a lifelong fan of Zenit, and he took any negative news about his favorite team as a personal insult. "The game has not even started yet—I am going to watch it tonight."

Artemov loved to watch live Zenit games against Moscow's teams, whose defeat by Zenit was always the talk of the next day, unless, of course, the president, also a long-time football fan, invited him to watch together, in which case, Artemov's allegiance to the nation's capital's team always dominated.

"That's the most curious thing, Mikhail Vasilyevich. These events are 'predicted' to happen before they actually happen. And the predictions are very accurate."

"Oleg, don't you think you are insulting my intelligence?" Artemov was visibly irritated, and Kolobkov regretted that he'd started with Zenit's defeat, as the thought clouded his boss's mind. "Unless the game is fixed, there is no way anybody knows the score one day prior to the game, and there is no reason for Zenit to fix the game."

"That was my initial reaction too, Mikhail Vasilyevich, when I looked at the info on the first day. There was a breaking news item about a game between Lokomotiv and Ural, which ended two to two. But not only did the site predict the score accurately, it also described two red cards for Ural and a penalty kick that brought them to a tie at the end of the second period. You cannot fix a game with such a level of accuracy. I went to the stadium yesterday and watched this match—it would be humanly impossible to rig the game with such precision."

Artemov thought for a whole five minutes in complete silence. Kolobkov, being quite familiar with his boss's thinking process, refrained from adding anything else and patiently waited for Artemov to resume his questioning.

"What other events does this site talk about?" he finally asked.

Kolobkov gave a full account of all other events that were supposed to take place and compared the previous day's prediction with yesterday's actual events.

"Oleg, if I hadn't known you for the last ten years, my reaction would be that you are hallucinating."

"And I wouldn't blame you for that," Kolobkov said. "There are many questions that arise with that site: Who exactly is behind it, how they get the material, what is fixed, and what is prognosed, and then how do they do it? What is their long-term plan, and who else is using this? There are, of course, many more questions that we need to answer. But we have an initial lead."

"Who is working on that?"

"Zverev's team—this is his highest priority, and he assigned his best people to it."

"Good. You said this site is a multinational effort. Who? Americans and Brits? Chinese and North Koreans? Iraqis? And how do you know it is multinational?"

"That's another fascinating point, Mikhail Vasilyevich. We succeeded in penetrating the London headquarters of Eaglewood Solutions. Our man there befriended Brandon Leland, who was considered to be a key person in Europe reporting directly to Jeffrey Rogers. It turned out Leland is only a button pusher."

"Button pusher reporting to Jeffrey Rogers himself? You gotta be kidding me!" For the second time, Kolobkov had surprised Artemov with his report, and Artemov was known as a man never in the habit of being surprised on the job.

"Yes. Ahh, I mean, I am not kidding you. Leland's sole responsibility is to come into the headquarters at midnight and push a button in an isolated office that only he and the highest corporate management can access. All this button does is pull up this Breaking News of Tomorrow website. They pay him a high salary to secure his loyalty. There is also a unique feature that is built into this website. That's the real reason behind Leland even being employed—there must be a real person that accesses this website. Zverev conducted multiple tests with automatic access to the site. None succeeded unless there was a person that manually called up the site. He even tried a robot and a digital image instead of a person—the same result: the site could not be accessed unless there was a real person trying it."

"Strange, but let's assume this. Why do they need this Leland guy to do that? Why not continue accessing this site from the US, where Eaglewood has most of his development?"

"Here comes an interesting part again—this site is very location-based," replied Kolobkov.

"What does this mean?"

"The news that you receive in different places varies depending on the location. Some might be the same, some might be different. Yesterday, we checked the results from Moscow, Yekaterinburg, Berlin, London, and Saint Petersburg—on average, about 30 percent is worldwide news, and the remaining 70 percent is local events."

"That's why Eaglewood has offices in so many cities around the world."

"Exactly, and we checked that each Eaglewood office employs a button pusher similar to Leland. Most interesting, Eaglewood established his offices in cities that have stock exchanges, and also in big, strategic cities that have a lot of important industries and key corporations. Our guy in London suggested this idea, and it appears to be correct. That's what leads us to believe that the team behind the Breaking News of Tomorrow site is multinational and well-coordinated."

Artemov fell into his thoughts again and, when he returned to the conversation, asked, "Can we reverse engineer the code from this site?"

"We haven't succeeded yet, but we will continue to work on it. We do not understand how the browser renders the code upon invocation. This site is the work of really advanced hackers, and besides the resulting entries in a browser, we cannot yet get any clue about its technology."

"You said you have a lead as to who is behind this site. Elaborate."

"The camera feed from the Eaglewood office revealed that they are gathering intel on a particular professor of astrophysics from MIT, a Nobel Prize laureate, Jeremiah Jeremei. We don't know how he is involved with the site, but every time Eaglewood logs into his computer at midnight to read the Breaking News of Tomorrow, he obsessively looks for information on this professor afterward. We established surveillance in Cambridge, both physically and electronically.

"There is another person in the picture. There is this journalist at their local TV network, named Rachel Sorrow."

"What about her?" asked Artemov.

"She is obsessed with Eaglewood. Her boyfriend is FBI Special Agent Joshua Koppelman, and she also employs a private investigator to spy on Eaglewood. We checked her out—apparently, she reported about the first big round of layoffs before Eaglewood announced them. She must be aware of the site."

Artemov stood up from his desk and started to walk around his office, without saying a word. Kolobkov was looking at him, knowing that a new series of orders would come shortly. He wasn't mistaken: ten years under the command of Artemov had taught him his boss's habits.

"Oleg, the president believes that our tech team is the best in the world and that we can play games with Americans whenever we want. What I see now is that Americans are playing games with us. The president won't like it at all. Do whatever you can to crack this site. This is now a matter of top national security.

"Also, I want you to monitor all the results of the site from all key strategic places and compile a daily report of predictions as well as actual events afterward and everything you found on this professor and whoever he works with. I want you in my office every day at nine o'clock with that daily brief and progress report.

"If there is anything that might compromise our national security, I want you to call me right away, no matter the time. The president is very concerned about Michael Eaglewood's attempts to hijack our economy, and I want to hear about any potential threat immediately.

"And, Oleg, if this reporter and her boyfriend are of any disturbance, you know what to do."

"Clear, Mikhail Vasilyevich," Kolobkov replied and stood up. "I am on it."

He turned around and exited the office, closing the door behind him.

"Natalia Ivanovna," he said to Artemov's assistant of many years, Natalia Serebrennikova, who didn't raise her head from typing some memo. "Mikhail Vasilyevich wants to see me daily at nine. Please reserve fifteen minutes."

"Until when?" she asked.

"In perpetuity," Kolobkov replied.

Serebrennikova stopped typing, raised her eyes at Kolobkov, and, with little wonder, nodded her head. "OK."

The stern look on Kolobkov's face left no doubt that something big was happening. As he was ready to take off, the intercom on Serebrennikova's desk awakened to life.

"Yes, Mikhail Vasilyevich?" she answered.

"Natasha, tell Oleg that we are going to watch the football match tonight."

Kolobkov smiled, feeling the change in Artemov's mood, and said, loud enough for Artemov to hear: "You aren't gonna love it, Mikhail Vasilyevich! We'll kick Zenit's ass."

CHAPTER 37

Artemov hated late-night calls, as they always meant one thing—a national security issue demanding immediate attention. He hardly had any personal life, despite having a family, as family outings were canceled more often than they were carried out. His friends were mostly nominal—government and military personnel that he was connected to via work, and whenever they were killed in action, dismissed, discharged, or retired, in most cases, he lost contact with them and rarely felt any void. Yet he wouldn't change his life one bit, as for him, serving one's country was the noblest of any profession.

It took Artemov less than two seconds to wake up and bring his mind to full alertness. His wife didn't even move on her side of the bed, having learned many years ago to ignore night calls and her husband's sudden disappearances.

He answered the phone on its second ring and went to his office. "Artemov here."

"Mikhail Vasilyevich, sorry for the late-night call." Kolobkov's voice was concerned. "I thought you would rather know it immediately and not wait till the morning. We just received intel from the Breaking News of Tomorrow site. You should be aware of it now before it's too late. Let me read it."

Kolobkov cleared his throat and read aloud:

A SECRETIVE PLOT TO TAKE OVER RUSSIAN KEY INDUSTRY SECTORS

Four prominent Russian oligarchs, Alexander Dubrov, Dmirty Atamanov, Evgeniy Suzhdenko, and Sergei Sharkov, each holding major ownership in some of the key sectors of Russian infrastructure, engaged with world-renowned billionaire Michael Eaglewood in an attempt to sell their holding to Eaglewood Solutions. The negotiations are taking place at Dubrov's residence at Ibiza, where the other three oligarchs and Duke Houston, president of Eaglewood Solutions, are in the final stages of the negotiations. If the deal goes through, it will prompt a series of difficult questions about the sovereignty of the Russian economy.

"How reliable is this intel?" asked Artemov when Kolobkov finished, still painfully remembering Zenit's shameful defeat.

"I have a strong belief it's solid," Kolobkov said. "We checked that all four of them are in Ibiza, and each arrived discreetly without leaving too much of a trace. Atamanov and Sharkov came on their yachts from different places, and Suzhdenko drove from France to Spain and then took a short private flight to

Ibiza, avoiding passport controls. Houston, on the other hand, was vacationing in Ibiza for a whole week prior with his new wife. My guy told me that Atamanov was seen early yesterday playing eighteen holes with Houston at Golf de Ibiza."

"Sons of bitches," said Artemov, referring to all of them—to the four Russians, who in his opinion, betrayed their country even by merely entertaining the idea of the deal; to Houston, who was Eaglewood's right-hand executive; and to Eaglewood himself, for even daring to look in the direction of Russia.

"Just a second, Mikhail Vasilyevich," said Kolobkov, closing his phone's microphone with a palm. He shortly returned to the call. "Sorry, a new intel just arrived—as we speak, Houston and the oligarchs are at Dubrov's residency. The deal is in the making right now."

"Thanks, Oleg," Artemov replied. "Good job! Anything else?"

"No, Mikhail Vasilyevich, that's all."

"Good, go to sleep now," Artemov said and hung up.

Artemov started to pace in his office, which always helped him to think and clarify a variety of potential solutions prior to making critical decisions. No doubt, this deal should not go through, not even partially. His intuition had told him it would be a matter of national security when the phone rang, and such issues weren't taken lightly. His mind ran through multiple options for solving this crisis, from the most appealing and easiest ones, which could be immediately executed with his single command, to more complicated ones, which relied on diplomacy and public relations. Weighing all the pros and cons, he came to a decision, and, sighing, dialed a number, which he rarely dared to call at this hour.

The office of the president of the Russian Federation never slept, and its primary resident, in Artemov's opinion, should now be woken up to make a long-distance call to a small Spanish island to convincingly explain to his four constituents the true meaning of Russian patriotism.

MIKE SAT IN the car returning from his additional hearing at the capitol. He looked at his phone, which immediately buzzed with incoming messages and voice mails. He scrolled through his texts and saw one from Houston: "Please call ASAP."

"Evening, Duke," he said when Houston picked up his phone. Houston's voice clearly indicated his frustration. "Something went wrong?"

"You bet."

Mike listened to the Duke's report without interrupting, a negotiation that initially proceeded according to plan, with all sides agreeing to the principal terms. But then, suddenly, Dubrov took a phone call and then excused them from the discussion, and all four Russians went to a separate room and talked about something. Then Atamanov exited the room and abruptly ended the meeting. The Duke did not understand what had happened, but it was clear that the reason for the Russians' sudden change of heart was this late-night phone call. Houston was furious, getting out of Dubrov's residency, but despite a strong desire to break somebody's head, or even better, to break all four of their necks, he succeeded in keeping his calm and bade everybody good night in a pleasant and friendly manner.

"This call changed everything," Houston concluded his report.

"Can it be just theatrics?"

"I doubt that. The look on Atamanov's face was of genuine concern."

"Duke, I want to see this deal go through. We need it. Let's go back to the table and increase the offer. If you need—double it."

"That's ridiculous. We should walk away."

"The whole foundation of the company is built on this ridiculous idea. You know this. I don't mind sounding ridiculous, but I don't want to be ridiculed. Let's go back to the negotiations and nail it." Mike motioned for the driver to turn around and go back to the hotel. "Let's talk tomorrow morning. Good night, Duke."

ON HIS WAY up to his residence, Mike requested a light dinner with mineral water to be brought to his room and immersed himself in nonstop emails, pausing only to take a few bites of the sandwich or sips of the water. The time slowly but surely approached midnight, and Mike opened his browser and pulled up the site. Strictly at 12:01 a.m., the Breaking News of Tomorrow page loaded, and Mike impatiently scrolled through all the entries until his eyes fell on the one he was hoping to find—news from Russia.

His heart sank when he read the title: "The Takeover of Russian Companies by Michael Eaglewood Failed." He carefully read the whole item; it didn't leave any room for a different interpretation. With heavy heart, unaccustomed to loss, Mike texted the Duke: "Back off from negotiations; everything is canceled."

He angrily slammed the laptop's lid, shoved it aside, and went to lay down on the bed, staring at the ceiling without blinking. Nobody could ridicule Michael Eaglewood, nobody.

CHAPTER 38

Koppelman was quickly walking toward the end of the street, watching the crowd. The line to the Yakiniku Japanese BBQ truck suggested a long wait, but 2,000 online reviewers all agreed: the wait was worth it. The truck staff was diligent, efficient, and friendly, but regardless of how fast they worked, their efforts weren't sufficient to cope with all incoming hungry office workers, who on such a lovely day were willing to spend most of their lunch hour waiting in line.

Koppelman loved this truck's food, and on his slow days, he was frequently found standing in line. The patience of people all coming with a simple goal to get their lunch, with an abundance of options around, yet willfully agreeing to quietly stand in a line for a $15 box, sometimes with a wait as long as twenty to thirty minutes, tranquilized him. Dealing with thugs—corruption, grand theft, and murders—this crowd of waiting people, unified in their unsophisticated desire to get their lunch, had a magic effect on him and brought calmness and serenity.

Rachel was supposed to be here at noon, but it rarely was her habit to meet him on time. Somehow, her brain always made a hard cut—she was very punctual for business meetings and more often than not late to her social happenings. This lunch meeting wasn't an exception, and after so many years, Koppelman had just adjusted.

Koppelman had just three people behind him order their food ahead of him, still waiting for Rachel, when he finally spotted her. A single look at her gait was enough to recognize that she was seriously pissed off—fast pace, head down, and quick, short puffs of a cigarette, one after another, without any gap between them, all this pointed to severe distress. Koppelman had only seen Rachel in such a mood twice, and in both cases, it wasn't pretty. In her job, not getting what she was after, being unable to publish everything due to many constraints, such as requests to keep sources anonymous, which castrated her from bringing the real spice to the story, was rather a typical conclusion of an investigation, despite popular belief. That never caused her such a mood—that was the trade-offs of her profession.

Even when she was in good spirits, Rachel wasn't a big eater; seeing her approaching the truck, Koppelman knew she wouldn't even consider lunch. He got to the truck window, and to the cashier's tremendous surprise, he asked for two Cokes.

"Man, you stood all this time for a Coke?" asked the cashier.

"Sorry, not hungry anymore," replied Koppelman. He paid for two cans of Coke and went off toward Rachel.

"That son of a bitch took over the network!" Rachel said to Koppelman when he caught up with her, skipping any greetings.

There was only one person who could match that description and cause such a reaction, so Koppelman asked, "Eaglewood?"

"Who else?" Rachel threw out the butt, which had burned down to the filter, and took a new cigarette from her pack. "Thanks for the Coke."

"Sure. What happened?"

"That stealthy son of the bitch persuaded Charles Tucker, our chairman, to sell the company! I just got out of a meeting with Tucker; he wanted to notify me personally before everybody else knows."

"That's quite a development!" said Koppelman, now fully realizing the reason for Rachel's mood. She'd just lost her job.

"This maniac wants to shut us up! We are the biggest antagonists to everything he does, and instead of doing the right thing, he just decided to buy us off and install censorship! I am so done here!"

"I see. Do you think that's the reason he bought the network?"

"What else? That's the only reason to force us to shut up. I am so pissed off, Josh, you don't even know!"

"Well, Rach, I can see that," Koppelman replied. "So what do you plan to do?"

"My first instinct was to tell Tucker I am done. But I am not a little girl anymore. I need to be responsible. I don't exactly remember what my contract says, never gave too much thought to the termination clause, need to read it first. But I don't want to work even a single day for Eaglewood. So today might be my last airing."

"Hmm." Koppelman didn't have anything to say. The prospect of Rachel moving out of the city saddened him.

"I didn't see this coming, but then, I should have seen this coming: this bastard has only one way to deal with criticism—he buys it off."

They continued to walk on the street without any specific direction, in total silence, for ten minutes.

"Your last broadcast on the network should be about Eaglewood," Koppelman finally said. "That would be the most appropriate Rachel Sorrow finale."

"It would be. I can spin old material, but I don't have anything new. I cannot talk about the takeover yet—gave my word to Tucker."

"Well, I can help you with that," said Koppelman.

Rachel abruptly stopped and turned toward Koppelman.

"Talk to me, Josh!"

"You know, we run our own investigation into some of the dealings of Eaglewood, mostly concerning his political donations and recently his potential collusion with Russians. Nothing solid yet, we just know Duke Houston is in constant contact with several Russian oligarchs that run half of the country's economy.

"Anyway, one of the executives of Eaglewood Solutions, Andrezj Linowski, looks like a very depressed guy. You know of him, right? He is one of the cofounders. Goes by Andy. Most of his days now he spends heavily drinking in the Night Glow, a secluded pub in the southern suburbs. You might look for something new there."

"That's golden, Josh! Thanks!" She hugged him like a happy child hugging their good friend upon receiving a long-awaited present, turned around, and ran off toward her car.

Koppelman watched her small retreating figure and wondered what would come next for her. He, too, turned back and walked toward the Yakiniku Japanese BBQ truck—by this time, the queue had dissolved.

THE NIGHT GLOW was an upscale pub in the southern suburbs that treated its wealthy patrons with discretion. It opened at three p.m. to allow early birds to wash down their daily excitement prior to returning to their dull homes, and it stayed open as long as the last person was willing to stay, never pressing its patrons to conclude their business. The bright bar, glowing blue, which gave its name to the establishment, was in the middle of the venue. It was staffed by three barmen, and the perimeter was divided into poorly lit niches, which allowed guests to converse privately and unseen.

Rachel entered the pub and went straight to the bar, choosing an entrance-facing stool. There were only three couples in the niches and one lone man at the bar at this hour, but Rachel's looks did not attract this man to flirt with her.

Slowly drinking Coke and fiddling with a bowl of peanuts, she finally saw Andy Linowski entering the pub, accompanied by two bodyguards, who surveyed the venue and sat at the bar. A young barman with a long ponytail and multiple piercings in his ears, nostrils, lips, and tongue didn't even ask them a question; he just nodded to them like an old friend and put a glass of sparkling water in front of each of them. Andy went to the farthest niche, and a waiter brought him a double scotch on the rocks, treating him like a regular.

Rachel waited for the waiter to leave Andy, stood up, took her Coke, went to Andy's booth, and unceremoniously sat across from him. One bodyguard was immediately upon her: "Excuse me, ma'am, this place is taken. Please return to your seat."

"That's OK, Jackson, Miss Sorrow does not mean me any harm," said Andy, recognizing the reporter.

"Good evening, Mr. Linowski," said Rachel when Jackson returned to his barstool. "I see you know who I am."

"Call me Andy, please. There is no Mr. Linowski here."

"OK, sure, call me Rachel."

"Alright, so how can I help you, Rachel?" Andy had not touched his drink yet.

"Andy, I won't beat around the bush with you. I know that you developed quite a disdain for Michael Eaglewood, and I really hope you can help me. I sincerely believe that Michael Eaglewood is a dangerous man, and I want to take him down. I need your help with that."

Andy looked taken aback by such bluntness. He took his drink and sipped it silently for a long time, not looking at Rachel, as if she did not exist. She realized that since he had not sent her away immediately and told her to mind her own business and stop bothering him, which he could easily have said and accomplished, given his two bodyguards, that this was not a lost cause and her crazy idea might even work. She patiently waited for him to resolve his inner struggle, praying that his solution would include talking to her. Andy finished his drink, and the waiter quietly appeared with a refill of his glass without being asked, which Andy finished in a single gulp. He put the glass on the table, finally looked directly at Rachel, and said, "He is not evil, but I think he became delusional in his quest."

He waved the waiter over for another refill, drank it in a single gulp, and said, "Shoot, what do you want to know? I don't care anymore."

MIKE SAT IN the kitchen with a big cup of green tea, spending his evening as he usually did—working. Jenn complained of a headache, which had become the norm after her birthday, and retreated to the bedroom after putting the kids asleep. Mike knew she was angry at him for something, but he wasn't able to guess the reason. Everything was as usual. They hadn't argued, and he was behaving the same way he always did, so the reason behind her evident unwillingness to spend any time with him was unclear to him. He noticed that she used any excuse to retreat to either the kids' room or bedroom, but did not understand why. Her irrational behavior annoyed him, but he was just too busy now to deal with that—with the Russian failure and with the QQBC takeover, his plate was full, and the last thing he needed to worry about was his wife's whims.

The old wall clock interrupted his thoughts, and with a loud creaking sound that could wake up the dead, as Jenn had once remarked, it announced ten o'clock at night. Mike clicked on a remote that was lying on the table, and a TV on the wall came to life, the opening theme of the *City Night* filling the kitchen.

"Good evening, ladies and gentlemen, this is Ben Wolf with *City Night!* For a long time, we've witnessed the rise of Michael Eaglewood and his empire, Eaglewood Solutions, and we have seen how his investment deals influence American and world economies, one sphere after another. Despite multiple investigations undertaken by Congress in search of corruption and anti-trust issues, despite numerous protests, despite several attempts to block some of the most critical acquisitions, Eaglewood Solutions, spearheaded by its founder and CEO Michael Eaglewood, continued its march toward total domination. It took one journalist to start a quest to understand the source of Eaglewood's power, and today Rachel Sorrow is primed to bring the answer to this question. Ladies and gentlemen, stay with us, as the discovery Rachel Sorrow made will both shock and amaze you."

Mike left the table and came close to the TV. After commercials, the camera zoomed in on Rachel's face, showing the determination of a wounded animal. Her eyes gleamed with mischief and, slowly, talking to an audience of one, she said, "Tonight, we will all discover…the Breaking News of Tomorrow."

Mike froze in place and stayed motionless long after the program ended.

The old clock loudly announced midnight.

A new tomorrow had just started.

EPILOGUE

The idea materialized late at night. The last three days proved to be a nightmare as things spun out of control following Rachel Sorrow's program. It was impossible to predict, yet it should be impossible not to. He felt confused. Something was wrong, but it was too elusive to pinpoint. And for the last three days, he'd tried hard. Now time was running out; that was clear. Especially with all these people hiding in the shadows, following him everywhere he went.

Fearing the worst, he picked up the phone and dialed. It took three persistent attempts until his call was answered.

"Eaglewood," said a man on the other side, finally picking up the phone.

"Michael, this is Jeremiah Jeremei from MIT."

"Good evening, Professor!" There was no sign of surprise in Mike's voice. "You are, of course, aware that your site is now public knowledge."

"I am glad you are not playing games and not trying to pretend you don't know who I am. I didn't expect this would happen, Michael, and it would become public knowledge. You were supposed to be the only one. You know I put up all possible guardrails to protect it."

"Why me, Professor? What was so special about me?"

"Oh, there were many reasons why I chose you, but let's talk about it next time."

"It took me seven years to finally get to the source of the site, Professor."

"Yes, I am aware. I was fascinated by your progress, Michael. You did a remarkable job."

"Thank you. I didn't expect this turn of events. There are a lot of things I have to ask you."

"And I believe you deserve all the answers, regardless of how shocking they will seem to you."

"Nothing can shock me now."

"I willingly believe you. Anyway, the reason for my call is because I need your help now. I'm afraid this thing got out of control. They are after me. I see them everywhere now, and I'm afraid something will happen. Something terrible. We need to meet and talk. I will answer all of your questions."

"Who are 'they?'"

"I am not totally sure. I have my suspicions, but I would rather be sure before I say."

"I can come to Cambridge next Monday. I must complete some things first. Otherwise there will be a disaster. This Sorrow announcement created huge turmoil. But I will be at your lab on Monday morning."

"Sure. But not at my lab. It's in another place. Call me when you land here."

"I understand. Good night, Professor."

Professor Jeremei hung up. Four days till Monday, too long. It might be too late. But he didn't want to show Mike that he was very concerned. There was a lot of work to be done in these four days. He felt tired, but sleep was out of the question.

He went to the window to close it, the late-evening air giving his tired body a chill. He noticed someone in a parked car watching his home. The professor closed the window and the blinds and returned to his desk.

It was already midnight, and The Breaking News of Tomorrow automatically displayed on his screen. He reached for the light switch, turned it off, and sat motionless, reading the entry: "A world-renowned physics professor at the Massachusetts Institute of Technology, Nobel Prize Laureate Jeremiah Eliah Jeremei, was found dead in his West Cambridge house."

He opened the lowest drawer in his desk and took out a pistol. There was little doubt at what would happen next, and for whatever was coming, he was ready.

DESPITE INCREASED SECURITY scrutiny, the threats reached Mike Eaglewood everywhere. They penetrated his emails, popped up as banner ads on arbitrary internet sites, and appeared as unsolicited text messages on his phone. Just hours ago, a drone had succeeded in sneaking past the guards, landed on his lawn, and exploded. Thankfully, no damage was done, but the incident added a significant amount of discomfort to his already shaken mind after the last week of turmoil.

Mike closed the blinds, turned off the lights, and switched on the TV in anxious anticipation of the day's news.

The news anchor stumbled and glanced sidewise, forgetting for a moment the network's protocol. His expression showed genuine bewilderment at what his news director was telling him through the earpiece. The anchor coughed, finally looked directly at the camera, and in a solemn voice announced, "Ladies and gentlemen, I am going to interrupt the program, as we just received breaking news."

The screen flickered, and the regular programming gave way to a newsfeed from Cambridge, Massachusetts. The camera first focused on residential houses in a West Cambridge neighborhood and then eventually moved to a reporter who looked highly disturbed, as if the news concerned her personally.

"This is Rachel Sorrow, reporting from Cambridge, Massachusetts," she began. "The police just announced the murder of one of the most prominent faces of modern science, Nobel laureate and MIT professor of physics, Jeremiah Eliah Jeremei. Professor Jeremei was found dead from a gunshot wound in his chest in his house in West Cambridge.

"Professor Jeremei, forty-seven years old, was well known in the science community, but he acquired world fame for a series of provocative science experiments, eclectic behavior, and a lifestyle more befitting a young rock star than a scholar of high acclaim. The police found Professor Jeremei following an alert from a neighbor who reported earlier today hearing sounds of a struggle and several gunshots. The motive behind the murder is unknown, and there is no immediate suspect. Professor Jeremei is survived by a mother and two sisters, who are also world-renowned scientists on their own merit."

THE ROOM PLUNGED into darkness when Mike turned off the TV, which was the single source of light. For a long few minutes, he sat motionless, contemplating his next steps and trying to estimate the needed level of security. If they got Professor Jeremei, nobody was safe. How much had the professor told them, he wondered, and how much had they figured out themselves? Time was running against him, and as Mike had learned in the last decade, time was always running against you. Of all people, Professor Jeremei was the most protected. If anything, he should be the one who was entirely immune to these assaults, yet they'd succeeded, which Mike believed should be impossible. *Am I next?* he thought, willing his heart not to start beating any faster.

He continued to sit in complete darkness for another hour until the old wall clock in the kitchen announced the beginning of a new day. Ignoring his initial impulse to check the news, he made possibly the worst decision he ever had, yet it was the right thing to do. He pulled his cell phone from his pocket and clicked on a number saved in his speed-dial. The call went to voicemail, much to Mike's surprise, as he expected it to be answered on the first ring. He hung up and called a second time, with the same outcome. He took a deep breath and spoke to the answering machine: "You know it was you who killed him, even if it was not you who pulled the trigger. We should talk ASAP. Call me."

He clicked on "1" to confirm the recording and held the phone in his hand, knowing that once the message was listened to, the reply would come. Three minutes later, the phone vibrated in his hand, and its screen identified the caller.

"Your phone might be tapped," Mike said without any greeting. "Find a clean one and call me back. You opened Pandora's box, Rachel." He hung up without giving her a chance to reply.

Still in darkness, he moved around the room, made sure all the blinds were closed, and opened his computer. He knew that the next few hours would be critical, but he already had a plan.

ACKNOWLEDGMENTS

Every book has a story behind it. Mine is about a hat.

One day in July 2020, I was driving home, listening to the radio, which broadcasted a chain of unfortunate events that happened in the world. You surely remember these days when the pandemic death toll rose, businesses collapsed, and people went crazy from being confined in their houses. And I thought about what would happen if we knew the next day's events ahead of time. But as it happens quite often, the thought was fleeting, and soon after I arrived home, my mind became occupied with more pressing questions.

Until a few days later, when I woke in the morning still remembering a dream: I wrote a book about tomorrow's news. I could hardly wait until Irina, my wife, woke up, and I could share my excitement with her.

My wife hates mornings. It takes her tremendous effort to get up. Except for one time. This time. She momentarily rose in the bed with a burst of laughter:

"There is no way you can write a novel in English, which is your third language, learned in adulthood! Dear, are you in your sound mind?"

I guess I wasn't, since in the evening, sitting on the pool patio, sipping a glass of wine, and watching our kids learning to head dive, I mustered my courage and asked my wife to give me an opportunity to describe my idea. Knowing me, she realized that it's better to give in now and hear it out than to subject herself to my nonstop attempts to force her to listen anyway. And, I think she reasoned with herself it would be more bearable to do it with a glass of wine and happily playing kids in the background.

And I talked, and talked, and talked, and the more I talked, the more she loved it, and we brainstormed it for hours and even involved the kids. And then there was a verdict:

"I really love the idea. It's interesting and refreshing. But…" Why is there always a but? "But this is a NOVEL! You need to create characters, make them compelling, describe what they ate for dinner, what they think, and where they spend their time! It's a novel, for God's sake, not a blog! You never wrote fiction before, not even in Russian or Hebrew, let alone in English!"

"But why?" I tried to protest. "Look at Nabokov!"

It was the wrong name to mention. I can talk about anybody, but Nabokov, her sacred writer? What a foolish man I am!

Being wiser than me, all Irina did was to measure me from up to down (or maybe it was from down to up, I don't remember the details now), and with a smirk, said, "Well, if you succeed to write this book, I will eat my hat!"

So I got all I needed: the approval, the encouragement, and the final reward!

I procrastinated, as I did, unfortunately, with too many things in my life, until one day, a few months later, after finishing two inspirational books, I opened a laptop and started to write. Excited, I couldn't conceal this from Irina and instead rushed to show her the pages.

She read them slowly as if deliberately trying to torture me. And then she said, "You can write. But the real question is—would you?"

"Yes, absolutely!"

She thought for a long time and said, "Well, then you should. I will fully support you and even release you from your most hated tasks at home, if that's what would help you."

What?! Being creative pays off! I definitely got a better part of the deal—writing in my office instead of loading a dishwasher or solving a mystery of a stolen sock from the dryer.

Fast forward, and here is the book, only because my wife promised to eat her hat.

So my biggest thanks go to my lovely wife, for being such a great support, for believing in me, and for letting me engage in this crazy endeavor despite being almost absent from the family scene for a good few months. Thank you for giving me constant feedback about everything and everyone, for reading my first, second, and third drafts, for gently criticizing them when needed, and for praising me when you thought the praise was almost deserved. There are not enough words to thank you!

My thanks also go to my kids, who gave me an opportunity to realize my dream. I know it is the time taken from you. While it's impossible to compensate for it with anything, I hope that you saw that even an impossible task might become possible if you have a burning desire to make it (I can see their grunt: again,

Daddy, you are lecturing and discussing the lessons learned even in the acknowledgment section? Sorry, guys, I cannot help it!)

My mother-in-law was the second person to read the book in its entirety in the first manuscript. Bella, I value your feedback so much! Thank you!

And, of course, huge thanks go to my father-in-law, Efim, whose dinner stories made their way to the book as dinner stories of Sergei Zharkov, a funny father of one of my characters. Sergei's stories are true and described as closely as possible to how they were told around our family table countless times.

Special thanks go to Diane O'Connell, my editor, for explaining to me what a POV is, among other, not less important, concepts. Diane, I consider my discussions with you to be my literary education.

Thanks to the publication team at Paper Raven Books for the book's production! I hope it will be a great success. Cross my fingers.

Huge thanks go to my close friends for not reading this book! Guys, I still love you! You push me to work even harder!

And last but not least, THANK YOU, my reader, for reading this book and giving it your time and effort. I hope it didn't fail your expectations. As a debut author, I cherish each and every one of you and hope that if you liked the Breaking News of Tomorrow, you would like the following novel too.

P.S. As I found later, Irina was true to her word. She covertly ordered a cake decorated with an edible hat for my birthday and ate it! A deal is a deal. And then she rechallenged me, promising to eat a second hat if the book was published. But as I learned in twenty years of being together, to really secure my win, the mere publication isn't sufficient. It must be a success! While I guess the Pulitzer Prize is not on the radar for this book, the fact that you read the book and even finished the Acknowledgement section leads me to believe that your Amazon review will count toward success.

So, please, please go to this title's Amazon page and tell Irina how much you liked it. Good reviews will make it. Well, I hope.

The hat must be eaten!

www.ingramcontent.com/pod-product-compliance
Lightning Source LLC
Chambersburg PA
CBHW021434310726
48971CB00005B/1361